The Last of Days

By *Paul Doherty*

Novels
The Death of a King
Prince Drakulya
The Lord Count Drakulya
The Fate of Princes
Dove Amongst the Hawks
The Masked Man
The Rose Demon
The Haunting
The Soul Slayer
The Plague Lord
The Love Knot
Of Love and War
The Loving Cup
The Last of Days

Non-fiction
The Mysterious Death of Tutankhamun
Isabella and the Strange Death of Edward II
Alexander the Great, The Death of a God
The Great Crown Jewels Robbery of 1303
The Secret Life of Elizabeth I
The Death of the Red King

Series
Hugh Corbett Medieval Mysteries
Sorrowful Mysteries of Brother Athelstan
Sir Roger Shallot Tudor Mysteries
Kathryn Swinbrooke Series
Nicholas Segalla Series
Mysteries of Alexander the Great
The Templar Mysteries
Matthew Jankyn Series
Alexander the Great Mysteries
Canterbury Tales of Murder and Mystery
The Egyptian Mysteries
Mahu (The Akhenaten-Trilogy)
Mathilde of Westminster Series
Political Intrigue in Ancient Rome Series

Visit www.headline.co.uk or www.paulcdoherty.com
to find out more.

The Last of Days

PAUL
DOHERTY

headline

First published in 2013 by
HEADLINE PUBLISHING GROUP

2

Cataloguing in Publication Data is available from the British Library

ISBN 978 0 7553 9784 6 (Hardback)
ISBN 978 0 7553 9785 3 (Trade paperback)

Typeset in Sabon LT Std by Palimpsest Book Production Limited,
Falkirk, Stirlingshire

Printed and bound in Great Britain by
Clays Ltd, St Ives plc

Headline's policy is to use papers that are natural,
renewable and recyclable products and made from wood grown
in sustainable forests. The logging and manufacturing processes
are expected to conform to the environmental regulations
of the country of origin.

HEADLINE PUBLISHING GROUP
An Hachette UK Company
338 Euston Road
London NW1 3BH

www.headline.co.uk
www.hachette.co.uk

As always, to my beloved wife Carla.

Historical Characters

The House of Tudor

Henry VII (1485–1509): victor of Bosworth, founder of the Tudor dynasty

Henry VIII: King of England (1491–47)

Henry Fitzroy: Duke of Richmond (1519–36): bastard son of Henry VIII by his mistress Bessie Blunt

Edward VI (1537–53): Henry VIII's sole male heir by Jane Seymour

Mary (1516–58): daughter of Henry VIII and Catherine of Aragon

Elizabeth (1533–1603): daughter of Henry VIII and Anne Boleyn

Henry VIII's wives

Catherine of Aragon (died 1536)

Anne Boleyn (executed 1536)

Jane Seymour (died 1537)

Anne of Cleves (divorced 1539)

PAUL DOHERTY

Katherine Howard (executed 1542)
Katherine Parr (died 1548)

The House of York
Edward IV: king 1471–83
Edward and Richard: sons of Edward IV, both mysteriously disappeared whilst lodged in the Tower of London
Elizabeth of York: daughter of Edward IV, wife of Henry VII, mother of Henry VIII
Richard III: king 1483–85, brother of Edward IV

Henry VIII's ministers
Thomas Wolsey (1473–1530): Cardinal Archbishop of York, Henry's principal minister before falling into disgrace
Thomas Cromwell (1485–1540): chief minister to Henry VIII, executed 1540
Thomas More (1478–1535): humanist, scholar and statesman, executed 1535

Henry VIII's Council 1546–47
Edward Seymour: first Earl of Hertford, courtier and general
Thomas Seymour: brother of the above, courtier and admiral
John Dudley: son of Edmund Dudley (executed by Henry VIII), courtier and soldier
Sir William Paget: self-made courtier and secretary to the Council

Thomas Wriothesley: chancellor under Henry VIII

Thomas Cranmer: scholar, Henry VIII's confessor and Archbishop of Canterbury; presided over Henry VIII's divorce and his break with Rome

Stephen Gardiner: scholar, Bishop of Winchester; a conservative, secretly a Romanist who wanted England to return to the Church of Rome

Thomas Howard: third Duke of Norfolk; one of Henry's principal ministers

Henry Howard: Earl of Surrey, son of the above, executed 1547

Foreign rulers

Charles V: Holy Roman Emperor, nephew of Catherine of Aragon

Francis I: King of France, contemporary and rival of Henry VIII

Prologue

In the wilds of Lincolnshire, at the very heart of the Fens, there once stood a sprawling gloomy tavern called the Hoop of Hades. God knows why, but this place had acquired a fearsome reputation as the gathering hall for devils. The tavern once served local villages totally annihilated during the Great Pestilence. Now, according to legend, on St Walpurgis Eve, the vigil of All Saints, a local necromancer could summon in all the demons and ghosts who roamed the surrounding wastelands. I freely admit, demons from Hell do not frighten me. I have met so many in the flesh, I would hardly turn a hair if an evil sprite popped up to confront me in a Cheapside alleyway. Nevertheless, this legend fascinates me, because in order to achieve this great summoning the necromancer had to use a chamber at the heart of the tavern called Haceldema – 'the Place of Blood'. An interesting conceit which I can only report, as both tavern and chamber were burnt to the ground during the Great Revolt against His Malignant Majesty King Henry VIII in that unholy Year of Our Lord 1536.

This journal, by my good self, Will Somers, is my gathering place. I was born in the year of terror 1485, when the present king's father toppled Richard III at Bosworth. To be sure, I have travelled far since then, in body as well as soul. I first glimpsed the light of day at Much Wenlock, in Shropshire. In my tenth year, my family moved to Easton Neston in Northamptonshire, where I entered the service of a local lord, Sir Richard Fermor. I graduated as his minstrel, fool, jester, innocent; whatever men wish to call me. In 1525, the year Rome was savagely sacked, I met our present King Henry at Greenwich. My master, Sir Richard, allowed me to perform at a royal banquet and there I pitched my standard. In brief, I made Henry laugh until the tears poured down those smooth, round royal cheeks and those light blue eyes, which later froze into icicles of pure terror, brimmed with merriment. Henry threw coins at me, bribed my master and cosseted me like a woman with her babe until I entered his service.

Oh, those were the golden days when the royal lion was magnificent in size, spirit and strength. A prince amongst princes who would stride out, one hand on my scrawny shoulder, the other looped around the arm of More, Wolsey or Cromwell. Of course he eventually sent all of these to the scaffold; as the skies clouded black, Henry's heart turned hard and the laughter finally ended.

All men talk to themselves, either directly or in

private. Henry talks to me. I have become his listening post, his whipping boy; a ready, always attentive audience for the royal tantrums, temper, tears and troubles. So, with Henry's knowledge, now, in these last of days, November 1546, I have begun this journal. Some twenty years have passed since I met the Merry Monarch of Greenwich, who has now shape-shifted to become the Malevolent Monster of Westminster. This journal will be my Haceldema, my place of blood, my gathering place, like that long-vanished tavern chamber. (I trust my own heart. Henry is plotting, and when that comes to full flower, blood will flow.) Here I will summon all the demons, and God knows their name is legion. First comes harsh-faced John Dudley, Viscount Lisle, son of a traitor, who has climbed through the tangled branches of politics' thorny tree. A dog of a man, a brutal but brave soldier, Dudley has pitched his standard alongside that of two other soldiers, Edward Seymour, Earl of Warwick, sly and subtle, and his proud-faced, womanising brother Thomas. These two have gained access to the Council because their sister, Henry's queen Jane Seymour, died giving birth to Henry's only male heir, the puny nine-year-old Edward. Others appear. Whey-faced Thomas Cranmer, Archbishop of Canterbury and, very rarely now, the King's conscience. Sir William Paget, vixen-eyed and sharp-featured; a self-made man, Paget has risen to be secretary to the Council and strives to maintain harmony amongst the wolf pack. Last, and certainly the worst of the wolves, Sir Thomas Wriothesley, the constant coat-turner and time-server who likes nothing more than to see a man (or, more deliciously, a woman), writhe in agony.

This league of self-serving, bloodthirsty opportunists are the reformists, dedicated to making the break with the Church of Rome deep and permanent. Confronting them are the Howards of Norfolk, led by Thomas Howard, third duke, a man steeped in years and guile. Norfolk is a heavy-eyed, long-faced hypocrite. At court he drapes rosaries and relics around his neck, but in his bed at Kenninghall he keeps his blowsy mistress, Bess Holland. Norfolk, like Paget, is secretive; both observe the rule 'Never tell a secret to more than one person'. He is always accompanied by his son, who is a far better man. Henry Howard, Earl of Surrey, is a roaring boy, a soldier, a courtier, and above all, something more lasting: a brilliant poet, whose verses dazzle the mind and catch the heart. With his wayward eye and foppish ways, he has one vice: an overweening arrogance. Perhaps Surrey has not forgotten, as Henry certainly has not, that the Howards fought against the Tudors at Bosworth, and that his grandfather won England's greatest victory of the age, the destruction of James IV and all the flower of Scottish chivalry at Flodden Field. While the Seymours crouch close to the throne through poor dead Jane, the Howards crawl more slowly. Norfolk's daughter was married to the King's only bastard son, Henry Fitzroy, Duke of Richmond, but poor Fitzroy, of weak stock, died young, and his widow, if gossip is correct, has certainly caught our king's lecherous eye. In politics, the Norfolks are like the others: self, self and self again. In religion, they hark back to the Church of Rome. They are guided in this by the jug-eared, proud-hearted Stephen Gardiner, Bishop of Winchester.

In the antechamber beyond, to continue the metaphor, others wait. Princess Mary, sallow-featured but kindly-eyed, constantly mourns her dead mother, Catherine of Aragon. Henry's sixth wife, the prim, pure Katherine Parr, also mourns, or so I think. She grieves at being locked and chained to her royal husband, whilst secretly cherishing, perhaps, the unmasked admiration of the lecherous Thomas Seymour. Somewhere too, but deep, deep in the shadows, stands Balaam, son of Beor, the man with the far-seeing gaze. Oh yes, Balaam the spy, the scurrier, the twilight man, always cloaked in the dappled shadow of secrecy. He is Princess Mary's link with those abroad who watch like hawks the maze of treacherous politics that has become the English court, and those rash or brave enough to thread that maze. All these assemble here in this journal, my Haceldema. They wait to dance attendance on their dread lord, the Master of Menace, the leader of the swirling, dangerous masque, Henry the King. No longer is Henry the golden-haired, fair-bonneted chevalier, resplendent in face and form. No, he has grown gross and heavy, eyes black slits in his podgy, moon-like face. A slow-moving mass of murderous deceit. *'Hola!'* as the Spanish say; the King has arrived and the swirling dance takes another sinister turn.

2 December 1546

I s our king dying? This constant question opened the doors of darkness and agitated my heart even as I returned to Westminster today. Henry, once the proudest monarch and the most glorious prince, is certainly declining, his sun setting in tawdry splendour. I was still pondering upon this when I disembarked at King's Steps to be met on the quayside by Sir Anthony Wingfield, Captain of the Spears, His Majesty's personal bodyguard of halberdiers. Scarlet-faced Wingfield, moustache and beard all bristly, questioned me closely about my journey along the river. He listened to my replies, nodded sagely and led me deep into Westminster Palace towards the King's secret chambers. It was late afternoon and the light was dying. Squares of pure wax glowed in their silver dishes. Torches flared beneath their caps in the cobbled yards, lamps glittered along the galleries. We passed empty chambers and rooms, the dwelling place of ghosts, though the palace kitchens we went through seemed merry enough, their fleshing tables heaped with slaughtered larks, storks, gannets, capons and pheasants. Master Bricket, master chef and a very valiant trencher-man, explained how he was preparing a stew of sparrows, gelatines, and game pie with a mess of cucumber lettuce and succulent herb purslane, all favourites of the King.

Deeper into the palace we went, where the floors of the chambers were strewn with fresh rushes, moist and piquant to the smell. The royal presence chamber I passed lay empty. The royal table on the dais was unattended, though steaming dishes were still served for the King by bare-headed courtiers who scuttled and bowed as if they really were in the presence of His Dread Majesty. In the antechamber councillors clustered in their dark-furred robes, only the white of their cambric shirts and the glitter of jewellery catching the light. And yet, a true hall of shadows! A contagion, a miasma seems to infect Westminster Palace, a place crammed with the forfeited chattels of those caught up in the furious thunder around the throne. Henry's court remains steeped in dark deceits and false favours, a shadow court paying service to a shadow king.

The King's sickness seems to infect the elegant galleries, their ceilings marvellously wrought in stone-work and gold. The news of his weakness creeps like a ghost past the wainscoting of carved wood and a thousand resplendent figurines in their countless niches. Everything appears tarnished. The heavy gold- and silver-thread tapestries are moth-nibbled. The thick glass in the mullion windows is stained and dirty. The courtyards, herb plots and gardens overlooked by these same windows remain weed-choked. The gilded butterflies of the court whisper how the King is past caring; oh, how wrong they are! He cares very much. He reminds me of a boar, heavy and shaggy-coated, hunted and wounded, so even more ferocious and dangerous for that. Memories of the past throng the dark chambers of Henry's marble heart. Is he trying to exorcise them? Is that why he wants me, Will Somers, hollow eyes in a lean face, shoulders hunched, in constant attendance upon him, as I have been for the last twenty years? I know Henry. He may be failing, but he is still plotting furiously, and that is why I keep this journal. I wish to chronicle these times, as well as record any coming storm.

This King is never more dangerous than when he broods. He worries about the ghosts of executed traitors that throng Westminster, unwilling to leave the goods seized from their estates: the purple-embroidered velvet bed coverings trimmed with gold that once belonged to Buckingham; the chamber furnishings of Edward Neville; the robes of the de la Poles, not to mention the fourteen thousand pounds of gold and silver, crosses and chalices looted from Cromwell's house at Austin Friars. Memories of those who served and failed him haunt my master. He mumbles how the ghosts of all the Thomases ring his bed at night: Wolsey, More and

Cromwell. They are brought by Thomas Becket, whose sanctity and relics the King so resolutely destroyed, blowing Becket's blissful bones from a cannon. Henry wakes in the dead of night and complains of these creatures of the mist, who cast no shadow in the moonlight, noiseless in their tread, fresh from the wastelands of the dead where no bird sings. All this rests heavily on our king, though not on his Council, that pack of ravenous wolves, greedy for power, those pernicious bloodsuckers of fallen men. As I passed through the chambers, I glimpsed my lords Dudley, Seymour, Wriothesley and others, Achitophels incarnate, all seemingly busy on this or that. In other rooms scurriers, couriers and messengers lounged booted and spurred, their horses ready in the freezing courtyards below to take messages across Henry's ice-bound kingdom.

A place of shifting murky light is how Goodman Balaam describes the palace. Long deserted galleries, fitfully lit; antechambers where those who move do so like the slippery shades of shape-shifters. The King's own inner chamber was closely guarded, its door half open. Inside, my lord Paget, that master of Hell, fur cloak still gleaming with river wet, as were his bonnet, beard and moustache. Paget's eyes glowed with cunning. Had he also been busy in the city and just returned? As always, I acted the humble commoner overcome by his surroundings. I kept my eyes down, shuffling my feet. In truth, the royal chamber is luxurious, hung with tapestries, chairs covered with cloth of gold, stools capped and cushioned with silk and taffeta. The purest candles glow and pots of smouldering dry herbs scent the air. Nevertheless, none of these can stifle the rank odour from the straw-covered urine flasks in their holdings or the stench of the close stools, their potted cisterns covered in black velvet fringed with silver. One of the King's trams, or moving chairs, stood half covered with tawny silk in a corner beneath a crucifix. His Satanic Majesty himself, clothed in a white bed shirt, his head towelled, sprawled on the great bed with its tester of scarlet, curtains of crimson and taffeta and counterpane of silk serge with golden-fringed pillows of the softest down. He lay back against the bolsters, a writing tray before him. On a table to his right were his rings and bracelets, placed there because the King's hands and joints are mightily swollen. These precious items, as always, caught my eye: rings set with diamonds, rubies and emeralds, all looted from ransacked monasteries. Precious stones of all kinds, including the Great Sapphire of Glastonbury, hacked from golden crosses. I suspect such plunder plays on our king's conscience.

Oh, how the mighty have fallen! His Majesty of England is no great prince now but a mass of bloated flesh and dry broken skin. I try to recall him in his prime. A painting by Master Holbein hanging in one of the royal palaces boasts of a time when this king was haughty and regal, fearing neither God nor man. All has changed. Gone are the gowns of scarlet and gold brocade, the crimson cloak and jewelled daggers.

No more the skirts slashed and puffed with white satin and clasped with jewelled brooches. No magnificent collars of twisted pearls and ruby medallions, no velvet cap jewelled and plumed with red and white feathers. The King is much declined, his eyes mere slits, black and gleaming. He uses glasses or spectacles, which he removes as he lifts his head; his lips are flaking, his cheeks and jowls sag and the skin of his face and hands has turned a puffy grey, dried and cracked, its bleeding dirtying the sheets and counterpane. The stench from his body is offensive, and now, as he moved, fresh gusts of putridity wafted towards me. His Majesty was studying a document; he pushed this away and lay back as Physician Huicke, with Paget, Seymour and Dudley fawning behind him, made the most humble obeisance.

'Good Dr Huicke, good sweet Will.' The King's voice was piping and laboured, like that of a marsh bird, as if his very breath had to squeeze itself out. 'Good sirs, I am indisposed with fever again.' His Majesty glanced swiftly at me standing there in my green hooded jacket fringed with white craul, my red stockings pushed into dirty boots. For a few heartbeats he seemed to drop his mask of suffering, as if he was relishing playing the patient, those sunken slit eyes bright with malice. God be my witness, the chamber itself harboured a menace, as if foul spirits curled like vipers behind the tapestries, ready to lunge. Henry is the proudest of men and the self-styled most glorious prince, but he is a better mummer than I. I recalled the legends about him. How he had been likened to the Mouldwarp of ancient prophecy, a hairy man, a royal devil with a hide like goatskin who would first be praised before being cast down by sin and pride. His Majesty has certainly lived his life in war and strife, and in these, the last of days, danger still presses in from every side. Those who approach Westminster are terrified. They hang rue around their necks as an amulet against witchcraft and put sprigs of mountain ash and honeysuckle in the harness of their horses against the evil that allegedly seeps from the King's decaying flesh.

His Majesty is certainly sick in both mind and body. He can no longer hunt, mount a horse or even climb a step. He has, according to himself, the worst legs in the world, and has to be carried up and down stairs and move in a travelling chair from chamber to chamber. He has two of these chairs, one upholstered in gold velvet and silk, the other in russet, each of them complete with brocaded footstools, for the royal legs are grossly bloated and bruised. The physicians, in their long, fur-sleeved gowns and black velvet caps, hover like carrion birds. They wave their urine flasks and, like the fools they are, constantly examine the King's water and close stools. Balaam's spy in the Bucklebury Place spice market, a man who moves easily among the apothecaries and herbalists, has devised a list of the potions, plasters, poultices, medications and elixirs being served to His Majesty: capathol water and rhubarb pills, tablets of rasis to fend off the plague, onions for his belly and greasy fomentations for his piles. Herbal mixtures and soft poultices are laid against His Majesty's head, feet, neck, spleen and anus. The King's face is swollen like a pig's bladder, his back is humped, whilst his legs, ever since a fall some years ago, throb like pangs of fire from open ulcers. He has concocted his own pulses made from marsh mallows, linseed, silver, red coral and dragon's blood, mixed with oil of roses and white wine. Yet despite all this, he is much fallen away, so unwell, considering his age and corpulence, he may not survive the winter. Sin, death and Hell have pressed their seals on this king, and all their retainers flock to attend on him.

I do not rejoice in such ruin. Henry reminds me of one of his tawny-coated lions kept in a cage at the Tower; Princeps was its name, a veritable prince amongst beasts, but it grew mangy, weak and wounded, though still dangerous. Henry the Magnificent, the striker-down of popes and princes, surveys his past and, believe me, mourns for what could have been. If only he'd begotten sons; not just sickly baby Edward or young Fitzroy, his bastard, now buried deep, but a pride of young lions to seal this kingdom as Tudor's fief once and for all. If a scribbler poet wrote a tragedy about this king, this is what he should describe: what might have been. How Henry strove for this dream yet, in the end, failed so disastrously. A tyrant, yes, but if I sift amongst the years, I detect a true greatness and majesty, though deeply flawed and heavily tainted by so much blood.

'I am ill.' The King's voice grew more strident, like the spoilt child he is. Eyes pleading desperately, he beat his fists against the bloodstained counterpane, demanding Physician Huicke attend him at once. Paget and the others withdrew, leaving only Huicke and myself. I helped the good doctor pull back the sheets and lifted the royal nightshirt to reveal the gruesome condition beneath. In truth, our king is a bolting hutch of beastliness. Ulcers perforate his legs, open fissures that Huicke tries to treat with horse hair and silk filament, tightening the skin around each ulcer so as to make it weep. The stench from the festering wounds is offensive. His Majesty lay cursing quietly, though now and again he would cry out for this person or that, some of whom are dead.

Next Huicke treated the King's bowels and belly, the latter so swollen and extended the stomach alone is fifty-five inches in circumference. His Majesty, laughing weakly at some comment made by me, complained bitterly how his bowels were so tight all journeys to the close stool had proved futile. He was then turned on his stomach, legs apart, his body sprawled like that of a huge sow on a fleshing table, much extended like a corpse left for days on a battlefield. No more than a great flabby sack of flesh, horrid to see, foulsome in smell, bruised and marked a purplish-blue.

'I am suffering,' His Majesty cried out, 'because of my sins against the innocents.'

'What innocents?' I retorted, thinking he was referring to Stafford, Duke of Buckingham, or the other great lords and ladies executed during his reign. The King, however, did not reply. He stretched out a puffy hand, picked up a set of coral Ave beads and began to thread these carefully through his fingers. I recognised them; they once belonged to the King's mother, Elizabeth of York.

'Your Majesty?' I insisted, hoping to distract him. 'What innocents have you sinned against?'

Henry beckoned me on to the bed, pulling me down beside him. 'The princes,' he murmured. 'You know, Edward and Richard, the sons of my grandfather, Edward IV of York, the nephews of the usurper Richard.'

'But we have the truth of that,' I replied hoarsely. 'Thomas More?'

The King's eyes did not flicker; they remained cold, hard black stones in that hideously white puffy face.

'More claims that Richard the Usurper killed the princes in the Tower.'

'Not so, not so,' murmured the King. 'More was wrong on that, as he was about so many things.' He stretched out, ignoring Huicke, who was working on his ulcerated legs again, a mass of dirty red blotches and festering scabs. 'Those two boys died of a fever. They were walled up in a chamber in the royal lodgings; the room is still there. It contains two skeletons.

I swear to God,' Henry continued, 'once I recover, I will remove those corpses and give them honourable burial.'

'Why hasn't someone done that before, Your Majesty? They were your mother's brothers.'

'Both princes died of the sweating sickness during the brief bloody reign of their usurping uncle. Richard was trapped. No one would believe their deaths were the result of a plague.' Henry heaved a great sigh. 'After all, they had been in his care. They shouldn't have been in the Tower to begin with. In the summer heat, that fortress is a midden mess with evil vapours from its stinking moat.'

'And your own father?' I asked.

Henry forced a laugh. 'Trapped also, Will. After his victory at Bosworth, my father entered London. He became affianced to Elizabeth of York, the princes' sister. For her sake, he made careful search for her brothers. The secret chamber in the royal lodgings at the Tower was opened and the remains of the two boys found. My father could not publish what he had discovered without raising the suspicion that he may have been party to their murder. Yorkist sympathisers still thrived in London. It would be only a matter of days before common report would claim how both princes were hale and healthy until my father arrived. In the end, the hidden death chamber was walled up again and kept secret, its whereabouts known only to my father and his closest councillors. The secret was bequeathed to me. I swore on my mother's soul that one day I would give her brothers honourable burial.' His Majesty, beating his fists against the bed, continued to bemoan the problems bequeathed to him by his father. At last, growing tearful, he recollected himself, asking what hour of the day it was.

In truth, His Majesty does not bemoan the deaths of two Yorkist princes. Oh no! What he truly fears is that once he dies, his own three children, Edward, Mary and Elizabeth, young and vulnerable, will themselves be spirited away to that sinister fortress to be walled up or secretly murdered. And where will Tudor then be? What reward for all of Henry's dalliances, alliances, wars and the great tumult he's caused in his own kingdom and beyond?

The King grew agitated. Huicke begged him to be at peace. The physician then had His Majesty's body anointed with oil, and delivered an infusion through the anus by means of a pig's bladder to which a greased metal tube was fixed. Despite the King's moaning and retching, a pint of lightly salted water mingled with herbs was also given, followed by a mixture of soothing honey and pap to lessen the soreness of his angry red piles.

After a while the King pronounced himself better, comfortable enough to sit in one of the moving chairs whilst Huicke brought in servants to change the bed sheets. His Majesty waited, a furred cape about his shoulders. He demanded his spectacles and had me bring in his tray of numerous clocks and timepieces, fashioned like miniature books or set in crystals and adorned with rubies and diamonds. He studied these carefully, as if fascinated by the time, before waving his hands for me to take them away. Only once did he stare long and hard at me, eyes as glassy and empty as those of a dead pig on a butcher's stall. He seemed lost in thought, gazing dully around, smiling briefly when I told him some crude jest about a cardinal and a lady of Rome. Dr Huicke mentioned how he intended to visit the Queen at Greenwich. The King simply grunted. Huicke then gave me the ingredients for a poultice for the ulcers on the King's legs before he was curtly dismissed. I was aware of others clustering around the door outside, impatient to present themselves. I felt the pot of court intrigue was bubbling merrily, though with what I could not say, except that the King instructed me to tell all the others to stay withdrawn.

For a while he waited, listening to the sounds fade in the gallery outside. Then he turned to me, that large moon-like face, those bloodshot piggy eyes, the pursed lips all petulant with unspoken grievances.

'How long have you been with me, Will?'

'Twenty-one years, nine months, two weeks, three days and six and a half hours.'

The King gestured at me to sit on the stool beside him.

'Is that candle straight?' he asked.

I turned, and as I did, he grasped the slender white cane close to him and brought it down time and again across my back. Despite his weakness, and my quilted jacket stuffed with flock, the blows hurt. As always, the King made sure he never cut my skin, though this time he missed and scored my neck. I felt the welt rise even as Henry, coughing and spluttering, threw the cane down. He breathed noisily, his fat-jowelled face quivering.

'You were busy,' he rasped. 'Now you are insolent.'

'I am always busy, sire. I am your conscience, your eyes, your ears. I listen to conversations that would never be uttered in your presence or that of your loyal councillors or spies. Terrible things they say about you.' I was thoroughly enjoying myself. Do I hate my master? Yes. Do I love my master? Yes. I might be his whipping boy, but I am also his friend, sometimes his enemy and always his father confessor. My stool is his mercy pew. I shrive the King of his worries and his anxieties. For over twenty years it has always been so. He regards me as the world turned topsy-turvy. I reply that we have a great deal in common because he has done the same. He rejected Rome, but he also poured scorn on Master Luther and Master Zwingli. I chide him. I grieve him and he beats me. I give him good counsel and he provides me with robes every quarter, a bulging purse of coins and, above all, his protection. He likes to bestow upon me some of the goods of those he executes. He even gave me Thomas Cromwell's fine purse, snatched from the great man's corpse when it lay spouting blood on Tower Hill scaffold. Henry demanded that the executioner hand it over or face the same axe he wielded. I always wear it on my belt, the purse once filled by the great despoiler.

'I remember Cromwell.' The King clapped his hands like a child and grinned, showing his yellow and black teeth in bloody sore gums. 'I can read your mind, Will.'

'Thank God you cannot,' I retorted, 'otherwise you'd know how I truly feel about you.'

The King's hand dropped to the white wand on the floor beside him.

'If you try and beat me, I will run away like any apprentice boy from his master.' I jabbed my finger at him. 'You cannot read my mind. You watch me. You saw me touch my purse; it's empty because of the bribes I've paid to collect the gossip you want.'

Henry's shoulders sagged. He made a sound as if sucking on a sweetmeat.

'I remember my good Thomas.' His lower lip quivered like a child's; tears filled his eyes. 'I could do with Cromwell now, Will.'

'He gave you wise advice.'

'Howard,' Henry spat the name out, 'Thomas Howard, Duke of Norfolk, advised me to turn Cromwell out. He hated him. He blamed him for my marriage to that ugly cow Anne of Cleves.'

'Hypocrite, hypocrite, you now call her your sweet sister!'

Henry snatched up the cane more swiftly than I'd anticipated. I tried to dodge, but he still lashed my shoulders. Then he tapped me on the top of the head as if I was some kind of performing dog.

'Stay here,' he murmured. 'Do you know, Will, what Surrey said when Cromwell lost his head? Surrey, Norfolk's proud brat?'

'"Now that foul sow is dead",' I retorted, rubbing my shoulder. '"So ambitious of other men's blood, now he is stricken with his own staff." That's what he said. You almost did the same with your own sword to your most hated enemy, Cardinal Pole. You would have had him executed along with the rest.'

'Friend of the Howards!' Henry took up the story. Oh, how my monstrous master loves to reminisce! 'Pole called Cromwell the messenger of Satan.' He sniffed. 'The day will come, Pole once declared, when Cromwell will feel the same pains of all those he has sent to die. On that day Londoners shall witness one of the most joyous entertainments.' Henry turned to the table beside him. He picked up a silver necklace and threw it at me. I caught it deftly. 'You can't keep it,' he pouted, 'it's mine.'

'No it isn't,' I replied, admiring the insignia on the central pendant. 'It belonged to Margaret, Countess of Salisbury, daughter of George of Clarence, niece to both Edward IV and the usurper Richard III.' I do love taunting His Majesty. 'She claimed to have better rights than you to the throne. She was also the mother of Cardinal Reginald Pole.'

'I know, I know,' the King moaned. 'Why do you remind me of that? Pole still refuses to return to England;

he moves from university to university. Do you know, Will, when I divorced Catherine of Aragon, he at first supported me?'

'He then changed his mind,' I interrupted, 'like so many did. He condemned your execution of More, Fisher and the Carthusians. He likened you to the tyrants Nero and Domitian of Ancient Rome. Little wonder he will not come home!'

The King did not stretch down for his cane, so I moved a little closer. 'He said you did not deserve your title of Defender of the Faith. How you had torn to pieces and slaughtered all true defenders of the Faith. How you had been led away, like Solomon of old, by your passion for Anne Boleyn, whose head you must sever if you were to rid yourself of all your offences against God.'

'Well I did cut her head off.' The King forced a smile, more of a grimace in that fat face. I recalled a line from a song about someone who can smile and smile again and still mean murder. Henry closed his eyes, head drooping; he may have been nodding off, or he may have been brooding about Cardinal Reginald Pole, one of the few men he really fears.

His Majesty certainly did not forget Pole's insults. The cardinal's younger brother Geoffrey was arrested, and after two months of strict confinement and brutal interrogation in the Tower, he accused his own family of treason. Geoffrey later tried to commit suicide, but was released to live terror-stricken for all his days.

Reginald's other brother Henry was executed on Tower Hill. Their mother Margaret, the aged Countess of Salisbury, was also confined so closely in the Tower, she greatly protested that she lacked the necessary apparel to change and keep herself warm. The countess refused to confess to any treason, and was so strong in her denunciation that her interrogators complained they had not dealt with her like before, proving to be more strong and constant than any man. She did not face trial, but was dragged out of prison to the scaffold on Tower Green, where she refused to lay her head upon the block, saying that it was for traitors, and she was no traitor. She kept twisting her head, screaming at the executioner that if he would have it, he must get it as best he could. He did so, hacking and cutting the old woman's head, neck and body.

Before her execution the good countess had taunted His Majesty about the faith of his own family. His parents had devoted themselves to relics and pilgrimages, so why had he rejected such cherished beliefs? She reminded him that his father had treasured a piece of the True Cross brought from Greece, as well as the leg bone of St George, to whose memory the old king had been most devoted. That his mother, Queen Elizabeth, had sent purses of silver to Our Lady of Walsingham, the Rood of Grace at Northampton and Becket's shrine, not to mention Our Lady of Eton, the Child of Grace at Reading and the Holy Blood at Hailes Abbey. His Majesty never replied to such tauntings. Now, in his last days, he fears Reginald Pole, a cardinal living in Venice. Reginald has sworn great vengeance and has taken a blood oath that if Fortune ever turns her wheel and he returns to England after His Majesty's death, he will have the King's corpse dug up and his bones blown from a cannon as His Majesty has done to so many of this kingdom's sacred relics. In truth, Reginald is a man after my own heart; I keep him close in my secret thoughts, one of the few men to truly frighten our nightmare king.

According to reports, His Majesty has, out of fear of what Cardinal Pole intends, issued strict instructions in his will about his own secure interment in a pure marble sarcophagus, once the property of Wolsey, that now resides in St George's Chapel, Windsor. He also, according to Princess Mary's spy Master Balaam, hired a professional assassin, one Ludovico dall'Armi, a Venetian, to kill the cardinal. However, Ludovico murdered two other men in a vendetta and His Majesty had to use all his good offices with the Doge and council to save the assassin from being garrotted.

'Cromwell!' Henry roused himself, voice powerful like it used to be. 'Cromwell swore to make Cardinal Pole eat his own heart.' The King moved to grip the arms of his chair, hands sticky with blood. He picked up a goblet of water and sipped noisily at it. I wondered if Dudley and the other wolves would come snuffling at the door. They had been warned often enough to stay away. If the King wanted them to whisper and to plot, to play hazard or chess, he would ring that damn little bell, which, like the cane, is never far from his reach. 'Norfolk destroyed Cromwell.' Henry's voice was now nothing but a whisper, a trick of his whenever he recalls the past and wishes to be absolved of all blame. 'I can't bring Cromwell back,' he turned, grinning at me out of the corner of his eye, 'but I will avenge his ghost.' He wiped his nose on the back of his hand and fell silent.

I knew the story well enough. Whatever he claimed, the King had agreed to his minister's destruction, so Norfolk had spoken privately to the captain of the guard and instructed him to arrest Cromwell after dinner on the appointed day and take him to the Tower. The captain wondered very much at this, but the duke insisted he need not be surprised, for the King had so ordered it. On the chosen day, as was the custom, the Council went to Parliament at Westminster. When they came out and were about to cross the yard to the palace for dinner, the wind blew Secretary Cromwell's bonnet to the ground. Now the courtly convention is that when a gentleman loses his bonnet, all those with him must doff theirs, but on this occasion the other gentlemen did not. Cromwell noticed this and exclaimed: 'A high wind indeed, which blows my bonnet off but keeps all yours on.'

They pretended not to hear, and Cromwell took this as a bad omen. They went to the palace and dined, and all the while they were eating, the other councillors did not converse with Secretary Cromwell as was customary.

Once they had finished, the rest of the gentlemen went to the Council chamber. Now it was Cromwell's habit after dinner to go close to a window to hear petitioners once the others had left. As usual he remained at his window for about an hour, then joined his colleagues to find them already seated.

'You were in a great hurry to get seated, gentlemen,' he declared. The other councillors made no reply, but just as Cromwell was about to sit down, the Duke of Norfolk exclaimed, 'Cromwell, do not sit there. There is no place for you, a traitor, to sit amongst gentlemen.'

'I am no traitor,' Cromwell retorted.

With that the captain of the guard came in.

'I arrest you!' he declared.

'What for?' cried Cromwell.

'That you will learn soon enough,' Norfolk jibed. Then the duke rose and said, 'Wait, Captain, traitors must not wear the Garter.' He ripped this from him, pushed Cromwell to the door and the guards took him to the Tower.

I know the story by rote. I should do. The King has recited it often enough.

'Why?' I asked abruptly. 'Why did you really destroy Cromwell?'

'He failed me, Will. Melted like wax in the heat of my temper. He roused the beast in me. He should have known better. What did Thomas More say to that courtier who said I was as playful as a bear? To be careful lest the fun prove fatal and turn to—'

'Murder?'

Henry leaned across and snatched away Salisbury's silver necklace.

'Cromwell begged for your mercy,' I added, eager to distract him.

'And he got it.' Henry pulled a face. 'For seven weeks he languished in the Tower, wondering if he'd be dispatched to Hell by the headman's axe or burnt to a cinder as a heretic at Smithfield. Norfolk wanted that. He said he'd arrange for the faggots to be green and supple so they would burn slowly. He was insistent that Cromwell should have no gunpowder tied around his neck nor, when the smoke billowed, be quietly strangled by the executioner.' He raised his hand. 'Will,' his voice was almost pleading, 'I showed Cromwell great mercy.'

'No you did not.' I pushed back my stool. 'You gave him the sweeter, swifter way to judgement by making him confess to certain secret conversations he'd had with you which proved you never consummated your marriage to the German, Anne of Cleves. You could then separate from her without offending her brother and the other German princelings.' Henry was now quietly sobbing to himself. He likes to reminisce, then to justify. He is fearful of Cromwell and the rest of the ghosts; he complains persistently of how they haunt him day and night. He has even made careful search on reports about strange events and sightings at the Tower, where, according to the testimony of members of the garrison, the earth-bound souls of the King's victims cluster about while their headless bodies lie crammed and rotting in arrow chests beneath the flagstones of St Peter ad Vincula. Even more disturbing are stories from Blickling in Norfolk, once the home of Anne Boleyn. The ghost of the executed queen has often been glimpsed there, walking close to the great lake. She has even spoken to some local villagers, claiming she is searching for something she will never find.

'So, you went into the City.' Henry's blood-streaked fingers curled in the light of a square of burning beeswax.

'I went to St Paul's, that house of news, the mill of chatter and rumour which provides grist and grain for all those who take it.'

'And?'

'The lawyers and merchants parade arm in arm, faces close together along Duke Humphrey's Walk.'

'But what do they say?'

'Oh, how silent you have fallen . . . they wonder about the succession.' There, I had said it, a word that bubbles the fires of fear in our dread king's heart. I decided not to wait for his questions.

'They talk about the Princess Mary, daughter of your first wife, the Spanish Catherine. She is still popular because of her mother. Some people claim she has already been removed. Others chatter how imperial war cogs lie off the coast ready to whisk her away, of conspirators milling in houses close by where she lives, waiting for the sign to move.'

'I would like to see Mary soon.' Henry's voice was all sweet and cloying. 'I did her wrong, but there again, her proud Spanish blood wouldn't make her bend. What else do they say? Come on, Will, you must have heard the chatter?'

'You have only got yourself to blame for there being so little!'

Indeed he has. The recent Treasons Act has declared that 'If any person or persons do maliciously wish, will or desire by words or writing, or by craft imagined, invent, practice or attempt any bodily harm to His Majesty, he is guilty of high treason and shall suffer the full penalty of hanging and disembowelling.' Speculating about the King's death could provoke this. Those who are prudent heed such grisly warnings posted the length and breadth of both this city and the kingdom. It is now no novelty to see men slain, hanged, quartered and beheaded for trifling expressions later interpreted to have been spoken against the King. Indeed, when a man is a prisoner in the Tower, none dare meddle with his affairs unless to curse him, for fear of being suspected of the same crime. At court a man can neither speak nor be silent without danger. It is certainly perilous when the truth can be twisted into error by the altering of one syllable, either penned or spoken.

'What, Will?' bleated the King, clapping his hands. 'What else?'

'How your courtiers turn on each other. How my lords Seymour and Dudley play cards with you, but in the antechambers beyond they circle like wolves and search for the least sign of weakness in their rivals. A true carnival of blood! How your lords hide their naked villainy with scraps from Holy Writ. They seem the saint when in truth they play the devil.' I sighed to disguise my grin. 'People do not know what will come of it except that it is wise to plan for the worst because the best will provide for itself. How at court reformers and Romanists clash; even the bible, on which your councillors swear their oath of loyalty, has become a battleground. They say new men compete against the old, and some of the latter will never rest until they have done as much evil as they can to all who supported Cromwell. Yet even if this is settled, there are others, fresher yet, who will begin the bloody carnival again.' I paused. 'Do you really want to hear this, sire?'

'Nothing but divisions.' Henry grunted. 'Nothing new, it's safer that way. Continue, do not spare yourself.' He smirked. 'Or me!'

'Allegations of treason and treason yet again are thrown and hurled back, and if this does not suffice, the mere suspicion of treason can bring a man down. How the Lord Mayor of London has been commissioned to enquire secretly into all who speak ill against you or your Council. They say you are out of your wits yet you remain dangerous. What may be made today can be unmade tomorrow. Old men, new men, commoners or nobles. Have you not said there is no head, be it ever so fine, you could not make fly?'

Henry chuckled, clapping his hands. 'Remember, Will,' he hissed, 'it's best to lead men with love, but it is a sad reflection on human wickedness that most must be led by fear. Go on! I see you enjoy yourself!'

'In truth, never have you made a man but you later destroyed him with either displeasure or the sword. Brutal death has shattered anyone noble, whilst fear has shrunk up the rest.'

'And the succession?' Henry picked up the white wand and tapped it on the floor, pushing at the Turkey rugs like a shepherd would lambs with his crook.

'They say Princess Mary is illegitimate; that you made her so.'

'And I have changed that.' Henry glared at me. 'You know that. She is second in line if Heaven's own imp,' his voice trembled, 'my beautiful Edward dies without issue.'

'But you made her so.' I couldn't keep the anger out of my voice. Henry knows I am partial to Princess Mary and even more so to Lady Jane Bold, Mary's pretty fool. 'You see, Your Majesty,' I continued remorsefully, 'what can be undone then redone can be undone again.'

Henry lifted the cane and sighed. 'And the Princess Elizabeth?'

'What do you think? Little red-haired Elizabeth.' I emphasised every word. 'The gossipers call her the Great Whore's Daughter.'

Henry covered the side of his face with his hand. 'So the graveyard yawns,' he murmured. 'All the old ghosts are coming back. Ride on, Will,' he said wearily, 'tell me what the common tongue wags.'

'All the ghosts.' I felt the anger drain from me; the Princess Elizabeth was a sweet child, but one haunted by her mother's ghost. 'I plucked down a handbill posted at St Paul's Cross stirring up all the old insults spat out eleven years ago. How the Abbess of Whitby called Anne Boleyn a common stud, a goggle-eyed harlot. How she should have been burned as a common strumpet, how she was intimate with Henry Norris, the red-haired,' I emphasised the description, 'knight of your secret chamber. Indeed, how when Archbishop Cranmer ruled that your marriage was null and void, he made a slip of the tongue, claiming Elizabeth to be Norris's child. How Boleyn rendered you impotent, a witch with a spare teat. How when Anne was arrested, the ladies of her chamber were put to the torture. One of them was called Margaret—'

'I know this, I know this.' Henry's voice was all a-tremble, and for a moment he dropped his hand to show the tears glistening on his pasty skin. In truth, I am never too sure about our king's tears. He can cry at a blink, then act all marble-hearted. He worries about his daughters, yet this is a father who, on hearing how prim and proper the Princess Mary was, encouraged his old drinking partner, the one-eyed Francis Bryant, to approach her and say something salacious to discover her response. Princess Mary herself told me about this, as well as about her years of exile from both her mother and her father. How Boleyn had threatened to kill her secretly by poison, or, if the King left England and Anne was regent, to have her head taken on Tower Hill. Strange, strange, strange! Sometimes I think Henry likes to be reminded that if his wives failed, it was not his fault but theirs.

'One of these ladies,' I continued remorselessly, 'called Margaret, described how Anne searched London for the best-looking singer and dancer and found him in young Mark Seaton. How she fell in love with him and begged this old woman to bring him to her every night.'

'Enough, enough, I know this tale well enough.'

'Except, Your Majesty, the gossipers say that the only difference between Mary and Elizabeth is that although both were made illegitimate by statute, only one of them really is.'

'If I caught such a gossiper . . .' The King, eyes closed, rubbed his hands as if he was secretly watching the most grisly disembowelling at Tyburn. As he sat slouched in his chair, now and again a wince of pain would crease his puffy face. He looked mice-eyed. I also noticed that he grasped an insignia of the Garter, its ribbon besmirched and torn. I moved and glanced round at a book lying on the floor between the King's chair and his great four-poster bed. I recognised 'The Book of the Knights of the Garter', those who gather every year in St George's Chapel, Windsor. Henry had been busy. The tattered, stained insignia certainly belonged to Cromwell, the one Norfolk had ripped from him. The King had been reminiscing. I rose, picked up the heavy calf-skin book, turning the thick stiffened pages to the list of knights inscribed since his own coronation. Many of those names were now scratched out. Beside each of them Henry had scrawled in his own hand, 'Oh traitor!' I wondered how much I really dared tell him. Henry was weakening, his body failing, but that cunning mind was as sharp as ever. If I flattered him, he'd sense that and flail out with his cane, or, even worse, banish me. Despite being a mountain of lies himself, he had a nose for dissimulation.

'Any more news from St Paul's?' He leaned over and snatched the book from my hands. 'You went into the markets, the taverns. Tell me, Will, what did you find? What are you keeping in that journal I told you to begin?'

'You may read it yourself, Your Majesty.' I had already secretly determined he would not.

'I don't bark when I have my own dog. Moreover, Will, you use the shorthand Master Cromwell taught you; he claimed you were one of his most able pupils. I could never understand it. So, cut to the chase, what is happening amongst the common herd?'

'Unrest seethes like a fire bubbling beneath a pot,' I replied slowly. 'Rumours quicken. A Buckinghamshire man in open court claimed you were no better than a knave whose crown was only fit to play football with.' Henry started at the relish in my voice. I lowered my head. 'In Warwick, at the market cross, a travelling

35

tinker proclaimed Your Majesty a worse tyrant than Nero. When ordered to keep the King's peace, he retorted, before he fled, that he did not give a turd for the King. Strange prophecies are circulating: how the white hare shall drive the fox to the castle of care and the swift greyhound shall run under the root of the oak and there'll be such a gap in the west that all the forces of England shall have enough work to stop it.'

'What does such nonsense mean?' Henry snapped.

'Chatter from Somerset says this riddle predicts a war of religious fervour. A trader in Buckinghamshire muttered to a merchant who is sweet on one of the maids at the Lamb of God how dreadful dragons will land on the coast with a host of bare-legged chickens, a reference perhaps to a rebellion in Ireland. Marvels have also been reported, omens for the future.' I hid my grin. 'A dead fish, the like of which has never been seen before, a veritable monster thirty yards long, lies beached on the northern coast beneath the soaring battlements of Bamburgh Castle. Recently the Severn flowed in continuously for nine hours so water flooded the Guildhall at Bristol, whilst above it a ball of fire the size of a human head streaked the sky. A comet with a trail of flame as long as a Munster man's beard was also glimpsed in the skies over Norwich, or so they tell me.'

'And Monsieur Odet de Selve and my lord van der Delft, you mixed with their men? What did they babble? Did they allude to comets and stars, beached whales or a baby born with two heads? Is it true that Monsieur de Selve still complains about the cold? What does his master say, the noble Francis? Come on now, Will, tell me!' Henry beat the arm of his chair with his wrist.

'Sire, according to the French ambassador, the noble King Francis finds you the hardest friend to bear, at one time unstable, at another time obstinate and proud. You think you are wise but he considers you a fool. He judges you to be the strangest man in the world. But there again,' I grinned, 'he would say that, wouldn't he? We hold Calais and Boulogne.'

'And I'll go back there,' Henry whispered. 'I am designing new ships, Will. I have told my smiths to cast bigger guns and mortars to hurl pots of wild fire against the French. Is there any news about the Genoese?'

I decided not to reply to that: far too dangerous! Henry can be shrewd but at the same time so easily duped. Quite recently a Genoese, slippery as a Lincolnshire eel, proposed to construct a monstrous mirror on the top of the keep at Dover Castle. The machine would reflect whatever was happening along the French coast, so any hostile craft leaving the ports of France would be seen long before it ever reached the English shore. The King, and even Heaven must wonder why, believed the charlatan and sent him south with purses bulging with gold, but after that, no more: no man, no mirror.

'And my lord van der Delft, the Imperial ambassador? What do his men say?'

'That you set your lords at each other's throats like a pack of fighting dogs straining on their leashes. How you allow them to turn on each other so you can berate them all.'

Henry covered his mouth with his hand and giggled like a girl.

'How you pull back one pack and let the other take the lead. How you stir the pot, one day this way, the other that. The envoys complain bitterly about the huge bribes paid for spying on you. How there is no certainty which path you will follow. How you are King Janus looking this way, then that. How you condemn Rome and support the reformers on Monday, but on Tuesday persecute the reformers and secretly weep for Rome. How you are ever-changing, ever fickle.'

'That is not true.' Henry pulled at the rug covering his legs.

'You know it is,' I retorted. 'Didn't you receive the papal envoy recently and talk about a general council? Then you met the French. I was there! You secretly discussed a plan whereby France and the Empire would join you in a general denunciation and refutation of the power of the Pope.'

Henry thought this was amusing; he sat chuckling to himself. Huicke must have given him some opiate to dull the nerves and numb the pain. Nevertheless, I was curious. Henry was leading somewhere, but there again so was I: an opportunity to discover what was being plotted.

'What else did they say? I mean about my councillors?'

'Oh, how they plot against each other. And worse.' My voice sank to a whisper.

'What, Will?'

'Your Majesty, what if they unite to plot against you?'

Henry searched beneath the gold-encrusted rug and brought out a jingling purse. He tossed this at me; a fleck of blood from his fingers splashed my hand. As I grasped the purse, the King abruptly seized my arm, nipping the skin. 'There you have said it,' he murmured, 'the heart of the darkness.' He let go of me. 'Will, I meet the Council later this evening. You must be there in your accustomed place. First let me sleep for a while; bring me some white wine.' I rose and filled a brimming goblet, which the King supped, talking to himself in a chattering whisper I couldn't follow, although I caught the names 'Boleyn' and 'Cromwell'. He put the wine down and dozed for a while. Now and again he would mutter, at one time crying out for his mother and then calling for Tom, but whether this was Wolsey, Cromwell or More I couldn't say. I sat back and studied him, his mouth slightly open, saliva dribbling down. I was mindful that I was watching a snake that had been lying dormant but was now ready to strike. Henry was about to give the wheel of fortune another viciously swift turn. He talks about the past, but he does not concern himself too much about that. He often informs me how he and God are on the best of terms and he has no problem with his conscience. Others would definitely disagree.

A darkness certainly broods over this kingdom. On my travels I do not recall having ever seen its people so morose as they are at present. They do not know whom to trust, and Henry himself, having offended so many, mistrusts everyone. He is still inclined to his amours, despite his age and ailments, at least in the eyes of his subjects. A porter at Syon was recently hauled before the Council for saying that the King kept a bevy of mistresses for his own amusement at a secret manor close by. A broadsheet published privately by 'a Sanctuary Man at Westminster' claims how a William Webbe, whilst riding out near Eltham, his pretty wench behind him, met the King coursing his hounds. His Majesty, according to Webbe, plucked down her muffler and kissed the wench. Indeed, the King, liking her so much and being puffed up with lechery, vainglory and pride, took the doxy for himself. On account of this Master Webbe has sworn bloody vengeance against the King, as have others. He certainly has his enemies. Little wonder Westminster and Whitehall are closely guarded by engines of war, gentlemen pensioners with their pole-axes and archers by the score. More dangerous, Balaam's spy in Bucklebury claims, there may be a plot to murder the King by slipping a poison into the potions and powders given to him, yet I've seen no proof for this.

The ubiquitous, all-seeing, far-gazing Balaam maintains that the cause and the root of the King's growing malignancy is not so much his amorousness; indeed, so Balaam reports, that is catered for most delicately by Her Grace the Queen, Henry's sixth wife, formerly the Lady Katherine Parr. According to Balaam, who can snout scandal as a hog would a truffle, the lovely Katherine conforms perfectly to the mirror of womanly excellence. She proves to be an ape in bed, a shrew in the kitchen, a saint in the church and an angel at the board. No, Balaam argues, the King's true malignancy is his insufferable pride. He will not be checked. Henry recently roared at his Council that he has the right of everything not because so many agree with him but because he, being learned, knows the matter to be right. His Demonic Majesty rejoices in wearing a gold bracelet studded with jewels and inscribed: '*Plus tot mourir que changer ma pensée*' – 'I would rather die than change my mind'. My Satanic master is, in his own view, the One Supreme Head and King, having the dignity and royal estate of the Imperial kind. He wields power, plenary, whole and entire, and so enjoys above all others authority, prerogative and jurisdiction. 'God has not only made us King,' he proclaims, 'but has given us wisdom of policy, and other graces in plentiful so necessary for a prince to direct his affairs to his own honour and glory.'

I stared at Henry, his great bulk overspilling the chair, the towel wrapped around his head slipping down, his face all twitching, lips still moving. I wondered what he was dreaming about. Was he truly sleeping, or was his brain teeming like a box of squirming worms devising some devious stratagem? If that was the case, someone would die. I gazed around the chamber, so luxuriously opulent. Glowing tapestries, a maze of many colours, covered the walls, silver and gold candlesticks, spigots, precious cups, goblets and dishes caught the eye. So much death had been plotted here. I shivered, rose, crossed to the hearth and placed two finely cut scented logs on the dying fire. A jakes pot in the corner caught my attention; its linen covering had slipped to reveal the squalid filth inside. I went across and pulled the cloth back over, but the smell was so offensive I hastily snatched a pomander and held it against my nose. I walked across to the thick, mullioned-glass window, which shimmered in the light of countless candles. I pressed my face against its cold surface. In the courtyard below, councillors were arriving. I glimpsed the white lion of Norfolk in the fluttering torchlight. Steel gleamed, the sound of voices and the stir of horses carried faintly. Snow was falling, thin, meagre flakes to wet the ledges and cornices.

'Some wine, Will?' Startled, I turned quickly. The King, now very much awake, was staring at me curiously. 'Have you eaten?' He gestured at a tray of sweetmeats next to a flagon of German wine, the jug carved in the shape of a dolphin. I went across, carefully filled a Venetian fluted glass and brought it over to the King. He gulped the sweetmeats and greedily drank the wine. He thrust the glass back into my hand and spluttered, staining my hands with the contents of his mouth, at the same time declaring how both jug and glass had once belonged to Edward Stafford, Duke of Buckingham.

'You wouldn't remember him, Will, a great lord. He hated Wolsey the Red Man, and Wolsey hated him. One day Buckingham had to act as ewerer. He deliberately poured the water over Wolsey's purple silken slippers. I cut his head off, Will, snipped it as you would a flower.' The King brushed his lap, snapping his fingers. 'Bring me the chess board.' I did so. Henry, all energetic, balanced it on his lap, sweeping the pieces into a bowl half full of mouldy fruit. He grabbed four of the crown pieces, placed them on the board and gestured at me to draw closer, as if we were two conspirators in some dingy tavern.

'Here am I.' He took the largest piece and placed it on the board. 'Thirty-seven years a king, now in my fifty-sixth summer. Physician Huicke tells me I might die.' He snorted through his nose. 'One day I will, and so shall he, sooner than he thinks if his care doesn't improve. Next in line,' he picked up another of the chessmen, 'the golden boy, Heaven's own child, my darling son Edward. Nine years old, fair-haired, grey-eyed, with a pointed chin. The say he is the very image of his mother, Queen Jane, a Seymour through and through but still a Tudor. Do you know, Will, there is a vicious story that I was so desperate to have a son that I ordered the physicians and midwives to rip open the Queen's stomach and pluck him out.'

'Did you?' I asked before I could stop myself. The King's fist, fingers now all decorated with heavy rings, smashed into my face, a stinging, cutting blow just beneath the left eye. His lips were curled, his rotting yellow teeth more like fangs, spots of anger high in that flour-like skin. And those eyes: no longer narrow like those of a pig, but fully open in their raging fury. I fell to my knees.

'Your Majesty. I jested.'

Henry rocked backwards and forwards in his chair.

'Are you keeping that journal, Will? The one I asked you to write at the beginning of this week?'

'Of course, Your Majesty.' I felt the King's hand on my head. He grasped my scrawny brown hair, forcing me to look directly at him. The fury had faded. He released me and gently stroked my bruised cheek.

'I need you, Will.' Tears filled his eyes; his jutting lower lip trembled. 'I need you to listen to me and give me good advice. You are my Everyman. Oh, go on. See to your face.' I crossed to the lavarium, dipped a napkin in the cold water and, holding it to my cheek, returned to the stool.

'Edward is nine,' the King continued conversationally. 'Soon I will create him Prince of Wales, yet it will be five or six years before he can beget an heir, whilst his constitution is not strong. He is tutored in the faith I want.' I was tempted to ask what that was; Henry's faith changes every day. Instead I kept my mouth firmly closed and nodded wisely.

'Should Edward die,' Henry moved another piece on to the board, 'there is Princess Mary, but she has Spanish blood and is an avowed papist. Apart from the Norfolks and Stephen Gardiner, Bishop of Winchester, she would regard members of the present Council as her sworn enemies, traitors to herself, to her church and to the memory of her allegedly blessed mother. Then there's Elizabeth, the child of contention, whose legitimacy is suspect, whilst her mother, according to gossip, was nothing better than a goggle-eyed whore.'

I tensed. Henry was no longer meandering or wandering but studying a problem that had hounded him for most of his life. He grasped my arm as if we were the closest of friends. 'Just over sixty years ago, Will, my father crushed the Yorkists at Bosworth and killed the usurper in mortal combat. We Tudors came into our own. But time passes. Master Luther called me Squire Tudor, nothing better than a Welsh farmer. Look at our Council! You see my suspicions? If a Tudor can become king, why not a Dudley, why not a Seymour . . .?'

'And above all, why not a Howard?'

'Aye, Will. Why not? Norfolk's grandfather fought for the Yorkist Richard at Bosworth. God knows what dreams the Howards dream as they creep and crawl towards the throne. They offered two of their women, Anne and Katherine, as my wife and queen. They dream dreams about inviting Cardinal Pole home, of restoring ties with Rome. Perhaps they even plot a marriage between a Howard and one of my daughters? However, let us not forget the others, such as Edmund Dudley, Viscount Lisle, Lord High Admiral, so fervently supported by my brother-in-law Edward Seymour, who wrote to me recently,' the King closed his eyes, '"I can do no less than recommend the Viscount Lisle to Your Highness, as one who has served you heartily, wisely, diligently, painfully and obediently as any man I have ever seen."' The sneer in the King's voice was clear and stark. 'Dudley! I executed his father. I threw his head to the people to please them. Has he forgiven me and forgotten that?' Henry's voice crackled. I sensed the danger he was hinting at. Would Dudley invoke the blood feud? That was the ongoing difficulty: so much bad blood between all of them. 'There is division. The reformists, Dudley, Somerset, Wriothesley and that master of secret practices Sir William Paget; and on the other side the Romanists, the Norfolks and their good friend Gardiner.' The King raised his hands as if weighing something in the scale, his smile rich in malice. 'Which ones first, eh, Will? But enough. Go.' He gestured. 'See to your face. At the appointed time join us in the Council chamber.'

I withdrew from the royal presence. The gallery outside was dark and cold, lit by lantern horns and oil lamps placed in niches. There was a rank smell. A sense of menace cloaks that long, glittering gallery, dappled in shadows, the light juddering and flickering. In dark recesses and shadowy corners stand the Spears, the King's personal halberdiers; their presence proves a grim reminder of swift arrest and even swifter punishment. I walked quickly, my footsteps echoing like a drum beat. A figure darted out of one of the chambers to my right. Sir William Paget grasped my shoulder and pushed me into the Chancery of the Secret Seal, the King's own writing office. Dark and closed, the walls panelled in stained oak, the floor covered with special rope matting over which thick taffeta had been stretched to deaden sound. Across the room, beneath a small oriel window filled with painted glass looted from Peterborough Abbey, where Catherine of Aragon's corpse lies interred, stood the King's great chancery table. A clerk bent over this, busy with a roll of vellum, beside his elbow a carved wooden block. Paget coughed, even as the bell in the King's chamber rang out its demands. The man glanced over his shoulder; I recognised William Clarke of the Chancery. Whatever he was working on swiftly disappeared into a black leather bag bearing the Royal Arms.

'Your royal master calls.' Paget tried but failed to keep the sarcasm out of his voice. The clerk jumped up like the startled rabbit he resembled, with his snub nose, twitching mouth, thinning hair and bulbous eyes, which sometimes have the stare of a mad March hare. He scuttled out of the room; Paget closed the door behind him, his clever, secretive face a mask of concern. The Chief Secretary of the Council was plainly dressed, a buttoned cap over his thick auburn hair. A lockram falling band, coarse but clean, circled his throat. He wore a brown coat tied with a belt of white horse hide whilst his breeches of russet sheep's wool stretched down to stockings of white kersey thrust into battered leather boots. He removed his heavy gauntlets and placed these in a wicker basket close to the hearth, where a merry fire crackled.

'Gardening.' He answered my enquiring look. Paget is a keen horticulturist. A man who plots as he prunes, who conspires as he cuts, who will walk a garden and be busy plotting his own secret way through a maze of intrigue. I stared at the window, against which white snowflakes floated.

'In this weather?' I asked.

'Not planting, Will. Now is not the time for that. As Ecclesiasticus says, there is a time for planting and a time for pulling up.' He let the menace drain from his voice and grinned. 'In truth, I have just taken possession of some apple trees, which those galleys at the King's Steps have brought from France. Nothing like planting.' He winked. 'Or planning.'

'Or plotting?'

'True, Will, the future always beckons.' Paget fumbled at a hanging thread on his coat; he loosened the horse-hide belt. I became distracted by the beautiful ruby, no bigger than a coin, deeply embedded in the oak panelling just above his head. I recognised the Ruby of France taken from Becket's shrine at Canterbury. A precious stone of unique powers. The writing office was dark, the light from the capped candles fitful, yet the scarlet radiance of that precious stone shone like a beacon through the shifting shadows.

'All things change, Will.' Paget followed my gaze.

'For the better, I hope, Sir William. What do you want with me?'

'The King, His Majesty?'

'Ask him yourself.' I stared at this smiler who always carried a dagger beneath his cloak.

'I will do so tomorrow. What agitates His Majesty?'

'People who ask questions, Sir William, so why not do it yourself?'

'Will,' Paget leaned forward, his saturnine face creased in a frown, 'I am not your enemy.'

'Are you my friend?'

'I could be. Sooner or later you may need one.'

'I have friends.'

'Ah yes, the Lady Jane, the innocent, the fool, the jester in Princess Mary's household. She who likes to wear blood-red petticoats.'

I simply stared back.

'And you also consider the Princess Mary to be your friend?' Paget rounded his eyes. 'She too has friends. She also has agents, couriers, men dispatched from her ally, Cardinal Pole in Venice.'

I kept my face impassive, concealing my unease. Paget rose, walked to the desk and returned with a scroll. He undid the red ribbon.

'This is a report from one of my agents in York. You know how the northern march, the border shires still lie bruised from His Majesty's forceful suppression of the Pilgrimage of Grace ten years previous, when Norfolk, with his son Henry of Surrey, caused such dreadful execution upon a goodly number of its inhabitants.' Paget shook his head. 'Norfolk swept through the rebels with sword and fire, hanging them on trees, disembowelling and cutting them, their quarters boiled and tarred, festooned in every town as a fearful warning. Men and women were hanged on poles in their own gardens, from the signs of village taverns, on the branches of churchyard yew trees or along the highways beyond.' He clicked his tongue. 'Most of the victims were poor men, their womenfolk being forced to creep out at night to steal back the corpses. They then kept these cadavers shrouded and hidden in their cottages until the royal levies passed, even though the corrupting flesh spread further pestilence amongst the living.'

Paget paused and crossed himself. I did not reply. He was quietly reminding me that my family, the Somerses, not to mention my former patron Sir Richard Fermor, had been caught up in this bloody tempest, as had the kin of my sweetheart, the Lady Jane Bold. Worse, I knew Balaam had been, and still is, active in those northern parts. Paget was threatening me ever so subtly.

'His Majesty still fears the north and a possible alliance between the border shires and the Scots,' he murmured. 'Resentment at the King and his Council continues to seethe along the marches. A broadsheet was recently pinned to the door of Durham Cathedral, a centre of unrest in the great rebellion.' Paget glanced down at the report. '"Since the realm of England was first a realm", this begins, "there never was in it so great a robber and pillager of the Commonwealth as our present king. We of the spirituality" –' he glanced up, grinning, 'the writer poses as a former priest – "are oppressed and robbed of our livings as if we were his utter enemies as well as those of Christ, guilty of our Saviour's death."' He tutted under his breath before continuing. '"In such an ungodly way this king handles innocents as well as learned and goodly men, not only robbing them of their livings and depriving them of their goods but also thrusting them into perpetual prison. It is too great a misery to bear and more to be lamented than any good Christian here may abide."' Paget paused. 'Can you believe this, Will? Listen, it goes on: "This king has also pillaged his nobility, using their wealth to construct towering palaces in which he enjoys and revels in his filthy pleasures. Our king is mired in vice, more vile and fetid than a sow which wallows and befouls itself in every stinking place. He has given himself up to the filthy pleasure of voluptuousness. He violates every woman at his court, neglecting the sanctity of marriage, and has taken to himself the wives of fornication."' He stared at me.

'Treason,' I conceded. 'What happened?'

'His Majesty's justices and commissioners in those

parts were furious. They tore down the broadsheets and organised the strictest search for its author, who proclaimed himself as Balaam, son of Beor, the oracle of the prophet, the man with the far-seeing eyes, the one who hears the Word of God. He sees what Shaddai makes him see. He receives the divine answer and his eyes are open.' Paget shrugged. 'Balaam's pursuers were not successful, and so Balaam, that man with the far-seeing gaze, struck again. A masque was staged in the great space before Durham Cathedral, the spectators drawn in by proclamations and rumours. The players gathered all visored and cloaked to perform a parable of the times. They even produced forged licences from the Council to warrant this. The stage was set up, great casks rolled out in front of the cathedral door. On one barrel sat God, clothed in white with a glorious sun mask. A pilgrim, garbed in dusty grey, face all painted red, approached God's throne. The pilgrim pointed to the cathedral, recently pillaged by the reformists and stripped of its statues, pictures and reliquaries.

'"How is it, Lord," he asked, "that you are alone? What has become of all your saints?"

'God answered, "They've all left, there are none here. They have departed to Spain, France, Flanders, Italy and Portugal."

'Pilgrim then replied, "Well, since you are alone, I shall not stay here either. I want to go to a place where you are surrounded by a more merry company." He turned to the other barrel, where Lord Satan sat enthroned, cloaked in purple, a gold mask on his face, a silver crown on his head. He too was alone, so the pilgrim asked him:

'"How is it that you are alone? What has become of all your devils?"

'To which Satan replied, "They've all left because they have so much work to do in England!"'

Paget glanced at the light fading against the oriel window. 'Balaam is a troublemaker, an agitator, a man who will end up being burned, boiled or hanged at Smithfield. I was in Smithfield this morning, Will. I watched Dr John Ashdown, a papist who won't take the oath, being burnt alive. They took him to a gibbet between two platforms and tied chains around his waist and hung him up suspended by the middle. He begged to have his hands freed, which they did, before starting a fire beneath him. The air turned smoky black, bitter-sweet with the reek of burning flesh. The skin of the poor man's legs bubbled and broke. I could hear the hiss of his body fat wetting the flames. Only when the fire reached his chest did the victim cease his writhing and hang still.'

'God have mercy on all such sinners,' I prayed. 'You must be greatly discomforted, Sir William. No wonder you plant apple trees, a soothe for your soul?'

'Or my belly. I retired for dinner to a nearby tavern and fed fairly well on a beef pie sopped in ale and capon sauce. Afterwards I returned to Smithfield; the crowd had dispersed and the gibbet was nothing but a smouldering, blackened wreck. Ashdown's remains had been taken and buried in the nearby hospital, though certain ladies, faces masked, were digging with pots and spoons about the execution spot, searching for scraps and globules of the dead man's corpse to preserve as relics.'

Paget watched the effect of his words on me, smiling with his mouth, eyes unblinking.

'I don't like seeing people die, Will. Nevertheless, I was His Majesty's witness, and today he determined that if he showed himself hard on papists and Romanists, he must be equally ruthless with reformers. Lambert came next, late in the afternoon. A leading member of the reformist party, he had openly attacked the sacrament, claiming the presence of Christ was only symbolic. He was questioned cruelly by the bishops but refused to recant. Condemned to burn, he was taken out of prison at four in the afternoon and carried to the house of a certain lord, deep into the inward chamber, where he was admonished for the last time because his end was near. He remained cheerful, however, and comforted. On being brought out of the inward chamber into the hall, he saluted the gentlemen present and sat down to sup with them, showing no manner of sadness or fear. Once the meal ended, he was immediately carried off to the place of execution. I was there, standing on a bench beneath an elm tree with some pie crusts in a napkin. Lambert was lashed to a stake on a high platform and the fire lit, but the flames were not allowed to do their worst swiftly and expediently. After his legs were burnt to the stumps, the fire was doused to no more than a few fiery coals. Guards either side used their halberds to raise Lambert on their pikes. The flames were then strengthened, and Lambert, his finger ends flaming with fire, was lowered to burn until the inferno reached his chest, before being raised yet again. The stench of the billowing black smoke, the screams and the horrid sounds proved too much. I gave my crusts to a beggar man and left.'

Paget picked up his gauntlets, examining them as if for the first time. He shook his head as if genuinely grieving. 'Nobody is safe, Will, be they sane or moonstruck. Take the case of Mr Collins, recorded in the Acts of the Privy Council. He had a wife of excellent beauty and comeliness, but notwithstanding that, she was light in her behaviour, of an unchaste condition. She left her husband for another. Mr Collins took this very grievously, more heavily than reason would allow. At last, being overcome with exceeding sorrow and grief, he became quite mad, and entered a church where a priest celebrating mass was about to raise the host. Collins, being out of his mind, and wishing to imitate the priest, took up a little dog by the legs and held it over his head, shouting out to the people. For that, despite the poor man's senses being turned, the King ordered him to be examined, tried and burnt at Smithfield, the dog alongside him.' Paget fell silent. I knew his reference to those who are moonstruck or witless was a jibe at me. My status as a fool, as the King's jester, would not save me from Henry's wrath. This dark soul and master of politics was making his presence felt. In that chamber I secretly acknowledged that of all the wolves gathered around my failing master, of all the wild hogs snouting at the royal trough, this man, together with Chancellor Wriothesley, was the most dangerous.

'And there are other dangers, aren't there, Will?' Paget persisted. 'The settling of grudges and grievances. You have heard the story about Robert Packington, a man of substance, discreet and honest? No? Well, Packington dwelt in Cheapside, the main thoroughfare of this city, graced with shops, stalls and the stately mansions of the wealthy. Surely a place of safety – yes? Well, every day at five o'clock, winter or summer, weather fine or foul, he would go to pray at a church once called St Thomas Acres, recently renamed the Mercers' Chapel. One grey, misty morning, Packington was crossing the street from his house to the church when he was brutally murdered with a pistol, its discharge being heard by a great number of labourers standing at the end of Soper Lane, though they did not glimpse the assassin. Only later did Dr Incent, Dean of St Paul's, confess on his deathbed that he, growing tired of Packington's railings against Romanist clergy, had hired an assassin for sixty crowns to kill the merchant.'

'Master Paget.' I moved restlessly on my stool. 'You

have now alerted me to all the dangers. Are you finished, or is there more?'

'Will, I am trying to be your friend; I wish you were mine. I am trying to warn you, or shall I say advise you. I know all about Balaam, as he calls himself, son of Beor, the man with the far-seeing eyes, who sees what other people can't see. That's how he describes himself, isn't it? A man who flits like a little fly, a veritable will-o'-the-wisp. Was he Packington's assassin? Whether he was or not, one day Balaam will be caught. He will be racked in the dungeons beneath the White Tower and he will confess.'

'To what?'

'To whatever I tell him to.' Paget waved a hand at me. 'Perhaps he may tell me about how you, he and the Princess Mary's fool and jester, the Lady Jane Bold, meet in a tavern in Whitefriars. What is it called, the Bowels of Hell?' He paused. 'You do most tenderly care for the Lady Jane, don't you? You always have. Both she and you support the Princess Mary, Catherine of Aragon's daughter. You all think you are safe.' He shook his head. 'Very few people have studied our king as I have. They think they can play with the Great Beast. Well, you were absent when this occurred.' Paget was now talking quietly, as if to himself. He glanced under his eyebrows at me. 'Of all men I reckoned to be safe, surely that would be Thomas Cranmer, Archbishop of Canterbury, the priest who brought about Henry's divorce from Catherine of Aragon so he could marry the great lust of his life, Anne Boleyn. Now, as I said, you were absent from court when this happened, the King having dispatched you on some errand or another. Anyway, despite all the archbishop had done for him, the King allowed Gardiner and Norfolk, those two cheeks of the same arse, to launch an attack on Cranmer. Oh yes!' Paget wagged a finger at me. 'They came into the King's presence and accused Cranmer most grievously. They alleged that he and his learned men had so infected the whole realm with their unsavoury doctrines that almost all the land was becoming diseased with detestable heresy to the great danger of the King, as it might produce the same commotion and uproar as it had in Germany. They insisted that the archbishop be committed to the Tower so that he might be more closely examined.' Paget pulled a face. 'His Majesty was most reluctant in granting this demand, but they persisted, claiming that no man dared level an accusation against Cranmer unless he was first committed to prison. Once this was done, they assured the King, men bold enough to tell the truth according to their consciences would come forward. Upon this persuasion, His Majesty reluctantly agreed that they should summon the archbishop next day before them and, if they found just cause, commit him to the Tower.'

Paget refilled his goblet. I had heard rumours of what he was telling me. Once I'd asked the King himself, but he simply lifted his cane and shook it at me. Paget was correct. If Cranmer could be threatened, the Keeper of the King's Soul, why not his fool, his jester? Henry might beat me, but he is also my shield, my bulwark. I am his creature, but there again, so is Cranmer, so was Cromwell, and all that trail of ghosts who now haunt His Malevolent Majesty. Would Henry sacrifice me upon the altar of fickleness? And if he died, would others consider me an embarrassment, to be dealt with in a welter of blood-letting? Terror prowls Henry's court, and in that shadowy chamber, I felt its fingers brush my soul.

'The King, however, had designs of his own.' Paget continued. 'At midnight on the day the archbishop was to appear before the Council, Henry sent one of his confidants to my lord at Lambeth demanding that Cranmer immediately adjourn to the royal presence. The archbishop was in bed, but rose straight away, dressed and repaired to the King, whom he found in the gallery at Whitehall. Once he had arrived, Henry revealed what he had done. How the Council wanted to commit Cranmer to the Tower on certain charges levelled against him. "I have granted their request," the King declared, "but as to whether they have done well or no, what say you, my lord?" The archbishop humbly thanked the King that he had given him warning before-hand. However, Cranmer added, he was very content to be committed to the Tower for questioning on his doctrines so that he might be heard. His Majesty was astonished at this and immediately cried out: "Oh Lord God, what fond simplicity you have, to commit yourself to be imprisoned so every enemy of yours can take advantage against you. Don't you know how, once they have you in prison, three or four false liars will soon be sent forward to witness against you and condemn you? These same accusers, because you are now at liberty, dare not open their lips or appear before you. Oh no," the King continued, "I have better regard for you than to let your enemies overthrow you. So tomorrow, after you come to the Council – and have no doubt they will send for you – when they reveal this matter to you, demand that, being one of them, you have as much favour as they would enjoy themselves. Insist that your accusers be brought before you. However, if they refuse and persist on committing you to the Tower, then appeal from them to me and give them this ring," which he handed over to the archbishop. "By this token," the King added, "they will know what I mean. I use this ring for no other purpose than to revoke matters from the Council to myself." And with this good advice ringing in his ears, Cranmer, after his most humble thanks, departed from His Majesty.'

Paget sat, head cocked to one side, as if listening to sounds from outside. He was telling the truth. I knew about this ring and the King's use of it. I also felt a cold dread. I confess that deep in my soul I always thought I was safe, inured to the King's dreadful games of the soul. Was this what Paget wanted to disturb?

'Listen now.' The King's Chief Secretary leaned closer. 'The next morning, according to the King's warning and his own expectations, the Council summoned Cranmer to be at their chamber by eight o'clock. When he came to the Council door, however, he was not permitted to enter but was told to remain outside for at least three quarters of an hour, many others going in and out. The matter seemed most strange to the archbishop's secretary, so he slipped away to inform the King's physician, Huicke. Huicke, not believing this, hurried to the antechamber and found it to be true that Thomas Cranmer, Lord Archbishop of Canterbury, had been forced to wait outside the door like some menial servant. The physician went directly and informed the King. "What is that?" exclaimed His Majesty. "By the mass, so my lord of Canterbury has become a menial, a serving man, to stand for almost an hour before the Council allow him entrance? How dare they serve my lord so?" Then His Majesty in a fit of rage lifted his hand, pointing his finger at the ceiling. "I shall talk with them by and by."' Paget now had his eyes shut, reciting what he had apparently learnt by heart. I feverishly searched my own memory about his whereabouts. Hadn't he been absent on an embassy to Paris?

He opened his eyes. 'Shall I continue, Will? Eh? A lesson for both of us?'

I nodded.

'The Lord Archbishop was summoned before the Council. They revealed that a most serious complaint had been levelled against him, both to them and the King. How he and others of his household had infected the whole realm with heresy so it was the King's pleasure that they should commit him to the Tower, where he could be carefully examined on what he had written and preached. Cranmer insisted that his accusers appear with him there and then before any further punishment was imposed. Although he argued most eloquently, he could make no headway, and they insisted that he be confined to the Tower. "I am sorry, my lords," Cranmer eventually declared, "but you drive me to this necessity. I appeal from you to His Majesty, who by this token has taken the matter into his own hands." Opening his wallet, he took out the ring and showed it to them. Immediately one of the council, Lord Russell, swore a great oath and said, "Did I not tell you, my lords, that ill would come of this matter? I always knew the King would never permit my lord of Canterbury to have such a blemish and be imprisoned unless it was for high treason."

'The Council, now terrified out of their wits, immediately adjourned to the royal presence, taking with them Cranmer and the ring he had produced. When they came into his privy chamber, the King said, "Ah, my lords, I always thought I had a discreet Council, but now I see I am much deceived. Why have you handled my lord of Canterbury so? What are you making of him? A slave? Shutting him out of the council chamber amongst the serving men? Would you like to be trapped like that?" After such taunting words the King added, "I would have you all consider my lord of

Canterbury as faithful a man towards me as any in this realm and one who in many ways is cherished by the faith I owe to God. Therefore," the King tapped his chest, "whoever loveth me loveth him."

'The Duke of Norfolk immediately went down on his knees and answered for the rest. "Your Grace," he declared, "we meant no harm or hurt to my lord of Canterbury. We only requested that he be confined to the Tower so that he might, after his trial, be set at liberty to even greater glory." His Majesty simply smirked and tapped Norfolk gently on the side of the head. "Very well, very well," he replied, "but I pray do not ever use my friends so. I can clearly see how the world goes amongst you. There is a lot of malice from one to the other. Let this be avoided, I warn you." Then, turning on his heel, he left the royal chamber. The Romanists on the Council had no choice but to shake hands, every one of them, with the archbishop, against whom never again did they raise a word.'

'Were you one of those, my lord?'

Paget scratched his ear, rubbing his lobe thoughtfully. 'I simply describe what happened. I learnt a most valuable lesson that day.' He held up finger and thumb slightly apart. 'So close, Will. Never mind the royal praise; Cranmer was that close to joining all those others our king has used and abused, be it Buckingham, Wolsey or Cromwell. Good Lord, the list gets longer by the year.' He rose and crossed to the dresser. He filled a goblet, thrust it at me. 'My father was a bailiff, Will.

Strictly speaking, a serjeant at mace, employed by the City of London; now I am Chief Secretary to the King's Council. I believe,' he went back and sat on his chair, 'that one should never tell a secret to more than one person, and that includes my beloved wife. The present secret is that our king is weakening; he can't even relieve himself without the use of some assistance.'

'Be careful, Master Paget.' I deliberately used the common term. 'His Majesty might not be as ill as he seems.'

'But one day he will die. What is so pressing is what he will do before he dies. Whom might he remove? And after His Majesty does join his fore-fathers, what might then happen to a jester whom nobody wants? Who consorts with the Princess Mary and her Spanish, Romanist ways. Who is besotted with that same princess's maidservant, the Lady Jane Bold. The jester who knows the true identity and whereabouts of this mysterious Balaam, the man who commits heinous treasons.'

I glanced up at that ruby glowing through the dark. 'What do you want, Master Paget?'

'His Majesty, I understand, talks about the princes, the sons of the Yorkist Edward IV who disappeared into the Tower?'

'Yes?'

'Will, my good man, His Majesty is deeply worried not about long-dead children but about his own: the Spanish Mary, Boleyn's daughter Elizabeth and his son young Edward, not yet ten years old. When Henry dies, will they be swept into the Tower and,' he shrugged, 'die of a fever or some other fatal accident?'

'And who would do that?'

'More importantly, whom does the King think might commit such heinous treason?'

'I cannot say, can you, Master Paget?'

'Why, the family His Majesty always fears: the Yellow Jackets, the People of the White Lion, the Howards of Norfolk. Look,' Paget stilled my protests, 'do you really think any of us are safe from Norfolk, a seasoned commander, and his son Surrey, England's proudest boy? All his life Henry has feared their shadow. He has tried to dominate them. Two of his wives were Howards, and they betrayed him. Worse, he believes they made a public mockery of him. The King has not forgotten that, and why should he? The Howards of Norfolk are even more dangerous now, with the King failing, his heir a minor. Remember the verse: "Woe to the kingdom whose ruler is a child"?'

'And what has this to do with me?'

'Why, everything! You, like everybody at court, must choose your side. One day the reckoning has to be made.' He blinked. 'And where your heart lies, so might your head.'

He paused at the ringing of the bell from the royal chambers, followed by the scurrying of feet along the gallery outside. 'Warn the King about the Howards.' He stretched out a hand. 'You will keep me informed of what you do and where you go? You will tell me on which side of the fence you stand? Time is short, Will.' He pushed his hand closer. 'Yes?'

'Yes.' I clasped his hand even as I breathed a prayer against my own lie.

'Good.' Paget rose, rubbing his hands. I am not the fool he thinks. He was clearly not convinced. He turned, staring at me from heavy-lidded eyes. 'Shall we see you at the Council meeting?'

'I am not a member.'

'No, no, you are not,' he agreed. 'You are certainly not.'

Dismissed, I slipped back into the gallery, now filling with retainers hurrying here and there. I needed to withdraw from the bustle of the court. Soft as a shadow, I scuttled up the various staircases to the chamber the King has allocated to me. A restful place, its walls painted with the story of the Prodigal Son, whilst two new tapestries describing the tale of Noah and his Ark decorate either side of the door. Woven matting covers the floor, stretching to a small four-poster bed draped with deep red silver-fringed curtains. All around the room stand coffers and caskets, chests and trunks, their lids thrown back, spilling out the robes I still like to wear. I have my own close stool specially provided by the King, a New Year's gift made of iron with a remov-able brass basin beneath its velvet-covered seat, beside this a small lavarium with bowl, jug and linen cloths.

The palace gong farmers had been busy that day and I wanted to ensure that they'd done their task as well as I had done mine. They had. I eased myself, then washed my hands and face, savouring the beautiful smell from the small tablet of Castilian soap Princess Mary had given me on my name day. I slipped into the quilted-back chair that serves my chancery table. I do like my room, I am proud of it, my home, my manor house. I have searched it thoroughly; no eyelets or peepholes have been carved for people to spy or eavesdrop. I enjoy the warmth of the fire and the glow of light from the constantly burning great lantern horn on its table. I closed my eyes, breathed out, then stared around my little kingdom. I dress soberly, though I love to receive doublets of worsted lined with samite, coats, capes and hoods of Lincoln green fringed with red craul, or heavy cloaks of blue wool lined with weasel fur. Another chest holds my painted costumes for court revelries, a crown and mask, together with a gilded mace and chain for my days as Lord of Misrule. Suits of brocaded silk edged with red linen, armour of flimsy board and even a fine hobbyhorse are all mine. Such items litter my chamber, deliberately so. I can tell at a glance if any Judas man, some court spy – and God knows they thrive like fleas on a turd – has been busy sifting through my possessions. Not today.

I picked up a posy from a basket on the desk and sniffed its fragrant aroma. I should be – well I am – a contented man. I have progressed far since I left the service of Richard Fermor of Easton Neston in Northamptonshire. I have undoubtedly prospered. I have gold and silver coins hidden away against any lean times with the goldsmiths along Cheapside and Poultry. Three fine horses and two sturdy sumpter ponies are housed in the royal stables, mine to use whenever I wish, on personal business or when King and court move from one palace to another. Friends are many, or so it would seem. I can pick and choose, for people regard me as the King's fool but also as the King's favourite. Above all I have the Lady Jane Bold, well cared for in the household of Princess Mary, a resident for the last eleven years, having once served Anne Boleyn, that woman of infamous memory. After she went to the headsman's block everything became ruined, dark, deceitful and morose.

I fished beneath my jerkin, took out the locket, snapped it open and stared at Lady Jane's sweet face. Vain as a peacock she is. Like me she spends her money on costly raiment: striped purple satin gowns, their pleats lined with buckram, bodices of fustian or crimson satin; kirtles striped with gold, jerkins of blue damask. Behind all this love of glorious show, Lady Jane is a closed book. She talks little about her past, be it personal or her time at the court of Tarquin and Semiramis, as she refers to the tyrant Henry and the lustful Boleyn. Jane is of medium height, with lustrous brown hair and bright dark eyes. She has perfectly formed features except for her pretty mouth, which she always twists in a slight pout, as if disapproving of the world. She is deft in conversation, skilled at listening and, whatever her mood, looks most interested. Oh she can act the simpleton, yet she is shrewd of wit, sharp of tongue and eagle of eye. She can mimic and imitate, be it a prattling preacher, a counterfeit crank, a drunken doxy or a boisterous bawdy basket. I recall her once turning on a buttery man who tried to steal a kiss from her. She called him a pickled lard and said he should do a tub fast: doused in a hot tub of water for an entire day whilst being starved of food and drink, the cure for anyone suffering from the French disease!

Jane and I are more than close. Once, during a royal progress to Dover, we secretly met before a hedge priest and exchanged our pledges. Now I drew her recent letter from my pocket, scrawled in the deepest black ink. We had not met for days. Jane wondered if I was playing truant with my bed. I recognised the cipher contained within the strange lettering. She wished to meet with me along with Balaam, Princess Mary's agent, that will-o'-the-wisp, mischief incarnate, the Devil in taffeta. I do not know his real name. Balaam has Moorish features, Hispanic, with jet-black hair, glittering eyes and a narrow sallow face. A dagger man born and bred. Jane believes his family once served Catherine of Aragon. Certainly he hates the King with a loathing beyond all comprehension and, as Paget described, never fails to stir up malicious mischief against the Great Despot.

A true scurrier in the cornfield is Balaam, hither and thither on Princess Mary's business, not to mention that of Cardinal Pole, who keeps in constant communication with the Romanists, the papists, the secret Catholics who yearn, as Norfolk does, for the old ways. Paget is correct. If Balaam is ever caught, it will be Tyburn or Smithfield for him. Nevertheless, he is the master of disguise, a true shape-shifter. Last time I met him he was pretending to be a physician, a herbalist, glittering gorgeously like the man on the moon. Bracelets decorated his wrists, his beringed fingers boasted St Vincenza's rocks, a silver case for instruments hung from his girdle with a gilt spatula thrust in the ribbon band around his feathered hat. When we met, he was audacious and bold, strolling into the Bishop's Mitre in Gracechurch Street, a tavern well furnished with all kinds of comfort, a place constantly frequented by sheriff's bailiffs, council men and their horde of hangers-on, spies and informers. On entering, he immediately demanded that the tavern master put an end to the din in the great yard beyond, where mastiffs had been set on a bear and a bull. I must admit, the noise was hideous: the cheering, the growls, the hellish barks and yelps as the mastiffs were tossed, their fall broken by their masters armed with sticks. Balaam's effrontery carried the day. He then proclaimed to all those gathered in the packed tap room that he was not the type of physician who gloried in the juice of a hung tortoise, the scrapings of an alligator or some other ill-shaped fish. He promised he would eschew all such ploys. 'Fingers are the best instruments for a physician,' he declared. 'Why, he should have a lion's heart, a lady's hand and a hawk's eye. I do not believe,' he added, 'that a tumour can be removed by stroking it with a dead man's hand, or that the skin of a salamander protects the flesh from the sun or that a spider swallowed alive in treacle is a sure protection against the ague. Nor do I accept that a steeple struck by lightning is the work of the Devil seen entering through the belfry window . . .'

I smiled at the memory but wondered how Balaam could be so elusive. Paget was undoubtedly hunting him, be it in London or in the north, which brought me back to that secret furtive meeting in the royal chancery office. Paget had been trying to frighten me, as well as discover where my loyalties lay. He was not so much hostile, but reminding me that nobody was safe. He was speaking the truth. Saintly Thomas More once said, long before his fatal clash with the King, that if it could win Henry a town in France, his head would roll. John Fisher of Rochester had been confessor to the King's own grandmother the redoubtable lady Margaret Beaufort, but that had not saved him from the axe. Richard Whiting, the eighty-year-old Abbot of Glastonbury, had been revered by the King as a living saint, but Whiting was dragged on a hurdle to the top of Glastonbury Tor and hanged like a common felon. Hadn't the King of France muttered how he would not let Henry of England marry one of his dogs, let alone a French princess? Paget was a realist; he was trying to elicit my help but he was also warning me not only about the present but also the future.

I also wondered about William Clarke, the chancery clerk with Paget. What had he been working on before he scuttled like a rabbit out of the light? However, a knock on the door disturbed me and a tousle-headed page bawled that the Council was about to gather. I greedily drank a pottle of beer and hastily ate some of the hardened bread left on a platter. Then I hastened out along the torch-lit galleries, the dark oaken rails, balustrades, panelling, newels and banisters gleaming in the light. Shadows moved, prompting memories. I paused briefly at the top of the stairs, recalling a recent visit to Hampton Court. How the servants there complained about the ghost of Katherine Howard, who had lost her head because of Thomas Culpeper. She had been confined there, hysterical with fear. On discovering the King was in the chapel, she had raced along the galleries to beg for his mercy, only to be caught and dragged screaming back. The servants claim her ghost still haunts the path she took, and her screams have woken many at the dead of night. But that is Henry. Where he goes, a whole legion of ghosts dolefully follow. I glanced out of the window. Darkness was falling. Smells floated, the savoury tangs from the kitchens mingling with the perfume and fragrance from herb pots and capped braziers. I continued on and reached the great council chamber. Anthony Wingfield, Captain of the Spears, glimpsed my pass, confirmed by the King's own seal, and I entered that long, cold room.

Torches, candles and tapers had been lit. Catherine wheels, their spokes lined with glowing cubes of beeswax, had been lowered. A fire roared in the carved double hearth. Candelabra placed along the centre of the great oval-shaped table glowed magnificently, yet for all this, still a cold, sombre room. Brilliant tapestries glow in a myriad of rich colours, but I am always fearful of that chamber. Whatever the hour, whatever the season, a sense of impending danger dulls the spirit, a malevolent malice, constantly lurking in the perpetual shadows. I hastened to the King's end of the table and climbed the stairs to the music loft, murky and ill-lit, though a place that provides an excellent view of the entire chamber. Henry often places me there, asking me to watch, to note the expressions and attitudes of his councillors, the glances between them and who whispers to whom. I once protested that I wasn't his spy. The King promptly beat me and banished me to my chamber, saying I would be whatever he wanted me to be. I was not his spy, he later breathed at me. (I remember the gin fumes; God knows he loves that drink.) He praised my memory and said my quick eye and sharp wits would catch what he might miss. I replied that in which case I should be the King and he the fool, upon which Henry promptly cuffed my head and tweaked my ear until I screamed in pain.

The tide of such protests has passed. I am the King's

creature. The Princess Mary has begged me never to forget that. So I stood cloaked and hooded in the shadow of that music loft. I sensed something would happen as the wolf pack gathered. Oh, they all swaggered in, jewelled bonnets and caps on their heads, heavy cloaks not quite covering their decorated, embroidered stomachers and waistcoats of silver cloth or quilted with gold. The light picked up the jewels on their doublets as well as the water on their cloaks. Gauntleted and booted, they stamped their feet and clapped their hands against the cold. A cheerful, merry group, like powerful merchants gathering for a banquet in the Guildhall, but this was different. The Dark Lords, the Masters of the Twilight, the Shadow-bringers were clustering in all their pomp and might. Thomas Cranmer, Archbishop of Canterbury, was the only visible exception, dressed in a white surplice under a heavy black mantle, a square cap of the same colour and material on his ageing head. A grey man Cranmer, with his seemingly colourless eyes, his dull shaven face always twisted into a mournful pull, lips pushed forward as if his tongue is too big for his mouth. He wore the archbishop's ring and rested on a silver-topped ebony cane. One crow amongst the peacocks, all a-glitter with their precious rings and collars.

Bonnets, hats, gloves and cloaks were doffed and thrown at waiting servants. Mulled wine richly garnished with cinnamon, mace and cloves was served in elegant pewter goblets wrapped in snow-white napkins. Trays of soft bread, buttered and covered in diced meat, were also offered. The lords of the Council, busy in their preparations, ordered their chancery clerks to place their writing cases on the table. Each seemed to know his own place. Greetings and salutations were exchanged, hands clasped, lips curled in smiles, heads shaken in knowing nods, confidential morsels softly whispered. All this was shadow and no substance, a mere ritual. The pack was simply milling about. The smiling faces hid devious, sharp minds. Wits were being honed. Opponents secretly but carefully scrutinised for any weakness. Everyone kept an eye on the door through which the King would enter. Physician Huicke appeared dressed in his costly black furred robes and physician's cap. Diamonds winked on his fingers, broad gold bracelets shimmered on his wrists and the silver medallion on his filigreed necklace glittered with the jewelled snake of Aesculapius. This too was only a pretence. Huicke's narrow, ill-tempered, whiskered face shimmered with fear. Truly the hunt at court was on, but who was hunting whom?

I moved to get a clearer view of the rest. The Seymour brothers, Edward and Thomas, the former newly created Earl of Hertford, bristling men of war who would take to fighting on land or sea as a bird does to flying. Hertford is fresh out of Scotland, where he has been busy burning, slaying and ravaging to his heart's content. Thomas has been roaming the seas chasing pirates, though court gossips claim he is no better than the men he hangs. Edward and Thomas are so alike, with their broad brows, staring protuberant eyes, thick sensuous lips and luxurious hair and moustaches. Both men stood gossiping with that other leader of the pack, John Dudley, the Viscount Lisle, his harsh, lean, bony face all shaven, his hair cropped close like the soldier he boasts to be, claiming that he is more at home on the battlefield than he is at court. Dressed completely in black, Dudley has the look of a Tower raven, constantly moving, head turning to watch the rest of the Council. The King enjoys the company of these three because he also likes to act the bluff, sharp-tongued, cynical soldier himself. He loves to challenge them to dice, hazard or cards whilst gossiping about the conduct of war. However, if present chatter is correct, His Majesty is not too favoured with the younger Seymour, a rash, impetuous man, a roué and rake who'd be more at home in the French court, where the dissolute gallants leave the corpses of hanged men in the beds of their mistresses as a clever conceit. English courtiers are more brash and aggressive; their tempers flare more easily. They breathe harsh words and commit violent acts. Dudley once exchanged fiery words with the Bishop of Winchester and struck him full in the face, for which he was expelled from court for an entire month. My lord of Hertford, the elder Seymour, also exchanged violent, injurious words with Wriothesley, the Lord Chancellor, though he did not suffer any such exile.

In truth, my king loves to watch his dogs curl and

fight. Chief Secretary Paget has the measure of our royal master. He realises that Edward Seymour, Earl of Hertford, uncle to the king-to-be, will take the ascendancy and, according to gossip, has persuaded Hertford to follow his advice in all proceedings. Paget uses Hertford as his dog to menace the Romanists and their mastiff Henry Howard, Earl of Surrey, son of the old Duke of Norfolk. Surrey is a poet who believes he is free as the air he breathes. He has already spent a month in the Fleet for challenging Sir John Leigh, the King's Justice, to a duel. He has also clashed with Hertford, striking him violently within the precincts of the court, for which he nearly lost his hand. Despite these strictures, he cannot restrain his heady will. Years ago, he went on a night attack against the wealthy of London, breaking their windows and hurling obscenities at them. When confronted with his crimes, Surrey retorted that he'd acted so that his victims might learn from the stones passing noiselessly through the air and breaking in suddenly upon them about the punishment that, as Scripture tells us, divine justice will inflict on impenitent sinners. Surrey is a wayward, haughty soul who led his troops to defeat before the walls of Boulogne. So frenetic did he become at his misfortune that he demanded his officers stick their swords through his guts and make him forget that day. Many now wished they had. His soldiers blame their defeat chiefly on him, their leader, whose head and heart are swollen with pride, arrogance and impetuous confidence in his own unreasoning bravery. Little wonder Paget has abandoned Surrey the hot-head and turned to my lord Hertford, who can act so moderately in all things (apart from dealing with my lord Surrey) that all believe him to be their own.

In fact the two Howards, Norfolk and Surrey, and their ally, Stephen Gardiner of Winchester, were the last to arrive in the council chamber. The three stayed away from the rest as if eager to inspect the cupboards of plate studded with precious stones and pearls that stand further down the hall. I've closely studied Master Holbein's painting of Norfolk. The duke is shown in all his glory grasping the golden baton of the Earl Marshal in one hand, the Lord Treasurer's white staff in the other. A sallow, clean-shaven face, the dark hair unfashionably long, a hawkish visage with hooded eyes, finely shaped brows and pointed chin, lips tight as a miser's purse. Thomas Howard is one who hides his seething ambition. A petty man in so many ways, he is deceptive and deceiving, well steeped in the dirty devices of the court and most skilled in weaving sinister designs. He complains constantly of a queasy stomach and loose bowels, yet lives to prove the English proverb that 'a creaking gate hangs longest'. He is like a tree that bends to every storm, a gambler who took up primero, a game introduced by Henry's Spanish queen, and became so skilled as to empty His Majesty's purse many a time. Norfolk is a reed shaking in the wind but one that has dug its roots deep, long and tangled. His own wife

Elizabeth, daughter of Edward Stafford, Duke of Buckingham, said of him: 'He can speak fair as well to his enemies as to his friends. He neither regards God nor his honour.' He can change like a loosened weathercock on a village steeple. A man of contrasts, he'll feed the hungry yet wears his dressing gowns until the fur is rubbed clean. He once proclaimed, 'I've never yet read scripture, nor ever will read it. It was merry in England before the new learning came. Yes, I wish all things were as in times past.'

In so many ways Norfolk is a memory of things long gone. He wears relics around his neck and revels in his ownership of fifty rosaries. Nevertheless, whatever his coarse boasting, he patronises scholars such as Skelton the poet, Leland the historian and the great classics scholar John Clarke of Magdalene, who introduced Norfolk's son, Henry of Surrey, to the beauties of Petrarch and other poets of that ilk, as well as grounding him firmly in Latin, French, Italian and Spanish. It was Clarke who set Surrey along the road to be the great glory of His Majesty's court, as well as the most arrogant man in England. Surrey is tall like his father and so is easily recognisable. He has a long, serious face, thick auburn hair, tightly compressed lips and a slightly flared nose. What is immediately striking about him is the cast in his right eye, a defect he feels most sensitive about. I have read some of his poetry where he makes reference to it. In his paintings they try to disguise such a defect, because an eye turning outwards, according to popular lore, indicates cunning, deceit and treachery. He will need all such vices in this present time.

I noticed that Paget, now dressed in his satin and silks, a jewelled bonnet on his head, did not greet the Norfolks, seemingly busy moving from one councillor to another. Wriothesley, the Chancellor, that viper incarnate, did sketch a bow towards them, and to his former patron Gardiner. Thomas Wriothesley! Now there's a man I truly fear. Yes, I, William Somers, formerly of Northamptonshire, the fool, the jester, the innocent. I am a soul who at times loses all wit and sense, the sort of fool who will add water to the sea or bring a firebrand to a burning house. True, I make mistakes and take false shams for true substances. Yet I can also be discerning, and that is a thing to be at Henry's court! I live in times when one Christian tears at another in those darkened chambers beneath the Tower. Yes, those dungeons, with their so-called licking walls, because the damp on them is the only refreshment available to the dry lips and cracked throats of the prisoners. Often the only reason they are there is because they no longer believe that God kissed Mary in Galilee, or they deny that royal Henry has the same power as the Bishop of Rome. Such prisoners are at the mercy of wall-eyed, fiendishly faced torturers, who hack and tear in the name of the gentle Christ who himself was hacked and torn. I truly admit, as I would on a book of the Gospels, I do not understand the heart of it. Such days of terror in a world of uncertainty.

I love my Jane. I would become truly hand-fast and warm with her in bed, but we are fools, innocents, and what might she conceive? That troubles me. When I am away from her I have to listen to the poisonous pourings of a half-mad king who seems to delight in dispatching all those his love touches to a violent death. Nonetheless, that same king, at certain times, will sit upon the floor of his bedchamber and sob like a child for what he has done and must do again. Little wonder I become anxious and afraid. Fear turns both belly and bowel to water. Demons in human flesh prowl my waking hours, and none is worse than Thomas Wriothesley, he of the dark russet hair pressed down under its flat-rimmed bejewelled cap, that curly beard and moustache cultivated in an attempt to hide his aggressive jutting jaw, and his eyes, milky blue, like those of a baleful cat.

Now and again in my teasing mood I have asked the great lords of the Council what they desire. Good governance? Honour? Titles? Lands? Wealth? Power? All are there. I asked Wriothesley the same question, only once, in the gardens of Hampton Palace. Swift as a snake, he grasped a bee in his thick gloved hand, squeezed it until it cracked and dropped the corpse at my feet. 'To crush my opponents, Will,' he murmured. Wriothesley is absorbed with death. Like all such men, strangely enough, he couples this with a detestation of women. He loves to interrogate, to question: a man who fences with his own shadow, a hell-hound who lives to hunt others to a gruesome death. A smiling villain, a dove-feathered raven, a wolfish ravenous lamb. He is false of heart and bloody of mind, a pig in sloth, a snake in stealth, a wolf in greediness, a dog in madness and a lion in hunting. I secretly call him Legion because his soul must house a veritable mob of demons. Nowhere is this more apparent than when some poor woman falls into his power.

Anne Askew was one of these; Balaam told me the story. Askew was young, beautiful and learned, of honourable birth and ancient lineage and a convert to the reformist faith. She was, for that reason, ejected from her Lincolnshire home by her husband. She then resumed her maiden name, journeyed to London and devoted herself to the propagation of that faith, for which she was patronised by the Queen's sister Lady Herbert, the Duchess of Suffolk and other great ladies of the court. Indeed, report has it that the Queen herself received books from Askew in the presence of Lady Herbert, which would have brought both under the penalties of the statute against reading heretical works.

Now the opinions of Mistress Askew are neither here nor there, but when Gardiner and Wriothesley learnt of her relationship with the Queen, they promptly ordered her arrest. She was cruelly confined in prison, where the ladies of the court, perhaps even the Queen herself, made the mistake of sending her monies, goods and other items for her sustenance. Immediately Wriothesley closed in. Askew was put to the rack to reveal the names of those who had sent her money. She refused to answer, only saying that it had been delivered by 'a man in a blue coat', whilst another 'dressed in a violet coat' had brought a purse, but she could not say who had sent these. Wriothesley racked her cruelly because she refused to confess or name supporters at court. The racking continued until the strings of her eyes and limbs were strained and she swooned into a dead faint. The then Lieutenant of the Tower, Sir Anthony Knyvett, ordered her release.

Once they had roused her with water, they made her sit for two long hours on the floor with Wriothesley, who whispered false promises and threatened bloody menaces if she did not tell him exactly what he wanted. He enjoyed it, rocking backwards and forwards, sometimes solicitous, at other times threatening. Askew was racked again, pinched and hurt until her joints popped out. Eventually Sir Anthony Knyvett intervened and instructed her to be taken down. Wriothesley, not at all happy that Askew might be released without confession, commanded Knyvett to strain her on the rack again, but the lieutenant refused, saying the weakness of the woman would not bear it. Wriothesley turned on him cursing, adding that he'd report his disobedience directly to the King. Knyvett still objected, so Wriothesley, throwing off his gown, actually manned the rack himself, questioning Askew closely but unable to break her and only ceasing when her bones and joints were almost plucked apart.

Finally Wriothesley gave up his attempt and returned to court. Sir Anthony Knyvett, upset and frightened by his threats, took a swifter barge to speak to the King before Wriothesley did. Ushered into the royal presence, Knyvett went down on his knees and sought His Majesty's pardon, then showed how the whole matter stood. How he had stopped the racking of Mistress Askew and had been threatened by the Lord Chancellor with His Majesty's displeasure. The King, patting Knyvett on the shoulder, said he'd done right, granted the lieutenant pardon and ordered him to return immediately to supervise his charge.

His Majesty, of course, was once again playing the two-faced Janus. He expressed his greatest displeasure that a female, a lady, should be exposed to such barbarity, yet he did not condemn or punish the perpetrators, nor did he intervene to preserve Anne Askew from further tribulation. In truth, according to Balaam, the King himself had ordered Anne Askew to be stretched on the rack, being furious against her for having brought heretical books into the palace and imbued his queen and others with her false doctrine.

Wriothesley and Gardiner then spread their net wider. Certain gentlemen of the court – William Morris, the King's usher, and Sir George Blagge from the privy chamber – along with Lascelles, a gentleman from Nottinghamshire, were arrested, confined to Newgate and warned by Wriothesley's men how they were all marked for death and so should pay heed to their lives.

So confident were Gardiner and Wriothesley that they could purge the court of all reformists that they struck hard and high. George Blagge was a great favourite with the King, who would honour him in moments of familiarity with the endearing appellation of 'his little pig'. Apparently His Majesty did not appear to be aware of Blagge's arrest until it came to signing the warrants for execution. He immediately sent for Wriothesley and berated him for arresting a man like Blagge and daring to interfere with retainers of the royal privy chamber. He instructed the Chancellor to draw up a pardon. Blagge was promptly released and swiftly trotted off to thank his royal master, who on seeing him cried out:

'Ah, my little pig, you're safe again.'

'Yes, sire,' replied Blagge, 'but if Your Majesty had not been better than your bishops, your little pig would have been roasted long ago.'

Mistress Askew was not so fortunate. Tortured and broken, she had to be carried to Smithfield on the day of execution in a chair because she was unable to stand on her feet. Two others died with her. Anne Askew was lashed to the central stake, bound around her middle with a chain to keep her upright. A priest came forward to deliver his sermon. Mistress Askew shook her head, saying, 'There really is no use.' The priest persisted, despite the cries and protests of the crowd, which proved so strong the execution ground had to be specially railed off. I, the King's witness, was close by on a bench near St Bartholomew's, where Wriothesley, Norfolk and the others had gathered. There was some alarm because the rumour spread that the victims had gunpowder about them. The lords were frightened that any explosion might send the faggots flying about their ears; Norfolk however pointed out that the gunpowder was not laid under the wood but about the victims' bodies, so there was no danger from the fire at all.

Once again Anne Askew and her companions were invited to recant. All refused. The Lord Mayor stood up and shouted: *'Fiat iustitia!'* – 'Let there be justice'. Then the fires were lit. Askew and her two companions were soon consumed by the flames. Wriothesley stayed till Askew was no more than smouldering ash. He savoured that.

Wriothesley was also the King's choice to send to Hampton Court when Queen Katherine Howard fell from grace. That silly popinjay, with a host of women from both her chamber and household, was swept into prison. Wriothesley interrogated them all about the Queen's passionate trysts with Dereham and Culpeper. Oh how he enjoyed himself! He took the greatest pleasure in almost frightening to death the aged Duchess of Norfolk, Lady Rochford and the rest. He would enter their chambers with the torturers jangling their chains behind him. He would listen to their screams, occasionally jumping up and down, dancing with pleasure, before leaving to regale the court with what he'd done. Once, overcome with revulsion, I conquered my fear and asked him why he took such delight. He just stared at me, that great chin trembling, those milky blue eyes full of dreadful joy.

'Master Somers,' he replied, 'I am the King's rat-catcher. I trap rats for him, and who cares about them?'

Well I did, and I told him so. Wriothesley pushed me along the gallery where we'd met, grabbed my shoulder and pulled me into a window recess.

'Will,' he whispered, eyes rounded in mock innocence, 'your Lady Jane was in Boleyn's household. You know, the great goggle-eyed whore. What did Jane know about those nightly trysts with Master Smeaton, Sir Henry Norris and even Boleyn's own brother George? I mean, while we are investigating queens, shouldn't your friend be seized and taken in a sealed barge to the Tower? Oh, the ladies hate that! Katherine Howard, all fearful, kicked her lovely legs till the tops of her stockings showed, her thick lacy petticoats going back. Oh Will,' Wriothesley closed his eyes as if savouring a delicious meal, 'how that firm, queenly little body struggled against mine.' He opened his eyes, chin thrust forward, 'So what did the Lady Jane know about all that, and what did she tell you?'

I broke free of his grip. I confess, perhaps I don't know how to love; that feeling is difficult to describe and even harder to explain. But hate? Oh, thanks to Wriothesley, I know how to hate. If he ever falls, I want to be there when he's dragged kicking and screaming from the barge as it docks before the great gates near St Thomas's Tower.

Nevertheless, standing there in the music loft above the council chamber, I also took great comfort in how I had thwarted him over the present queen, Katherine Parr. Gardiner and Wriothesley certainly failed to trap Cranmer, but they were not finished, and engaged in further wicked intrigue towards their real quarry, the Queen. The Queen's sister Lady Herbert had already been secretly denounced to Henry as an active instrument in subverting his edict on heretical works. Wriothesley subtly pointed out that Anne Askew, the recently burnt heretic, had also been patronised by Lady Herbert and others of the Queen's chamber. The King was not pleased. The attack had gathered strength, a subtle malignant plot. Wriothesley fed His Majesty information that his consort received and read books forbidden by royal decree. Time and again Gardiner and Wriothesley continued to argue that everything the Queen expressed or insinuated must be seen in the light not only of heresy but of treason.

Now I know our king; I have studied him most closely and I have very good reason to do so. Henry's anger is always the most deadly when he broods over an offence, and as I assure myself, this king does brood. It nearly cost Katherine Parr her life. The Queen had become accustomed during those hours of domestic privacy with her husband to converse with him on theological subjects, in which they both took great delight. Naturally they disagreed, but the ready wit and honeyed eloquence of the Queen only gave spice to these discussions. I have it from the gossips amongst the ladies of the chamber, as well as a gentleman in the King's household, that His Majesty was at first amused and intrigued by such debates. Katherine gradually became aware not only of her husband's physical sickness but of his deep guilt over a horde of unrepented crimes, in particular about Catherine of Aragon of blessed and beloved memory. Her Grace proved keen to provoke her husband to a sense of sorrow, a realisation that one day he would have to account for what he had done. Moreover, the Queen was swift to realise that the King was neither Romanist nor reformist but wished to mould religion in the light of his own conscience and will, which she herself could not accept.

Now, as God, his angels and my good self realise, anyone who tries to advise His Majesty with spiritual advice, be it Romanist or reformist, treads a very dangerous path. John Fisher, Bishop of Rochester, tried and paid the price. Thomas More, once Lord Chancellor, attempted the same and lost his head. Cromwell, Anne Boleyn and others had all stumbled along that murderous runnel leading to execution in or around the Tower. Her Grace the Queen thought she could avoid such danger and quietly challenged the King's infallibility, pointing out that he was assuming for himself what he condemned in the Bishop of Rome.

One day, in the malignant presence of Wriothesley, the Queen tried to discuss with her husband a proclamation the King had recently issued, forbidding the use of the translation of scripture, which he had previously licensed. The King was tired and depleted, the ulcers in his legs inflamed and painful. The Queen, unknowing of this, persisted in the matter too closely, even though the King showed tokens of anger and abruptly cut the matter short. Her Grace then made a few other pleasant observations and withdrew. Once she was gone, the King's fury erupted.

'A good hearing it is,' he shouted, 'when women become such clerks. Much to my discomfort in my old age, I am to be taught by my wife!'

I do not know whether the King was trying to trap the Queen or not, but Wriothesley, along with Gardiner, could not resist the opportunity and began to breathe a malice which, only a few days earlier, they'd kept so well hidden. They flattered His Majesty, I witnessed this, on his theological knowledge and judgement, declaring that the King 'excels the princes of his age and every other age as well as all the best doctors of divinity'. Consequently it was most unseemly for any of his subjects to argue with him so impudently as the Queen had just done. Indeed, it was most grievous for any of his councillors to hear it, since those who heard such bold words spoken in defiance would themselves not scruple to act so disobediently. Gardiner, hard eyes watching the King, added softly that he could make great discoveries about the truth if he was not deterred by the Queen's powerful faction. And chattering the like, Wriothesley and Gardiner so filled His Majesty's suspicious mind with fears that he gave them permission, under warrant, to consult with others about drawing up articles against the Queen to charge her with heresy and treason.

Wriothesley of course thought it was best to begin with the women of her chamber, particularly Lady Herbert. He proposed to accuse them of breaking the Act of Six Articles, which defines this kingdom's faith, and so organised a search of their closets and coffers. He hoped to find incriminating evidence against the Queen; once he had, she could be taken by night in a sealed barge to the Tower. The King agreed, and the matter was secretly carried forward, though the Queen had no knowledge of the dangers gathering about her. Despite my pleas, His Majesty continued to behave politely whilst Gardiner and Wriothesley drew up an act to attain his wife, a bill for her impeachment in Parliament. I decided to act, and anonymously sent her clear warning of the horrid danger.

The Queen, once informed, fell into a hysterical agony. She was accustomed to occupying an apartment close to the King and lapsed into one fit after another, her shrieks and cries reaching his ears. The King, incapacitated with pain, sent me to visit her. I comforted her and returned to inform His Satanic Majesty that his wife was dangerously ill, her sickness being caused by a malady of the mind. I urged him to see her. The King immediately insisted that, because his legs could not sustain him, he be carried into the Queen's chamber, where he found her heavy with melancholy almost to the point of death. The Queen however had the wit and shrewdness to show a proper degree of gratitude for the honour of the royal visit, which, she assured His Infernal Highness, greatly revived her spirits. She then confessed how distressed she was at having seen so little of His Majesty lately and that her apprehension had deepened as she may have unintentionally given him offence. The King, fat face beaming goodwill, replied graciously and encouragingly with many tender touches. The Queen, as if tutored, behaved in a humble and ingratiating manner, supplicating the humour of her husband.

Once he had left, the King turned to me and Huicke, quickly informing us in great detail about what was being plotted against the Queen. I have no proof of this, but I suspect that Huicke immediately went to Katherine and advised her about the great danger still threatening and how she might escape it. Our queen is no fool and recognised the source. Her own ladies have no love for Wriothesley; one of these owns a pet dog called Riotously, which she teases and taunts outrageously in public.

The Queen certainly felt under threat. Once the meeting with the King was over, she ordered new locks for her coffers and boxes, whilst the religious books that had been brought in by her ladies, those donated by Anne Askew, were either hidden in the garderobe or smuggled out to a safer place. There were other dangers. Katherine Parr, Lady Latimer as she once was before her marriage to His Majesty, was a widow. She is a pretty piece, small, pert-faced and dresses so elegantly. Now a comely widow with a rich inheritance is as attractive as a honeycomb, and no lesser person than Sir Thomas Seymour, brother to the Earl of Hertford, paid court to her. In my view, and those I trust, Katherine Parr was much taken with Sir Thomas. Under different circumstances she would have married him, but of course, the King's eye and favour fell on her and she had no choice but to bow to his imperial will. Sir Thomas, under the prompt direction of his elder brother and Master Paget, decided to quit the field and leave His Majesty to his pleasures. Now Katherine Howard, late queen of this present king, was executed for not revealing previous amours and relationships with young men of the court. Gardiner and Wriothesley hoped they could discover the same about Lady Parr, but could not.

I do sense a shifting danger in all this. One day our King of Hades must join his forefathers, but who will manage the kingdom for his heir? The Council? Yet there again the Queen-widow has rights; could she not be appointed regent? And if she is made regent, does Sir Thomas hope that he can control her and so master the young king? The younger Seymour is a bloodsucker, a bottled spider, twice as fit for Hell as any of them; his tongue could out-venom a viper and he is a danger to the Queen. Only the good Lord knows whether

Wriothesley, that royal rat-catcher, mentioned Seymour or the Queen's childlessness to further disturb the King's humours.

I did my best to mollify such rumours. The King had visited his queen and shown he was benevolent towards her. The following evening the Queen found herself well enough to reciprocate and so visited the King in his own privy chamber. She came attended by her sister Lady Herbert, the King's young niece Jane Grey carrying the candles before them. His Infernal Majesty welcomed his wife most courteously but slyly turned the conversation to the controversy regarding religion, hoping perhaps to draw her into further heated debate. The Queen – and her flattery would have choked me – cleverly avoided the snare, declaring that she was but a woman, imbued with all the imperfections natural to the weakness of her sex. Consequently, in all matters of doubt and difficulty she must refer herself to His Majesty's better judgement, because God, she continued her face all prim and proper – and the Lord only knows how she kept it so – 'has appointed you to be the Supreme Head of us all, and from you, next to God, will I learn'.

'Not so!' our royal hypocrite retorted. 'Aren't you becoming a theologian, Kate, to instruct us and not to be instructed by us, as sometimes recently we have seen?'

'No, Your Majesty,' the Queen replied. 'If Your Majesty has so construed my meaning, how much

mistaken! For I have always maintained that it is prepos-
terous for a woman to instruct her lord. Moreover, if
I have ever presumed to differ with Your Highness on
religion, it was partly to obtain information for my own
comfort regarding certain finer points on which I stood
in doubt. At other times because I understood that, in
conversing with you, you were able to pass away the
pain and weariness of your present infirmity. All this
encouraged me to boldness in the hope of profiting
from Your Majesty's learned discourse as well as
soothing you.' Oh, clever, subtle woman! I learnt that
evening how cunning Katherine truly is.

'Then if this is so, sweetheart,' our King of Pharisees
replied, 'we are the most perfect of friends.' The Devil's
own liar then kissed her with much tenderness and gave
both her and her ladies permission to depart.

Wriothesley and Gardiner had no knowledge of this
meeting and continued their plot, singling out a time
for her arrest. On that day the King, recovering from
his ailments, sent for the Queen to take the air with
him in the gardens. She came attended by her ladies.
The royal couple walked and talked, but then
Wriothesley, with forty of the guard, entered the garden
with the hope of carrying the Queen off to the Tower,
the Chancellor having not the slightest information
about how the King had changed. Our ever-fickle
Majesty received Wriothesley in a burst of indignation
and saluted him with the unexpected address of
'Beast!', 'Fool!' and 'Knave!' then sternly ordered him

to withdraw. The Queen, when she saw the King angry with his Chancellor, had the sense to intercede for him, saying that she'd become a humble suitor for Wriothesley as she deemed his fault was occasioned by a mistake.

'Poor soul, Kate,' retorted our mendacious monarch, acting his much-loved Solomon role, 'you little know how much evil this man deserves at your hand. On my word, sweetheart, he has been a very knave.'

Afterwards I remonstrated with the King that Wriothesley should be severely punished, even removed from the Council. Henry, for his own strange reasons, disagreed.

'Gardiner, Bishop Gardiner of Winchester, is the prime mover,' he declared. 'He is the one to be punished.'

Wriothesley suspected, God knows how, that I had been instrumental in saving the Queen. I waited for another opening to strike at him, but none occurred. The weasel-souled rat-catcher decided to make his own submission. Grinning at me with his eyes, he knelt solemn-faced before the King, stretched out his hands and pleaded, 'I shall have good cause to be sorry to my innermost heart for all my life if the favour of you, our most gracious master, fails me. I pray, I beg, I plead your clemency will temper that.'

Only the Lord and his angels know who put Wriothesley up to that. He knew he had done a wicked thing and he was no more sorry than the cat who'd swallowed the cream. Henry of course loves to appear merciful and compassionate, especially when he is accosted personally. I remember one dire story of a man whose son was hanged. The King passed him at court and stopped. 'If you had pleaded with me,' he remarked, 'I would have pardoned your son.' And then he passed on. The King loves such occasions just as he never forgets an enemy. He had certainly not forgotten Gardiner, nor the fact that Thomas Seymour had secret designs on Katherine Parr.

My sleepy meditations and reflections in the music loft were brought abruptly to an end by the ostentatious entrance of the wand-bearing royal chamberlains, resplendent in their livery. These loudly announced the imminent arrival of the King, who shuffled into the chamber, a great, hulking shadow, breathing noisily, face all creased, leaning on a staff that rang like the beat of a funeral drum as he edged into the light. Henry was garbed in a beautiful long robe powdered with gold and silver crowns and lined with snow-white fur, velvet buskins on his feet, the bejewelled flat cap on his head sporting a blood-red plume. He stomped across the floor to his waiting chair. Assisted by his chamberlains, not speaking a word to anyone, he lowered himself down on to the thick cushioned seat. I was standing behind him. I could not see if he winced at the shooting, burning pains of his haemorrhoids or the suppurating ulcers on his legs. The Council were also denied such pleasure. Once the King entered, they doffed their hats and sank to one knee. Henry kept them waiting. He snapped his fingers and snatched at the goblet of white wine a chamberlain hurriedly brought; he slurped this noisily, belched loudly then slammed the goblet down on the table before him.

'My lord Cranmer, my good friend,' the King emphasised the last three words, a warning to the Romanists, 'intone the prayer.'

Cranmer, in a shaky, reedy voice, began the 'Veni Creator Spiritus', which the rest of the Council soon joined in. Once finished, however, Henry kept them kneeling, even as the Spears, the royal halberdiers, the King's own bodyguard, filed ominously into the council chamber, the naked steel of their pole-axes glinting in the light. That constant sense of dread deepened. These royal axemen had accompanied so many who had enjoyed Henry's favour to a waiting black-draped, sealed barge on the Thames. The councillors continued kneeling, bonnets off, heads bowed like those who had to kneel on the scaffold on Tower Hill. Henry breathed out, a noisy gasp, before greedily sipping from his goblet. I stared down at that great frame, a doom-bearing mound of festering flesh, cunning brain squirming like an eel in the muddy, sluggish waters of court politics. The silence grew baleful. Some of the councillors such as Norfolk, the knobbly joints of their old legs straining against the pain and discomfort, found it hard to maintain their genuflection. Somewhere in the palace a bell boomed, followed by a loud cry, which abruptly died.

'My lord Thomas Seymour,' the King rasped, 'you are no longer sworn to this Council. You have no need to stay. Begone.'

The younger Seymour raised his head. Paget, kneeling beside him, gently touched that blustering, lecherous soldier on the arm. Seymour's brother Edward coughed, a warning to his impetuous sibling to rein in both his tongue and his temper. Everyone knew the reason for Thomas's abrupt dismissal. Queen Katherine Parr resided at Greenwich, exiled from the royal presence. Seymour still carried a torch for her in his heart. He had stupidly interceded for her to join the court to keep a merry hall at Westminster over Yuletide. This was the King's response. Seymour rose, bowed from the waist and walked to the door, the high heels of his riding boots rapping the floor.

'My lord Seymour.' The errant nobleman paused. 'If I were you, and I am certainly not,' Henry did not even turn in his chair, 'I would tread much lighter.' Seymour almost tiptoed from the chamber, the King's guarded warning ringing like a death knell over the heads of his councillors.

'My Lord Chancellor?' Wriothesley raised his head, face all fearful. 'Did I not,' Henry was now pointing at Gardiner, who, to ease himself, was leaning back on his heels, 'did I not command you, my Lord Chancellor,' Henry kept jabbing his finger at the hapless bishop, 'how that person can no longer be amongst us?'

'Your Majesty,' Gardiner gabbled, 'I simply came to

offer money, benevolences from the clergy.' He gestured with his hands as if supplicating the very air.

'Then I accept it,' Henry replied.

'Your Majesty,' Gardiner babbled on, 'my apologies, my humble entreaties . . .'

'Had your previous doings been as agreeable as your present fair words,' Henry bellowed, 'you would have no cause to speak.' The King raised a hand. 'As it is, we see no reason why you should bother us any further.'

Now Gardiner is a fearsome man, with frowning brows, deep-set eyes, a nose like a buzzard and great paws like the Devil. They say that when he passed through Winchester recently, he grew deeply offended when the people didn't pull off their caps for him and make courtesy at the cross carried before him. He turned to his servants, saying, 'Mark that house! Take this knave's name and have him imprisoned!' No doubt Bishop Gardiner harks back to other days, as he himself said, 'when the realm lived in faith, charity and devotion. When God's word dwelt in men's hearts and never came abroad to walk on men's tongues. Now jesters, railers, rhymers, players, jugglers and simpering prattlers take upon themselves the duty of both administrators and officers to set forth God's word.'

Gardiner did not act so confident now. He staggered to his feet with no one to assist him and bowed towards the King, who, having downed more wine, belched in the bishop's direction. Gardiner scurried from the chamber.

'He has gone,' Henry bellowed, 'because my lord bishop cannot be managed. He is like a horse or a mule without bridle. Moreover, I know things about my lord Gardiner.' He nodded, finger wagging. 'Discord!' he thundered. 'Discord here, discord in Parliament. Tell my beloved commons I thank them for their recent subsidy in defence of Boulogne. Yet,' the King continued, 'the perfect love that should bind ruler and subject is being bitterly marred by disputes amongst themselves. Charity and concord are not even found amongst you,' the King bellowed, 'but discord and dissension weigh heavy in every place, even here. One calls the other heretic, an Anabaptist, whilst the other replies with "Romanist hypocrite". Are these tokens of charity amongst you? Are these signs of fraternal love? So all men are in discord and few, or none, preach truly and sincerely the word of God.'

Some of the councillors, I am sure, must have been sorely tempted to retort that the King himself was a constant source of such discord, but silence is best. His Majesty then went on to reprove his kneeling councillors for their lack of order, for allowing others to slander priests and bishops, for failing to seize those who rebuked and taunted preachers in the pulpits with their fantastical opinions and vain expositions. The King reminded them how, although he'd permitted his subjects to read Holy Scripture, this was only to inform their own consciences as well as to instruct their families and children; it was certainly not to make scripture a railing and taunting stock against priests and preachers. The Bible was meant to enlighten; 'Instead,' His Diabolic Majesty thundered, 'that most precious jewel, the word of God, is being disputed to rhyme, song and jangle in every ale house and tavern.'

Henry let his words roll like a volley of cannon. He then lapsed into silence. He had seized an issue as he would his cane and lashed his fighting dogs.

'Now, my lords, I have spoken my mind. Pray take your seats.' He snapped his fingers. 'Some wine? Sugared wafers for my Council. Sir Anthony,' he turned to his captain of halberdiers, 'I no longer have need of you.' He paused. 'As yet.'

The Council, hiding their groans and moans, took their seats. Paget's creature, William Clarke, hastened in. More lanterns and candles were lit. Chancery satchels were opened. The King now acted all courteous and kindly, addressing several members, though I noticed that he did not even glance at the Howards. The formal meeting began. Paget soon proved his reputation as the master of dark politics! I scrutinised him carefully. Although he proved to be the busiest, he acted pliant but not petty, cautious but not cowardly, popular but not people-pleasing, correct but not condemning. In truth, Paget is a realist. Our king will die, that is a fact. Young Edward will succeed, that is a fact. The elder Seymour is the young heir's uncle, with an entree to the royal privy chamber denied to others. Dudley is a soldier who can whistle up and deploy the thousands of mercenaries garrisoning the royal castles and ports. Paget, I suspect, will not try to control the Council or the heir apparent, but he will control those who do. In the meantime he will flatter the King.

Paget began with news from France. How the King's great rival Francis was sickening, his body swollen with the pox, the effect of consorting with so many women, for King Francis, Paget murmured, did surely sup at many fountains. He reported how the French king was now racked by dreams and fantasies of his silvery youth and persisted in visiting certain rooms, forests and glades where he had carried out his greatest conquests. How he became angry when he heard that his sons were already toasting his death and plotting what to do next. He lost his temper and went to their chambers to find his sons had fled, leaving nothing but soiled table linen, napery, unwashed cups and platters, which Francis hurled from the window.

Henry pronounced himself delighted, as he always is when he hears about the ailments and discomfitures of his rivals, especially the King of France. 'I should send him good Dr Huicke.' He coughed in his laughter as he gestured at Huicke sitting so forlornly at the end of the council table. 'Now . . .' The King turned to the business in hand.

I watched and waited for at least an hour. The price to the King for this display of royal power was costly. Once the Council meeting was over, Henry returned to his own secret chamber, the room all neat and sweet-smelling. He dismissed his household men, even Huicke, who only stayed to prepare a certain potion, then stripped for bed, pulling over his bloated, blood-blotched torso a thick linen nightshirt with a matching purple woollen mantle; around his balding head he wrapped a towel, clasping the folds with a brooch, then, cursing and retching, he lowered himself on to the close stool. He sat straining, head forward, those narrow little eyes unblinking. Once finished, leaning heavily on me and grasping the polished walnut post, he climbed into the great four-poster bed. For a while he just lay back against the bolsters, savouring the goblet of white wine I served. I thought he was drifting off to sleep, but he stirred and abruptly asked what I had thought of the council meeting.

'You frightened them,' I replied. 'Which was your intent.'

'Terror more likely, Will. Horror piled upon horror.' He gave a twisted smile. 'I must leave this kingdom safe, yet look at me now.' He leaned forward and ruffled my hair. 'Only you do I trust.'

He paused as the door of the chamber opened and John Roberts, Yeoman Extraordinary of the Secret Chamber, a sly-eyed rascal whom I do not trust, allowed in the King's spaniels. Yapping furiously, these circled the bed, unable to jump such a height, for which the King was grateful, as these excited little dogs often tread on his legs. At last I quietened them to lie on their cushions in the corner. Behind me, Henry was bemoaning the loss of Catullus, his favourite spaniel, who'd died suddenly two weeks earlier, found in a pool of vomit on these same cushions.

'Will?' he called out. I crossed to his bedside. Henry had slipped on to his red, swollen nose a pair of those German spectacles he orders by the dozen, as he often loses them. 'Will?' He passed me a docket ordering thirteen items in gold and silver gilt, mazers, goblets and jugs, from Morgan Wolf the royal goldsmith, and asked me to decipher a number on the docket, as his sight was failing. Ever since I entered his service, over twenty years ago, the King has been impatient with clerical work, hence his utter reliance on Wolsey, Cromwell and the rest.

I clarified the entry for him and noticed how the docket had been signed with the King's dry stamp. This was a small, carved wooden block impressed on parchment by a special hand-press, which would leave an imprinted imitation of Henry's signature to be later ink-filled by William Clarke, that ubiquitous clerk of the Privy Seal, and witnessed by Sir John Gates, or Sir Anthony Denny, another of Paget's creatures. Now to uphold probity, all such transactions are recorded in a special ledger inspected by the King. Both stamp and ledger are kept in a black, leather-bound casket held by Henry himself. Previously I had witnessed nothing untoward; now my thoughts milled like a shower of falling arrows. I recalled Clarke busy with Paget in the royal chancery, his sly furtiveness. The King was growing weaker, his eyesight was failing. He was impatient, as he always has been, with the outpourings of his writing office. Did he – could he, I wondered – control the dry stamp? Were there two stamps, one the King used and another fashioned by Paget and his agents for their own devious, secret reasons? To forge the King's seal and signature was high treason. I had no proof for my anxieties, just a hidden fear. After all, if my suspicions proved correct, the Council could use such a dry stamp to snuff out a person's life like the wick of a candle.

'Will? Will?' I broke from my reverie and stared at the King's swollen, vein-streaked face. 'Go back into the City tomorrow,' Henry pleaded piteously. 'Discover what you can. Snatch up the gossip about me.' He lay back against the blood-flecked bolsters. 'Afterwards cross the river with Huicke to Greenwich. Visit my queen. I do miss her lithe white body, fresh and warm, ever so obedient. She reminds me of Boleyn, my little night crow. She is not stale or frozen, yet I do not trust her. During these days, I will not have her close, but watch her!' Henry's lower lip thrust out, trembling; his narrow, bloodshot eyes brimmed with tears. 'Will, I trust no one except you.'

'Your Majesty, the dry stamp?'

'Oh fool, what about it?'

'How do you know that you see every document sealed with that?'

Henry waved a hand. 'Not for now, fool. More pressing business. My queen, does she expect to be regent? Is that snake Seymour hoping to slide between her thighs? Oh why am I without friends?' He squeezed his lower lip between finger and thumb, peering plaintively at me.

'Why did they get rid of poor Cromwell? Ah well,' he sighed, 'go out, sniff about and come back, little dog. Discover the mood of the City. I draw my strength from it. Remember!' He gripped my wrist. 'Once you leave the Queen, do not let Huicke out of your sight.' Henry stretched back against the bolsters. 'I must sleep now.'

And so he did. I lay down on the cushions amongst the spaniels. I was woken in the early hours. Henry was shouting and crying, bellowing at the cowled, empty-hooded shapes he claimed were crowding around him.

'I was in Mount Grace,' the King gasped, his sweat-soaked face glittering in the nightlight. 'You know, Will? The Carthusian house up on the Yorkshire moors? I was standing in the nave. Along its transepts either side ranged a row of hanged men, bodies twirling, the nooses attached to brackets in the wall. A cold breeze swept the ruins and ruffled their robes. Then they began to chant, I think it was them, a hymn from Maundy Thursday, "Tenebrae Facta Sunt" – "And Darkness Fell". That was it, Will, "a great darkness over the whole earth". My horse stood alongside me. I went to climb into the saddle when more ghostly shapes emerged like columns of black smoke pouring out of the ground.' Henry gasped and sighed.

I did my best to comfort him, dabbing his face with a napkin soaked in rose water. I made him drink a little opiate mixed with wine. Eventually he slept, and so did I.

Yeoman Roberts roused us early the next morning. The King roared at him to take the spaniels, now all frisking and yapping, and stay outside until he'd finished his matins.

'Will, Will!' Henry whispered like some little boy conspiring against his tutors. 'Come here, come here!' I went and sat on the edge of the bed.

'Your Majesty is comfortable?'

'His Majesty's arse is paining him with all the fires of Hell. I woke again to lay siege to the close stool.' He grabbed my shoulder and squeezed it until I yelped. 'You were sleeping like a babe. I stood over you, Will.' His eyes glittered with a malicious glee. 'No, no, I didn't piss on you as I've done before. I was tempted to, but why spoil a good jerkin, eh? Instead I looked down at poor Will Somers, hair sweat-soaked against his scrawny face, that small hump on your back that makes you look like a snail all curled up.'

I did not reply; Henry was in an ugly mood.

'Now,' he thrust a small purse into my hand, 'I shall tell Huicke to meet you in what tavern, at what time?'

I glanced across at the hour candle Roberts had trimmed the night before. I wanted to be free of Westminster for a while.

'The Lamb of God in Cheapside, opposite the Guildhall, when the market horn sounds for the last quarter of the day.'

'Good. Accompany Huicke to Greenwich, where he will meet my sweet queen, then escort him back here. Do not let him out of your sight once you have seen the Queen.' The King wiped his fingers, their cracked skin seeping blood on to my jerkin. 'Go, Will.' He smiled. 'Who knows, you might meet the Lady Jane . . .'

'Tonight, after dark. I will meet her . . .'

'Just be careful. Now go.'

4 December 1546

I left the royal quarters, pushing my way through the throng of retainers, servants and others gathering in the galleries and antechambers beyond. Within the hour I had washed, changed and left the palace. I showed my letter of pass to the halberdiers who patrolled everywhere. I was intrigued by Henry's forced jollity; it meant he was plotting. I also wondered what he meant by the warning to be careful. Did he know about Balaam, Princess Mary's man, slipping like a weasel in and out of the city to cause mischief and to bring his mistress letters of support and encouragement from the Emperor Charles V or Cardinal Pole and other exiles abroad? Was he concerned that I might betray secrets to Balaam? But what secrets did I really know, except that Henry was plotting? As usual, everything he did was dappled in light and shadow. Was he plotting mischief against his queen? At the previous night's council meeting he had struck at the Romanists, removing Gardiner, the bishop who dared to conspire against Katherine, from his royal presence. Yet the younger Seymour had also been exiled, and why had Paget been so keen to probe and question me?

Such questions could only be posed, not answered. 'Sufficient for the day is the evil thereof' and '*Carpe diem*', 'Seize the day', are my mottos. The King wanted to know the mood of the City, and so did I. His Majesty uses me. If I have one gift, apart from my jests and sallies, I am a good listener who prompts confidences. In many people's eyes I am like the old and infirm; I don't really exist. Small in stature and slightly hunched, I pose no threat, real or imagined, against anyone. I recall Thomas More's famous dictum: 'I think no man evil, I say no man evil, I do no man evil.' A good rule to both live and die by.

Today, with Advent drawing on and the Christmas festivities fast approaching, I immersed myself in the City. First I talked to the watermen along the Thames, especially those commanding the royal barges (one of which is still reserved for my use), beautiful craft: the glass windows in their resplendent cabins exquisitely ornamented with painting and gilding, made even more gorgeous by garlands of artificial flowers of green sarcanet, their branches of eglantine powdered with blossoms of gold. These watermen informed me how the King is failing; that is why his craft lie berthed and idle at Whitechapel Steps. They loudly bemoaned the lack of business along the waterways. The gilded barges of the London Mysteries, which always accompany the royal entourage in a joyful and ear-splitting cacophony of trumpets, drums and flutes, with guns and squibs hurling to and fro against the blackness of the night, also lie silent. The steeples of the score of churches lining the Thames remain eerily peaceful: the wardens have no reason to call out their ringers to salute the King and afterwards pay them threepence to quench their thirst.

The river certainly seems to reflect the sombre mood of this city. Winter's high tides have brought flooding and muddied the water, so thick you can pluck haddock with your hand from beneath London Bridge; the fish float upon the water, their eyes blinded by the heavy river sludge. Some of the watermen hoped the Thames would freeze as it did ten years ago, so hard that His Majesty and his wife-queen Jane Seymour, now cold in her coffin beneath the paving of St George's Chapel at Windsor, crossed in sumptuous pageantry from Westminster to Greenwich. Yet this December of God's year of 1546 is bereft of such frozen beauty. The swollen Thames is used only by those who have to man the tilt barges that nose their way forward, their deep hulls crammed with livestock for the markets: boars (live 8p, dead 4p), calves (5p live, 2p dead) and poultry (5p for 20 or 3p for the same number dead). Such bills demonstrate how high prices have risen, another complaint of the riverside people as they sit in the warm fug of the Fisher of Men tavern just south of Westminster.

THE LAST OF DAYS

The watermen have certainly noticed the changes, especially the ominous silence now shrouding the steps to Whitehall and Westminster Palaces. Not even the great barges of the ambassadors of France and the Empire have been glimpsed. Whilst the guards, as one bargeman dramatically proclaimed, have been doubled, and throng so thickly that the dim light of winter glints off their pikes, morions and breastplates.

I was intrigued by this character. Narrow-faced and hot-eyed, a man educated in his horn book. One of those emerging preachers who has studied the scriptures, newly translated, and believes that God has inspired them to proclaim true religion, which, if the facts be known, has more to do with Master Calvin and the Genevans than Archbishop Cranmer and Lambeth Palace. This waterman had assumed the name of Ezekiel, which, I am sure, was not his true title conferred at his baptism. He was certainly full of ale and ready to pontificate on all things, human and supernal. He trusted me, and as I've written, who sees any danger in a grotesque? Moreover, council spies and Judas men would soon be recognised in such a tavern and immediately tossed into the freezing river.

'And the King?' I asked. 'His Majesty's silence?'

'I can only report what other tongues wag,' Ezekiel replied lugubriously. 'The rumours have begun: "The King is dying! The King is dead!" The brothels, whore-houses and strumpet shops recently closed by royal decree, those abodes of filth and debauchery,' his lips became slobbery and wet, 'now thrive joyously. They know the King is failing and his council too divided to act. Once again red candles glow behind latticed windows, inviting customers to share the joys of the sisterhood in all their satin and taffeta, that glorious throng of city prostitutes with their bare breasts and painted nipples.' This self-proclaimed prophet was now thoroughly enjoying himself. 'My dear mother of blessed memory would mourn such decadence, but she lies dead for many a day, buried beneath the harsh coldness of St Michael's, Cornhill. She always warned me against these bath-houses and molly shops.' Ezekiel wagged a bony finger in my face. 'Such places boil, stew, then spread all forms of gossip about our king and this seeps out to the surrounding alehouses and taverns. The talk is always hushed, since the Law of Treasons, recently amended, has made it a heinous crime to even imagine the King's death.'

I sat round-eyed, mouth gaping, as if awestruck by his knowledge and skill. Others now joined in. The cause of His Majesty's weakness was hotly discussed; the conclusions reached would certainly not have pleased my hellish master. The King, so one waterman whispered, was a wasteful dissolute in all his ways, a deflowerer of virgins. He, the great lecher, who banned all lewdness in the stews, kept his own privy cupboard of prostitutes and procurers in a solar above a gatehouse. Yet the fellow could not even inform us where that gatehouse stood!

Such chatter, I reflected on leaving the Fisher of Men, spreads like a deadly pestilence, heavy in the air. Nothing can stop it, not even the fog-bound river, for rumours creep across London Bridge, the only span over the Thames, eight hundred feet long, connecting the City with Southwark at Fish Street. I constantly marvel at its grandeur. The bridge certainly proclaims London's darkening mood. The magnificent gatehouse on its southern approach is a forest of spikes thickly festooned with the heads of executed traitors; these range black and gaunt against the sky like onions on toothpicks. On 15 November 1546, no fewer than thirty-five heads, eyes and lips pecked sharp by the kites, decorated the gatehouse rim to peer sightlessly in all directions. Those who live in the handsome, well-built mansions along the bridge whisper that there is certainly room for more, a tale taken up by the pin-makers who have their stalls there. I pretended to purchase and eavesdropped on their words. They claim the King is dying and the Great Lords are gathering, whilst the City mob, that beast with many heads, is ever ready for mischief. These same pin-peddlers talk most comfortably, their treason cloaked by the sound of the Thames. The river thunders through the twenty stone arches, lacing the protective starlings with all the dirt it carries. The thudding of the water competes with the soaring water-mills, their great fans clacking noisily as they fight to harness the tide. Words are easy to hide beneath such clamour, whilst the bridge is always a place of darkness. The houses and shops built on either side lean across like conspirators to block the light, the only break being a few ancient cornerstones, each called Jesus, where the drawbridge waits to be raised for some high-masted ship. The common chatter here is whose head will next decorate the spikes. Whoever it is, the skull will rot away to softness. Eventually some enterprising trader will take it down and hollow it into a drinking cup, to be sold as a sure remedy against noxious fumes to metal workers at the Tower mint.

What else did I learn? I listened and observed sharply. I have found that rumour moves like an army pillaging a city. It breaks into strands, snaking up the narrow rutted lanes past the posts and chains at Holborn Bar, across muddy ditches and foulsome streams full of the greasy bones of measled hogs as well as the heads, entrails and hides of pig and calf. More importantly, the clacking gossip creeps along Fleet Street, that land of ink, to form an invisible bridge between the broadsheet sellers who work with dirty fingers at their printing presses and those more skilled who sell such news at St Paul's and Westminster. Naturally, few dare put their names to what they think. Government men swarm like fleas over a diseased carcass, whilst those who know add that the King has been ill before and still recovered. Nevertheless, rumour piles upon rumour. Tower troops apparently guard the roads leading in and out to the City, while a strict watch is being kept at Queenhithe and along the other City wharves. Couriers, armed and swift, have been sent to the ports, where the council surveyors are out in force. Speculation about the King boils feverishly in the one-storey cottages as well as the three-level mansions of loam and lath along the twisting trackways of Pudding Lane, Bread Street and Milk Street. People claim to know someone who knows someone else, whose nephew is a friend of an ostler in the royal stables. He was the one who definitely told them about the King's health in the Mermaid in Pater Noster Row, or was it the Pegasus along Cheapside or the Bull's Head in East Cheap? It's always the same: 'The King is dying.' The gossipers stay wary and weasel-eyed. They do not want to be arrested by the bailiffs with their iron-tipped staves and hauled off in Newgate fashion to rot in that ancient gaol close to London Wall. Once there, they are doomed. They will only leave to make the final journey to the derelict leper house at St Giles Field, where they'll sup their last refreshment from a deep-bowled cup before being hanged to strangling on the Tyburn gibbet. They will choke and dance whilst the executioner, with all the skill of a flesher, plucks out their steaming bowels to the horrified delight of the crowd.

No matter how humble your station, I discovered, a gossiping tongue can bring pain and humiliation. I walked down Cheapside, marvelling at the wealth of this city and what can be found there: sweet wines of Crete, oil from Calabria, Moorish carpets, buttons and bells, hats and spices, hawks' bells, birch rods and candles, condiments and sweetmeats. London truly is an array of contrasts. The ground about these richly stacked stalls is infected with the entrails washed from the nearby scalding houses, whilst I glimpsed a beastly body shamelessly defecating in the open street. Further down Cheapside, at the Standard, two women, one heavy with child, were being nailed by the ears to the stocks for calling certain parsons 'puffed up porklings of the Pope'. London is like a vast sea, full of gusts, dangerous shelves and fearful rocks, ready at every storm to sink or cast away the weak and inexperienced.

Perhaps I should not be so prejudiced. I recently received news from Paris, where, even in the royal lodgings, chamber pots are rare and, for want of any alternative, men have to urinate on the fire. They do this everywhere by night and day. Indeed, the greater the nobleman or lord, the more readily and openly will he do it. Nor must I forget the noble French king's celebration of the winter solstice on the day following Christmas last. The city authorities erected in the Place de Grève a towering pyre around a sixty-foot-high tree stacked with kindling and straw. On top were placed a barrel, wheels, flowery garlands and baskets containing two dozen cats and a fox to be burned alive for the king's pleasure. Trumpets blared as His French Majesty sparked the conflagration with a wax torch wrapped in red velvet. Afterwards he sat down to enjoy the spectacle whilst dining on a confectionery of dried fruits, scented sweet tarts and other sugared delicacies. Cities change, human nature does not.

Life in this city continues as normal, or apparently so. The water flows through the lead pipes and conduits in Hog Lane, Cheapside and elsewhere. Traders barter, metals are tapped, tubs hooped, pots cleaned, coaches and carts rumble along the narrow streets, the houses on either side, sagging with age, supported by posts and poles. Taverns are busy, be it the Sun in Splendour or the Face in Heaven. The streets, at least until the curfew sounds and the beacons flare in the church steeples, ring with cries of 'Hot peas!', 'Small cords!', 'Milk fresh as the dawn!', 'Clear water!', 'New brooms!', 'Sweetmeats!' Beggars swarm like shoals of fish. The bold-eyed cross-biters and pimps search for conies: customers desperate for a feverish tumble in some dark corner before moving back to the taverns where the horse boys hold the mounts of those too precious, too tender or too idle to work. Such young gallants always bring gossip.

Others, wanting to be more knowledgeable, slink into that den of thieves, the cathedral of St Paul's, the haunt of nips and foists, the trading ground of butchers, ale-conners and fishmongers, as well as costly courtesans in the company of their apple squires. Here the curious can bathe in a river of chatter whilst keeping a wary eye on the delators, the professional informers clustering thick as lice on a foul hog's hide. The old St Paul's is gone, the glory dismantled. Of all its former chapels, shrines, paintings, carved marbles, work of silver and gold, gilt-edged relics, nothing is left. Only bare white-washed walls and a few crumbling stone tombs. A bleak place where people speak of the winter being so harsh it affects men's moods, including the King's. The air is so cold, deer have been found frozen in Epping Forest, to the north of the city. There is talk of the last summer, so very hot, with the sweating sickness, and of fresh diseases rife in the capital, be it a postume on the brain, swelling of the head, terrible dreams, the falling evil, the palsies, the cramps, limpness of limbs, bloodshot eyes, scabbiness and itch, diseases in the ears, sneezing out of measure, breathing with a wheeze, colic and rumbling in the guts, worms swelling the navel, the pain of a stone, pissing in bed, consumption, leanness or bleary eyes. The air is thick with pestilence. Indeed, the Angel of Death hovers so close, priests have grown busier than doctors.

I was so taken up with my observations I startled in alarm as a figure brushed by me and a piece of parchment was pushed into my hand. The shadow was gone before I could even exclaim. I unfurled the scrap. Balaam had struck, providing the time and place of our meeting later that day. I am sure he disappeared, though I felt I was being watched, even followed; just a suspicion, a prickling along the nape of my neck. However, even when I stopped and turned quickly, I could see no one. Slipping and slithering on the frozen mud, I walked on, deeper into the noisy, smelly throng of Cheapside. Smoke fumes, odours and fragrances swirled in the freezing air, so cold even the beggars strove to cover every piece of flesh against the nipping frost. The feast of Christmas is approaching, yet in that busy thoroughfare I detected a real change, a sense of mourning and consternation that the old ways had gone. Many churches have lost their statues and relics. They do not know what to do. Priests, parsons and vicars are confused; the Church is now the Tower of Babel rather than the sheepfold of unity. They cannot decide if mumming, carolling and all the rest of the festivities are permitted. If the music of sackbut, viol, schawm and other instruments is allowed. They wonder if it is acceptable to stage a tableau depicting Gabriel meeting Mary, or to dress in tawny coats, red hoods and silver masks to play out the visit of the Magi. Is the Blessed Sacrament reserved? Should there be a sanctuary lamp and bells be rung, and if so, when? Can the altar be incensed? What vestments may be worn? During mass, when the bread and wine are consecrated, are they truly the body and blood of the risen Christ, or only tokens of Our Lord's Last Supper? Can there still be wrestling in the churchyard during which church ales are served, and is it right to bestow a bleating ram on the champion wrestler? What vestments, if any, should be worn in God's Acre? May the faithful bring flowers and candles to pray for their dead? Is it permitted to re-create the stable of Bethlehem in figures or in masques? Is this still valid or popish idolatry? After all, it was encouraged by the Franciscans, who, because of their deep hostility to Henry, have been dissolved and banished.

I felt this deep confusion as I moved among the crowds coming out of churchyards and cemeteries, listening to their chatter and whispering. Now and again some fiery speaker like Ezekiel would deliver a short homily on what he thought should be happening. Of course such sermons were always brief, over and done with before the sheriff's men arrived. Some churches still ring out the Angelus bell, reminding the faithful of devotion to the Virgin; many now reject this as superstition. Even the dead are caught up in the confusion. Some coffins are borne to their last resting place with taper, candle, incense and psalms, beadsmen finger their rosaries and whisper an Ave. Others are hurried along the frozen lanes without pomp or prayer as if the mourners are ashamed of their dead. In the cage on top of the Cheapside Tun, an imprisoned nightwalker had collapsed. Someone had placed a bowl of water on his chest as well as a feather beneath his nose to discern whether he was still alive and breathing. An argument had also broken out about whether a priest should be called. One bailiff shouted that the fallen man should be shrived, whilst another ridiculed such papist nonsense.

I passed on and reached the Lamb of God, where Huicke, all resplendent in his dark robes, was waiting patiently for me. The physician is a strange character, a fellow of Merton, principal of St Alban's Hall. According to Balaam, he alarmed the university

authorities by dismissing the old schoolmen as destroyers
of good wit, though he was later appointed to the Royal
College of Physicians, their censor no less. Like the
master, so the servant; Huicke had attempted to divorce
his wife Elizabeth. Dr John Croke trialled the case and
found in favour of the wife. Huicke then appealed to
the Privy Council, and the case was heard by my lords
at Greenwich. After listening to them both face to face,
the Council exonerated Elizabeth of any blame and
vigorously condemned her husband's cruelty and deceit.
The King, a patient of the good doctor, could not resist
mischief. He used the occasion to become his own
physician's comforter, confessor and councillor. Huicke
trusts the King, truly the mark of a fool! No better
proof of the proverb that 'nothing masks deceit better
than soft and tender flattery'!

We decided to leave immediately for Greenwich. A
hideous journey across the freezing, fog-bound river
with craft warning each other off with bells, horns
and flaring lanterns. The Thames was ugly, grey and
swollen. I was pleased that Huicke had arranged our
passage in one of the royal barges with cushioned
seats, albeit soaking wet, beneath a protective stern
canopy. The swell of the river, the barge sinking and
rising before juddering sideways, rendered me sick.
Huicke made matters worse by chattering about how
dry seaweed was a sure preventative against the
mal-de-mer. When he started to describe how to chew
it, I held up a hand and, turning away, vomited

generously over the side, much to the amusement of the oarsmen. Never was I so pleased to glimpse the red-roofed turrets of Greenwich Palace and pass through its majestic yawning water gate. I leapt like a deer on to the narrow quayside, where servants carrying torches escorted us up the slippery steps into the palace. For a while we waited in an antechamber, where we were served mulled wine and portions of apple tart. I balanced these sitting on a stool next to Huicke, fending off the Queen's greyhounds, their wet muzzles buttering my fingers. Huicke chatted about how we would not be long; later that evening he must attend a meeting of the Privy Council to be held by Seymour in his mansion on the Strand.

'A meeting of the Privy Council,' I exclaimed, 'in Seymour's house! All council meetings must be held in the palace.'

'That is what His Majesty ordained.' Huicke's voice turned officious. 'So that's the way it should be.' I nodded wisely, as I am expected to, and so often do. Naturally I wondered why the King had given his consent. My heart skipped a beat. I know Henry as well as any man does, I recognise the signs: the tears, the swift changes of mood, his devil-may-care attitude to matters of state, only to turn abruptly, spinning like a coin. Henry was plotting something, and this visit to Greenwich was part of it, as were my instructions not to let Huicke out of my sight. However, the greyhounds were pressing even closer, so I gobbled my apple tart and drained my posset. A chamberlain came for us and we were ushered into the Queen's privy chamber.

Queen Katherine Parr is rather small, with delicately marked features. She has hazel eyes and auburn hair and was wearing a round crimson velvet hat (she had been recently walking in the park) edged with pearls under a gold band studded with jewels, which kept her hair in place under a white veil. A double row of pearls shimmered around her slim throat. She was garbed in a richly brocaded dress of silver and green with a girdle of gold hung with jewelled pendants around a still slim waist. She was reading a book of her own thoughts, 'The Lamentations of a Sinner', which she presented as a gift to Dr Huicke. The Queen smiled obligingly at me. The lady does not really know what debt she owes me from when Gardiner and Wriothesley were hunting her. I never told her, whilst the King's memory is always shaped to suit his whim. How can he confess that his own fool was sharper than he – or had more compassion towards her?

For a short while we discussed certain herbs and poultices on which she is an apparent authority. The Queen however seemed ill at ease, eager to be alone with Huicke. Now and again she'd break off as if distracted by the bedchamber itself, with its richly carved black oaken panelling and tapestries of brilliant beauty. She seemed particularly taken with a gorgeous central hanging. I, being sharp of eye and keen of wit, studied this intently. At the centre of the tapestry was a medallion surrounded with flowers wrought in twisted silk and bullion. Above this a spread-eagle floated, around its throat an imperial crown, whilst in each corner of the hanging reared heraldic dragons in red, purple, crimson and gold. This long, heavy tapestry hung down the wall where there was no wainscoting. I noticed it move as if shifted by some secret draught and wondered if the hanging concealed a hidden door.

I was then dismissed, told to sit in the small ante-chamber with only one of the Queen's henchmen present. I remembered the King's instructions not to leave Huicke's side, but what choice had I? The room had been cleared; it was truly deserted even of the Queen's beloved greyhounds (nourished on milk) and her parrots (fed on hempseed), whilst nowhere to be seen were the many minions she had constantly around her. Once I was ushered out, the door to the Queen's bedchamber both closed and locked behind me, I grew even more intrigued. The chamber-man offered me some mead in a gilt cup. I, in return, proffered a coin and said I would sip provided the fellow joined me. Of course he did. I performed the office, filling both cups and sprinkling a little potion into that of the chamber-man, a mild sleeping powder which, because of my constant attendance upon the King and his sudden moods, I always carry with me. A short while later the servant was dozing in his chair. I swiftly locked the door to the antechamber and pressed my ear against that of the bedchamber. I heard chairs being moved, the clink of jug against cup, murmured greetings followed by laughter as more logs were placed upon the fire. Others had secretly entered the bedchamber through that hidden door. I heard many voices and, beneath the hum of conversation, recognised one: the younger Seymour.

I strained to hear. The conversations were whispered, though I heard Surrey's name. Balaam had reminded me previously how Surrey and Seymour had clashed when they had fought together before Boulogne. Balaam believes, and I agree, that the recent attack on the Queen had its origins in the Howard faction; were the Seymours now plotting their revenge? I heard footsteps, the click and crick of a door being opened, more voices, but these remained muted. I listened keenly and heard two men speak, then the Queen answer. I am sure I caught the drift of words about 'the death of the screech owl'. I wondered if I had misheard, but the phrase was repeated before the voices faded to a whisper. I then stepped back, though in such a way that I could see into the chamber when the door was opened. Eventually it was, and Dr Huicke, all flushed and hot, strode out. I am certain that in the chamber beyond I glimpsed the shadow of a man standing very close to the Queen. Huicke, however, was all bristle and bustle, snapping his fingers at me to follow him out of the palace.

We had to wait a while for a royal wherry. Huicke was full of talk about the King, chattering like a bird of the dawn about the royal symptoms as if eager to divert me from his recent meeting with the Queen. He confided that some people thought the King suffered from the French disease, the Great Pox; he waved an admonitory finger beneath my nose.

'They say His Majesty suffers from that.' He tapped my right nostril. 'How there's a bruise or mark on the King's face here, a sign of the disease, but that is nonsense! His constant fevers are due to the ulcers on his legs caused by a fall from a horse some twenty years back. Look at his children,' Huicke continued, 'no trace there of the pox. A fable.' He snapped his fingers and shouted at the wherryman to hurry. 'A sheer fable based on a story about how the late Cardinal Wolsey, the Red Man, tried to infect the King with such a contagion. Yes, yes,' he continued, 'that's how the indictment put it: "that the same Lord Cardinal, knowing the foul and infectious disease of the Great Pox had broken out upon him in diverse places on his body, came daily to His Grace whispering in his ear and blowing upon his most Noble Grace with his most perilous and pestilential breath to the great danger of his Highness. But God, in his infinite goodness, provided a better cure and protection."' Huicke seemed very satisfied with that. He glanced away, rocking backwards and forwards on his feet, whispering to himself. I truly wondered why he should raise the matter of the Great Pox. Had such a scourge been discussed during this secret meeting in Greenwich? Was the Queen herself concerned that in her ministrations to the King she might have become infected? I decided however not to press the matter further. We climbed into the wherry and took our seats under the hooded canvas covering near the stern.

Physician Huicke remained all a-tremble and once again explained how the ulcers on the King's legs were the source of his ill-humours. Recalling what I had glimpsed in the Queen's bedchamber just before we had left, I diverted the conversation back to Her Grace. Did she not have a love of herbs and skill in physic, having had to nurture two old men, previous husbands, in their dotage? Huicke rejected that, pointing out how Lord Brough had been the same age as Lady Parr when they'd married some seventeen years ago but he had proved sickly and died. And Lord Latimer? Huicke smiled grimly. The royal physician seemed eager to extol the virtues of the Queen. He described how ten years earlier, during the Pilgrimage of Grace, the great rising in the north against Cromwell and all his doings, Latimer had been taken hostage by the rebel leader Robert Aske and forced to be his mouthpiece during Aske's most treasonable negotiations with the King. (Balaam of course has told me all about that, as he became a gentleman in Aske's company, though one swift enough to avoid the royal pursuivants when Aske was taken, hanged, quartered and disembowelled.) Latimer, Huicke explained, was compelled to go south and treat for the rebels with the King. His Majesty furiously demanded that this hapless envoy reject Aske and submit to royal clemency. Latimer did so, but once the rebellion was over, he was a broken man, remaining in London to be nursed by his wife.

Huicke was now gossiping so much, I suspected he had swiftly drunk a deep bowl of claret, but why? What was the physician frightened of? He kept chattering how the Lady Parr, as she was then, first won the King's attention by pleading for a kinsman, Sir George Throckmorton, a victim of Cromwell's rapacity. Indeed, she'd been visited by the King and given presents by him months before her husband's lingering death. And my lord Thomas Seymour? (I decided to test the waters.) Hadn't he also been hot in the pursuit of the soon-to-be-widowed Lady Latimer? Huicke just smiled knowingly and, tapping his nose, turned the conversation back to the King and the treatment of his ulcers. He dipped into his wallet and drew out a script of parchment detailing a poultice the Queen herself had drawn up. I would have liked to study this, but Huicke thought better of it, putting it away, whispering how the Queen was concerned that His Majesty might return to the hunting park at Oatlands to try and hunt the stag during the grease season, which would do his health no good.

Still gossiping, we disembarked at the King's Steps and were at once approached by the Norfolks, father and son. Of course both ignored me but chattered for a while with Huicke, explaining how they were leaving London before the Christmas festivities 'on king's business'. Surrey, arrogant and impetuous, the cast in his eye most marked, discussed the condition of his wife, Lady Frances, who was expecting their child. Norfolk, his long, cunning face twitching, kept dabbing at his dribbling mouth, bemoaning how cold Westminster felt and how he looked forward to keeping merry hall at his own palace of Kenninghall. I was tempted to ask if it was more the warmth of Bess Holland he was pining for, that brazen-mouthed, big-bosomed strumpet he'd installed in his bed to the exclusion of his wife Elizabeth, daughter of the great Buckingham. Eventually they moved away. Huicke, whispering to himself, preceded me into the warren of galleries leading back to the royal chambers. Servants were busy pushing paste balls soaked in herbs into the mouse holes at the base of the wall panelling. The corridor reeked of a tang that reminded me of the salt pans along the coast.

When we reached the King's privy chamber, Henry was sitting in his scarlet and gilt throne chair looted from Fountains Abbey. The abbot's thick winter robe, lined with ermine, was wrapt closely about his shoulders, his head protected against the cold by a flat jewelled bonnet which Catherine of Aragon had taken from the corpse of James IV of Scotland at Flodden Field. The King glanced up from the makeshift bed table across his lap. Paget and his creature Denny were with him. Denny is all sweet-faced and earnest, a handsome man with copper-gold hair, moustache and beard; his merry eyes crinkled in welcome, though Paget glowered like the basilisk. I smiled and bowed at Denny. I rather like him, especially as he does me no hurt. A

Norfolk man, a scholar, he once confided in me: 'If two deities did not command me, the King and my wife, I would surely return to my studies at St John's College, Cambridge.' He certainly served his wife, the Lady Joan; they have ten children. To house them all Denny was, as Keeper of the Palace, given custody of three mansions close to Westminster named, rather appropriately, Paradise, Purgatory and Hell. I always tease him about which of the three shelters the Lady Joan. A born courtier, Denny had comforted the King over his mockery of a marriage to the German Anne of Cleves, declaring: 'The condition of princes on matters of their marriage is infinitely worse than that of poor men, for princes have to accept what is brought to them whilst poor men are most commonly left to their own choices and devices.' Henry was profoundly impressed. Denny could do no wrong because he had portrayed Henry as the victim. Poor Cromwell, who'd arranged the marriage, climbed the scaffold at Tower Hill while Denny was given a strong hand up the ladder of royal preferment.

I heard a cough and glanced across the chamber. A man, dappled by shadows, lounged in the window seat. He was dressed like a soldier in leather jerkin and thick serge hose, one booted leg swinging, spurs clinking faintly. I peered closer and recognised the bald head and unshaven face of Sir John Gates, the King's roaring boy. If politics should ever come to swordplay in a darkened runnel, or a dagger beneath the arras,

Gates is your man. He can whistle up his ruffians to form a posse: mercenaries from Spain, Portugal, Italy, the Rhineland duchies and even a sprinkling from North Africa. At Henry's court, danger swirls like a perfume; you can grow so skilled at its detection that you can pluck it from the very air. I sensed it then. The whisperings at Greenwich about the screech owl, Norfolk and Surrey leaving the court just before Seymour held a meeting of the Privy Council in his own house. And now these three cunning courtiers closeted with their king.

'I really must do something about his corpse.' Henry broke the silence. He had taken the bonnet off his head and was inspecting its rim.

'Who, Your Majesty?'

'Why, Paget, James IV of Scotland. After Flodden Field, old Norfolk brought his corpse to London, beautifully embalmed, and it was never sent back. It still lies here, in one of the cellars.' Henry peered at me. 'You've seen it, haven't you, Will?'

I recalled that cadaver embalmed like a doll lying in its casket in a wine cellar to the north of the palace, a sombre, dreadful sight: the corpse of a once magnificent king left lying like a piece of old furniture.

'You should send it back, Your Majesty,' I agreed. I watched those shifty eyes blink. 'The servants say that James's ghost haunts them, crying for burial.' Henry grinned. He has no intention of ever sending that corpse back to Scotland. James IV once held a resplendent court. A warrior much loved by the ladies, he had dared to challenge Henry by invading England, only to meet the bloodiest defeat. Of course what rankles with Henry is that the great English victory was not won by himself – he was busy chasing French horsemen around Normandy – but by old Norfolk, the present duke's father, and Henry's queen, Catherine of Aragon.

'Ah well.' Henry closed the jewelled calfskin-bound ledger he had open before him, placing it in the black coffer. 'The dry stamp is being handled validly.' The King winked at me. 'Gentlemen, I must ask you to withdraw. Good physician Huicke, please leave what you have brought from Her Grace the Queen. Somers, stay for a while and amuse your king.'

The rest withdrew, Huicke backing out bowing. Denny smiled at me; Paget gave me that hard, calculating gaze of his whilst Gates rose and swaggered across reeking of leather and sweat. He still wore his sword belt with his hanger, a long stabbing dagger in its brocaded sheath, a rare concession, a mark of trust since very few are allowed to carry weapons into the King's presence. Gates gave me an arrogant look; he reminded me of a falcon on its perch, those cruel eyes, that hooked nose and narrow slit of a mouth. Outside in the antechambers and galleries voices rose and fell as Paget issued orders. Henry sat up in his chair, head back, face all shadowy.

'Your Majesty.' I broke the deepening silence. 'What is happening?'

'We have seen the days, Will, haven't we? Do you remember old Wolsey and the tricks you used to play on him? How he once asked you to better yourself and you promised you would. He asked how. You replied that you'd live in Ipswich and be a butcher's boy like he was.' Henry sniggered.

'And do you remember,' I retorted harshly, 'how John Dudley was only six years old when you executed his father, *your* father's loan collector. You killed him and his comrade in sin, Empson; you did it to please the people.'

'One of these days, Will, your head will fly.'

'Your Majesty my feet will be swifter. I am not the threat. I fear some trickery with the dry stamp. The Privy Council meet in Seymour's house tonight. Your own physician Huicke will be present.'

'Let them be. Cromwell became Earl of Essex, vice regent of the Church of England, and where is he? Wolsey was a cardinal, he even sought the triple crown of St Peter, and where is he? Buckingham was the greatest duke in England with his host of spears, and where is he now? As for Huicke, he is my spy, not the Council's, so I will know what happens. Now, you were with him at Greenwich?'

'Not all the time.' The white wand came hissing out of the darkness, striking my shoulder, a searing blow scraping my cheek. I screamed, jumped to my feet and backed away.

'I commanded you.' Henry leaned forward, his

swollen face contorted, the folds of fat so creased his eyes became small black pebbles in a pasty waste of puffy skin.

'Your Majesty, I had no choice. Your wife the Queen was insistent. She wanted to consult with your physician, Huicke, on a personal matter. I—'

'True, true.' Henry threw himself back in the chair, the cane slipping from his hand. 'I am still master of the game, Will. I know what I am doing. Huicke will tell me. Now,' the King indicated the piece of parchment listing the ingredients for the poultice, 'you can swear that from the moment you departed the Queen's chamber that scrap of parchment never left his hands? Whom did you meet?'

'The Norfolks, for a brief while on King's Steps.' Henry simply groaned, waving a hand. I picked up the Queen's prescription: linseed, vinegar, rosewater, long garden worms, scrapings of ivory, pearls powdered until they are fine, red lead, red coral, honeysuckle water, suet of hens and fat from the side-bones of calves.

'Your Majesty?' I glanced up. 'Is there anything wrong?'

'Tell me, Will, what happened at Greenwich?' The King listened carefully, nodding his head quickly, as was customary whenever he concentrated. 'The screech owl,' he whispered. 'Who is that? Is it Surrey, Norfolk's brat?' Just the way he spat these words out created a stab of fear. I recalled him ignoring the Howards at the recent council meeting, their exclusion from the proceedings at Seymour's house, their haste to leave Westminster.

'Surrey's arms boast an eagle,' I offered. 'The reference to a screech owl could be an insulting reference to that.'

'Tell me, Will; you know the lore, the folk tales. What is the screech owl?'

'According to tradition, the bird acquired its name from its cry because its mouth speaks what overflows from its heart; what it thinks inwardly it utters with its tongue. It is regarded as loathsome because its roost is filthy from its droppings, just as a sinner brings all who dwell with him into disrepute through the example of his own wicked behaviour. The screech owl is heavy with feathers to symbolise an excess of flesh, and like an evil spirit is always bound with a heavy laziness, the same laziness that renders sinners idle and unwilling when it comes to doing good. The bird lives day and night in cemeteries, just like sinners who revel in their sin and the stench of human corruption. It also hides in caves like a sinner reluctant to cast off the darkness, hating the light. If other birds see the screech owl they make a great cry and attack him vigorously, just as a sinner recognised in the light becomes an object of mockery for the righteous as he struggles in the toils of his own sin. Other birds tear out his feathers and wound him with their beaks, as the righteous who hate the fleshly deeds of a sinner curse and attack his excesses. The screech owl is unhappy because its heart is heavy with the habits and vices it nurtures.' I enjoyed reciting that. I know all about the bestiary, be it the basilisk or the unicorn. I also entertained my own suspicions as to whom it really referred. The King sat silent.

'Is it,' he asked, as if he could truly read my thoughts, 'a reference to me? Is that how my goodly wife, that bastion of prim virtue, truly regards me? You suspect Thomas Seymour was with her today, don't you?'

'Possibly, Your Majesty. If he was, that makes Huicke a traitor.'

'Or a very frightened man,' Henry replied. 'And Huicke can easily be frightened. They are all terrified of the Seymours. Though one thing at a time. Unlike you, Will, I am no fool. The court expects my death. The Council discuss it daily.'

'Even though it is treason? Sir Walter Hungerford was condemned to death for speculating about your death.'

'Don't quote him,' Henry snapped. 'So many do! Hungerford was exceptional. He bribed two priests to raise demons to inform him of my death. He was a born fool. He was executed the same day as Cromwell.' The King yawned, revealing yellowing black stumps in blood-tinged gums. I glanced away.

'Hungerford was executed not just for treason.' Henry yawned again. 'He also buggered a servant and raped his own daughter.'

'Huicke could be replaced,' I declared, eager to divert the King.

'And who would fill his place? Physician Wendy, who in turn will be threatened and bribed? No, no,' Henry sighed, 'I realise how these things go with them – I mean my courtiers. I am just suspicious.' He paused. 'The Act of Poisons was enacted some fifteen years ago, wasn't it? After Richard Roos, for his own wicked, damnable reasons, tried to poison the entire household of the Bishop of Rochester.'

'Oh yes, I remember him. Roos was boiled alive in Smithfield. You forced me to go and witness it.'

'Did you?'

'No. I sheltered in a nearby tavern; that was bad enough. Roos's screams were horrific. Smithfield, I understand, stank of boiled fat for days afterwards. Why?' I was becoming increasingly alarmed at this macabre conversation. 'Do you believe you are being poisoned?'

'Catullus,' the King replied, 'my dear dead spaniel. He gnawed on a poultice after it had been smeared with one of the Queen's recipes. I left it on a stool; the dog chewed it and died.'

'But sire, there are many medicines that can be applied to a wound but are not to be swallowed.'

'So you are a physician now, Will?'

'No, I am trying, as I often do and fail, to be your conscience. Are you really saying your queen is trying to poison you?'

'Or her would-be lover, Thomas Seymour?'

'You have proof?'

The King's lower lip began to quiver, fat jowls shaking, tears starting.

'Will,' he began to sob, 'how do you think I feel? I have proof that my beloved wife is pining for another man, waiting for me to die, hoping she will be left as queen regent. If that is the case, why should she, or Seymour, baulk at shortening my life?'

I was tempted to reply that this was also a queen who had cared tenderly for him and had been walking in the garden when Wriothesley and the Spears arrived to haul her off to the Tower. How Wriothesley would have loved to bully such a fine lady into a hysterical fit. I kept my lips sealed. I recognised the danger.

'Over seventy years ago, Will, we Tudors won the crown by the edge of the sword! Why shouldn't someone else do the same, sweep away little Edward and my daughters?' Henry's whole bulk heaved. He reminded me of an old mastiff preparing to attack. 'But who?' he demanded. 'The Howards? The Dudleys? The Seymours? I have cared for them all, favoured the Seymours because of Jane, their poor sister. I have overlooked Dudley's lowly, tainted origins. As for the Howards, they fought against my father, yet I made Surrey the constant companion of my bastard son, Henry Fitzroy, Duke of Richmond. I even married Fitzroy to Norfolk's daughter, and now they betray me.'

'Who does, sire?'

'They all pull lady faces and wag lady tongues but they have dragons' hearts; they are wolves garbed as lambs, hawks who act the dove. Never mind, never mind.' Henry's voice became brisk. 'I have much to attend to; my Council will be returning here.'

Dismissed, I returned to my own chamber and drew out Balaam's message, thrust into my hand earlier in the day. Balaam and Lady Jane would come suitably cowled and visored to the Bowels of Hell, an ancient three-storey tavern close to the old friary of the Carmelites, Whitefriars, not far from Puddle Wharf and the Temple Gardens. Balaam promised to be there after the witching hour, waiting for me in the Vespers Chamber overlooking the garden at the back of the tavern, a suitable place for escape should flight become necessary.

I left after lamp-lighting. I hired two armed luciferi to carry lanterns before me as I hurried through the crooked, narrow lanes. Darkness had fallen, an icy blackness that drove all good citizens from the streets and melancholy wastes. A bristling breeze sent the tavern and shop signs creaking eerily. The only light was the occasional flaring pitch torch pushed into some crevice or holder. Here and there bonfires raged as the rubbish heaps were soaked in oil and fired into a furious conflagration which drew in the legion of beggars from the mean streets and lanes. On doorposts tallow dips in their lantern boxes glowed a dull yellow, their cheap odour mingling with the insidious stench of refuse, dung and above all that stink of rancid oil that seems to drift everywhere. We passed open doors revealing narrow nooks of rooms, their walls blackened by time: pillars and rafters worn, floors tainted and sticky with rotting straw, windows mere slits stuffed with old rags and pieces of rubbish. I was nervous because such a night-time foray is a rare event. Nevertheless, the creatures of the dark, the night-stalkers and sewer squires, glimpsed the steel of my escort and slunk away.

Eventually we reached the Bowels of Hell, a stark, forbidding tavern standing on the corner of a trackway leading down into the heart of Whitefriars. Of course the curfew means nothing here. I knocked on the side door and it quickly swung open. A shadowy figure led me across a gloomy taproom. The place reeked of rancid cheese; the rushes underfoot were a squelching slush through which vermin scampered and squeaked. A rickety staircase led up to the main gallery. My shadowy guide knocked on the door to the Vespers Chamber. Balaam, he of the long dark face, cynical eyes and mocking mouth, was waiting. He was sitting at the head of a well-scrubbed table where platters of dried meat, fresh bread and pots of hot herbs and vegetables mixed together had been laid out with goblets of water and a stoppered jug of white wine. He rose to greet me. He was dressed in a dark brown robe like that of a Benedictine monk, whilst the chamber he had hired seemed like his cell. Its walls and floor were clean and free of any covering; a Spanish crucifix hung over the hearth where a fierce fire roared. Pots of incense curled scented smoke, which provoked memories of masses offered.

Balaam whispered his greeting and we exchanged the kiss of peace. He then went to the door and his escort brought up the lovely Jane Bold, my sweetheart, my true reason for living. Oh Lady Jane! Small and petite, her face even prettier framed by its furred hood. I gave her the warmest hug and a saucy kiss on those lovely lips. She gazed bright-eyed at me and we kissed again until Balaam coughed. I took the Lady Jane's hands, brushed them with my lips and escorted her to a chair. All three of us gathered around the table.

For a while we satisfied our hunger, Jane, in her soft country voice, telling me how she felt and what she had done, how she had brought her mistress's greetings. I listened intently and grasped what she wasn't saying. All power now lay at Westminster. The households of Princess Mary, the Princess Elizabeth and the Lord Edward were isolated, allowed to sink into a boring, humdrum existence. Winter had sealed the roads, whilst the Council determined what messages travelled along them. In return I told the usual tales. How Henry's mood was improving. How he missed his elder daughter. How he hoped to travel to meet her and looked forward to sharing the festive season with her. Jane nodded as she listened; she knew it was fiction, as would her mistress. Everybody was waiting to dance to Henry's tune, as they had for the last thirty years, only now Henry had hidden himself deep in shadows. This time

Balaam would demand the stark truth on other matters. I fed the Lady Jane sops of food until Balaam tapped the table with his goblet.

'The Lord be with you,' he breathed.

'And with you too, brother,' I retorted.

'Master Will, the King, how is he? Please be blunt.' He grinned. 'Even treasonous! The Princess Mary is being starved of all real news.'

'I shall speak directly. The King's torso is obese, gross. The fat around his neck threatens to choke his breath and he has a great hump here,' I half turned, indicating my own back, 'between the shoulder blades. His skin is yellowing, thin and as easy to crack as a communion wafer. Wounds and cuts heal very slowly if at all. His face is now moon-like, dragged down by folds of fat beneath his eyes; the same swell around his hips. He complains of constant soreness to his ribs and back; his bowels and anus ache so much, the pain of easing himself licks like tongues of flame.'

'And his mind?'

'Sharp as ever. Just as changeable. Just as dangerous. He trusts no one, but sometimes gives the impression that he trusts everyone. They are all fearful. Henry has a nightmare that when he dies, all will be swept away.'

'And the Council?'

I told Balaam everything I had seen and heard in the King's secret chamber. This was not betrayal; I could tell from Jane's face that if the King was fearful, so was the Princess Mary. I relayed my conversation with Paget, particularly his description of Cranmer's brush with death.

'I have heard of that,' Balaam murmured. 'Rumours, snatches of conversation. Now that would disturb the humours of a man like Paget. Dudley and the Seymours are soldiers, but Paget is a true student of Machiavelli. He has studied Henry closely. In many ways Paget reminds me of Thomas More without his saintliness.'

'But why discuss the King with me?'

Balaam toasted me with his goblet. 'Will, you are the King's close companion. Paget wishes to see which way you will jump. If he has approached you, he probably has had similar conversations with other members of the Council. I would wager a purse of silver that Paget is prepared, should the King die, to concede supreme power to Seymour and Dudley on the one condition that they are guided and advised by him.'

'Paget is also hunting you,' I warned.

That master of shadows simply smirked. 'Cromwell tried the same, and where is Cromwell?'

'Where is this leading?' Jane demanded. 'Surely it is the King's mood that is all important?'

'Shall I tell you?' Balaam shuffled his feet. 'If Master Paget studies our king, then so do I, and that includes the paintings. I have glimpsed one; you may have seen it, Will: Henry seated in all his glory under a cloth of state. On his right stands the Prince Edward, Henry firmly grasping his hand. On his left, Queen Jane Seymour, as if she has been lifted from the funeral hearse and made to stand beside her king and her seven-year-old son whom she hardly glimpsed before she died. Further away, to the right and left of the King, stand his two daughters, Mary and Elizabeth, almost indistinguishable.'

'I have seen this painting,' I broke in. 'I cannot recall who executed it; a strange painting, timeless. Young Edward is depicted much older than he was at the time. Queen Jane died in childbirth, yet she is there, as if summoned back from the dead. Even more curiously, at either side of the painting there is an arch leading into the great gardens of Hampton Palace. Under one arch stands you, Jane, in your red petticoats, in the other myself garbed in a green jerkin and rough hose.'

Jane too was nodding excitedly. 'I too have seen this,' she murmured. 'It hangs in the presence chamber at Whitehall.'

'And there is the other painting,' Balaam declared. 'On one occasion, Will, you described it to me, from the King's book of hours, very peculiar.'

'What is this?' Jane turned to me.

'A curious painting,' I replied, 'where the King is depicted as old, ill and overweight. Shown in the guise of King David, he squats close to a Welsh harp, one of the instruments His Majesty is most skilled at. In the foreground stands myself, the King's fool, with my back to him in an attitude of rejection. I am dressed in a coat of green cloth, its hood lined with fur; on my belt hangs Cromwell's purse. My hair is cropped, my face unshaven. On my left shoulder perches a monkey, which is searching my scalp.'

'Master Balaam, why do you mention paintings?' Jane asked.

'They show the King's mind,' he retorted. He paused, listening to the wind whipping the shutters and carrying the dull cries of the night.

'How?' I started at the hideous screech of a rat caught in the jaws of a cat along the gallery outside.

'Remember, Will, remember, Jane.' Balaam was not being pompous, but voicing something he'd milled and sifted in his own devious brain. 'Remember,' he repeated, 'all paintings have to be approved by our king. The first painting is significant. Henry in his splendour with his long-dead wife next to him and his son brought to boyhood. Queen Jane just stands there like a statue, whilst Henry grasps Edward's hand to demonstrate complete ownership. On either side, much further away, his two daughters, whom Henry really didn't want but who he will tolerate and use to his best advantage. Nobody else is depicted except, my respects to both of you, the two court fools. Do you represent, at least in Henry's eyes, the rest of the world? Look at that painting again, Will. Jane is correct: it hangs in the presence chamber at Whitehall. There is no cross, no crucifix, no altar, no bishop, no priest, no clerk, no courtier; nothing but Henry, his queen, his three children and his fools. Nothing else exists for him; that's his world and how he regards it.'

'And the second painting?' Jane asked. 'The one in the book of hours?'

'Henry is neither Romanist nor reformer but simply the King,' Balaam declared. 'The verse in this painting is from Psalm 52: "In his excess the fool said there is no God." The painting underscores this. Will is the fool who represents those who hold that no God exists and so turn their back on the true God, so evident to see: Henry and the royal house of Tudor. Henry,' Balaam concluded, 'has the arrogance to assume the role of King David, God's anointed, a man, as scripture says, after God's own heart. David's bloodline is sacred because from it came Christ the Lord. Henry sees the same replicated in his own lineage.'

'A prince who had many women,' Jane murmured, 'who slew his enemies but remained God's beloved.'

'That's why Henry allowed himself to be depicted as old and overweight – it's the truth, but so are the King's claims to be what he most desires.'

I touched Balaam's hand. 'Which is precisely what?'

'His Majesty,' Balaam replied, 'believes in neither the God of Rome nor that of Luther, Calvin and Zwingli, but only in himself. He is obsessed with his own lineage and house; he will destroy anyone who threatens them.' He went on to say that if the King survived his present illness and returned to government, he would carry out reforms and purges the like of which had never seen before. He would destroy everyone: the Howards, the

Seymours, Dudley, even Cranmer. No one would stand in his path.

Balaam maintains that His Majesty the King is approaching the same form of princely madness as the emperors of Ancient Rome. Henry believes he is God, or at the very least, God's will on earth, and therefore cannot be checked or opposed; hence his depiction as David of scripture. Outside of Henry the king, there is no God, so he will dictate the true tenets of established religion.

'Remember,' Balaam sipped at his goblet, 'this is nothing new. The seeds were planted many years ago. In 1530, so the Princess Mary tells me, the King held a meeting of the English church in St Edward's Chapel, Westminster. They discussed the translation of the Bible. Henry asserted that the welfare of his subjects' souls was his, not the bishops' responsibility. He would decide on what translations, if any, were to be made and how they would be distributed. No other monarch has ever claimed such a right.' Balaam gave that lopsided grin. 'A few more steps,' he murmured, 'from being the keeper of God's word to being that word himself.'

He went on to say that the screech owl was not Surrey but the King himself, a dark, lonely, dangerous soul. His councillors had now recognised the lurking danger and were plotting furiously to counter it.

'Once,' Balaam declared, 'I stayed in Rome. I visited a haunted house where, allegedly, two statues of cardinals of the Santa Croce family descend from their pedestals at night to walk dolefully in a rattle of chains. I investigated that house. I discovered an oubliette lined with sharp pointed stakes, all around a mass of skeletons, one of them in armour with a dagger driven through the helmet. I also found an embalmed corpse walled up in a niche.' He paused, clicking his tongue. 'It's the same here,' he murmured. 'England is a haunted house full of devious devices, traps and secret cells with corpses hidden away and ghosts that walk the dead of night.'

'A ghost story!' Lady Jane exclaimed.

'England is a ghost story,' I retorted. 'The court is its haunted place. Ghosts lean against the wall, stand by the threshold and peer through the window.'

'Old resentments,' Balaam declared, 'buried griev-ances, dashed hopes, murderous resentments, Henry knows all this. He will not exorcise the ghosts but will try and kill them. I truly believe that. He will turn on one party then the other. The one he believes to be the most vulnerable will be smitten first.'

'And who is that?' I asked.

'Why, the Howards of Norfolk!'

'And what charge could the King or the Council level against them?'

'Not from without, Will, but from within. Holy Scripture says a house divided against itself cannot stand, and the Howards are riven with dissension.'

'True, Norfolk is alienated from his wife. Surrey has clashed with both his father's mistress Bess Holland

and his sister, the widow of the King's bastard son, Henry Fitzroy, but how can this be treason?'

Balaam was about to reply when a clatter of steel echoed from outside in the freezing night air. The chamber fell deadly silent. Balaam hurried across to a window. He pulled back the shutters, slashed a cut in the stretched pig's bladder covering the narrow gap and peered out.

'Men, hooded and visored,' he whispered. 'They carry staves and pennants. Council men! Somehow our meeting has been betrayed.'

I felt a chill. I was responsible. Paget knew of my visit here. We had done no wrong, but if we were taken, questions would be asked. I rose, and was gesturing at Jane to follow when the chamber door was flung open. A group of men, heads and faces covered in white sacks with rents for eyes, nose and mouth, slipped like ghastly nightmares into the chamber. Lady Jane gave a scream, cut off as Balaam pressed a gloved hand against her mouth.

'No fear,' he whispered, 'no fear. These are my men. What news?'

'Council men,' one of the masked men replied. 'About twelve in number. Mine host is keeping them dancing on the threshold. They carry no warrant but demand entrance to search. We had best leave, but not through the garden.'

He led us out of the chamber, along the ill-lit gallery then down stairs and shaky steps until we reached the dingy, smelly cellars beneath. The floor was slippery and stained by the beer and wine that had leaked from the barrels, tuns and vats, the cold night air broken by the constant squeak of mice and rats. Torchlight flared. We waited anxiously whilst a great cask was pushed aside to reveal a door built into the wall; that was quickly thrown open. Balaam, sword in one hand, a flaring torch in the other, led us into a warren of evil-smelling passageways and ancient sewers cut beneath London's streets. We fled like bats down those dark tunnels. Now and again, I am certain, we passed skeletons, a heap of snow-white bones glittering in the passing light before the darkness swallowed us again. On one occasion Balaam made us stop, the blackness all around us, to ensure we were not being pursed and there was no danger ahead. I stood clutching Lady Jane's hand, eyes tightly closed. Balaam's ghost story and the sights we'd glimpsed had upset my humours. I was not sure whether I was dreaming or not. Faces came out of the dark. Edward Seymour with his craggy features and popping eyes; Thomas his brother, with his bristling moustache and beard; Dudley, fox-like and predatory; Paget, slapping those garden gloves against his thigh whilst studying me intently. Balaam murmured, tugging at my cloak, and we moved on.

Ghosts haunted that place of shadows. I abruptly recalled a story of how the King had apparently entered a chamber at Hampton Palace and come face to face with all his victims: Anne Boleyn, sharp-featured and laughing shrilly; Katherine Howard clasping her neck to show how small it was; Cromwell clutching his beads and pleading piteously for mercy; Wolsey in his purple cardinal's robes weeping that he had served his king better than his God; More and Fisher all reproachful; the Carthusians of Charterhouse in their bloody robes. Henry had fled screaming like a demented child. Such a memory rendered me highly anxious. I was so relieved to be free of that gloomy vault, out through the taproom of a riverside tavern and on to the snow-swept quayside. We made our hasty farewells. I embraced Jane, whispering my love into her ear, kissing her on the lips, cheek and brow before Balaam plucked her away, ordering some of his escort to see me safely back to Westminster.

I slept fitfully and woke famished, so I rose and, pushing aside all cares, broke my fast on a chine of beef, a joint of mutton, buttermilk, six eggs of chicken and a pottle of beer followed by a little salted fish with melted butter poured over it. I tried to see the King but I was turned away from the privy chambers by that arrogant oaf Roberts on the orders of Sir William Paget. The yeoman curtly informed me that I was not needed and should look to my own affairs. I replied that I had gossip from the city for His Majesty. Roberts just shrugged. He said he had his orders and I had mine. I had no choice but to return to the kitchens and my good friend Master Bricket, the master cook. Bricket knows my weakness.

I love the life of the kitchens. There is nothing more soothing than to be swept up in the lavish preparations for the King's table. I helped to prepare the royal meal: soup, roast capon, boiled beef, chicken pasties, roast pork, fish, almond tarts and baked apple. In the evening we prepared stewed fruits, and oysters from Colchester augmented with eggs, cream, butter, onion and herbs. Bricket surpassed himself making subtleties of almond paste and sugar in the shape of the Virgin and the Angel Gabriel. A minstrel, hired by the Lord Chamberlain, joined us. I listened to his stories about a bleak castle set in the middle of a wild forest where outlaws prowled clothed in Lincoln green, but soon grew tired of this and asked for something romantic, a lilting country tune so I could evoke the past. Afterwards I went to the palace bath house, its roof and walls hung with sheets, the bath itself warm with rosewater, herbs and a sponge for me to sit on. I cleansed myself and returned refreshed to my own chamber.

I was content to relax and reflect on what Balaam had said. If Henry was about to move, and he certainly was, on what grounds could he strike at the Howards? They were powerful. They had done nothing to incur the King's anger except by being who they were. How could Henry find evidence against them? They had their estates, their palaces, their retinues. I glanced at a painting on the wall and felt a chill of apprehension. The picture showed a married couple, long-dead courtiers, husband and wife sitting so amicably close together.

I recalled Balaam's words about how a house divided against itself could not stand. To outsiders, the Howard family are like a fortress, but within, have not Norfolk and his wife gone to war? I have glimpsed Norfolk's wife Elizabeth, daughter of Stafford, Duke of Buckingham, at the Howard house in Lambeth. A fine-boned, full-faced lady with reddish hair and eyes as sharp as a jackdaw, a pleasant visage though with a slightly receding chin. She has long, slender fingers; I remember them grasping a scarlet missal with a gold cross in the centre. She wore a hood in the English style edged with a band of jewels, peaking high in light red velvet from which fell a full train of dark material. I recall it well because an acquaintance, someone who'd served Chapuys, the former Imperial ambassador, remarked how the duchess's appearance evoked memories of Catherine of Aragon, the very source of all that redoubtable woman's troubles. Such a chance memory emphasised Balaam's prediction. When the King moved against an opponent, he always destroyed them from within, be it Anne Boleyn's musicians or Katherine Howard's ladies. Norfolk's household would be a fertile furrow to plough, the source of dissension being the old duke's rejection of his wife.

At first, according to court gossip, Elizabeth's marriage to Thomas Howard seemed happy enough. She bore him three children, Henry, Mary and the younger Thomas, but the bane of her life was Cardinal Wolsey, whom her father Buckingham hated with a passion beyond all others. Buckingham publicly called Wolsey a butcher's churl and, as royal cup bearer, refused on one occasion to pour water for him, instead spilling it all and spoiling the cardinal's purple silk shoes. Hatred for Wolsey was common amongst the lords. Howard himself drew a dagger on the good cardinal and, on another occasion, declared he would tear Wolsey apart with his teeth. Howard could dissimulate; Buckingham, however, could not; little wonder Emperor Charles called him 'the proudest Buck in England'.

Eminent for his high birth and large revenues, Buckingham built a fantastical pile at Thornbury on the Welsh march, a monument to his own greatness. He rode high in the councils of the King, but was ruined by his ever-clacking tongue. Believe me, at the English court Fate never undoes a man without his own misdirection, and when it does, its first stroke is always at the head. Buckingham preened himself so magnificently that people considered that if the King should die without a male heir, the duke might easily obtain the crown. A dangerous saying. His Majesty took note. Buckingham was arrested and arraigned before Norfolk's father, the victor of Flodden, for plotting the destruction and death of the King. The Norfolks wept at the thought of Buckingham being condemned but still pronounced the verdict of death. Buckingham had to surrender to the sheriffs and a guard of five hundred men. On Tower Hill he recited the penitential psalms, took off his gown and, blindfolded, laid his head on the block, where he died miserably but with great courage. The Norfolks, both father and son, wept and wailed, then comforted themselves with large portions of Buckingham's chattels and estates. This was slightly before my time, but the story was common knowledge. Henry often comforted himself by personally itemising the fallen duke's personal possessions, which he kept close about him.

Elizabeth, the duchess, so common report has it, never recovered her wits after her father's brutal and sudden fall. Perhaps she glimpsed for the first time the deep hypocrisy of Norfolk, her husband, who emerged as one who had conspired with both king and cardinal to bring him down. Buckingham did not go like a lamb to the slaughter but, from the bar of his court, rounded on those who had plotted his destruction, declaring that of all men living he hated Howard the most, regarding him as a man who had done his utmost to disgrace him in the eyes of His Majesty. Elizabeth never forgave nor forgot; some thirteen years later, as the King began to press for a divorce from his Spanish queen, she proved resolute in her defence of Catherine. Norfolk once warned Thomas More that the wrath of the King meant death, to which More replied that if that was the case, the only difference between them was that he would die today and Norfolk tomorrow. Such was the Duchess Elizabeth's attitude. She did not fear the King's wrath. She had no time for political subtleties or pastime with good company, the joys of the tennis courts, tilting yards, bowling alleys and dicing tables, of bawdy doggerel and games of courtly love. The constant masques, dances and banquets in the royal palaces, with their unalloyed service to Venus and Bacchus, repelled her. The duchess loudly proclaimed that she had no patience for those who showed her fair face to conceal false heart, who cried 'All hail!' when they intended all harm. Men and women of the court who'd doff their bonnets to her in greeting, but who would quietly pray to see her head leave her shoulders. Courtiers who would make a leg to her and bow with all reverence yet would have those same legs broken to see her dead and hurried to the grave.

She herself was guilty of no such deceit. Angry at both king and husband, she openly espoused Queen Catherine's cause, and that of the Princess Mary, so I hold the duchess's name in the highest regard. Lady Jane once informed me how Norfolk's wife filched letters from her husband's own chancery which provided information about the King's secret designs to have his marriage to his first wife annulled. The duchess carefully copied these and sent them to the Queen cleverly concealed in an orange. She publicly informed the Queen how Boleyn's court strove to entice the duchess over to theirs and declared that even if the world tried, she would remain faithful to her. She encouraged Catherine to stand firm, telling her to have good courage for her opponents were at their wits' end, being further off from their design than the day they first began. The Duchess of Norfolk openly realised she could be the ruin of her family, and her fidelity to the Queen certainly cost Norfolk dearly. She was eventually exiled from the court, judged as speaking too freely and declaring herself for Catherine more than was liked.

Lady Jane was party to all the gossip and rumour learnt by her mistress the Princess Mary. She narrates with great gusto how there was even a secret plan for Anne Boleyn, when the King's cause seemed weak, to marry young Surrey. A marriage of convenience to satisfy Boleyn's ambitions whilst allowing the King free rein with her. Norfolk always tried to weave his family close to the Crown, and his wife's persistent refusal to even consider such a squalid arrangement enraged him further; to be sure, my lord of Norfolk's fiery temper is more hasty than is needed. Duchess Elizabeth remained obstinate in her stubbornness. She refused to bear Boleyn's train when she was elevated to the title of Marchioness of Pembroke, and ignored the summons to join that same lady's retinue during her crossing to France. She did not attend Boleyn's coronation or the christening of her child, the Princess Elizabeth. Norfolk, distracted out of his wits and fearful of the King, begged Henry Stafford, his wife's brother, to take her back. Stafford refused, saying his sister's wild language was constant and he had no power to prevent it, whilst her presence in his house might cause great danger for him and all his kin. He did not deserve that and he could only pray that God would send his sister a better mind.

Matters were certainly not helped by my lord of

Norfolk, who was greatly seduced by the charm and beauty of Bess, the daughter of Lord John Holland, his chief steward. Bess eventually became the lady of the house at the duke's principal manor of Kenninghall. This proved too much for Duchess Elizabeth, who turned on her rival, calling her 'a churl's daughter, a washer of nursery pots, a drab, a quean, a harlot'. Twelve years ago, during Passion week, all thought of Christ's suffering and death was ignored in the duke's residence. The King, smirking behind his hand, told me the story. The duchess refused to suffer the Holland bawd and her harlots, so the duke locked her in a chamber, taking away all her apparel and jewellery. On hearing this, the reformist Bishop Latimer openly preached at court how it was part of the penance of being a woman to suffer in bearing children, as it was to be subject and subservient to their husbands, because women were underlings and, as such, must be obedient. The duchess certainly refused to accept such advice and her husband became lost in a marvellous sorrow and indignation at her obduracy.

The duke was already mired in controversy. Unable to help either the King or Boleyn, he had become Anne's enemy. She openly resented him, especially his remarks about how the conflict over the King's divorce from his Spanish queen was caused by Satan and nobody else. How Satan had been the inventor and source of all that dispute. Norfolk, fearful lest Anne Boleyn and her faction would turn the King's heart from him, banished his wife to Redbourne, one of his Hertfordshire manors. Even there, the duchess sustained her litany of sorrows and objections, dispatching letter after letter to the King, Master Cromwell and her husband. She insisted that Kenninghall belonged to her and not to Holland; that she, the duchess, was a noblewoman by birth and raised to live daintily. She described physical attacks on her when Norfolk sent Holland and other harlots to bind her until blood seeped out of her finger ends. How they tortured her and sat on her breast until she spat blood. So ill was this treatment that it had weakened her health; she became sick in autumn at the fall of a leaf as well as the spring of the year. She protested how she'd only married Norfolk out of duty to her father, as her real love was Neville of Westmoreland, and how her husband, even when she was pregnant, had assaulted her. She received no comfort from her children and publicly proclaimed that no mother bore so ungracious an elder son and so unnatural a daughter. The duchess fled to the King when he was hunting outside Dunstable, but what could His Majesty say about the holiness of marriage vows? In truth, and I was the King's audience, Henry secretly but gleefully recounted Norfolk's woes. He and his drinking companion, the one-eyed Sir Francis Bryant, laughed at the duke's misery until their cheeks were wet and their sides ached. Elizabeth, despairing of the King, importuned Cromwell for protection, claiming that even if she was allowed to go home, she might be poisoned because of Norfolk's love for his harlot Bess Holland.

The duchess had chosen well. Norfolk hated Cromwell, the upstart blacksmith's boy from Putney who in turn twisted and turned to trap Norfolk as Wolsey had Buckingham. Cromwell was ever greedy for any morsel of possible treason by Norfolk. The duke had to swallow, even choke on his pride and account to Master Cromwell for what he regarded as the truth of the matter. Surely this must have been the bitterest egg to bite! The duchess arrived in London and stayed at Austin Friars. Cromwell wrote to Norfolk that perhaps he should also come so Cromwell could mediate between the two. How Henry laughed at that! Norfolk, furious, dismissed his wife as wilful, saying that he would never come into her company because she had wrongly slandered him, claiming that when she was in childbed with their daughter for two days and nights, he had dragged her out of that bed by the hair of her head, thrown her about the house and, with his dagger, scored a wound to her head. Norfolk protested his innocence. He claimed to have witnesses that the scar on his wife's head was from fifteen months before she was delivered of the said daughter; it was in fact a cut by a surgeon in London for a swelling when drawing two teeth.

Henry was beside himself with merriment at such details. He cuffed my ear and said he would replace me with Norfolk and his wife, for such a masque was better than anything I had ever presented. On one occasion, at Greenwich, deep in his cups, he insisted on playing such a drama out. Closeted in his chamber, he made Bryant, who could mimic all he met, take the role of Norfolk, with me as Bess Holland and himself as the duchess. I grew tired of such revelry so Henry struck me, loosening a tooth. Bryant drily remarked that now I and the duchess had something in common. Henry roared with laughter, gave me a purse of silver and, drunk as a sot, declared we should all make peace before collapsing on the bed with his spaniels.

In the end, Master Cromwell realised that Norfolk would never take his wife back and, at the King's secret order, conceded he could do no more in the matter. The duchess, in full despair, wrote to Cromwell shortly afterwards saying that, from now until ever, she would never petition the King or any other to ask for her husband to receive her. The King thanked God for that! The duchess proclaimed that she had made her plea and received nothing in return. She insisted that she had done no wrong except reveal her husband's shameful handling of her and concluded that she would never go home, for if she did, her life would be short. Henry, now bored with the proceedings, ignored her protests. However, he would never forget. Norfolk's most dangerous enemies were in his own household. Henry, like the predator he was, would study this. The great Buckingham was destroyed by his own son-in-law. Could circumstances repeat themselves?

23 December 1546

When Henry strikes, it's always swift, like a peregrine swooping from the clouds. The victim does not even realise the danger until the talons close about it. Anne Boleyn was busy with her May Day celebrations. Cromwell joined his fellow councillors after dinner. Queen Katherine Parr was tending to her sick pained husband. And so it is in these last of days. I kept no journal for a while as there was nothing to describe, nothing to note until late this December the Year of Our Lord 1546. I had been excused, increasingly so as the King became closeted with Dudley and Seymour. Life became still, if not serene. The King locked in his chambers would host neither wife nor children, so why should he see me? I thought he was resting, plotting or both, only to discover that the carnival of blood was picking up pace. The Howards of Norfolk have fallen! Swift and brutal, both father and son were taken up and committed to the Tower. Henry Howard, Earl of Surrey, had come up from his country residence to Whitehall. The King, much recovered, ordered his arrest, telling the captain of his guard to take the earl most secretly and swiftly. On Thursday afternoon, 9th December, entering the palace after dinner, Surrey glimpsed Sir Anthony Wingfield, Captain of the Spears, walking towards him down the stairs of the palace.

'Welcome, my lord, to Whitehall,' Wingfield declared. Nearby a dozen Spears waited in an adjoining corridor. The captain was eager to take the earl towards that trap, well away from his own household men. 'I want you to intercede for me with the duke your father,' Wingfield continued, plucking at the earl's sleeve, 'on a matter in which I need his favour. If you would be so kind as to listen to me . . .?'

Surrey graciously conceded. They had hardly disappeared from the hall when the guards ran out, seized the earl and hurried him without attracting notice on to the quayside and the waiting barge. He was taken to Blackfriars and then up to Ely Place in Holborn to the residence of Lord Chancellor Wriothesley, the man with the milky blue eyes of a cat. Here he was detained for ten days, interrogated and questioned most closely. Thomas, Duke of Norfolk, on hearing this, hastened to London from his palace at Kenninghall to enquire after his son, only to be seized himself. Some allege that father and son had some ambiguous discourse about the King whilst the latter was ill some weeks ago; the object of their discussion seems to have been the government of the young prince. Any hope of their liberation is very small. The duke was deprived of both staff of office and his Garter before being taken to the Tower by water. According to Balaam, who learnt this from a gentleman in Wriothesley's retinue, the Imperial ambassador van der Delft declared it pitiable that persons of high rank and noble lineage should have undertaken so shameful a business as to plan the seizure of the government of the King by such treacherous means. Others gossip about a Howard plot to murder either the King and his heir or the entire Council; the evidence for this is a letter written by Surrey to a certain gentleman full of threats and menaces. The case against Surrey certainly presses hard. Even though he has always been so generous with his countrymen, there is no one well disposed enough to regard him as innocent.

The fall of the Howards is proof enough that the reformist coven have obtained such influence over the King as to lead him according to their fancy. Indeed, in the days since I last wrote, courtiers who used to refer foreign envoys directly to the King are now of a different aspect and inclined to please the Earl of Hertford and Lord High Admiral Dudley more than anyone else. Indeed, these two have entirely obtained the favour, grace and authority of His Majesty. Nothing is done at court without their intervention. Council meetings are regularly held in Lord Hertford's mansion on the Strand. Balaam, that greedy gull for information and rumour, claims the custody of the young prince and the government of the realm are being daily entrusted to Hertford and Dudley, whilst the misfortunes that have befallen the Howards spring directly from them. Rumours fly as thick as the snowflakes that now carpet the palace gardens. How Surrey has been taken on two principal charges: first that he had the means of seizing the castle of Hardelot when he commanded His Majesty's forces at Boulogne, and neglected to take it; the other that he said there were some in England who made no great account of him but that one day he trusted to make them very small. Whether he intended, plotted or wished the death of His Majesty or his son is not certain. I regard such accusations as false and spurious; the Princess Mary, Balaam and Lady Jane would swear the same.

The reformists are certainly gleeful. They view Norfolk and Surrey as the bitterest enemies of their word and claim that both are guilty of secret attempts to restore the Pope and the monks. This latter allegation masks a greater danger. I, Balaam and the Lady Jane secretly met a gentleman of the Princess Mary's chamber, a former priest, Lydgate, who, so it is said, is the princess's envoy to Cardinal Reginald Pole. According to Lydgate, many Romanists believe that in the eyes of God, the young prince has no right to succeed. Henry was solemnly excommunicated by the Pope, and his marriage to Lady Jane Seymour was clearly against the law of the Church; thus any child from such a marriage could never be a true Christian monarch. It is hinted that Surrey, England's proudest and most foolish boy, has been confined because he might stir up such a commotion against the young prince after his father's death. Indeed, it is claimed that he was already hot on this business, hence his unexpected return to London with certain henchmen of his household, all armed and ready for war. I do not believe this. Surrey always had such young bloods in his company.

Now, excluded from the royal presence, I haunt the royal kitchens, warm and friendly and a deep well of juicy gossip. Scullions and spit boys, servitors and pastry cooks do not, as with myself, exist in the eyes of the great lords of the soil. Naturally, such lowly people snout out rich truffles of gossip. Stories about Surrey's henchmen echo chillingly true. How two of them were found garrotted behind the stews along Southwark side. How another was knifed over a game of hazard in a tavern nearby whilst five more took a barge close to the Priory of St Mary Overy but never reached Queenshithe. River accidents, especially when the sea mists roll in thick and heavy, are common enough. The corpses of all five young men, frozen blue and bloated with filthy water, were plucked by the scavengers from the reeds further north and given hasty burial in some common place for strangers. The warning was clear. No Howard, retainer or henchman, was welcome in London.

Surrey himself and his father are certainly not ill-used.

The earl is confined to comfortable house arrest at Ely Place. As for Norfolk, I visited the Bosom of Abraham, a spacious tavern that serves the garrison at the Tower. Mingling there with warders and other minions, I learnt that Norfolk is not imprisoned in some fetid hole but in Beauchamp Tower, chambers usually reserved for the King and the royal family. Certainly he is not hidden away. He is even provided with pens and manuscripts. Sir Walter Stonor, the new Lieutenant of the Tower, has allowed him to keep two servants close to him, whilst buckets of sea coal are provided for the fire in his chamber, together with at least six dozen candles, yards of black satin, furred buskins and tapestries to warm the walls. Norfolk has a feather bed with a bolster, two pillows, thick blankets, quilts and sheets, as well as special utensils including a flagon, salt shaker, cups and goblets from the King's own jewel house, and is served hot meals from the Tower kitchens.

Nonetheless, the axe has truly fallen. The Howards are taken. They have fallen so low that Wriothesley and his allies on the Council could dispatch a party of horsemen, led by Sir John Gates, that royal bully-boy, Sir Richard Southwell and Wymand Carew, to Kenninghall to plunder the Howard palace. Of course they realised there would be women and children present, so Dr Huicke was included in the comitatus issued by the Council on Sunday 12 December between three and four o'clock in the afternoon. They reached Thetford on Monday night and were at Kenninghall by daybreak on the 14th. They galloped up to the gatehouse with the startling news that the duke and his son were taken. The steward was absent organising some form of muster, so they called the almoner and ordered that the gates at both front and back be locked. They then demanded to speak with the widowed Duchess of Richmond and Bess Holland. These had only just risen but nevertheless hurried down to meet their unexpected visitors in the dining chamber. Huicke, on his return, informed me how the young duchess was so perplexed and trembling that she was on the point of collapse. On recovering, she reverently knelt and humbled herself to the King, saying that although by nature she must love her father, whom she always regarded as a true subject, and her brother, whom she believed to be a rash man, she would conceal nothing but declare in writing everything she could remember.

It was not a pretty sight. Huicke offered his ministrations, but Sir John Gates – and no man's pie is free from *his* greedy fingers – was merciless. He and the others, all booted and spurred, cloaked and cowled, stood in the dining chamber with these women on their knees and advised them to use truth and frankness but not despair. My foreboding was correct. Henry had marked down the Howards for destruction, but the means were not a legion of Judas men and council spies; rather Howard's own family. He had studied them all and knew what keys to turn in which locks. If admissions of treason were elicited from the likes of the King's own former daughter-in-law, how would the Norfolks fare?

Gates and his coven were greedy for confessions but also for plunder. They became frustrated when they ransacked the Duchess of Richmond's coffers and closets to find nothing worth taking. The duchess explained how she had sold her jewels and all her precious objects to pay her debts. However, when they turned to Bess Holland, Norfolk's mistress, they found a wealth of girdles, beads, buttons of gold, pearls and rings set with diamond stones, which they swiftly listed. At the same time they sent servants to the duke's other houses in Norfolk and Suffolk warning the retainers there that a careful audit would be made. They also dispatched couriers to Bess Holland's well-furnished house in Suffolk. Afterwards they visited Surrey's residence on a hill outside Norwich called Mount Surrey, where he had built a great palace to his own honour and prestige.

Once these plunderers and ravishers had returned to London, the attack on Surrey began in earnest. At Princess Mary's secret request, I tried, I truly did, to plead with the King, but he was obdurate. My exile from his chamber had been imposed by Paget, that master amongst the shadows, who was weaving his own dark web whilst the King was busy with his. Henry lapsed into a sullen mood of deep sulks and terrible threats. He chose to completely overlook how Norfolk's own daughter, the Duchess Mary of Richmond, was the widow of his beloved bastard, Henry Fitzroy, who in turn had also been Surrey's close companion, whilst the earl's reputation as a warrior and leading poet of his day was never even considered. So why should I expect compassion from this King without mercy? This is the same Henry who openly rejoiced when Catherine of Aragon died in that haunted, benighted manor of Kimbolton. The same Henry who proclaimed his daughters as bastards and banished them from his sight even when he resided at the same palaces as they did. The chatter-mongers claim that our sinister king nourishes a hideous anger. Oh no, it's something much grimmer. There are occasions when Henry's soul simply dies; no hate, just nothing, a yawning cold emptiness. In his eyes, at such a moment in time, no one exists except Henry and God, perhaps not even the latter.

Yet while the King ignored my pleas, he ordered me to attend the hearing at Wriothesley's house in Ely Place where the wolf pack had gathered. Sir Thomas Wriothesley, his twisted face wreathed in smiles, posed as the lead questioner whilst the Seymours, Dudley and the others looked on. At first Surrey protested, but Wriothesley badgered him with questions, first asking about the earl's residences, particularly his palace at Mount Surrey and what he meant by such glories. He listed for Surrey what Surrey already knew. How his wardrobe boasted a gown of black velvet embroidered with a border of Venice gold; another lined with black velvet and satin from Bruges; a riding coat of green

satin with a fringe of silver; hose of black velvet embroidered with Venice gold and a whole fur of sables. How
Surrey also owned hats, jewels and brooches as well as
decorative swords, daggers and knives, collars with
knots of crown gold and a George medallion set with
diamonds. Surrey, sitting in that long panelled room lit
only by faint candlelight, seemed puzzled as Wriothesley
plucked up one piece of parchment after another,
detailing items such as an image of St George standing
upon a dragon with his sword, spear and shield weighing
forty ounces, and a vast array of golden chandeliers,
basins, ewers, pots, flagons, dishes, spoons and bowls,
as well as certain tapestries boasting the stories of
Moses, St Louis and the Jesse tree.

Wriothesley then went on to describe Mount Surrey,
with its remarkable view of Norwich, and its three
pavilions designed to resemble fortresses, all decorated
with military insignia and ornamental cannon. How the
Howard lion was depicted everywhere, be it on walls,
windows or plate; even on the banners flying from the
crenellated towers of his residence. Again Surrey just
shrugged, perplexed, as Wriothesley went on to describe
curtains and quilts panned with red and yellow silk and
a chair of state upholstered in purple velvet and satin,
as was the canopy of his bed, which was embroidered
with silver lions. Why, Surrey had even bought Turkish
carpets, Spanish blankets and bedsteads from Flanders,
whilst the walls of his house boasted tapestries that
would cost more than a fully rigged and armed warship,

all of the finest quality, displaying garlands of flowers, pomegranates, cucumbers, grapes and birds.

Surrey sat at the end of the long refectory table tapping his fingers impatiently. I, standing with the rest in the shadows, watched Wriothesley pause, long neck down, jutting chin pressed against his chest, then heard him whisper the words 'The residence and possessions of a prince, perhaps even a king?'

Surrey snorted with laughter, head going back. He was all tight with pride and honour, his right eye even more notably askew. He glared around and the real taunting began. Wriothesley touched on the question of Lady Jane Seymour, the King's third wife and mother of Prince Edward. How she had declared that she had no greater treasure in the world than her honour and would rather die a thousand times than tarnish it. Had not Surrey heard those words and mocked them? Had he not spread the story that the King had forced Master Cromwell, now adjudged a traitor and executed, to vacate his lodgings so Lady Jane could occupy them and use the private passage to the royal apartments? Had not Surrey implied, by such malicious words, that Henry's beloved late queen, mother of his darling heir, was no better than a Cheapside strumpet? Surrey hotly denied this.

Wriothesley then turned to the Pilgrimage of Grace, the great rebellion in the north against the King some ten years earlier. Had not John Fowberry, a servant of Surrey, taken part in this insurrection? To this Surrey just laughed out loud, saying that Fowberry, a rebel at first, had later redeemed himself by informing the Howards of the rebels' plans to take Hull. Wriothesley moved smoothly on, proclaiming how Surrey had twice listened to a song in support of both the Pilgrimage and the rebels, yet refrained from punishing the singer. Again Surrey just scoffed, indicating that he had heard many such songs; if every singer were hanged, there would be no men left alive. Wriothesley made a wry mouth and turned to Surrey's poems, most of which he had read. Had not Surrey composed a poem about an ancient king of Syria, a ruler steeped in blood who had fed and gorged himself on the plunder of his victims? Was he referring to any prince alive? The earl just glanced away. Oh, I could see the dark path opening up, leading to the pits, traps and morasses. Wriothesley was acting on behalf of the Seymours and Dudley, and behind them, the dark, menacing shadow of the King. The stage was set for the drama to be presented: Surrey was to be depicted as a truly dangerous traitor who saw himself perhaps not only as the protector-in-waiting but even as England's new prince. For this he was being hunted to death.

Wriothesley sighed and pronounced himself satisfied for a while, summoning servants to pour wine and serve sweetmeats. He and the others sat talking quietly amongst themselves, leaving Surrey at the end of the table to tap his fingers and stare wildly around. I and the other retainers murmured amongst ourselves. I heard the swell of damning whispers. How Edward Seymour, Earl of Hertford, had always been Surrey's bitter enemy. He too had served in the retinue of Henry Fitzroy, in the lesser office of master of horse. After the Pilgrimage of Grace, Hertford, amongst others, had expressed doubts about Surrey's loyalties. Surrey, learning about this, had hurried to Hampton Court, where he'd found Hertford walking in the park and had struck him, challenging him to a duel. Of course to strike a man at court, in His Majesty's presence, warranted the bloody penalty of losing one's right hand. Surrey was not punished in such a way but closely confined for a time at Windsor Castle. I studied Surrey. Did he, like Cromwell, Wolsey and the rest, not understand the real danger? He had not even been tried but was already condemned.

Once the wine and sweetmeats were served, Wriothesley rang his small handbell. The door in the far corner of the room opened and in came Sir George Blagge, the King's 'little pig', the same who so narrowly escaped being roasted as a reformist at Smithfield. Surrey pushed back his chair and would have risen, but Wriothesley's guards stepped from the shadows so he sat down again.

'Do you not remember George?' Wriothesley taunted. 'And your argument with him at Whitehall recently? You were full of venom against my lord Hertford. Master Blagge reminded you that those whom the King appoints shall be the most suitable to groom the prince in the grievous event of the King's death. To which you, my lord Surrey, replied: "My father is most suitable for such a task both because of the services he has done and because of his high estate." Do you remember that?'

Surrey, glaring at Blagge, refused to answer, so the King's little pig spoke up. 'You may remember well, my lord, because I answered that if that was so, the young king would be evil taught. Indeed, I declared that if the prince should be under the government of your father, or even yourself, I would thrust my dagger into you.'

'I do remember,' Surrey replied quietly. 'And then you fled.'

'Yes, my lord,' Blagge retorted, 'and because I opposed you, you took sword and dagger and hurried to my lodgings. Fortunately my house has a stout door, which withstood your efforts to break it down, but you stood outside, shouting that I had been very hasty with you and you meant to teach me better ways.'

Before Surrey could protest further, Blagge was dismissed. Wriothesley, enjoying himself immensely, preened and shook himself like a cat ready to pounce. Oh how I hate that man; my heart seethes with fury at him. A good friend of Cromwell, at least until he fell from grace, Master Wriothesley is a disrupter and an iconoclast. At Winchester he revelled in shattering the cathedral's precious statues and ancient painted glass. Later, out of fear of the local inhabitants, he stole back into that same cathedral during the dead of night and demolished a tomb much loved and visited by pilgrims, that of St Swithun, whose feast day, so it is said, determines the weather of our clammy island. Worse, once finished there, Wriothesley took horse to nearby Hyde Abbey and, with the utmost sacrilege, destroyed and desecrated the tomb of England's first and some say greatest king, Alfred the Saxon. There's something horrid in Wriothesley's soul, if he has one: a destroyer who, I suspect, would dance with joy if the world caught fire.

At Ely Place Wriothesley posed like the master of the masque from the School of Night, a strutting player determined to delight his audience with fresh horrors. No sooner had Blagge left the chamber than Wriothesley rang his infernal little bell again. The door opened and another figure slipped in. Those gathered there, myself included, gasped at the arrival of Sir Richard Southwell, a supposedly close friend and neighbour of Surrey. He took his seat in the pool of candlelight and, at Wriothesley's prompting, declared that he knew certain things about Surrey touching his loyalty to the King.

'What things?' purred Wriothesley the cat.

'I saw it myself,' retorted Southwell, blood-red face all sweaty. 'On the seventh of October last at Kenninghall and again at Mount Surrey, a coat of arms treasonable to the King.'

'How so?' Wriothesley sighed as if cut to the heart.

'Because Surrey's arms were quartered with those of our saintly King Edward the Confessor.'

'But they have silver labels,' exclaimed Surrey,

recovering from his shock at seeing this Judas so eager to lead him up the garden path of treason. 'I have, my family has, always carried such arms; the labels show their difference from the royal insignia.'

'Silver labels or not,' replied Wriothesley, an expert in heraldry, 'such arms are still identical to those of the Prince of Wales.' He stilled the hum of conversation with a dramatic gesture. 'Are you, my lord, proclaiming yourself to be an heir to the throne, to have a claim on royal power?'

Surrey's passionate temper gave way to violence. He sprang to his feet and strode forward, affirming that he was a true man, demanding to be trialled by combat, offering to fight Southwell in a duel, armourless in no more than his shirt. Only then, I do suspect, did he begin to perceive the cloying web closing about him. Wriothesley, on behalf of his masters, had worked hard and well.

With the light fading, Wriothesley wanted to finish that day's business with more spectacles. No sooner had Southwell, Howard's Judas, disappeared than Judas' sister, Norfolk's mistress Bess Holland, swept into the chamber in a gown of tawny sarcanet that matched her auburn hair. A bold-faced, hot-eyed woman worried sick that the treasures seized from where she'd concealed them at Kenninghall might never be returned. A true treasure hoard: diamonds, rubies, white sapphires, gold, silver and pewter brooches depicting images of Our Lady of Pity, the Trinity and Venus Arising. Necklaces

and bracelets, jewel-encrusted crucifixes and a valentine
of gold with five diamonds, three rubies and eight pearls.
Other chattels included ivory sandalwood tables, silver
spoons and other such utensils, as well as a row of
girdles all strung with precious stones. Bess the Harlot
wanted them back and would sing any song for their
return. In that shadow-filled room, before her lover's
son, who had little time for her, she confessed all the
gossip and chatter of the Howard family. Care and
tribulation must have pierced Surrey's entrails, a growing
fear seized his mind, a cold dread drenched his soul.
What hope for him from such a false heart and lying
tongue? He held up a hand, interrupting Bess's opening
words.

'And the Lady Frances?' he demanded. 'How is she?'
Surrey's wife, Frances de Vere, daughter of the Earl of
Oxford, was enceinte, only six weeks off delivery.

Wriothesley replied, words dripping soft as melted
butter, something about the Lady Frances being well
comforted. In truth we had all heard about Gates's
ruffians. Surrey's children had been placed with others,
whilst Lady Frances had been unceremoniously hustled
into a chariot. When she complained about the cold, a
nightgown of black satin, much worn and edged with
squirrel fur, snatched from the old duke's wardrobe,
was thrown about her.

Surrey heard Wriothesley out, then whispered loudly
how this 'brace of lying knaves' would have their day
against him. He joined his hands, head bowed, as Bess

Holland, who had held her peace during the interruption, proclaimed her grievances in a voice like brass. How the old duke had told her that none of the King's council loved him because there was no noble born amongst them and because he truly believed in the sacrament of the altar, which they did not. How the duke considered that the King did not love him either because Norfolk was popular in the country, which was why he was not a member of the inner Privy Council. How His Majesty was so sick he could no longer endure and the realm was divided by differing opinions. 'The King is much grown in body,' Norfolk had confided, 'and cannot go up and down stairs but has to depend on devices.'

Surrey lifted his head at this; so far Bess had said nothing about him but only about his father imprisoned in the Tower. However, Wriothesley had summoned her for a purpose. She was closely questioned about Norfolk himself bearing an illegal coat of arms. She claimed she knew nothing about that; only that the old duke had found fault with his son's heraldic devices. There, I saw the deadly snare. Bess Holland would portray even Norfolk himself as deeply affronted by his own son's conduct.

'The old duke liked them not,' Bess confessed, 'and did not know from where they'd come.' She went on to explain how Norfolk had claimed that Surrey himself had the family arms wrong and ordered Bess to refuse to weave such a motif into her needlework. Because of that, Bess Holland declared, glaring down the table, the Earl of Surrey did not love her much.

Once Bess Holland was gone, Surrey shouting that she would stifle in her own midden heap of lies and calumny, certain councillors pressed forward, bending over Wriothesley, whispering to him and pointing at the window. Wriothesley shook his head and gestured towards the door through which Bess Holland had left, talking swiftly and excitedly, as if there were certain businesses that had to be finished on that particular day. He waited. The silence in the chamber deepened. All eyes were on that long table, the sheen of the candles glowing along its polished surface. Wriothesley, arrogance seeping through every part of him, slouched in his high-backed chair at one end, the Earl of Surrey at the other, like jousters in a tilt yard waiting for the next run. Further down the room, deep in the shadows, stood the rest of the Council, listening intently. Surrey asked for something to drink. Wriothesley lifted a hand, snapping his fingers. A servant placed a goblet brimming with wine in front of the earl, who gently sipped it, then glanced around and leaned back in his chair.

The door opened again and a woman entered the chamber. Only when she stepped into the pool of candlelight did Surrey suddenly rouse himself as if from sleep. He started forward, staring in disbelief as his own sister Mary, the widowed Duchess of Richmond, took her seat on Wriothesley's left, turning slightly to face her brother. A pretty, comely woman, the duchess was dressed in a dark blue cloak with a mantle of the same colour around her shoulders; a hood, slightly pointed, covered her hair. She pushed this back. Her gloved hands were first kept hidden, but she betrayed her nervousness by rubbing the top of the table, peering anxiously at Wriothesley though never once glancing fully at her brother. Surrey put his face in his hands, shoulders shaking, his sobs clearly heard. Wriothesley sat and watched. Surrey took his hands away, wiped his cheeks with his fingers and crossed himself.

Wriothesley, that purple-hued malt worm, was cunning. He did not question the duchess but simply gestured with his hand, saying that Her Grace had information that was of great value to the Council and of deep interest to His Majesty. The duchess began to talk like someone who'd learnt a speech by rote. She spoke loudly, her voice betraying little warmth, as she described how her father had wanted her to marry Sir Thomas Seymour, Hertford's brother. Surrey had also desired that, but not for her happiness or that of Sir Thomas; instead he had insisted she should endear herself to the King and so win his affection and rule there as others had. She had protested bitterly and refused such a task.

The duchess paused, playing with the fringes of her gloves as what she had said was savoured and digested by those listening. In truth I found such an allegation difficult to believe. That the Duke of Norfolk and his son wanted their own daughter and sister to prostitute herself to the King through marriage to another man! Wriothesley of course had schooled her in her statement, as he knew such an arrow would not miss its mark. Since the death of his bastard son, the King had always had an appreciation for the pretty young duchess and perhaps at a better time in a better place might not have refused her favours.

Surrey sat shocked, his back against the chair, head lightly twisted, mouth opening and closing as if he wanted to shout his denial but could not. The duchess then continued explaining how her father would also have liked her brother to marry the Earl of Hertford's daughter, but he had refused, saying that he would have nothing to do with such an upstart family. That these new men hated the nobility, and that once God called His Majesty away, Surrey would make them smart for their arrogance. Indeed, the duchess continued, her brother hated them all since he had been imprisoned at Windsor Castle. She then paused as if forgetful. Wriothesley leaned forward and whispered something. The duchess lifted her head and talked about heraldry. How Surrey had assumed the arms of his grandfather the Duke of Buckingham, an adjudged traitor. However, instead of the duke's coronet, he had put into his livery a cap of royal purple with powdered fur, whilst the crown, in her view, looked much like a royal crown, and underneath it a cipher that she took to be the King's 'HR'.

She gabbled on, saying that Surrey had confessed

how the King did not like him because of his failure at Boulogne; that he had dissuaded her from reading the scriptures and added that God must give his father long life, for once the old duke died, the Council would have Surrey's head as he had so bitterly cursed some of its present members. Eventually Wriothesley tapped the table, a sign that she had said enough. Even those hostile to Surrey realised the duchess was only rehearsing and repeating what she had been instructed to say. Once she had finished, she fled from the room, leaving her brother, a faint smile on his face, staring down at Wriothesley.

Surrey murmured something. Wriothesley leaned forward, cupping his ear.

'My lord, what did you say?' he demanded. 'Eh? Eh?'

'Just a line from a poem,' Surrey replied, 'about the froth of folly, the scum of pride, the shipwreck of honour and the poisoning of the nobility.' He lapsed into silence.

'What mean you?' Wriothesley shouted. 'What mean you by that? Do you have a mortal malice against these in this chamber?'

Surrey refused to reply.

'Is it true, my lord,' Wriothesley pushed back his chair, 'that you have a painting of yourself depicted full length, standing under an archway against a rural landscape?'

'I hired William Scrots, a Dutchman, the court painter,' Surrey replied, as if thinking about something else.

'And in that painting,' Wriothesley continued, 'are you not leaning on a broken column, your left hand resting on your hip, your right hand clasping a white glove?'

'I remember that.'

'And did you not ask the artist to paint a miniature of His Majesty's dead son, the Duke of Richmond, on the column plinth?'

'I did.'

'Why?'

Once more Surrey refused to answer.

'Why, my lord? Why should you put on a pillar, in a painting of yourself, an image of His Majesty's dead son? Are you alleging that you and he were the same? Are you implying that your relationship with the dead prince gives you a power and status that you would exploit if His Majesty, God forbid, should die?'

'It was a painting,' Surrey retorted. 'I have never abrogated to myself kingly or princely powers.'

'Do you not, sir,' Wriothesley plucked up a piece of parchment from the table, 'do you not remember how three years ago you lodged at Mistress Millicent Arundel's house in Laurence Lane? Is that true?'

'You know it is.'

'And do you remember that night of Sunday the twenty-first of January, the Year of Our Lord 1543? How, when the beacon lights had been lit, the curfew signalled and the bell of St Mary-la-Bow rung, you and your companions ran amok through the streets of Cheapside?

Armed with stone bows, you shattered the windows at the home of Sir Richard Gresham, former mayor of this city, and then abused others along Cheapside, Poultry and the Stocks Market. Afterwards you commandeered boats and barges rowing along the river, shouting obscenities and shooting missiles at the prostitutes who ply their trade along Southwark bank.'

'My lord,' Surrey leaned forward, 'that was hot-headed foolishness for which I answered before the Privy Council.'

'For some of it you did,' Wriothesley declared, 'but the maids of Mistress Arundel, Alice Flanner and Joan Wetnall, made depositions against you. They reported how the armorial bearings above your bed in the chamber you hired from Mistress Arundel were very similar to those of the King. Is that not so?'

'I cannot remember.'

'And when Mistress Arundel bought a knuckle of tainted veal from the butcher's, you sent it back with a sharp rebuke, saying that no one should mock a prince such as you. Are you a prince, my lord?'

'I cannot answer for what tavern wenches blather.'

'No, you cannot,' Wriothesley continued, 'but where did they get these imaginings from? How could a tavern wench blather that if anything happened to the King and his beloved heir, then you, my lord Surrey, would be king after your father?'

Surrey protested most vehemently once more. But for Wriothesley the day's proceedings were finished. The

Council had done its task most efficiently – or at least I thought they had. The Howards were divided and chance remarks were being turned into weighty matters of law. What concerned me, and this must have occurred to Paget, was whether the King would be satisfied with their destruction. Would he turn on someone else? If so, who? I hurried back to Westminster, but the King refused to see me.

In the days following, the interrogations continued, but now they were following a well-beaten track. Wriothesley received fresh depositions, the most damaging that of Sir Gawain Carew, who claimed that the Duchess of Richmond had informed him that Surrey had actively encouraged her marriage to Sir Thomas Seymour. How she should dissemble the matter and use it as a means for His Majesty to speak to her. How she should not refuse such invitation but leave the issue to rest so His Majesty would take occasion to speak to her again and again. Consequently, by passage of time, the King would take a great fancy to her. The duchess would become his mistress and rule both King and court like Madame Destampes did in France. Surrey had argued how this would help not only herself but all her friends and family. The duchess, however, had defied her brother. She said her family could all perish, that she would rather cut her own throat than consent to such villainy. Similar statements were made by others. Edward Rogers, an acquaintance of Surrey, repeated the established story.

How Surrey hated the new men on the Council and believed that when the King died, the protection of the young prince should lie with the Howards.

Such charges and depositions were repeated time and time again until Sunday 12 December, the vigil of St Lucy, a day popular in this city, with lights and candles and much gathering around the stalls and shops. The Council chose that day for Surrey to be taken to the Tower through Holborn, not riding with banners flying but walking surrounded by guards like a common criminal. Wriothesley's arrow sped true. He wished to divest the earl of any trappings of power, publicly proclaiming him a criminal, dispatched to the Tower to await judgement.

Only then did Balaam and I meet secretly in a tavern chamber. He sat warming his fingers above a chafing dish, his face much drawn and tired. He acknowledged that Surrey's cause was finished. Balaam was hot against the King, exclaiming that if all the pictures and patterns of merciless rulers were lost to the world, they might again be painted true to life in the story of His Despotic Majesty. He was certain that Surrey, now he was in the Tower, would never be freed or receive royal mercy.

'You see,' Balaam lifted his hands like a storyteller, 'imagine the mix they've prepared for him. Listen, Will. Surrey is accused of mysterious paintings, of changing his armorial bearings, of hinting that he is a royal prince. Above all, he stands arraigned of whispering that if something happened to His Majesty and his son Edward, then perhaps the Norfolks are the true heirs. Even so, if His Majesty dies, then it should be Surrey and his father who govern the young prince. Wriothesley, that father of villainy, has mixed this meal and served it to His Majesty, that swollen parcel of arrogance lurking in Westminster.' Balaam crossed himself. 'Remember what you told me of the King's mumblings about the blood of innocents? He is haunted by the princes in the Tower. He is fearful that his own son may become a similar victim, a young prince once seen and quickly forgotten. Can you imagine what His Satanic Majesty must feel after all these years of intrigue, of lechery, of divorce, of seeking an heir? Within days of his own death such plans might simply be smoke wafted away by the cruel winds of politics.'

'But the evidence against Surrey?' I asked. 'Surely it is meagre? That alone may weaken all charges.'

'Perhaps. There is another story,' Balaam declared, 'which is coming to light. How Surrey had a picture painted where the arms of his father were joined to those of the King surrounded by the Garter of St George. Where the motto of the Garter should have been, "*Honi soit qui mal y pense*", Surrey has inserted the phrase "Till then thus". Till then thus?' Balaam repeated. 'That could be viewed as a threat! That Surrey was biding his time until the right moment for his planned treason, the King's death. Surrey is supposed to have ordered the artist to put another canvas over it so it looks as if there is no other painting there. He shared all this with his sister, the Duchess of Richmond. She told the duke her father, who called his son aside and fiercely berated him, to which Surrey replied, "Father, our ancestors once bore those arms, and I am much better than any of them, so do not grieve about it." Norfolk retorted, "My son, if this comes to the ears of the King, he'll accuse both of us of treason, so keep it secret." "No one knows it, Father," Surrey replied, "but you and my sister. The painter is a foreigner who has now returned to his own country." The duke replied, "God grant my son that no ill may come of it. Do not tell your younger brother Thomas, he is too young to be trusted and might tell someone else who might accuse us. Bring the painting to me and let me see it." To which the earl replied, "Sir, that is impossible, another painting is over it."'

I was surprised: in all the gossip I had sifted, such a tale had not been told. I shook my head in disbelief, but Balaam assured me the story might well be true. More importantly, Surrey's sister, full of anger at her brother's marriage plans for her, did go to the King and informed His Majesty that her brother had such a painting. The King immediately summoned Paget and Hertford and told them what intelligence had come to his ears, and so the order was issued for the earl's arrest.

'Surrey,' Balaam concluded, 'may well have had a painting executed in which he allowed his fantasies full play; that is enough to send him to the headsman's block.'

I could only wonder at Henry's cruelty and cunning. He had used a Norfolk to trap a Norfolk. The Duchess of Richmond would be terrified witless. Whether she liked it or not, she had been cast as a woman urged to seduce the King into adultery. After all, was he not married? And was not such a proposal part of a Norfolk plot to seize government? This was treason on so many counts. What pity could the Duchess of Richmond expect from a monarch who'd considered poisoning his first wife, executed two others, cruelly rejected a fourth and diligently plotted the arrest of a fifth for treason? Margaret Pole, the Countess of Salisbury, and Lady Rochford had been shown none of the tenderness owed their sex. Others might blame Paget, Seymour or Dudley, but I recognised Henry's hand as the guilty one. He was using the same device against the Howards as he had against the Poles over a decade earlier: terrifying one member of a family in order to accuse the rest of treason.

'And now?' I asked wearily.

Balaam lifted his head. 'According to the Princess Mary, Surrey must escape and I must help him.'

'Why?' I asked. 'Why must Surrey escape? True, I feel sorry for him, and God knows he is guilty of foolishness and a devilish pride, but if that is treason, then we'd all dance at Tyburn. He is innocent . . .'

'Surrey is condemned already.' Balaam's face was all mournful. 'His trial will be a sham of shadows. Henry wants him dead and probably his old father too. The

Council also want the Howards and their Yellow Jackets destroyed before the King dies.'

I held a hand up. 'Master Balaam, I am a fool by profession, that is my trade. I am not foolish in wit. Why not state it clearly? The Howards of Norfolk still pine for the old days and the Church of Rome. They will be the best defence for the claim of the Princess Mary should young Edward die without heir. You know that, the world knows that. I am not a physician,' I continued remorsefully, 'but for God's sake, look at Edward, frail of body and not yet ten years old. London is swept by plagues and ailments. The Council are not only frightened of the Howards when the King dies, but terrified lest his heir follow him swiftly into the grave. Mary's claim is next. I know your mistress, Balaam. Cardinal Pole will return as papal legate. There will be peace with Rome, but above all, the Princess Mary will deal out judgement to the gods of Egypt. She will demand a bloody reckoning with these men of the reformed faith. Dudley, Seymour and their ilk would not survive a season.'

Balaam gave a lopsided grin and nodded. 'The Princess Mary,' he whispered, 'has given me my orders. I must attempt Surrey's escape.' He stretched out a hand. 'You are with us on this?'

I stared back. Balaam lives on intrigue; I'm simply its spectator. I watch His Malignant Majesty as I would that fierce lion in the Tower menagerie, fascinated yet frightened, but my heart's blood loyalty? This is to Lady Jane Bold and so the Princess Mary.

I clasped Balaam's hand. 'To the death.'

There, I was committed. I had crossed Paget's line. God help me. God help us all.

17 January 1547

Christmas, Yuletide, the New Year, Epiphany and the Feast of the Kings have all come and gone. Presents have been exchanged. Greenery placed on rafters and along sills and ledges. Hobby horses and fantastical creatures have danced and carolled with the Master of Revels and the Lord of Misrule. Yuletide logs have been cleared of snow and pulled into feverishly hot kitchens to be dried and prepared for the fire. Sweaty, red-faced cooks have wielded their axes and fleshing knives on legs of mutton, capon, venison and beef. Pheasant royale and princely goose have been prepared, along with a boar's head gilded gold, its mouth stuffed with boiled apples, all carried on precious plate escorted by cooks and their underlings from steam-hung kitchens to this great table or that. Now the mummery has gone like silver tinsel which shrivels and blackens. Christ has been born anew but is still ignored. The court observed both ritual and the rite, yet the message was lost. Masses were sung, but all were uncertain about what these actually meant and what was their use. Change and more change is imminent; what is doctrine and liturgy this year might be heresy and treason the next.

I met the Lady Jane secretly and gave her my presents: spice boxes, jewellery and a heart-shaped pendant. We kissed and cuddled, then kissed and cuddled again stretched out on some tavern bed. She brought me news about how the Princess Mary kept a merry hall over Christmas. I could give her little in return except that our plotting prince was busy, busy. It was as if the King had abruptly recalled who he really was, of the blood imperial and God's viceroy on earth, so why should he converse with a poor, lonely, witless hunched-back creature such as Will Somers? If Henry did not say that, I am sure Paget and Wriothesley did. Both had seen me at Surrey's questioning. They know full well where my sympathies lie. On the morrow of Epiphany, Wriothesley passed me in the gallery outside the palace chapel. He drew his dagger and pushed me into the deserted, incense-filled nave. He slammed the door shut, then shoved me so close to a window the Christmas holly along its ledge scratched my face.

'Mannekin.' He grinned down at me, pale lips curling back like those of a dog to display yellow teeth. I flinched at his stale breath. 'Mannekin, be careful. Do not put your trust in foreign princesses . . .' A reference to the Princess Mary. 'Restrain your prying and your peering. Do not upset your betters. Remember you are no safer than the Howards, or anyone else you might choose to name.'

I had little choice. What concerned me particularly over the Holy Season was the way Henry's mind seemed to have turned against his family. Neither the Queen nor his children were invited to spend the Christmas festivities with him. All doubts about Huicke appeared to have been put aside. He and others of his ilk, such as Physician Wendy and Thomas Alsop the apothecary, together with their legion of assistants, were busy in their attendance of the King, who proclaimed himself to be fine and in full fettle. I was left to my own devices. The weather had turned bitterly cold, with thick snow carpeting Westminster and both banks of the Thames. I had little opportunity to travel after the Christmas season so I joined Master Bricket, the King's chief cook, in his own steam-filled empire. I nicknamed Bricket 'Herod the Great' because, I jested, 'He rules the roast and is a pitiless murderer of innocents as he mangles poor fowls with unheard tortures, sparing neither hen nor chick and being particularly merciless to the newborn capon.' Never a true Christian until a hissing pot of strong ale has slaked him like water thrown on a glowing grid iron, Master Bricket is a redoubtable man, a true terror who scowls till his tarts quake, his custards quiver and his jellies shake. His kitchen is a merry place and a very useful refuge, as well as a fount of gossip. I learnt how His Majesty, on the day after

Christmas, had asked his council to produce the royal will, drawn up some three years earlier. When it did so, the King was swift to pounce, roaring that the version produced was not what he wanted and there was certainly one of a much later date. What this will decreed, however, I could not elicit, being dependent on gossip three times removed.

The other reason I frequented the kitchens was to meet Balaam, that cunning man of subtle wit. If you wish to hide and go in disguise, then do so in a crowd. The royal kitchens, butteries, pastry chambers, scolding rooms and store chambers are ideal. Such places are thronged with the many officers of the household, be it 'the serjeant of the King's side of fresh fat deer roasted' or 'the keeper of the white puddings of hog's liver': officious little men who thrive on flattery and obsequious-ness. Balaam was in his element amongst them. He arrived suitably dressed in honest but coarse garments, a black woollen hat and broad-toed leather shoes. He would chatter to me and yet who could study him in a haze of smoke or eavesdrop in a place where stillness was as rare as a thin priest? Of course the brimming news was Surrey and the plans to aid his escape. Balaam informed me all about this . . .

There is a chamber in the Tower of London built on the first floor in the western half of St Thomas's Tower overlooking the moat near the water postern that people call Traitor's Gate. Within that western wall is a large shaft that runs its entire length down into the moat.

This comfortable room was refurbished some fifteen years ago to accommodate Anne Boleyn as she prepared to journey to Westminster to be crowned; little did she know that she would be returned to that very same chamber to await execution. Surrey was also imprisoned there. He was well treated and, unlike poor Thomas More, was given pens, ink and parchment. The hapless poet boy returned to composing sonnets based on the psalms, writing about his desire for wings to escape the stormy blast that threatened to engulf him. Escape in fact was the only choice he had. The Londoners were cowed. Surrey's henchmen had either cooperated fully or were hiding in their lonely Norfolk manor houses. The memory of the malignancy that had befallen those henchmen who'd accompanied Surrey into London remained very fresh in the minds of many.

At Westminster the King, narrow black eyes sunk even deeper into the folds of his fatty face, ignored me and urged his Council on to another act of bloody, judicial murder. Surrey became completely isolated. Nobody wished to serve him. I have noticed this before. Whenever some unfortunate falls from grace, brothers, sisters, indeed all the victim's relatives, flee as if from the plague. Queen Katherine Howard had a gentleman of her privy chamber brought to her bed every night. There was so much puffing and blowing her maids could scarcely sleep. On one occasion the intruder was almost surprised by the nightwatchman, and when he grew more cautious, Katherine taunted him that she had a stream of lovers waiting outside other doors. At the time Katherine and her lover were feted and praised. Nevertheless, when they were swept up by the storm which overwhelmed them, the brothers of both these victims of Henry's anger, garbed in their finest clothes, paraded around London on horses openly rejoicing, a public show to demonstrate how pleased they were that royal justice was to be done. A means of proclaiming that they did not share in the crimes of their relatives and, more importantly, that they remained faithful and loyal to their sovereign.

And so it was with Surrey, England's proudest poet, the King's own champion outside Boulogne. Once he fell, no one came to stand beside him. Accordingly, Princess Mary, through her agents such as Balaam, found it very easy to use her good offices to introduce an adventurer, a Spanish mercenary called Martin, into Surrey's prison chamber to act as his servant. Neither the lords of the Council nor the King would like it if Surrey – and he certainly would – were to proclaim at his coming trial that he had been ill-treated. This Martin was under secret orders to assist him with any plan. He was a Spaniard, or of Spanish extraction, so it was easy to depict him as free of any Howard influence or allegiance.

Of course I wandered out to listen to the chatter, and the best place for that is the taverns and ale houses that throng Petty Wales and the area around the Tower. Here the keepers, turnkeys, grooms, ostlers and maidservants rub shoulders, eat, drink and revel. Naturally gossip about prisoners is rife, especially about the likes of Surrey. Apparently he soon grew to trust his new manservant and the plot to escape developed very swiftly, all being planned in a day and a night. Martin brought the earl a dagger, and Surrey decided to escape through the shaft in the western wall serving the garderobe; this ran down to the moat, which in turn was cleansed by the river. At times the tide came up, at others it receded, leaving the ground beneath almost dry. Surrey noticed how the lowest point of the tide was around midnight for that time of year. The only difficulty was that his two guards slept in the retiring room which housed this garderobe. Nevertheless, Surrey considered this shaft to be his only hope. Once he had the dagger, he revealed the particulars of his escape. He asked Martin to go to St Katherine's Wharf and wait for him there shortly after midnight. He was to hire a boat and stay until Surrey appeared. In the meantime, he was to approach Surrey's younger brother Thomas and ask for a certain amount of money to assist him.

On the chosen night, Surrey hid the dagger in his bedstead and waited his chance. He pretended he was ill and declared he would retire early to bed. The guards wished him well, adding that they would do their tour of duty before their return. Once they had left, Surrey prepared himself. Shortly before midnight, when the tide was at its lowest, he pulled back the closet lid and lowered himself down. At that very moment the guards returned. Surrey was unable to defend himself with the dagger he had secreted and was easy prey for the guards, who then called to others for help. The earl was ignominiously dragged out of the closet and placed in shackles. Martin the servant disappeared and was never heard of again. I learnt all this with sinking heart when I met Balaam in the Palm of Jerusalem, not far from the King's Steps. He assured me that he had made careful search for Martin, as had soldiers from the Tower, who had swept the quayside looking for any barge or wherry equipped to take Surrey away.

'I found nothing. They discovered nothing,' Balaam hissed. 'I don't know what happened to Martin. Was he seized and secretly murdered? I don't know. But both he and any money he may have collected from Surrey's younger brother have disappeared.'

'But if he was captured?' I urged. 'Could he not betray you and others of Princess Mary's household?'

Balaam shook his head. 'No, no,' he replied. 'Martin was met and paid deep in the shadows. He would not be able to recognise me or anyone else. We regarded him as a desperate man, hungry for money.'

'Then he was well fed!' I snapped.

I felt deeply uneasy about the so-called escape and the way it was so swiftly foiled, but I left it at that. Of course I tried to intercede with the King once again, but Henry was preoccupied. Now this tyrant King loves nothing better than preparing an indictment against those he has marked down for death. Henry appeared stronger, his wits keen, his mind sharp. No longer bed-ridden, he dressed in a simple blue, red and gold robe, stomping about his chamber. He had chosen his quarry and, like any predator, was simply measuring the distance between himself and his victim. In the King's eyes, Surrey had usurped royal authority, proved by the Howard use of the royal arms and insignia. The King became feverishly busy on establishing this, assisted by the court cat, Wriothesley, who considered himself an expert on heraldry. Books and manuscripts were produced. The King, fingers all bloodied, spectacles perched on his nose, drafted questions and objections to what Surrey had done. He only half listened to my pleadings, until on one occasion he abruptly paused and stared at me over the spectacles as if noticing me for the first time. God be my witness, I have never seen him look at me like that before, as if he was measuring my worth and found me totally wanting. His cold, soulless eyes peered at me, lips slightly twisted, and I knew someone had done me terrible damage. If I did not suspect already, I soon discovered who.

The King promptly dismissed me. I walked down the gallery, then jumped at the hand on my shoulder. I turned. Wriothesley beamed down at me.

'My lord?' I asked.

'Martinmas, Will? Isn't that the season when the lambs are slaughtered?' Wriothesley gave a crooked smile, eyes half closed in amusement, and walked off.

Martin! Wriothesley was hinting at so many things,

perhaps claiming that Surrey's servant Martin was his man, while the reference to the slaughter of the lambs was Surrey's planned execution. Surrey was truly beyond all mercy and compassion. He had been imprisoned, provoked to escape and captured.

Urgent dispatches were sent to the lords at Westminster. Surrey was more closely confined, put in irons, yet he still protested his innocence. Wriothesley, Dudley and the rest of their coven visited him in the Tower, urging him to confess, but without any profit. The Council had waited long enough. They were determined to convict Surrey yet equally scrupulous to achieve this by publicly honouring the process of law. Of course it was a travesty. Surrey had allegedly committed his crimes in Norfolk, so the bloody charade began there, in the great snow-bound hall of Norwich Castle with its lowering black beams draped in the banners and pennants of the Crown. An indictment of treason for appropriating the royal arms was presented to a grand jury assembled on the benches before the gold-festooned dais. The jurymen had been carefully selected; not a true friend of Surrey amongst them, a veritable gaggle of Judases. They had little difficulty in reaching their conclusion. The foreman, in ringing voice, declared the indictment to be *billa vera*, a true bill. A special commission of oyer and terminer, 'to hear and to decide', was established to sit at the Guildhall in London. Royal couriers, horses splashed with muddy slush, thundered to Westminster with the news. The rats poured in together. Surrey, shackled in the Tower, remained defiant, but his father, Norfolk, Thomas Howard, now in his seventy-fourth year, was different.

I tried once more to plead with the King. By now Henry was wary and suspicious of me. Wriothesley had done his job well. The King's mind had been turned. I recalled the fate of old Skelton, a former jester. How Henry had favoured him until Skelton went too far and Henry beat him to within an inch of his life. When I did meet the King, he was much improved and looking forward to the usual pre-Lent festivities. I enquired as to what revelries would be staged, what masques would be presented. The King just smiled to himself, tapping his fleshy nose and saying he would think about that. I asked him about the Queen and his children. Would they be joining him and wouldn't it be good if they lodged at court? Again the King tapped his nose. I suspect he would have liked Edward to visit him, but he could not invite his son without issuing an invitation to his daughters and the Queen.

Because I do not like Paget, or trust him, and I had dismissed what he'd told me at the royal chancery about the King's secret scheming. On reflection, I now beat my breast. Henry is certainly involved in some subtle strategy, but, as ever, I cannot decide what direction it will take. No doubt the Queen is out of favour. Henry does not wish to either see or meet her. He no longer requires her as his nurse. So what does he intend? I tried one final time to plead for Surrey and his father.

I will be honest: I did so at the Princess Mary's behest. In truth, the Howards of Norfolk may not be my friends, but they have never proven to be my enemy. Indeed, old Norfolk, when he used to gamble with the King, always gave me something from his winnings. On another occasion, before he and the King left for Boulogne, I made young Surrey laugh, a rare event, with a story about a Norfolk squire who made himself a fool over a milkmaid, a story I borrowed and refashioned from Chaucer. Surrey instantly recognised that. He rubbed my head, gave me two silver pieces and said it was a subtle conceit. I have pleaded for prisoners before and won the King's mercy; Henry likes that. Nothing soothes his pride more than to have someone on their knees begging for their life or someone else's. Isn't that how Katherine Parr saved herself? When Katherine Howard fell from grace, Norfolk sent a letter to the King distancing himself from his errant kins-woman and throwing himself on the King's mercy. I did the same, kneeling before the great throne-like chair, hands clasped. And my reply? The King pressed his foot against my shoulder and gently kicked me away. He did not even raise his eyes. He said he had no further need of me, and if he did, I would be summoned.

Others of course had also reflected. If the lords of the Council could not break Surrey, then they would try with his father, the great survivor. Norfolk has a gift of saving his own skin. He has lived through turbu-lent times. He was born in the year after the furious fight at Tewkesbury when the Yorkists annihilated their Lancastrian foes, wiping them out as you would a dusty slate. Thomas of Norfolk has seen it all. A page at the glorious court of Edward of York, he witnessed the treachery of Clarence, the mysterious death of King Edward, who died at such an early age whilst boating on the Thames, and the violent usurpation of Richard. His grandfather fought for that same Richard at Bosworth and was killed, whilst his father was carried off the battlefield a grievously wounded prisoner. But, as I have observed, the Norfolks survive, and Thomas Howard is the finest example of this. All his enemies – Buckingham, Wolsey and Cromwell – have been dispatched to ignominious death. Indeed, if Norfolk had had his way and the King not listened to me, poor Thomas Cromwell would have been burnt alive at Smithfield. I don't think that even Cromwell, for all his cunning, realised Norfolk's deep treachery; he can smile when he wants and be ever so humble. On one occasion he wrote to Cromwell, 'Since I saw you last you have most lovingly handled me. You will always find me a faithful friend.' A short while later he invited Cromwell to Kenninghall, and even promised he would find a 'buxom wench with pretty, proper tits' for his entertainment. Yet when Cromwell was arrested, Norfolk was the one who beat him down and humiliated him. When I frustrated Norfolk's attempt to turn Cromwell into a living torch, the duke secretly arranged for the most inexperienced executioner to be assigned to sever the head of the disgraced minister. In this he was successful. The creature Gurrea, along with his assistant, chopped at Cromwell's neck and head for nearly half an hour.

Now imprisoned in the Tower himself, Norfolk is no doubt wondering how he will survive the present crisis. As soon as he was arrested, he sent the most supplicant letters to Westminster. Such pleading letters to both King and Council continued, signed 'His Highness's most poor prisoner. T. Norfolk.' I read copies of these missives. Henry, however, would not be moved. Wriothesley constantly dripped poison into the King's ear. No, that's wrong. The greater truth is that this King believes what he wants to believe. He has determined on the destruction of the Howards.

I soon learnt to keep a still tongue, reverting to what Henry wants me to be, his congregation, his audience. I act like a dumb, submissive wife in a malicious, squalid marriage. He is the master and I am the slave. I become the part, nodding my head, gazing in admiration at his profound wisdom and insight. Henry has grown stronger, I recognise that. He stands as he used to, feet apart like some colossus, belly thrust out, great body encased in his robe. Such occasions sharpen my memory. Henry neither forgets nor forgives anything. Oh, I listened to the habitual tirade about the Norfolks at Bosworth. How they gained the great victory at Flodden. This was followed by the usual ranting and raving about the Norfolk women, Anne Boleyn and Katherine Howard, how both had made a fool of him. The honest answer would be that never was a man so eager to be gulled and wear the cuckold's horns. Henry gave such vent to his spleen about the Howard women, I did wonder if the rumours were true. We all know that Mary Boleyn, Anne's sister, was the King's mistress for a while. Rumours abound that she had a son by him, born short of wit and weak of mind. However, Henry then began to talk salaciously about Anne's mother, Elizabeth Howard. He even recalled a joke he'd made with his drinking companion, Francis Bryant, who had teased him about having both the hen and its chick. Other ugly jealousies and resentments emerged. Surrey's ability to compose beautiful poetry, his bravery in battle and love of show. God forgive me, I have served this King for more than twenty years. I have made one hideous mistake. I have underestimated that cancer of the heart, his aptitude for hatred.

Henry allowed the Council their way and they left Norfolk to wallow like a becalmed ship in some dreadful limbo. They'd already made their decision, or Henry had made it for them, that they would use the father to destroy the son. Wriothesley led the pack. This time he included the two Chief Justices, Sir Richard Lister and Sir Edward Montague. They decided to visit Norfolk in the Tower. The King, cuffing me sharply about the ear, told me to join him. I asked him why. I even gently teased him that he had lost confidence in me. Henry grinned maliciously. I was being sent for a host of reasons. I was the King's audience; he knew I would report back. He also wanted me to see his cunning at work, and above all, he was being cruel. He wanted to demonstrate that all my pleading had come to nothing. He recalled the old legal dictum that he used to pun about, 'The will of the King has force of the law.' Or, to paraphrase it, 'Will, I am the force of the law.' Henry is like that. Poor Margaret Roper, Thomas More's daughter, wanted to give her father honourable burial. After all, More was dead, head severed from his body. She still had to negotiate with the executioner and snatch her father's remains from London Bridge. Oh yes, Henry likes such grisly conclusions. He always insists that the relatives of his victims are not spared the consequences of royal decisions, so I was off to the Tower to witness this for myself.

A bitterly cold day. Snowflakes coated our faces and stung our eyes as we clattered through Lion Gate and into the inner bailey, dominated by the soaring White Tower. They were all there: Wriothesley, Dudley, Paget and the Seymours. They had summoned their ally, Sir John Gates, and set up house in the great refectory in the Tower's royal lodgings. They grouped around the banqueting table on the dais, close to a fire which roared up the stack and exuded a blast of heat supplemented by spluttering braziers and chafing dishes of sparkling charcoal. We broke our fast on capon, sliced and drenched in herb sauce, white currant bread, dishes of stewed vegetables and goblets of mulled wine heavily laced with nutmeg and cinnamon. Of course they ignored me. I was of no more interest to them than the two greyhounds nosing the rushes. Strange, I remember their names: Sallyforth and Parryswiftly; their keeper, a young boy, kept begging me for morsels of food to feed them. On one occasion I caught Paget studying me rather sadly. I glanced away as if interested in the greyhounds.

Only when the hawks were ready for their quarry did they summon Norfolk. He was brought from his chambers in a furred robe all stained and moth-eaten, shabby slippers on his feet. A veritable scarecrow of a man, no more haughtiness, his dirty grey hair and beard all a-straggle, blinking eyes deep-set in that long, furtive face. Ave beads and miniature reliquaries hung around his neck and hands. He shuffled into the refectory, hands outstretched in supplication.

Wriothesley stepped off the dais and exchanged the kiss of peace with this noble he truly despised. Indeed, if he'd had his way, Norfolk and his son would be kneeling with their necks exposed on the blood-soaked scaffold on nearby Tower Hill. Then he offered Norfolk a cup of posset, pouring it himself before taking the duke over to a deep window embrasure so the old man could be questioned by Huicke, who had also accompanied us. In truth, the lords of the Council hoped that Norfolk was failing and that the damp, dire miasma of the Tower would be more deadly than the headsman's axe. This was a strong possibility. The old duke complained loudly of constant catarrh, rheums in his joints, a bubbling belly and bowels as loose as water, an ailment, he added plaintively, contracted in the service of the King along the northern march. Once the physician was finished, Wriothesley invited Norfolk up on to the dais. An air of jollity and calmness reigned. The Council's bully boys and henchmen clustered near the door and around the hearth. More posset was poured, then Wriothesley led the assault on the old duke. He recalled Norfolk's years of court service, emphasising the King's generosity and magnanimity, particularly over Anne Boleyn and Katherine Howard, the duke's two errant nieces.

'I was swift to condemn them,' Norfolk protested.

'As you were to recommend them,' Wriothesley interrupted. 'But come, my lord, you know the treasons of your own son?'

'No I do not. I . . .' Norfolk fell silent as Wriothesley rapped the table. I watched that sly man with his reddish hair, moustache and beard, pale face and sloe eyes. He stabbed at the heart of the matter.

'My lord of Norfolk, even if you and your son are innocent, that is not important. What is pertinent is that the King believes you are guilty. You have served him long and well. You know what I say.'

Wriothesley let his words hang like the clanging of a mourning bell. Norfolk sat as if struck by a bolt, hands out on the table, fingers splayed, shoulders shaking as he tried to suppress a sob.

'Buckingham thought he was innocent,' Wriothesley

continued remorselessly, 'Wolsey considered he had done no wrong. What about More and Fisher? Thomas Cromwell, whom you hounded to the death, always believed he was the King's good servant.' He paused. He was closing off all the other paths, leaving only one gate free to open.

'Others, my lord, have openly and unreservedly acknowledged their guilt or thrown themselves on the King's mercy. Remember Cranmer, whom you hoped to take? He went to the King at the dead of night. Or Queen Katherine Parr? Didn't she save her neck by pleading on her knees, openly acknowledging her failings? Or your good friend Bishop Gardiner, before he was exiled from the King's presence for good? You must recall how the late lamented Charles Brandon, Lord of Suffolk, had the King's permission to take Gardiner off to the Tower. Indeed the order was issued, the death barge prepared, the halberdiers summoned. Gardiner's friends, however – you must have been one of these, my lord – informed our good bishop about the real and pressing danger. You must recall what happened? No? Well, our cunning prelate hastened to the King and humbly confessed to all the accusations levelled against him. He earnestly pleaded for His Majesty's pardon, which the King graciously granted. The following morning my lord of Suffolk protested to the King, who replied: 'You should have kept him from me. You know what my custom and nature is and always has been on such matters. I am consistent in pardoning those who neither dissemble or deceive but truthfully admit their transgressions.'

Wriothesley slowly sipped from his goblet. The trap was opening. Every other gate was locked fast against Norfolk; the only escape was what Wriothesley offered. God forgive me, God have mercy on us all. Norfolk walked straight into the snare and the trap slammed shut behind him.

'This,' Wriothesley pushed a parchment before him, 'contains all the allegations levelled at you, my lord. God be my witness, the case presses heavily against you. You, your son and your family have only one resort – His Majesty's clemency and pardon.'

'And I will be able to see the King?' Norfolk pleaded. He was now a broken man. From the moment of his arrest he had defended himself, but the ominous silence from Westminster had broken him. Now these lords of the Council were his only salvation.

In a matter of an hour it was finished. Norfolk had studied and signed his confession. By the following morning copies would be posted at the Cross at St Paul's and the Standard in Cheapside. The confession is not so much proof of treason but testament to the utter collapse of the house of Norfolk. And so it was done, signed by Thomas Norfolk and witnessed by the hounds who'd brought the old tusked boar to bay. Once the proceedings were over, Wriothesley picked up a mazer of sweetmeats. He thrust this into Norfolk's shaking hands and, one arm round the old duke's shoulders, escorted him from the refectory and pushed him into the hands of Sir John Gates's bully boys. The ruffians led Norfolk, the premier duke of this kingdom, off like a schoolboy who has not excelled but been awarded some piffling prize as a petty consolation. Good Lord, it would have brought tears to any eye. The door had hardly shut behind them and Wriothesley was organising his couriers and clerks. What can I say? I have read the documents. Norfolk had confessed to the same so-called treason levelled against his son, the misappropriation of the Royal Arms. In truth it is nothing but arrant nonsense.

The pack, however, were not finished. For a while all was business in the refectory, men entering and leaving. A bell chimed through the freezing air. I felt restless. I always do when I visit the Tower; that grim, narrow place provokes sharp memories. I left the refectory and wandered about. Frosty and freezing, the ice sparkling along the sills and coating the woodwork and cords of the great war machines, the catapults, mangonels and trebuchets so beloved of Henry. I went across to study the massive cannon and mortar but became distracted by the ravens, those sleek black birds, their cruel yellow beaks constantly spearing the ground. I heard shouts and cries coming from the refectory; soldiers and archers were assembling, gathering together with the Council's henchmen. I hurried back inside, taking my seat just before a figure cloaked and cowled like a monk was led in. The door slammed shut behind him. The mysterious figure, escorted by Gates's retainers, pulled back his cowl to reveal Henry Howard, Earl of Surrey. He stood defiantly, feet apart, hands hanging by his sides, his long, bony white face sharply offset by his russet hair and beard. He was the very opposite to his father, face full of pride, glaring fiercely at his gaggle of accusers, the cast in his eye even more pronounced.

'Your father the Duke of Norfolk has confessed,' Wriothesley yelled, 'to a whole litany of treasons.'

'No he has not.' The earl's voice was calm but carrying. 'He has been tricked, as have I.' He turned his back on them and walked to the door.

'We have much to talk about.' Wriothesley sounded shrill, white foam staining the corners of his mouth.

'I have nothing to say to you,' Surrey shouted back over his shoulder. 'Not here, not ever.'

God bless him, but the lords still had their way. The following morning, Thursday 15 January, the Year of Our Lord 1547, Surrey was committed for trial. An ice-bound morning which marked the end of the Howard family, their opponents eager to render it as degrading as possible. Surrey was not deemed a parliamentary lord; his earldom was a courtesy, so he was not to be tried in the solemn grandeur of Westminster Hall, where King's Bench and the other great courts sat next to both abbey and palace. Instead he was to be dispatched at the Guildhall like any other common felon, be it a housebreaker or violator of the King's peace. I had not been summoned back to the King, so I crossed to Greenwich and then returned to take lodgings in the Puddlicot, a tavern adjoining the ancient gateway of Westminster Abbey.

Surrey was roused early that Thursday morning and his chains removed. He had been stripped of his possessions, so the Lieutenant of the Tower brought him a black satin cloak lined with coney fur. Once all was ready, he was marched out through the Tower's Lion Gate, the noise of the royal beasts echoing like some discordant chant. At the gate he was handed over to the sheriffs' men; these formed a cordon around him, and they processed along the frost-hardened lanes. Crowds had gathered, not only at the mouths of alleyways and the windows of taverns and houses but on corners, church steps, even climbing on to the market crosses, braving the buffeting wind and the icy, slippery stonework. Immediately before Surrey walked the headsman, holding his execution axe with the blade to the front. If and when Surrey was convicted, the blade would be turned back towards him.

Snow was falling as the three hundred halberdiers, weapons at the ready, marched through the heart of London. If Surrey's enemies hoped to stir resentment against their foe, they were bitterly disappointed. Surrey was popular in the City even though he had been a scapegrace, a roaring boy who had feasted, revelled and rioted long after the chimes of midnight. The crowds, braving the bitter cold and sharp snow flurries, remained ominously silent. The procession reached the great cobbled yard of the Guildhall, dominated by the life-size statues in their frescoed porches: Christ in majesty, two bearded men representing Law and Learning and four female figures depicting Justice, Discipline, Strength and Moderation. Inside, the dimly lit court hall was ready, the galleries around it packed with people, including myself and Balaam, all anticipating the unfolding drama. The judges sat on their great throne chairs along the dais: Wriothesley, Paget, Dudley and Seymour. Immediately to their right were the jurymen who had been empanelled at Norwich Castle. To be sure, these included former friends of Surrey, but others, like Sir John Gresham, had clashed with the earl. The Greshams had never forgotten Surrey's frenetic revelry in London four years earlier, when the drunken earl and other rioters smashed the windows in Gresham's Cheapside mansion.

Surrey was escorted to the great bar before the judges. A bell tolled mournfully, marking the ninth hour, and the trial began. The clerk rose and, in a ringing voice, asked Surrey to raise his right hand. Once he did, the indictment was read: how Henry Howard, Lord of Surrey, had 'falsely, maliciously and treasonously' assumed the royal arms of King Edward the Confessor. Neither in law nor fact was there any justification for this because such arms, by right and law, pertained only to His Majesty the King. By his actions, therefore, Henry Howard had encompassed the 'peril, scandal and disinheritance of the said Lord King and the overthrow of this his realm of England' and was therefore a public enemy; the devil had seduced him from his allegiance and he deserved death. Surrey heard this out. He had been the first to offer to fight without armour to prove his innocence, so sure was he that God would protect him; now he was prepared to fight with words. When the clerk asked, 'Henry Howard, how do you plead?' The 'Not guilty!' reply echoed like a trumpet call of defiance through that cavernous, oak-beamed court.

'And how will you be tried?' asked the clerk.

'By God and the country.' Surrey delivered this in a tone that eloquently conveyed how the true verdict on him would be decided in years to come and not on this bleak January day surrounded by his enemies.

Only then were the jurors sworn in. Surrey could not challenge these, as the recent Treasons Act had abolished the defendant's right to question a juror. He could only defend himself, and he did this brilliantly for almost eight hours, until five o'clock in the evening. When Sir Richard Rich opened the case for the prosecution, Surrey rounded on him. 'You are false,' he shouted, 'and to earn a piece of gold you would condemn your own father!' He continued in the same vein: that he had never intended to usurp the King's arms, whilst everyone knew the Howards had a right to certain insignia. 'Go to churches in Norfolk,' he boasted, 'and you will see such arms; they have been ours for hundreds of years.'

'Hold your peace, my lord,' Paget interrupted. 'Your

intent was to commit treason, and as our king is old, you thought to become king yourself.'

'And you, Catchpole . . .' Surrey paused, allowing those in the gallery to laugh quietly at the earl's allusion to Paget's father, a mere city bailiff. 'What do you have to do with this?' He continued. 'You should hold your tongue. This realm has never been the same since the King put mean creatures such as you into its government.' Paget fell silent, and even from where I stood, I could see his deep discomfiture.

Dudley came next, accusing the earl of trying to escape from the Tower, an act which proved his guilt.

'I tried to escape,' Surrey swiftly retorted, 'to prevent myself coming to this situation in which I now find myself. You, my lord . . .' He was now quietly reminding Dudley about his own father. 'You, my lord,' he repeated, 'should know full well that however right a man may be, they always find a fallen man guilty.'

Surrey was like a hawk swooping on all the judges, pecking at their weaknesses, in each case the same: the father of the man accusing him. For the rest, he trusted in the classic defence: not to dispute the facts but to establish what were his motives. He was impressive. The mood of the court subtly changed. He established himself as a man of deep understanding, sharp wit and the most remarkable courage. He changed tactics, sometimes denying the accusations as downright lies and so impugning the credibility of his accusers, at other times demonstrating how his words could be interpreted to

pose no threat and so casting the prosecution as feverishly lying.

He dealt with witnesses in a similar fashion. One of
these described an argument with Surrey, who had used
hot words against him. Surrey simply pointed out that
the man's conduct was so disgraceful he richly deserved
what he received. When the allegation that he tried to
persuade his sister to become the King's mistress was
levelled, he did not bother to deny it but posed an angry
question: 'Must I be condemned on the word of such
a wretched woman?' He struck at the very heart of a
key witness: not what she said but what she had become,
a woman prepared to send her own brother to the
headsman's block.

Surrey outfoxed his opponents so cleverly that a
member of the commons, a gentleman of Essex, voiced
the attitude of the spectators that Surrey had depicted
himself as a man of great parts and high courage with
many other noble qualities. Most of the jury tended to
agree. If Wriothesley and the rest thought the play was
finished and all the rehearsed lines delivered on cue,
they were bitterly disappointed. On their retirement the
jury could not, did not reach a verdict. The judges
became so nervous that Wriothesley was dispatched to
Westminster to confer with the King. An interesting
development as His Majesty must have been alert and
very expectant about the outcome of the trial. He had
apparently demanded to be closely apprised of any
development, and a recalcitrant jury was one of these.

For judges to interfere with a jury's verdict they would need the royal assurance of protection, which they very swiftly received.

Wriothesley hurried back to Westminster and visited the jurors in their chamber. Of course it was a foregone conclusion, and what I write here I learnt from Sir John Clere, a juror, a former friend of Surrey, a firm adherent of the Princess Mary, a man who is highly regarded in many parts of Norfolk. Once Surrey's trial was over, Clere went straight to Greenwich and sought an audience with the princess, where Lady Jane was present. He related the sorry tale. Apparently the jury had found for, not against Surrey. At the time I accepted that was obvious, but to my astonishment, Clere revealed to Princess Mary that the judges also agreed with this. However, they insisted that Surrey had to be condemned, not because of the King, but 'that it was sufficient cause to make them say guilty because Surrey was not a man to live in a commonwealth'. I have reflected carefully on this; I catch its drift. Henry had struck at the Howards but the lords of the Council did not perceive it in that fashion. They were already reflecting on what would happen when the King died. Were they plotting a change of governance? Would this governance be Crown or commonwealth? Did the lords see themselves like the council of Venice or those other republics in Germany and northern Italy?

At the time, I understood what they preached: whatever his defence, Surrey was to be condemned. The jurors returned to the courtroom; even then they were not allowed to speak. When summoned by name, each replied that Seymour would speak for them, a subtle subterfuge; like Pontius Pilate, they washed their hands of any guilt. Seymour relished the part. After each juror stood, he shouted in Surrey's face, 'Guilty and he should die!' The verdict was greeted by shouts and cries of protest. Once order was imposed, Surrey broke the silence.

'Of what have you found me guilty?' he demanded. 'Surely you will find no law that justifies you. However, I realise the King wants to be rid of all the noble blood around him and to employ none but the lowest people.' He kept up this tirade until a guard silenced him. Then Chancellor Wriothesley, head, neck and shoulders veiled in black, rose and pronounced sentence.

'Henry Howard, you are to be taken to the place from whence you came; from there to be dragged through the City of London to the place of execution called Tyburn. There to be hanged, cut down while still alive, your privy parts to be cut off and your bowels to be taken out of your body and burnt before you. Your head is to be cut off and your body divided into four parts, the head and quarters to be set at such places as the King shall assign.'

The headman's axe was turned towards Surrey as he left the bar, the halberdiers closed around him and he was led back through the City to the Tower.

*   *   *

I finished this last entry to my journal late the following day, after Surrey had been condemned. I visited the Lady Jane at Greenwich and she informed me of what they knew about the machinations of the jury. I felt sick at heart and indeed sick in body, tired and depleted. I returned to Westminster. The situation has not changed. The King has no need of me. I spent two days in bed wrapped in blankets against the iron cold outside. To be honest, I am also frightened. Whatever the King is planning gathers pace. He will see nobody except the Council, and they are hot on finishing what they have begun. The Howards have been destroyed; the Romanists severely checked. Gardiner languishes in exile, locked firmly under house arrest. A Bill of Attainder has been introduced in the Lords proclaiming Norfolk and Surrey 'High Traitors' and ordering the complete forfeiture of all titles, houses, chattels, offices and lands. Norfolk has not saved himself; his confession was simply a trick to entrap. No mercy has been shown. No compassion or pardon exercised. From what I understand, the old duke's death warrant awaits signature.

19 January 1547

God forgive me, but today, 19 January in the Year of Our Lord 1547, saw the destruction of Surrey. Yesterday evening John Roberts, escorted by one of Gates's ruffians, banged on the door of my room. My heart leapt. Perhaps the King was summoning me. That was not the case. Henry was turning the knife. The writ Roberts thrust into my hand made it very clear. I was to be one of the King's witnesses at Surrey's execution the following morning. I could not object. Roberts waved a hand around my chamber.

'It will be very early.' He spoke matter-of-factly, as if he and I were planning to rise and journey to some fair. 'Master Somers, you'd best go to the Tower now. You must not be late. My good friend here,' he patted the ruffian dressed in half-armour, a man whose horrid soul was clear in his cruel eyes, 'will make sure you arrive safely.'

I was tempted to plead sickness, but that would be

ignored; this would prove to be a winter's evening in more ways than one. I packed a few belongings in a set of panniers and my escort took me down to King's Steps and the waiting barge. The river journey along the Thames is always to be feared, but never more so than in the depth of winter, the breeze sharp as a knife, the river swollen black and ugly. Thank God we kept close to the shore. I drew comfort from the beacons glowing in their steeples and the roaring bonfires of rubbish along the quaysides. We passed under London Bridge without harm and docked at Tower Wharf. Soldiers, men-at-arms and archers, all wrapped in thick cloaks, their weapons at the ready, guarded every approach, gateway and postern door. Torches flared merrily along the battlements. Despite both the hour and the season, I glimpsed the sheen of armour. The Tower had been put on a war footing, as if expecting an enemy fleet to come sailing up the river or an invading army ready to circle it about. I walked doggedly. I was aware of the various courtyards and narrow gulleys we passed through. Fires glowed. Braziers crackled. People hurried here and there, slipping on the ice. Shouts and cries. The neigh of horses in the stables and the barking of the guard mastiffs were all drowned by the roars and snarls from the royal bestiary.

I was given a chamber in the Salt Tower, with two guards outside. A spit boy brought me a surprisingly hot and delicious meal from the Tower kitchens: venison freshly slaughtered and well cooked, soaked in a spicy sauce with a mess of chopped vegetables, good white bread and a jug of the heaviest claret. I ate well and drank deeper. I did not change, but stretched out on the bed, falling into a deep dark sleep until I was aroused the following morning. Surrey was woken in his cell at the same time, the first faint light against the sky, and briskly informed that he was about to die. Poor boy; he protested, but the decision was made and sentence passed.

I waited outside with the other witnesses, stamping our feet, clapping our hands, drinking the posset that had been served on trays and pecking at the bread and salted bacon offered us on platters. Now and again one of the witnesses would walk away to ease themselves at the latrines. Guards and servants came hurrying up full of gossip about what was happening at St Thomas's Tower, where Surrey was being hurried towards his death. The fallen earl was not even given time to itemise and bequeath the paltry possessions he'd been allowed to keep in his grey-walled cell: a feather mattress, bolster, blankets and quilts, a silver flagon, and a gilt-edged salt shaker. Dressed in the same black satin robe lined with coney fur as he had worn at his trial, boots on his feet and a soft cap on his head, Surrey retained his dignity as the Lieutenant of the Tower, Sir Walter Stonor, bluntly informed him how the King, out of the depths of his mercy, had commuted the dire punishment for treason to simple beheading. After this he was brought down to us in the bailey.

Torches flared. Cresset torches spurted, their flames leaping eerily in the icy half-light. Surrey kept his face like flint. I glimpsed his pale skin and those strange eyes, a man almost hiding himself in the clothes he wore. He did not even glance at us but turned his back, staring up as if studying the parapet walk along the Tower. Orders were issued. We proceeded to the gatehouse. A freezing dawn, the snow and ice underfoot hardening while the river mist hung as thick as wool, turning the torchlight into a hazy yellowy glow. At the drawbridge Surrey was handed over to the two waiting London sheriffs, Richard Cernas and Thomas Gurlin, as the City of London owns the execution ground of Tower Hill adjoining the fortress. Retainers and henchmen of the lords of the Council were there, a few foreign ambassadors and some local tradesmen. I listened intently to the sheriff's men. The execution party was under strict instruction to proceed as swiftly as possible. Surrounded by City serjeants carrying torches, and preceded by the headsman, the blade of his axe held high towards Surrey, we walked along the line of the Tower to the black-draped scaffold, four feet high and reached by nine steep steps.

Surrey walked purposefully and climbed the steps, the executioner and sheriffs assembling behind him. The halberdiers promptly ringed the scaffold. A drum roll sounded, threatening and ominous. Surrey strode to the edge of the platform and began to address the small crowd. He was not going to submit or admit to being justly condemned. He never asked forgiveness from either God or the King, and all the conventional rituals were ignored. As during his trial, he loudly protested his innocence. He wasn't allowed to speak for long. The wind whipped away his words. Torches moved on the scaffold. A voice shouted and any further speech was drowned by another roll of drums. The drama of death swept on. Surrey held his hands up as if in prayer and loosened the clasp of his cloak. The executioner, as expected, knelt to beg his forgiveness. Surrey gave that; then he too knelt, to be shriven by a priest. Once finished, he was offered a blindfold. He refused. He lay down, stomach pressed against the black, water-soaked drapery covering the boards. He loosened his shirt further and stretched out his hands. Even as he positioned his head more carefully on the block, the executioner's axe swung up, a sliver of glistening steel, and the thud of its fall echoed down the hill.

Surrey was gone. England's premier poet and greatest earl, one of the kingdom's bravest men. The waiting death wagon, black and stark against the lightening sky, draped in funeral cloths and carrying the arrow-chest coffin, drew closer. Torchlight moved. Both corpse and severed head were lifted, the executioner wrapping the latter most tenderly as if he was swaddling it. I turned and walked away as the cart pulled off to the simple burial ceremony in All Hallows by the Tower.

*   *   *

I made my way back to Westminster. The sheer, bleak fog of death weighed heavily on me. Surrey's death was murder by another name. An earl, a leading poet, an audacious warrior had been executed for the sheer silliness of a foolish boy. Henry's court truly was a masque, a carnival, a sham, a pretence, and I had been part of the illusion. Henry the Magnificent, the Champion of the English Church, the Defender of the Realm against the power of Rome. Bluff Hal! Yet when I now look back down the passage of the years, I see it crammed by steaming corpses. What did it all amount to? A string of severed heads on the poles above London Bridge? The Mouldwarp manifesting his misery to the multitude around him?

The city I passed through was dark and filthy. No beauty caught my eye, but rather the frozen middens populated with vermin, scavenging dogs and snouting swine. Blood-soaked fish and meat stalls watched carefully by the nest of beggars in alleyways and runnels, their children waiting to snatch a gobbet of raw flesh, ready to risk their lives by scampering beneath the iron-shod hooves of the stable-fed stallions ridden by the great merchants and lords. On that day London seemed to be a city of the damned, bathed in the half-light of a winter night that would never fully pass. The freezing cold, the sour smells and hideous sights frayed my soul further. I avoided the pillories and the stocks, the whipping post and the bailiff's cart. I stopped at a tavern to down a goblet of wine. At the same time I tried to remember my love for the Lady Jane, lying with her under the sun in some green, supple-grassed meadow. My thoughts, however, kept going back to Surrey and the pack of wolves that had brought him down. When I was young I could never understand the hermits, the anchorites, the recluses who hid themselves away from humankind. *Oh Jesu miserere*, now I do! If you live alone, there's no other, no pain, no struggle for power, no victory, no submission, no hurt, no harm.

I was terrified, finished with a king and court where no one was safe. I drained my goblet of wine and downed another, then quickly made my way back to Westminster, determined to flee. Sir Anthony Wingfield, Captain of the Spears, prevented that. He was waiting in the gallery below my room, two of his men lurking in the stairwell. He must have guessed I would return, and God knows, that man can wait like a cat ready to pounce.

'His Majesty,' Wingfield leaned down, watery blue eyes glaring at me, 'His Majesty, God knows why, wants to see your ugly face. No,' he grasped my arm as I turned to go down to the royal privy chambers, 'not there. Follow me.'

I had little choice in the matter. The Spears, the royal halberdiers, swarmed everywhere and Wingfield is a man you do not cross. Red-faced, bristling and bustling, he is a man for orders; if instructed to fight the sun, he would do his best to comply. He led me through the warren of courtyards that make up the old palace. A place where time seems to have paused some hundred years ago. A dark, ill-lit maze of ancient chambers, rooms and halls. Paintings, their gilt frames decaying, the canvas faded, hang slightly askew. Here and there ancient weapons are nailed against the wall, such as the war axe of the Black Prince or the sword of his grandfather, dulled and chipped, put up as trophies and left to fade as dim memories. Cobwebbed statues stand in niches, now ignored under the new religion, the flower pots beside them full of dirty water, the flowers long corrupted to a black smelly mush. Lamps and candles glowed fitfully, making it a place of dancing shadows even though it was not yet noon. We crossed overgrown frozen gardens past sheds with turf for roof and ox-hide curtains for doors and shutters, the squalid hovels of those hired to rake and weed the ice-hard soil. The air was thick with the acrid smoke of their fires and sour with the stench of human refuse from the makeshift latrines. Thin-ribbed dogs barked and yawned at us. Mangy cats slithered out, then fled. The hide curtains were pulled back by grimy fingers holding cracked food bowls; pallid faces, framed by hoods and cowls, peered out at us.

We left one such garden, entering a gallery where the oak gleamed as it caught the shifting light, the air rich and sweet from the aromatics crushed and sprinkled on the many braziers. We were now on the opposite side of the palace, where the great storerooms of the Exchequer, Chancery and Court of Augmentations are supervised by an ink-stained tribe of clerks who scrambled aside at Wingfield's approach. Eventually he paused and opened a door; the steps inside leading down to the cellar were railed and covered with thick rope matting. The cavernous chamber below was well lit by a host of flambeaux and warmed by a row of glowing braziers. At the bottom of the steps halberdiers stood on guard; beyond, slumped on a great cushioned seat surrounded by huge chests, iron-bound coffers and metal-studded caskets, sat the King. On the floor next to him lay his two great walking sticks. He was dressed in a heavy blue and scarlet robe powdered with gold and silver, woollen purple buskins on his feet, a bonnet sporting diamond, rubies and pearls pulled down firmly over his head. He glanced towards me, peering through the murk, beckoning at me. Even from where I stood, I could see the blood glinting on those fat, splintered fingers.

'Come, Will,' he said throatily. 'Come join your king and sit amongst the dead.'

I did not understand what he meant. Wingfield pushed me forward and continued to do so until I reached my grim master. I immediately genuflected and felt a stinging blow to my right cheek. I glanced up at Henry; smirking from ear to ear, he slapped me again.

'Your Majesty?'

'Not for being what you are, Will, but for what you do.'

'Your Majesty?'

'Oh, I cannot be bothered,' Henry sighed, dropping a purse of coins before me, tapping me on the face, incensing me with his blood as he gestured that I should pick it up. I did so wearily and the King punched me on the shoulder.

'You saw him die?'

'You know I did.'

'Bravely?'

'You know he did.' Henry lunged at me, but I scrambled swiftly backwards.

'Sit down, sit down.' The King was breathing heavily. I looked around, and as Henry probably intended, my gaze was caught by the corpse, embalmed and gowned in a dark woollen robe of murrey, lying within a lead coffin. Startled, I rose and went to stand over the unburied remains of James IV of Scotland, killed that cruel day, 9 September in the year 1513, at Flodden Field, above ground now for almost thirty-four years. I stared at the reddish hair, clipped moustache and beard, the snow-white skin and faint pinkish lips. The dead king's hands were long, the fingers tapered, his cheeks slightly sunken. The smell from the remains was fragrant, like the aroma of a herb garden. In the dancing dim light it looked as if he was asleep.

'Your Majesty should bury him.'

'They started it,' the King murmured.

'Who did?'

'The Howards,' Henry replied. 'Thomas Howard now awaiting death in the Tower, the father of the traitor we killed today. Years ago, Will, he was Lord High Admiral and took two Scottish ships off the Downs. I refused to punish their captains or return the goods. James of Scotland saw this as cause for war. Come here, Will.' I did so tentatively. The King grabbed my arms, fingers digging into my flesh; I yelped at the pain. From the other end of the crypt I heard the sound of weapons being drawn and glimpsed the glitter of steel.

'No, no.' Henry pulled himself up close to me, grinning down like some moonstruck lover. 'No, no!' he repeated; his voice was strong, echoing off the grimy stonework. 'Will is no danger, just a prop.' And with one hand on my shoulder, the other gripping a silver-topped walking cane, Henry pushed me aside so he stood close to the lead coffin. He stared down at the preserved corpse.

'I come down here to talk to him. Do you know, Will, they dragged his half-naked corpse from the battle-field after someone recognised it? Others disputed that. You see, James . . .' Henry broke off as if addressing the corpse directly, 'was not wearing that iron chain around his middle. The chain of penance for rebelling against his own father.'

'Your Majesty?'

'A man for the ladies, weren't you, James?' Henry wagged a finger. 'You young fool. He crossed the northern march because the Queen of France, stupid woman, sent him her ring on the tip of a spear. She begged him to be her champion and invade the northern shires.' Henry stood rocking on his feet, hand firmly clasping my shoulder. 'Some people claim that James escaped from the battle, but he did not. I have him here. So strange!' His voice sank to a whisper. 'The Norfolks brought him to battle, trapped him at Flodden. He fought like a man possessed and got within a spear's length of Norfolk before he was cut down. A mass of wounds; his right hand hung only by a strip of skin. They disembowelled and embalmed him at Berwick. Look at him, Will, and weep! A prince whose throat once burst with rich words and vivid images. A poet, a troubadour, a warrior, but where is that now? Where is the chivalry, the minstrel song, the full-boobed wenches with their scarlet baskets of cherries? The Howards finished that, father and son,' he hissed. 'And they would have done the same to me. The fate of princes, Will. James was killed in battle, his father James III was murdered. He tried to put down a rebellion and failed. He fled and hid in a mill. He begged a peasant woman to fetch a priest to shrive him. God knows who the priest was, but he heard the old king's confession, then cut his throat.'

Henry gripped my shoulder and turned me towards another chest. 'Look too at the grandeur that was!' I stared in amazement. The deep, iron-studded coffer was filled with some of the sacred relics looted from various shrines. For a while he regaled me with scandalous stories about abbeys, monasteries and convents. How at Swaffham the Benedictine nuns were ruled by Prioress Joan Spilman, who had set up house with a runaway friar and sold all the convent's goods. After Henry dissolved the house, Joan had turned witless and lived out her life in an underground cellar in the local vicar's garden. Henry, hobbling from casket to coffer, then described some of the relics. There was the phial of the Holy Blood from Hailes Abbey: 'Nothing but honey mixed with saffron,' he muttered. He gestured at the Black Virgin of Willesden, an ebonised statue revered by former kings and queens. The golden jewels from the tomb of St Edmund. Mary Magdalene's girdle from Farleigh. The Rood of Grace from Boxley and the miraculous blossoms from Maiden Bradley.

Muttering to himself, the King moved slowly around the various chests. I watched him intently. I recalled the rumours of how he was accustomed to come here and talk to the embalmed corpse of King James. The cadaver should have been sent back to Scotland; it had first been entrusted to Henry's great friend Charles Brandon, the Duke of Suffolk, who sent it to the Carthusians at Sheen before it was moved here. I recognised that Henry was fascinated by James, a true ladies' man, married to Henry's ugly frump of a sister Margaret, a king so fertile in the sons he had produced, both legitimate and bastard. Henry's fascination with relics was also understandable; these were the bridge back to the old religion of his father and mother.

'Your Majesty,' I tried to keep my voice humble and suppliant, 'why have you brought me here?' I suspected he wished to justify himself. Henry hobbled back to his cushioned chair, gesturing at the stool close by.

'James of Scotland was once a great prince, feted by France, the papacy and the Empire, yet he died on a wind-blasted hill, his corpse now lies in a London cellar and his orphan child rules Scotland, or at least tries to. And the relics? Once they held sway over kings and queens and tens of thousands of souls. Now look at them. I read Augustine's "Confessions" recently. He argued how we are a veritable bag crammed with all sorts of fears, influences, memories and dreams. I was five, Will, five years old when Cornish rebels in their thousands occupied Blackheath. My father fought one pretender after another. Ten years ago the north rose in rebellion against me. Danger on every side.' Henry gestured at the lead coffin. 'What happened to James could happen to me and mine.' He leaned closer. 'Do you really think that the Howards would suffer the Council? There would be civil war, and if the Yellow Jackets were victorious, how long do you think my little Edward would last, or pretty-faced Elizabeth or your own brooding mistress, Princess Mary?'

'And how long do you think they will last with the lords of the Council?' I retorted, pushing back the stool, fearful of the King lashing out. He just smiled, the grin of a greedy, spoilt boy who was already plotting fresh mischief.

'I tell you, Will,' he leaned closer again, whispering hoarsely, 'there will be one king, one realm, one religion. So don't weep for Surrey or his father. Staring at that corpse, going through these so-called relics is a reminder of what can happen if we don't succeed and matters fail.' Then he added, almost to himself, 'I have not yet finished.' He held out a hand for me to kiss. I did so, and he drove his knuckles hard against my teeth.

'Go, Will. Wingfield will take you back.' He gently touched my face and stared sadly at me. I rose, bowed and turned away.

'Will?' I glanced back. Henry was grinning at me. 'Remember, I have not yet finished.'

Sir Anthony Wingfield escorted me back to my chamber. That was three hours ago. I have sat here and had food brought up by my friends in the kitchen. I have reflected on what the King said. He has often talked about fickle fortune, of his determination to rule and be ruled by no one else. At first I thought he might be expressing guilt, yet Henry never feels guilt. He often asserts how he lives in peace with his conscience, which is on excellent terms with God. No, I concluded, he was drawing strength for something else, but what? More remarkable was Sir Anthony Wingfield's conduct as he led me back. Wingfield is Henry's man body and soul, in peace and war. He has no dealings with anyone, yet something amiss occurred as we passed the royal chancery chamber. Wingfield was accosted by Paget's creature William Clarke; a hushed conversation followed. I am certain Clarke passed over a heavy pouch, a purse of coins, which Wingfield swiftly took. So why would that be?

4 February 1547

enry is dead! The King is dead! The Great Monster, the Prince of the Sun, that vast-framed man is no more! The Mouldwarp of ancient legend has gone into the dark. No longer will we hear his booming voice. Never again will he stride into a chamber and make all who wait there shake with fright. A prince who cuddled and cosseted me, who laughed uproariously at my jests and sallies, who showered me with gifts yet at the same time would beat, pummel, pinch and humiliate me. A lord whom I loved and served and at other times loathed with all my heart.

He died, according to reports, at two o'clock in the morning of Friday 28 January. On this matter alone I have to grieve, at least for a while. Death soothes many a pain, yet it is a heavy price to pay for peace. Whatever the King's sins, my heart still harbours memories, and these come sweeping back. Images and thoughts. Henry in his prime. Henry the King in his robes of silk slashed with different colours, a jewelled bonnet on his head, his great body encased in gorgeous robes sparkling with precious stones. Henry swaggering along a gallery, filling it with his presence, or standing on top of some steps, feet apart, hands on hips, carefully scrutinising all before him. Seasons and feasts: Christmas, Easter, Midsummer and Michaelmas. Banquets opened with the blare of trumpets as a gilded, painted boar's head was presented to the King. Masques and revelries where mummers leapt and danced, their faces visored, their painted bodies covered in coney skins and furry tails. Henry galloping on his beautiful stable-fed warhorse. Henry in the tilt yard. Henry in the forest. Gorgeous mock battles with Morris men armed with pikes and cross-bows. The sudden explosion of miniature sacks of gunpowder through which devils fled pursued by angels intent on strangling them. Henry roaring with laughter and throwing food, coins and precious goblets as a reward. Crowded halls at the dead of night, the torch-light battling against the inky darkness as he refused to leave the board for bed. Or like some mysterious paladin from Arthur's court, Henry entering the lists on the tournament grounds to joust and break a spear. He would abruptly appear in black armour, purple plumes nodding in the breeze, no escutcheon or insignia on either his breastplate or the huge kite-shaped shield which I sometimes carried as his squire. Henry emerged as a fearsome figure, some hell-born vision sitting firm as a rock in his high-horned leather saddle, his satin-coated warhorse black as night, its sharpened hooves pawing the ground. The spear would be slowly lowered, knight and warhorse moving in an ominous rattle, the lance, feathered with pennants, now fully couched, aimed directly at his opponent's heart. Oh the awesome beauty!

And these last of days. That powerful voice, those piggy eyes blazing with fury, snarling lips spitting a white frothy rage, the heavy footfall, the nipping, the beating, the pulling and pushing, and then the abrupt change of mood, the sly glance, the giggling behind the hand. *Kyrie eleison, Christe eleison, Kyrie eleison.* Lord have mercy, Christ have mercy, Lord have mercy! Whatever the nightmare he became, he was still my king. At times a good and generous lord, a man of vaulting ambition with the talent to match. I mourn his death. I grieve for what he might have been and, in the end, for what he truly was. Some might say I could have done more to soothe his fiery rages, temper his malice, check his pride. I ask you in all truth, what could I have done? I, scruffy Will Somers the fool? I did what I could in the circumstances, as I do now. I have recited the Dirige psalm, David's song of mourning. I have arranged for requiem masses to be offered privately by a chantry chaplain garbed in blue and gold, purple-tinted candles spluttering against the darkness, in the side chapel of St Michael's church. My present lodgings are draped in funeral cloths. I will perform the three-day fast. I will light tapers before a statue of the Virgin, if and when I find one.

So how did this all happen? How was I taken unawares? *Mea culpa! Mea culpa!* My most grievous fault. My own arrogance. My confidence that I was safe. Ah well, Satan fell like lightning from Heaven and so did I! On the morning of Saturday 22 January I left the palace to stroll in Westminster's crooked, narrow lanes. The guards had been strengthened. More cannon hauled from the Tower. Horsemen milled in the courtyards. I returned a short while later. I wanted to see the King, but Roberts, together with two of Gates's ruffians, turned me away. I went to my own chamber. I had hardly taken off my cloak and boots when the door was flung open and Paget and Wriothesley sauntered in, Gates dressed in half-armour behind them to guard the door. All three were casually and coolly arrogant. Wriothesley sat on my bed. Paget on my high leather-backed chair. Gates's burly figure filled the doorway. Menace and threats seeped from all three. Paget peeled off his elegant doeskin gloves, beating them against his thigh as he stared around.

'His Majesty is not well,' Wriothesley declared. 'He does not seek your company. We do not want your company, fool.' He wetted his lips, chin jutting out like a weapon towards me. 'Scuttling little Somers, hither and thither like a will-o'-the-wisp over the marshes. Well, my mannekin, now you are caught and held fast.' He grinned falsely at me. 'No more scurrying or scampering. You are detained.'

'On what charge?'

'Possible treason.' Wriothesley smiled, wiping his eyes. 'Treason.' He shrugged. 'Perhaps misprision of treason.'

'Nonsense!'

'Speculating on the King's death. You, little fly, are not fit company for His Majesty.'

'I want to see him.'

'He does not wish to see you,' Wriothesley murmured with mock sweetness. 'You are a fool, Somers.'

'And you are not a wise man,' I retorted, 'and what folly I commit I dedicate to you.' I pointed at his face. 'You wear your wit on your chin and your guts in your head.'

'I would cut out your tongue.' Wriothesley got to his feet.

'And sir, I'd still talk more sense than you.'

Wriothesley's face paled, those soulless eyes unblinking. Gates took a step away from the door. Paget, watching me closely, stopped playing with his gloves.

'All of you . . .' I could not control my temper, 'glass-faced flatterers. You are so full of oil even Satan doesn't want you. You'd set Hell on fire. Your very tears are Judas's children. You do not care for His Majesty. You are busy preparing a mess of malicious mischief. The Norfolks were your enemies, not the King's. Now you are rid of them, your malice plots more mischief against whomsoever,' I stopped for breath. These clever, subtle men had conspired well. At the time I did not know what they were plotting, but they had already sprung the trap.

'You will stay here,' Paget declared. 'Food and drink will be served. There's a garderobe in the gallery. Sleep, eat, drink and be merry, but stay here, Master Somers. Try and escape,' he pulled a face, 'and you will be one corpse amongst many fished from the Thames.'

Wriothesley sauntered towards me scratching his ear, then he lunged like a dog, driving his fist into my face. 'For your impertinence,' he snorted.

Then they left. Outside in the gallery I heard Gates's henchmen assemble to stand on guard. I nursed my face and accepted there was nothing to be done.

From then on, for the next nine days, I was a prisoner. The gallery outside was constantly thronged with Gates's city rifflers and a few Spanish cut-throats. One of these worthies of Spain brought me my meals, his scar-crossed face a mask of contempt about why he should serve someone so small and ugly. I was allowed to use the garderobe at the end of the gallery. I was permitted no visitors. I could not detect or discover any news except that from the mist-bound courtyard below, night and day, echoed the clatter of horsemen leaving and arriving.

The first I knew that something was seriously amiss was the cannon fire from the Tower booming through the frosty air, the first public signal that Henry had died. This was late in the afternoon of Monday 31 January, just as Seymour, Dudley and Sir Anthony Browne, Master of the King's Horse, galloped into the city. In their loving care, or so I was told later, was the King's only son and heir, Prince Edward, surrounded and protected by three hundred horsemen and a host of banner bearers. They rode directly to the Tower to be greeted by fresh salutes from the fortress's walls as well as from the warships moored strategically along the Thames. In the greying, misty fastness of the Tower, Prince Edward was proclaimed king.

At the same time Thomas Wriothesley, Lord Chancellor, that mummer from Hell, gave his finest performance before Parliament. He appeared all grieving and in deep mourning, tears soaked his face, emotion tightened his throat. He solemnly announced the King's death and declared Parliament to be dissolved, but not before Paget, equally stricken to the heart, read out the principle clauses of the King's will, declaring the succession to be his son Edward and, should he die without heir, then Mary by default, then Princess Elizabeth. In the meantime there would be no queen regnant; Katherine Parr was completely ignored. A regency council would wield power; the names of this council were obvious to everyone.

I learnt all this on the morning of 1 February. Wriothesley, this time more distracted, entered my chamber. Halberdiers crowded the gallery outside. The Lord Chancellor, pale-faced and red-eyed, was vicious as ever, but wary. I wondered if all was well with the wolf pack. In the end, after staring malevolently at me, he gave me an hour to leave Westminster Palace.

'Where should I go?'

'Your mistress, the Spanish Mary, resides at Greenwich with the widow queen.' Wriothesley stared at me, those milky blue eyes full of malice. 'Do you know, mannekin, I am not yet finished with you or with . . .' He caught himself. 'One hour,' he repeated. 'Master Bricket in the kitchen will provide both cart and carter. Do not come back.'

'Wriothesley?' At least he turned. 'The King? His Majesty?'

'One hour,' he repeated, then he was gone.

Thanks be to God, Bricket proved to be a good friend. He whistled up his legion of scullions from his steam-strewn kitchens. They helped me pack and carry coffers, chests, panniers and caskets, rolls of cloth and my chancery bags down to the cart in the main kitchen yard. Bricket warned me with his eyes and signs not to speak or question him. He whispered how he'd sent a courier across the river to advise the chamberlains at Greenwich that I was about to arrive, adding that he had already arranged for me to be conveyed there in his own small barge. A strange experience being released from that chamber. Once a part of my life; now I'd been thrust out like some dishonest servant.

The Council were certainly making their presence

felt. Captain Wingfield and the Spears thronged everywhere. I also noticed how important doorways and galleries were guarded by Dudley's henchmen, wearing his livery of the bear and ragged staff. He must have whistled up every single able-bodied retainer. The more I watched, the more I realised that Dudley and Seymour had assumed precedence over the rest. Perhaps that was why Wriothesley seemed apprehensive. The royal quarters remained closed and sealed. I gazed despairingly at a doorway that I used to casually walk through. Bricket, however, gripped my shoulder and guided me out of the palace, down to the freezing quayside, where the cart containing my possessions was already waiting. Only then, with the mist swirling about and the cries of the riverside strangely dulled, did he whisper about what he knew, and that was very little.

'On the Sunday, the day after you were imprisoned in your chamber, everything continued as normal. Food was cooked, served and taken to the royal dining room. Some of it was even carried up into the King's privy chamber.'

'By whom?'

'Roberts, Huicke, Alsop the apothecary. On a number of occasions even Dudley and Paget themselves. But no one except those sworn of the Council were allowed anywhere near the King. The Seymours particularly were very busy, especially Thomas.'

'But . . .' I gazed back through the drifting snow at the lords' retainers crowding near the main gate. 'Is

Thomas Seymour now sworn of the Council? You know, I know, everyone in the palace knows how the King deeply resented him.'

'I pretend to know nothing,' Bricket whispered, catching at the cuff of my jerkin, 'but on the twenty-fourth of January I learnt that Thomas Seymour was indeed sworn to the Council. Now come, Judas men swarm everywhere, it's time you were gone.'

I cannot really recall that journey across the tumultuous Thames, I was so deeply locked in my own thoughts. Servants awaited me at Greenwich. I was led like a dream-walker down galleries and passageways. I was shown a chamber in the royal quarters and told this comfortable, warm room was mine. Porters followed carrying all my luggage. Jane appeared. Once the room was empty, we just lay wrapped in each other's arms on the four-poster bed, its heavy, gold-fringed drapes and gleaming walnut posts capturing the light of the candles on their prickets. We lay together until a servant knocked shouting how Her Grace was waiting. We prepared hurriedly and left.

The servant ushered us into the privy chamber, where the Princess Mary greeted us. She was dressed in black taffeta lined with white lace at neck and cuff; a veil of similar colour and fabric covered her reddish hair. Small and quick in movement, Princess Mary finds it difficult to sit still; her unpainted face showed she'd been crying, those gentle grey eyes all red-rimmed. The King's elder daughter has her own unique beauty, though her harsh, deep, almost male voice does jar on the ear, and when she is angry, her furious shouting reminds me so much of her own dread father. Restless and irate, she explained how she had only been informed about her father's death late last night. Queen Katherine Parr had also been overlooked, having been given the news about the same time. Distraught and unsettled, the Queen had retired to her own chamber to quietly grieve. Mary however was furious at Wriothesley and others.

'I cannot tell you much, Will.' She forced a smile and ran a finger down my face. 'His Majesty, my father, is dead. I mourn, I grieve. My chantry priests will sing the requiems.'

'How?' I replied. 'Your Grace, how did your father die? When? Who tended him?'

'I do not know, Will.' Mary's voice fell to a whisper. 'The very tapestries of this palace have eyes and ears.' She sat down in a chair, shifting her Ave beads from one hand to the other. 'We must wait until Balaam arrives. He is busy as a ferret in a warren.'

Balaam did not keep us long. Later that very day he came swift and sudden like a storm sweeping up the Thames. Mary summoned myself and the Lady Jane back to her privy chamber, where the fire had been built up, chairs and small tables placed close to the roaring flames. Balaam was frozen through, quietly cursing the snow, vowing he would seek warmer climes. Nevertheless, once he had doffed cloak and boots and loosened his sword belt, he described what he had discovered since the day of my arrest. Apparently, on that same day almost to the hour, the King's chamber at Westminster became closely guarded, even more so than usual. Balaam, one hand extended towards the flames, the other holding a deep-bowled goblet of posset, described how he learnt this by mingling with the henchmen and retainers of the great lords in and around Westminster. He described how during these secretive days matters had been helped by the thickest mist of the winter curling along the river and shrouding everything in a dense veil of freezing greyness. Horses, hooves muffled, slid out of this gate or that. Couriers and grooms appeared no more than shadowy wraiths visored and cowled. Outside the palace, the few torches did little to disperse the gloom. Orders were also issued forbidding bonfires or the movement of carts without Wriothesley's permission. Inside the palace itself, passageways, galleries and stairs were also bereft of light, places of deep gloom, full of an inky blackness where candles and torches had either been doused or allowed to splutter out.

'Why?' Lady Jane asked.

'Simple enough,' I replied. 'Only those who know the palace well could move around stealthily and easily. Some furtive stranger, a spy or someone curious to discover what was happening, would stumble and slip and certainly arouse the attention of the guards. Like an army camp when the enemy is close, if the light is poor it means no one can thread the picket lines and move about at will.'

'That is true,' Balaam agreed. 'The palace was like an army preparing for battle, silent and secretive, guards and halberdiers patrolling everywhere. There was a sense of perpetual night; that and the icy weather reduced everyone to the same cowled figures. The guards were most vigilant. Everyone, even councillors, was stopped and ordered to show their passes.'

Sitting almost knee to knee in Princess Mary's chamber, thinking we were safe, again an arrogant mistake on my part, we listened to Balaam describe the dense fog of secrecy that spread and curled through Westminster. How entry even into the courtyards was subject to a special pass. I asked about Bricket and the cooks.

'Oh,' Balaam replied, 'they are all now terrified. Very few people are allowed to enter. No one is permitted to leave unless they carry a special warrant.'

'From whom?' I asked. Balaam just shrugged.

'Will, when was the last time you saw the King?'

'The day Surrey was executed, sometime in the afternoon of the nineteenth of January.'

Balaam nodded. 'Did he discuss what was happening?'

I recalled that macabre meeting in the Westminster cellar. 'Just his imaginings,' I murmured.

'According to what I have learnt,' Balaam drank some posset, 'the King was troubled about his will. He intended to include some who were not named before and put out the likes of Gardiner, whom Henry continued to curse as a wilful man not fit to trouble the King, his son or the Privy Council any more. Van der Delft, the Imperial ambassador, was trying to meet the King, as were others. Rumours were rife that His Majesty was ill. Others claimed his legs had been cauterised and the ulcers closed. Would that be true, Will?'

I replied how I had met the King in the royal cellars at the other end of the palace, which at least proved he was able to walk. Balaam nodded, saying that all this agreed with what he had learnt. How the King had appeared very alert, deeply concerned about the English garrison at Boulogne and their lack of supplies. He was also interested in his gardens, especially some apple trees recently imported from France.

'Did he,' Princess Mary asked, putting her hand to her face, 'ever ask to see his children?'

'No.' Balaam smiled sadly at her. 'Your Grace, as far as gossip has it, the King your father did not ask to see the Queen or any of his family, certainly not before that last week when Westminster fell under the iron grip of the Council. To be honest, Your Grace, God only knows what the King said or did during those last days of his life.'

The Princess Mary held a hand up for silence, staring into the fire. God forgive my arrogance, yet I could sense what she was thinking. The bittersweet, and not so sweet, memories must float like dark smoke through her soul. Once Henry had hailed her as the greatest treasure of his kingdom. Yet when locked in his lust for Anne Boleyn, he would not even speak to her. He declared her illegitimate, exiled her, humiliated her and, on occasion, left her vulnerable and exposed to the malice of others, who, if given leave, would certainly have executed her.

'Perhaps he was not in his right mind?' Mary shifted in her chair.

'The King,' Balaam soothed, 'must have been in great pain.' He sat chewing his lip

'What!' Princess Mary demanded. 'What did you hear, Balaam?'

'Oh, Your Grace, there are stories, vague imaginings, tittle-tattle, scraps of gossip. How the King's secret chambers and apartments were sealed for days.' He took a deep breath. 'Of course you heard the cannon fire from the Tower?' He didn't wait for us to agree. 'Well that was the first public announcement. Here,' Balaam stretched in his chair, 'is where we walk on firmer ground, but,' he paused, 'remember this is what is being proclaimed to all and sundry.' He rubbed the side of his face. 'You know how it goes. If enough people repeat a story time and again, then lo and behold, it is the plain and unvarnished truth.' He paused to collect his thoughts. 'It's common knowledge that the King met the French and Imperial ambassadors on the seventeenth of January. They were told not to tarry long as the King was greatly weakened. We know Surrey was executed on the nineteenth. The King was active enough. Silence descended till Thursday the twenty-seventh, when Parliament passed the Act of Attainder against the Howards, both father and son. The King approved of that; he also took the Eucharist from his confessor, John Boole. Now all this,' Balaam waved a hand, 'is the official story. On that same day the King weakened considerably. Rumours abound that his ulcerated legs had become a squelching mess, that he'd lost control of bowel and bladder, that the light hurt his eyes, his skin crackling yellow like cheap parchment all dried out.'

'So,' the Princess Mary intervened, 'once the attainder against the Howards was approved, my father's state worsened. He slipped swiftly towards death.' She shook her head. 'If Norfolk was condemned, why hasn't the sentence been carried out?'

'Perhaps the Council do not want the young king's reign to begin with the execution of an old man, England's premier duke. Or,' Balaam pulled a face, 'Norfolk is over seventy. We have had enough drama with the Howards. Perhaps Wriothesley and the Council just hope he will rot away in the Tower and die like some neglected old man in his hovel. They have what they want. Surrey is dead. The rest of his family terrified, their property, estates and movables all seized.'

'And my father,' Mary insisted, 'if he died early in the hours of the twenty-eighth of January, surely somebody warned him of his impending death?'

'No one dared. According to rumour, Wriothesley

and the others hung like ghosts on the threshold of the privy chamber. Late in the evening of the twenty-seventh, Sir Anthony Denny, First Gentleman of the Privy Chamber, entered and knelt beside the King's bed. Henry asked what the matter was. Denny informed the King that all human help was in vain and it was now time for His Majesty to review his past life and seek for God's mercy through Christ.' Balaam paused as if listening to the sounds of the night. 'I must be gone soon,' he suddenly whispered. 'The city is under close watch.' He rubbed his hands. 'Soldiers have raised chains on the streets. Barricades have been set up. Horsemen patrol Cheapside. War barges float along the Thames. Your Grace, it's best if I not be seen.' He grasped Mary's hand, raised it and kissed it like the good troubadour he was.

'Finish your tale,' Mary insisted. 'Although whether it's the truth is another matter. It seems to be . . .' she searched for words, 'so much hearsay.'

'After Denny had warned him,' Balaam decided to continue, 'Henry struggled to reply, asking him what judge had sent him to pass this sentence. "Your phys- icians," Denny answered. Henry promptly summoned these. They arrived with their trays of medicine but Henry, gasping and fighting for breath, demanded they leave. "After all," he rasped, "once judges have passed sentence on a criminal they have no need to trouble him any further, so begone." Denny then invited the King to confer with some of his prelates. "I will speak to no one except Cranmer," the King replied, "but not yet. Let me rest for a while and then I shall decide." He slept fitfully for about an hour, and when he awoke was feeling very weak. He ordered that Cranmer, who had withdrawn to his palace at Croydon, be sent for with all haste.' Balaam drained his goblet. 'Cranmer is no swift courier. It was now the dead of night, the weather was freezing, with savage flurries of snow. By the time Cranmer entered the King's chamber, Henry was speechless. Cranmer stretched out on the royal bed and grasped the King's hand. He begged Henry to testify by some sign that he still hoped in the saving mercies of Christ. The King stared at him, pressed Cranmer's hand and, a short while later, passed from this life to the next.'

Balaam paused at a bell booming through the mist-hung evening. I heard doors opening and shutting. I glanced at Princess Mary. She just sat staring into the fire, eyes brimming with tears. As for myself, I was more intrigued by Balaam's story. The princess was correct, it was like a scene from some miracle play: the Norfolks had been silenced and then the King's condition suddenly worsens. However, no one really talks to him, no one summons his wife and children, whilst hours are spent fetching Cranmer from Croydon.

'My father died early on Friday morning. They kept his death quiet for almost four days. Why?'

'Your Grace, they will argue that certain preparations had to be made. Your illustrious brother was brought into London, ports were sealed, the roads closely watched. The Council had to deal with its own schedule of business.' Even as I spoke I realised my own words sounded hollow. Such matters might take one or two days. Nevertheless, the King died in the early hours of Friday and his death was not made public until Monday. What did happen in those secret chambers at Westminster? More importantly, had the King, my royal master, really died in this rather peaceful way? I turned to the princess.

'Cranmer,' Balaam murmured, 'says he will not shave his face as a sign of mourning.'

'Will?' the princess asked. 'What were you going to say?'

'What must have occurred to your Grace, to Balaam, to Lady Jane and indeed everyone.' I emphasised the points with my fingers. 'First, the King said nothing before he died except that he felt unwell and would like to see Cranmer. Second, there are no witnesses to his death. Cranmer is summoned when it is already too late. The Queen and the King's children are not alerted. No one is allowed to view the corpse. Is that not so?'

'I have dispatched messengers to the palace. I am informed I cannot view my father's corpse; it is now being embalmed and prepared for burial. I believe the same reply has been sent to the Queen.' Mary sighed noisily, 'For the moment, there is little more to be done.'

We had just risen, preparing a collation of cold meats and bowls of hot stewed vegetables to be served on a table near a window, when the sound of pounding feet in the gallery outside startled us. The door was flung open and one of Mary's Spanish servants, the steward I think, burst in and fell to his knees in front of his mistress. Even as he spoke I heard the clash and clatter of steel, the sound of wood breaking, the shrieks of serving wenches. The steward was chattering in Spanish. Mary quickly silenced him with a gesture of her hand and turned to us.

'Wriothesley!' she declared. 'Wriothesley is here with Wingfield and a company of the Spears.'

Balaam at once drew sword and dagger, checking for escape routes. There was no other door. The chamber windows, shuttered against the cold, were too narrow for any escape. Already the halberdiers were in the gallery, the door crashed open and Wriothesley sped like some hunting dog into the chamber, Wingfield and his escort pouring in afterwards. Instantly I knew why he was here, or at least I thought I did. Princess Mary shouted her protests, spots of anger high on her cheeks. I caught the same passionate, flaring fury of her father. She demanded to know by what right they invaded the palace and forced her chambers. Of course this was Wriothesley. Our chancellor does not care for courtesy, honour or title. Swathed in a heavy coat with a ridiculous-looking bonnet on his head, he leered at me and the Lady Jane, who now huddled close beside me. He produced a warrant even as Wingfield drew his own sword and, accompanied by a group of Spears, halberds lowered, advanced threateningly on Balaam. I heard a clatter as Balaam's sword and dagger fell to the floor. Mary snatched Wriothesley's warrant.

'It bears the Council's seal,' Wriothesley bellowed. 'It gives me the power to search any house, palace or not, and to seize any persons suspected of being involved in treason.'

'Not here!' Mary snapped. 'My lord,' her voice became more placatory, 'my father the King is dead. I have just received such doleful news. I do not think this is either the time or the place.'

'Your Grace,' Wriothesley bowed, 'I mean no ill, but this present time is truly perilous, especially in a place like this, a royal palace. Your brother has yet to be crowned, this city seethes with unrest.' He pointed at me and Lady Jane. 'They have not been accused. No indictment has been laid against them, but I'm afraid I must take them into custody.'

'Custody!' the princess cried. 'What custody?'

'Your Grace, I am sure a few questions will clarify matters.'

'Then do it here.'

'No, Your Grace, that is not appropriate. Sir Anthony?'

Despite the princess's strident protests, the Spears closed in around us. Jane was clinging to me for life. Wriothesley was truly enjoying himself; that demon soul revels in such mischief. Deep in my heart I knew he might harm me but not the Lady Jane. Her terror was that she did not recognise that.

'And who is this drawer of weapons?' Wriothesley stepped round me. To my astonishment, Balaam lapsed into a tirade completely in Spanish, acting the part, flinging his hands in the air and shouting at the Princess Mary, who just as swiftly replied in her mother's tongue.

'What is this, what is this?' Wriothesley demanded.

'Master Hugo,' the princess replied, 'is an accredited envoy in the retinue of the Imperial ambassador. His Grace will not be pleased that one of his household is accosted and threatened.'

'Your warrant?' Wriothesley demanded.

Balaam correctly played the surprising role he'd assumed. Voluble in Spanish, he ignored Wriothesley and, hands extended, conversed with the princess as if he did not know what was happening, though clearly resenting Wriothesley. I was astonished. True, I was terrified by Wriothesley's arrival but I was equally startled at this abrupt turn of events. Surrounded by halberdiers, with the Lady Jane clinging close, I found it difficult to turn and watch what was happening. Nevertheless, the Chancellor's demand to produce the warrant was swiftly answered. Acting the interpreter, the princess explained what Wriothesley wanted. Balaam pulled a face, shrugged, scratched his head and muttered something beneath his breath. Neither I nor Wriothesley understood Spanish, but it was obvious that Balaam was cursing our intruder with a spate of filthy words. He looked as if he was going to refuse. Ignoring the Spears, he slowly picked up both sword and dagger and resheathed them, then opened the wallet on his war belt, took out a square of parchment and tossed this at Wriothesley's feet. The Chancellor picked it up and walked over to a lantern box. He read the document before carefully scrutinising the seal.

'The dry stamp,' he called over his shoulder. Balaam had the sense not to reply. Wriothesley was certainly suspicious. He scrutinised both seal and royal signature again, pronounced himself satisfied and handed the document back.

'Take these.' Wriothesley gestured to Lady Jane and myself. Princess Mary shouted protests. Balaam also contributed to the clamour, which echoed in our ears as we were pushed along the gallery and down the stairs. A thoughtful servant hurried up with our cloaks, then we were out in the icy cold half-light. We were hurried along the quayside down to the waiting barge and a nightmare journey across the Thames. Lady Jane, wrapped in both her cloak and mine, trembled like a babe. I shivered until Wingfield, a look of compassion on his harsh face, snatched up a rug the barge master had provided to cover his legs and threw it at me. I squatted, watching the lantern horns either side on the prow rise and fall. A trumpeter kept blowing his horn, a mournful, echoing sound, warning other craft to stay away.

At last we reached Queenhithe, where we disembarked and trudged through the streets to the hulking, ugly, evil-smelling mass of Newgate tower. 'The Stone

Jug' and 'the College of the Damned' are just two of the names given to that sprawling fortress of heinous horrors. I have reflected on what happened that evening. One day, God willing, I will reread it. Perhaps I will teach Lady Jane or some other close friend my cipher and allow them the same. Somebody should know what happened and learn a little more. Certainly I speak the truth. If there is a hell on earth, this can be found in Newgate. If there are degrees of torment in hell, Newgate will certainly display them. The prison is a living death, a grave, a tomb where you are buried before you are dead. A place of sweating filthy walls, its paved cracked floor crackling with the lice which multiply like the plagues of Egypt upon the putrid clothes and filthy bodies of the hordes of unwashed prisoners crammed into its squalid chambers, cells and holes. The reek and stench are suffocating. The clamour, the constant shouting and screams of those incarcerated there din the ear and chill the heart.

We were at once taken to the master's side, where Wingfield's halberdiers were replaced by burly, leather-aproned turnkeys. Wriothesley shook his head when the chain clerk produced the Black Book to record our admission. Now, though that demon did not recognise it, I took great comfort from that. Many years ago, I was hauled off to Newgate for some petty crime. The keeper and his gaolers are like carrion crows; they batten full and wax fat on their victims. They like to number every one and assess his worth so they can exact the fullest tribute. Wriothesley's refusal demonstrated that we might not be there for long, and I began to suspect that he did not enjoy the full authority of the Council for what he had undertaken. He did not want a written record explaining the reason for our arrest and committal to prison. Indeed, the more I studied him, the more I could detect behind his bluster and malice a strident nervousness, as if he too was frightened, but of what?

Wriothesley talked quickly and quietly with the keeper and we were taken to a narrow, cobwebbed room, its floor covered by a dirty, slushy straw which formed a mess around our feet. I sat on a bench opposite the door, pulling Lady Jane down beside me. I murmured comforts as Wriothesley slammed the door shut, grabbed a stool and sat before us. He continued to play his game of Hodman's bluff. He seemed hasty, impatient, and of course he would be. Princess Mary had her father's temper; she would not stand idle but be voluble in her protests. Already couriers would be hastening across to Westminster. I also wondered about Balaam. How could he have a diplomatic warrant? Who arranged that for him: the Princess Mary, the Imperial ambassador or someone else? At the time, that was not my prime concern. I just prayed the winds of this storm would shift swiftly and we would soon be released. I fought to steady my breathing, to calm my nerves. Princess Mary might protest, but this was still dangerous. If Wriothesley could trap us into treason, he would justify

THE LAST OF DAYS

his actions. Of that I was truly afraid. Nevertheless, I underestimated the Chancellor's malice. He could not resist spending valuable time on indulging his own cruelty and resentment.

Wriothesley was distracted by Lady Jane, slim and pretty, a maiden in distress, a comely damsel terrified out of her wits, his natural prey. For a while he berated us, our status, our patronage, 'two deformations' who had no right to be at court. A spate of furious, filthy insults spurted from his mouth until he paused, dabbing his fingers at the creamy froth on his lips. He lifted a hand as a chilling scream from elsewhere in the prison pierced the air. Lady Jane, now beside herself with terror, began to chatter nonsense. I was deeply concerned. My beloved is small and well formed, she can be merry and sharp of wit, but those wits can be easily shattered. She can become highly anxious, fretful, sometimes collapse at the confusion that rages within her. I was frightened this living nightmare might truly turn her humours.

'Hush now, hush now,' Wriothesley mocked. 'That's only a prisoner in the press yard suffering peine forte et dure. Some wretch who's refused to plead. He lies in the yard under great paving stones, starved of everything except foul water.' The Chancellor grinned. 'It might be him screaming, or there again,' he shook his head, eyes blinking as if genuinely perplexed, 'it might be his accomplice, some stupid wench, a doxy having her ears nailed to the pillory board.' He paused, sniffing noisily as if waiting to sneeze. 'The prisoner will eventually plead, then he will be taken to Tyburn Elms, where he will be half hanged, disembowelled and his entrails burnt in front of him. Afterwards he will be beheaded and his body quartered; that's what traitors suffer. You may wonder, as many do, how a man can survive being ripped open. Well, the executioner ties certain strands within the body so his victim will survive long enough to watch—'

'Wriothesley!' I screeched. 'What is it you want? Why are we here? You know we are no traitors.'

Wriothesley, jaw jutting, wagged a finger. 'Just one question, Will, only one.' His change of tone and mood surprised me, even more so as I caught a flicker of fear; there truly was more to this. Wriothesley delighted in frightening and terrorising us, but this masked something else. He swiftly glanced over his shoulder at the door, then back at us. 'The monster,' he hissed, 'is dead! Screaming and begging he was, Will!' He raised an eyebrow as if expecting applause.

'What!' I demanded. 'That's not what we heard. Are you out of your wits? Are you babbling about the King?'

Wriothesley leaned across, slapped my face then poked Lady Jane on the shoulder like some spoilt, malignant child. I resolved then as I do now: if I can, if I am able, I will kill this man. For a while he just sat staring at us, clucking his tongue. I held his gaze, wondering if this man was truly out of his wits. Ill, evil or both? I also felt strangely reassured. Wriothesley had brought us here to play some hideous game. In his narrow, soiled soul, if he has one, he truly hates myself and Jane not for what we do or say, but for what we are. He considers us freaks, less than human. Years of watching us being fussed and patronised had festered and now spilt over. Yet there was something else. Wriothesley could have seized me at Westminster, pummelled and harassed me there, so why not? Because he needed Lady Jane, to use her to frighten me, whilst he was also concerned about being overheard. He didn't want us in Newgate just to vomit his filthy spleen, but for something else. And what did he mean about the King screaming and pleading? Oh how the world changes so swiftly! A few days earlier he would never have dared say that. Wriothesley continued to stare at me, rocking himself gently backwards and forwards as if the Lady Jane's gentle sobbing was a sweet cantata to his ears.

'You should hasten,' I taunted, 'you really should. Princess Mary will be sending urgent messages to the Council. Our release is only a matter of time. What do you really want to know, Wriothesley?'

'What our late king said to you about me.'

'You should have asked him yourself.'

'Did he ever intend to move against me, I mean with Dudley and Seymour, or discuss any secret plans involving me?'

God be my witness. That poisonous snake of a man! I truly wondered what he was talking about. Of course, like any snake on the move, he twisted and turned.

That's Wriothesley. He had been with Cardinal Wolsey and deserted him. He should have gone to the Tower with Cromwell but saved his neck by testifying against his former master, who had taken him into his own household. Gardiner had been his ally, but Wriothesley deserted him in his hour of need. Perhaps that was it: had the King been plotting his downfall? I tried to cover my confusion, deciding that honesty was the best path.

'I know nothing,' I blurted out. 'I know nothing at all.'

'You could be questioned.'

'By what right? Where is your warrant?'

'I could frighten you,' he pointed at Lady Jane, 'or her, your little friend. Or,' he spread his hands, 'you could tell the truth.'

'I know nothing. Question me, torture me, I will still know nothing. You could bribe me with a house, lands and a pot of gold, my answer will be the same. But Master Wriothesley,' I deliberately used the same common term which the King would have done when he censured this man, 'you have miscalculated, haven't you? You are nervous and you should be. You were once Gardiner's friend and ally; do you think Dudley or Seymour will forget that? What guarantee do they have that you will not whisper council secrets to the Bishop of Winchester?'

Wriothesley abruptly stood up; I secretly rejoiced. Apparently all was not well with the late king's fighting dogs: they would turn on each other, and this sinister soul might be their first victim. He walked to the door and peered through the grille. He was agitated, plucking at the costly belt around his waist, muttering to himself, fingers fluttering the air. I do wonder if Wriothesley suffers fits of lunacy.

'What do you know?' He turned on me.

'Nothing you don't know yourself,' I taunted, 'and if I told you that, you wouldn't be any wiser for it.'

'Riddles.' He smiled. 'Riddles . . .'

A pounding on the door startled him. The hammering was repeated. Wingfield shouted for the door to be open. Someone echoed that. The door was flung back and Wingfield, accompanied by William Clarke, Paget's creature, strode into that miserable cell. Clarke at once produced a document, which he pushed into Wriothesley's hands.

'A writ of liberate!' he shouted. 'Signed by the Chief Secretary, Lord Paget himself. These two are to be released unharmed and delivered into the care of Princess Mary's household.'

'Sir Anthony?' Clarke turned to Wingfield, who'd retreated back to the doorway, the keeper of the prison behind him. 'Sir Anthony, if necessary, enforce the writ.'

Wriothesley examined the document, kicked the stool over and stormed out, muttering under his breath. Clarke stood like a sparrow, head cocked slightly to one side, a smile on his lips as he listened to the clash and clatter in the passageway outside. Once this had faded, he snapped his fingers and led us out of that hellhole along a warren of putrid passageways, across filthy courtyards, through the iron-bound gates on to the great concourse before Newgate prison. We had to wait momentarily, as the death carts had just arrived back from Smithfield and Tyburn Elms crammed with the cadavers of the hanged. A truly gruesome sight with their ghastly faces, twisted necks, limbs sprawled all frozen in a cruel death. Relatives and friends were pushing forward to claim their kin, only to be beaten off by the hangmen and their assistants, whose faces remained hidden behind macabre red masks.

Jane huddled close. I shielded her eyes from such ghoulish sights. Once the carts were gone, we followed Clarke into the fleshers' markets. The day's trading was done, the market horn had sounded. The butchers had taken down the gutted flesh of pig, chicken, duck, pheasant and calves. The offal tubs were being rinsed and the misty air reeked of salt, blood and rotting meat. Bonfires, lit to consume the rubbish, had drawn in the beggars with their scraps of mucky meat that they had managed to scoop up from the cobbles. Now fastened to makeshift cooking rods, these morsels were thrust into the flames, turning the air rancid with the reek of bubbling fat. Clarke led us past, striding down Cheapside, now and again looking over his shoulder to make sure we were not being pursued, and straight into the Lamb of God, where Balaam was sitting in the inglenook, toasting himself before a roaring fire. Clarke waved us towards him as he handed over a pouch.

'Two warrants from the Council,' he grinned, 'properly sealed. These will allow you to journey without impediment or obstruction,' he paused, 'as retainers in the Princess Mary's household, both you and your woman. But,' he held up a bony finger, 'not in any other.' Then he was gone.

Balaam acted all solicitous. He could see I was wary of him; indeed I marvelled at the change. The excitable Spaniard had disappeared; now Balaam was very much the master of the scene. He called for the wash-boy to fetch bowls and napkins so we could cleanse the filth from Newgate from our faces and hands. Lady Jane was beginning to recover from the horrors Wriothesley had inflicted. Still pale and shaking, she greedily drank a deep-bowled goblet of the richest burgundy, ate some diced chicken and manchet bread and promptly fell asleep. Helped by Balaam, I carried her to the cushioned settle to the right of the hearth, then we returned to the table.

'Spanish?' I abruptly asked. 'Are you Spanish, Balaam? Are you a friend of the Council? All of them, or just one or two? Does the Princess Mary know? No,' I brushed aside his interruption, 'as I have said before to many a person, I may be a jester, but I am not stupid. To be recognised as a member of the Imperial ambassador's household you need a warrant signed by the King – if it is the dry stamp – and ratified by the Council.' I extended a hand. 'Show me that warrant.'

'Will, Will,' Balaam smiled sadly at me, 'I cannot, not now. Perhaps one day, I assure you. I have already revealed too much.'

'Why not now?' I demanded of this shifter amongst the shadows.

'Wriothesley has just apprehended you. He had the arrogant insolence to invade Greenwich Palace, force the Princess's chambers, arrest you and throw you into Newgate. I suspect he threatened and menaced you; he certainly terrified her.' Balaam gestured at the settle. 'The Lady Jane is still suffering from shock. I know people locked in Newgate for a day and a night who came out baying at the moon. What if Wriothesley or even someone else tries again, subjects you to harsh torture, peine forte et dure? You would, as I would, as any of God's creatures would, break and tell them everything they wanted. These are murky times. We are like swordsmen in the darkest room, stumbling about, lashing out. We cannot distinguish between friend and foe.'

I drank my wine. Despite the turbulence in my heart, I recognised that this enigmatic man spoke the truth; Wriothesley had proved that.

'You could be as white and as pure as rain-washed bone,' Balaam leaned closer, 'and still be guilty. Days of thunder, Will, where you could be met by a sudden shoal of ferocious furies, a swarm of menace and malice. We all walk on the edge of death's dark park. Sin and charity stand thick together in the same field; the only time we can tell the difference is when they blossom, and that time may well be close. So tell me what Wriothesley wanted.'

Satisfied that Balaam was speaking the truth, I described everything that had happened, from our leaving Greenwich to the welcoming arrival of Clarke.

'I sped hastily,' Balaam murmured. He stared pitifully at the Lady Jane. 'I was anxious lest she break.'

'Wriothesley frightened her into abject silence.'

Balaam thrust his hand out for me to clasp,; I did so and he held mine fast. 'I swear, Will, by all that is holy, if Wriothesley ever falls, I will be there.'

'God hasten that hour.'

'Amen.' Balaam withdrew his hand. 'The Council seem united except for Wriothesley.'

'He cannot plot against them,' I replied. 'He doesn't have the skill, a bully who terrorises women . . .'

'No, no.' Balaam shook his head. 'Not him, Will. This has its roots, I am sure, in that mysterious silence that clouds His Satanic Majesty's death. I just wonder what . . .' He paused. 'You know the hymn well enough.' He waved a hand. 'Henry used Wolsey to destroy Buckingham, Cromwell to destroy Wolsey, Richard Rich to destroy More. Norfolk brought Cromwell down and Henry used Howard's own family to destroy Norfolk. Subtle and sly was our late but not lamented king. Norfolk himself is not executed.'

'He was saved by Henry's death.'

'Was he?' Balaam smiled. 'I wonder. Then there is

Gardiner, abruptly exiled by the King but never really punished, and finally our good friend Wriothesley.'

'What do you wonder?' I asked.

'Was Henry cut off in the middle of yet another of his murderous plots? Is that why he ranted and raved?' Balaam drained his cup. 'Here,' he got up, 'let me help you and Lady Jane reach Greenwich safely. The night is dark and cold. A few of my roaring boys will escort us.'

15 February 1547

In the succeeding days we were all swept up in the funeral preparations. I remained anxious about the Lady Jane, who still had waking nightmares of Wriothesley and that dank, dismal cell at Newgate. No invitation to visit the royal coffin to pay their last respects was issued to the widow queen, Henry's heir or his two daughters. Mary remained silent on that, white-faced and thin-lipped. Apparently no one was allowed near that cold, rotting royal corpse. Balaam reported how the chief apothecary, Thomas Alsop, and his minions had been given a veritable treasure to buy oil and herbs for when the body was embalmed: cloves, oil and balm, musk, myrrh, cinnamon, crushed rose powder and various other spices. A lead coffin within a huge solid elm casket was also constructed. Balaam tried to question those involved in the grisly task of embalming. My master was over six foot three, whilst the weight of his body must have been well above twenty stone at his death. He had rottenness in his legs, catarrh and rheums in his nose and corruption in his belly. Surely the cleansing of all this would cause some chatter and gossip? Yet, as Balaam admitted, he might as well have asked a stone statue to sing the 'Salve Regina'.

'They are fearful,' he reported to Princess Mary. 'They will neither say nay or yea, except for what a servant girl reported. One of the halberdiers was sweet on her. He told a story of how hundreds of pounds was also spent on oil of roses and other perfumes to sweeten the air around the royal privy chambers; how a hideous stench, an offensive reek polluted the air. More than that I cannot say.'

Balaam went back to his searches but could discover nothing else. The Council was tightening its grip on both city and kingdom. Ports and harbours were under surveillance, all roads into London closely guarded, whilst the Council's Judas men were as busy as rats in a hayrick. He did discover that old Norfolk, that duke of infinite cunning, had cheated the headsman's axe by a mere breath. His death warrant had been signed by the dry stamp on Thursday 27 January; the death of the King, or so it was said, had prevented it from being served.

'I heard another story as well,' Balaam declared. 'How Norfolk had bequeathed his lands in their entirety to Prince Edward, and how the King was delighted with this. In the end, they have left him to rot.' He rubbed his hands and stretched them out to the fire burning in the great hearth of Princess Mary's chamber. 'They'll let the cold, damp rigour of the Tower drain both life and health from him.'

'I wonder,' the Princess Mary declared. 'So smooth, so serene.' She answered my quizzical look. 'I mean for Wriothesley and his coven.' She pointed at me. 'Do you really believe it, Will, the story about my father's last illness and death?'

I thought of Westminster sealed and closed like any trap, horsemen galloping here and there. Dudley hastening to Hertford. Young Edward's swift arrival into London. Beneath it all a prickling unease, that matters had been, and still were, cunningly contrived.

'No, no.' I shook my head.

'*Flectamur nec flectimur*,' Mary murmured. 'Let it go. Let us bend and bend very low lest we break, then we shall see.'

I was reluctant to talk with Balaam present. I was still deeply concerned about his loyalty. I could understand the logic of what he'd claimed in the Lamb of God, yet here was a man who had posed in the northern shires as a rebel, an outlaw, a traitor put to the horn, hunted by the likes of Paget, but who still carried that warrant signed by the King and sealed by the Council. Little wonder, I reflected, that he had never been caught. Memories came and went of how he could slip so easily in and around the city and never be taken. I recalled King Henry once discussing certain spies in France; he had bitterly joked how he was not too sure where their loyalty lay, only to answer his own question by suggesting that it probably was for the prince who paid them the most. Was Balaam one of these turncoats? On one occasion I tried to speak to the Princess Mary about it, but she simply gave that cold smile, her usual sign for a polite refusal.

Something nagged at my soul like an importunate beggar. It was like trying to recall a nightmare; it plagues your sleep but you cannot recall the details. Lady Jane eventually jogged my memory. She soon recovered from her ordeal, returning to her usual pursuits. Now the Lady Jane likes nothing better than to learn and recite poems and sonnets which catch her heart. Copies of the late Earl of Surrey's commentaries on the psalms, written during his last weeks in the Tower, were now being sold by the various print shops in the City. One morning I found her reading Surrey's commentary on Psalm 73. She was sitting in the princess's pew in the small chantry chapel made available to her mistress at Greenwich. I sat beside her as she recited the verses in that pretty clear voice of hers. The words invoked Surrey in all his passionate energy. I recalled the way he had so bravely defended himself, then I abruptly started, so much so that I sprang to my feet, staring at the Spanish crucifix, all heavily wrought and intricately carved, placed on the black-and-gold-draped altar.

'Will?'

'Spanish!' I exclaimed. 'Martin, the man who was

supposed to assist . . .' I broke off and stared down at my beloved, then kissed her absent-mindedly on the brow and left the chapel. I found a lonely window seat overlooking the gardens, still held fast in a heavy winter frost. What if, I wondered, Balaam had been Spanish Martin? He had proved he could certainly act the part, a true shape-shifter, a master of disguise. If he had, and I was becoming more certain that he did, a patron or ally on the Council, he would have found it very easy to secure the post as Surrey's servant. After all, during those last days, the earl had been deserted by friends and family. Balaam could have disguised himself as Martin and been placed at the young earl's service, but what then? Had he urged Surrey to escape and then betrayed him? But why would he show such callous ruthlessness? In truth I could find no solution to the mystery; all I could do was promise myself to be more circumspect and wary with the man with the far-seeing gaze.

I have decided to continue this journal. I want to record what truly happened from the very start of all the mystery shrouding the last days of Henry. I agree with the Princess Mary. The official story of the late king's death is both *faux et semblant*, false and dissimulating. I pick at the story as you would loose threads on a piece of cloth. I have nothing else to do, and the mystery weighs more heavily on me than the King's actual death. For all the horrors he could heap upon his own subjects,

Henry had a deeply morbid fear of death. Did he truly slip away like some shadow under the sun? I cannot understand the business of Cranmer. According to the Council, Henry had been weakening, yet they delayed sending for Cranmer, allegedly at the King's request, until it was almost too late. They claimed Cranmer was in his house at Croydon, but what was he doing there in the depths of winter? Thomas Cranmer was the King's special confessor and confidant, Archbishop of Canterbury, the man who presided over his church. He had been in Westminster on 27 January when Parliament had passed the Bill of Attainder against the Howards. Surely, I argued to myself, Cranmer would have made constant enquiries about his patron and friend the King? Why didn't he stay in Westminster to be close to his ailing master? He could have lodged at the palace, at Whitehall or any of the royal residences. Moreover, if Cranmer did not make enquiries, which I would find very strange, surely the Council, of which he was a member, would have at least informed him about the approaching crisis. Instead, like some sorry actor in a play, he was kept hidden away deep in the shadows until summoned to play his part.

And what a dramatic role was assigned to him! Hastening into London in the dead of night, reaching the King at that very moment when Henry had lost the power of speech and was slipping into death. Yet who would challenge the word of the King's friend and confidant, the Archbishop of Canterbury? Few would know that only recently Henry had toyed with the idea of sending the archbishop to the Tower, a churchman whose leanings towards the reformists in Europe were making him less and less palatable to his king. Perhaps Cranmer was not the King's favourite after all? True, he and Cromwell had helped Henry break with Rome, divorce Catherine of Aragon and marry Anne Boleyn. He had ghosted the King's conscience during the crisis. However, he had also, for a short while, tried to defend Anne Boleyn, until the King snarled at him, and had been one of those who brought Henry dire news about the loose morals and lewd living of Katherine Howard. Henry would not forget that.

The King would also have been alarmed at stories about Cranmer's private life. How his supposedly chaste archbishop, when he was a scholar, had fallen in love with a maid at the Dolphin in Cambridge. Cranmer had married her secretly and, some claimed, carried around his 'holy wench', as she was described, in a stout chest pierced with holes. Perhaps the relationship between king and archbishop had grown colder. For his part, Cranmer, for all his humility, would not have forgotten how close he had come to following the likes of Bishop Fisher of Rochester and Houghton of the Charterhouse to the Tower. Consequently, if the story of Cranmer's arrival at the royal bedside well after the eleventh hour was a fable, Cranmer himself must have been party to such a fiction. Despite all the claims of close friendship, had the archbishop grown fearful of his king? And what would that fear induce him to do? Be party to a conspiracy involving others on the Council about the last days of their dread royal master? Was this what Wriothesley meant by his enigmatic reference to 'the monster' screaming and ranting during his final hours? Or was this just the vain imaginings of a sick, sad soul?

Moreover, why were Henry's wife and three children never brought to see him, either alive or dead? Were the Council trying to hide something? Even criminals condemned to death are allowed the courtesy of a visit from family and kin. To be sure, Henry's relationship with his wife might not have been harmonious, but his beloved son and heir? Mary and Elizabeth, whose rights he had so jealously safeguarded in his will? I recall Balaam's words about those paintings of Henry that emphasise the importance of his family. I could also plead my own case; I was close to the King but still cruelly excluded from his last hours.

I continued to listen carefully to chatter about the funeral preparations. Henry had published detailed plans for his burial in St George's Chapel, Windsor, the resting place of his grandfather, the Yorkist Edward IV, as well as of his beloved Jane Seymour. Wolsey, God rest him, had chosen the same place and commissioned the construction of a massive black marble sarcophagus. Henry had promptly seized this for his own use, yet all this was to be ignored. Henry would be laid to rest next to his beloved Jane, her brothers would see to that, but the coffin would be that speedily constructed lead shell in its elm wood case. There would be no lying in state, no viewing of the corpse. Haste was the order of the day. According to the published account, the apothecaries, surgeons and wax chandlers went swiftly about their business, sponging, cleansing, waxing, embalming and furnishing the royal corpse. By 1 February, the dead king's bowels and entrails had been removed, hastily encased in a chest and swiftly buried beneath the flagstones of Westminster Palace chapel. I could only imagine the embalmers busy digging and cutting the mouldering, messy flesh. Nonetheless, I was deeply surprised at their speed. The embalmed corpse, wrapped in thick velvet and samite sheets and bound with silk cord, was sheeted in its lead shell and placed in its wooden casket.

On the eve of Candlemas, 2 February, the entire coffin under its rich gold pall was brought to the prepared and lavishly decorated royal hearse standing in the royal chapel, the entire church hung in black cloth of the most precious fabric decorated with the King's arms and royal insignia. The hearse was ringed by eighty candles, each two foot high; all about it hung more banners, pennants and other heraldic cloths depicting the royal descent. The floor of the chapel was covered in black cloth, whilst at each corner of the hearse, more gorgeous tapestries celebrated the lives of St George, Edward the Confessor and others. An altar bearing a weight of silver and gold holy vessels stood at the foot of the hearse so that requiem masses could be celebrated continuously. The massive rail around the hearse also included twelve pews or stalls, three on each side, for the twelve principle mourners, led by that nonentity Henry Gray, Marquis of Dorset, garbed like the other eleven in special mourning habit, hood, mantle and gown.

Such preparations pricked my suspicions. The royal corpse left the King's secret chambers late on the afternoon of 2 February. Henry had died early on Friday morning of the previous week, but this had not been made public until the Monday, 31 January. Now of course preparations for the funeral may have been initiated secretly; even so the haste must have exhausted the apothecaries, carpenters and other workmen. Or had Henry really died much earlier? I was also surprised that Bishop Gardiner was designated as the chief celebrant bishop, ostensibly because he was the leading prelate in the Order of the Garter. More pertinently, he was a Romanist in persuasion and would not refuse to celebrate the sacrifice of the mass. Cranmer, Latimer and the other reformist bishops certainly would have refused. On reflection, the Council was playing a subtle game. They had tightly controlled the King, both alive and dead, during that last week of January. Now that he was gone, the breath out of his body, his corpse so swiftly hidden away, Dudley, Wriothesley and the rest seemed eager to draw in others. They deliberately did not appropriate rank and status for themselves in the funeral obsequies, but ceded these to other nobles such as Dorset, Oxford and Shrewsbury.

In the end, the King's coffin lay in state at Westminster Palace chapel for days, draped in gorgeous cloths brilliantly lit by thousands of pounds of sweet-smelling beeswax. Again the Council seemed eager to distract attention from those secret, furtive days at the end of January. No expense was spared. Ceremonies were ornate and rich. The mourners regularly gathered, suitably garbed in the pallet chamber, the bishops in all their pontificals in the sacristy. Requiem prayers were recited. The Dirige and Placebo psalms were sung. Both coffin and hearse were incensed till they were hidden beneath the sacred smoke. The Norroy King of Arms would repeatedly declare, voice ringing through that chapel: 'Of your charity pray for the soul of the High and Most Mighty Prince, our late Sovereign, Lord and King, Henry VIII.' I certainly did. Clustered with the Princess Mary and her small retinue I stood in that magnificent chapel bathed in half-light, clouds of incense drifting, bells clanging ominously, the sparking of flames shimmering in the oak and elm of the hearse and glittering in the costly silver and gold thread of the splendid funeral drapes and tapestries. The solemn requiem masses were sung, followed by votive masses to Our Lady, the celebrants vested in white, then those of the Trinity in the liturgical blue, followed once again by black-garbed priests chanting the continuous requiems.

Outside, in the City, thousands of poor Londoners gathered in Cornhill and Leadenhall to receive the royal alms of a groat each in memory of the King, a prompt to pray for the repose of his soul. This almsgiving lasted for most of the day, whilst the churches in every ward of London observed the funeral rite; this was followed by a similar liturgy in churches throughout the kingdom as couriers galloped along the roads spreading the news. The same messengers also carried orders to clear the highways between Westminster and Windsor of over-hanging boughs, overgrown hedges and anything else that might impede the planned progress of the royal coffin. Bridges were to be checked and repaired. Huge panels, decorated splendidly with the royal arms, were dispatched to scores of parishes along the route, along with sacks of grain to dole out to the parish poor so they would pray for the dead king's soul. God knows, he would need every prayer.

On 14 February, the funeral cortege left Westminster. The coffin was carried on a great gilded chariot, on its top a life-size effigy of the King. At Charing Cross an escort garbed entirely in rich black livery gathered to conduct the coffin out of the City, a majestic column of over a thousand mounted men and a similar number on foot all carrying torches. I, following the Princess Mary, was able to get close to the hearse to pay my respects, the closest I'd been since my imposed exile. Once again I was struck by the lavish preparations. If I had had my doubts about the Council's treatment of the King, I was now cynically convinced that they were determined to honour him in death, or at least publicly so. The effigy was dreamlike. A direct imitation of a king, on its head a black satin night cap over which had been placed the Crown Imperial, with collars of the Order of the Garter around its throat and thighs; gold bracelets, studded with pearls and jewels, circled each wrist. On one side of the King lay his sword, whilst in either hand rested the orb and sceptre of state.

We left Charing Cross, porters armed with heavy staves going before the funeral procession to clear the way. Hundreds of beadsmen garbed in funeral weeds chanted the psalms for the dead. Behind these came the banner men, their gorgeous standards displaying the red dragon of Tudor, the greyhound of Lancaster and the King's own household banner. A mass of people followed these: standard-bearing heralds with grooms leading the King's destrier, caparisoned in flowing cloth of gold, all ringed by the Spears dressed completely in black, halberds resting on their shoulders. Nonetheless, a cold, bitter, nerve-jarring journey. I kept myself cowled and cloaked as we processed across a countryside frozen in the icy grip of a frost so harsh it seemed it would never break.

17 February 1547

I have just reread what I have written. It was a pageant well devised by those cunning cozeners of the Council, I am sure it was. They were eager to divert attention from the secrecy surrounding the King's death with this public display over his burial. It was also a prologue to what was about to be played out at Syon on Thames, where the King's corpse rested on its final journey. We reached the former Bridgettine convent early in the afternoon, passing through lines of London aldermen to the great west door of the church, under its double arch and into the nave. Here the coffin was placed on the prepared gilded hearse. Standards were raised, candles lit, psalms sung and masses celebrated. Darkness fell and the horrors erupted.

The King's coffin was left on its hearse in that convent chapel. I considered the place to be an ironic choice: the King had roughly dispossessed its nuns, whilst his disgraced queen, Katherine Howard, had been imprisoned there after the scandal of her amours became public. Indeed, the King's coffin arrived at Syon on the fifth anniversary of that hapless queen's execution. Such a bloody memory quickened my own sense of deep dread at entering that ghostly place. I was lodged for the night with Princess Mary's household. I could not sleep, but tossed and turned. Eventually I made my way to the church, where the corpse door hung open. Inside, the nave was clothed in the deepest darkness except for a circle of light around the elaborate hearse and the coffin it supported. Countless candles fed this floating pool of glowing light. Other mourners had entered the church to conduct their own private death vigil. None of the lords of the soil; perhaps just the curious who wanted to tell their grandchildren how they had prayed at the midnight hour for the great Henry.

I crouched by a pillar and stared down at the funeral hearse. Once again I was close to my master. I dozed. I pondered memories. I said my prayers. I suppose I was half asleep, so I cannot truly describe what actually happened. I recall pulling my cloak closer around me and wishing I'd brought a blanket. The church was freezing cold despite the braziers crammed with blazing coal that stood around the nave. I moved to be more comfortable on the cushion, my only protection against an icy dampness which seeped through the ancient cracked paving stones. I tugged at the heavy cloak and pulled at my cowl, watching a freezing mist creep under the doors, its tendrils moving like ghostly fingers.

Suddenly I heard a crack, a wrenching from the direction of the glowing candles, followed by a heavy thudding, as if something had slipped and fallen. I half rose. Others, sleeping in their vigil, also stirred. The strange creaking from the candle-ringed hearse continued, then silence. The barriers protecting the coffin were high, providing a broad enclosure around it. As I crept carefully towards them, a most horrid stench caught my nostrils, an odour so foul it made my gorge rise till I began to gag and retch. From the coughing and spluttering echoing around me, others had also noticed this rank, fetid smell. God forgive me. The creeping horror of that nave killed all grief: that monstrous hearse rising up above the glow of candles, the sharp echoing of those strange noises, the foulsome stench of corruption heavy on the draughts that seeped through that ancient place. I stared at the huge dark mass of wood, gold, silver and steel which made up the late King's funeral ornaments. I guessed what had happened. The rotting, bloated corpse had swollen and burst so fiercely it must have wrenched open the lead coffin and the elm wood casket that contained it. I crept closer to the barrier and looked over. The offensive odour was almost impossible to bear. I heard the drip, drip of putrid matter seeping out and glimpsed the filthy puddles which caught the light. I could take no more. I turned, as the others did, and fled.

The following morning, after a fitful sleep in my narrow chamber in the old Bridgettine guest house, I stepped over the sleeping bodies of the two chancery clerks I shared the chamber with. Cloaked and booted, I made my way down across the mist-hung cobbles towards the convent church. A grey, cold morning. The only sound was the raucous cawing of the rooks and ravens that thronged the winter trees, their stark branches stretching like black fingers against the sky. At first I thought everything lay under a pall of silence, only to find the lychgate closely guarded by halberdiers. Through the shifting mist I could see others clustered around every door to the church. The halberdiers were grim and abrupt. No one could enter. I returned to my chamber, unlocked the small coffer I had hidden away and took out some silver. I returned and took up position where I could observe both corpse door and lychgate. The guards were now turning mourners away, telling them that there would be some delay before the funeral procession recommenced, as one of the poles on the hearse had snapped and had to be rectified. Everyone accepted this. I did not.

The morning drew on. The mist lifted. Eventually the corpse door opened and two royal serjeants of the carpentry hurried out. A short while later a local workman, by his smock and leggings, a felt cap pulled over his eyes, also departed. He carried a leather sack in one hand and a basket of tools in the other. I followed him as he left the convent and crossed the trackway. Ahead of him I could glimpse through the bare branches of the trees a tavern sign, the Keys of the Kingdom. By the time I entered the tangy, warm taproom, my quarry was seated on a bench before a roaring fire. It was still rather early; the taproom was fairly empty. I ordered a bowl of hot steaming oatmeal laced with honey and went to sit next to him. He introduced himself as William Consett, plumber. I gave him a false name, gossiped for a while, then put my bowl down. I took out some of my silver coins and placed them on the small trancher across my lap. Consett, red face all blistered by the cold, dark eyes watery, sniffed and gave a wry smile.

'I wondered what you wanted, and it isn't your pots and pans repaired.'

'The coffin in the church,' I replied.

'I was sworn to secrecy.'

I leaned closer and smelt the costly perfume generously daubed on his face, neck and clothes.

'They made you wash your hands and face thoroughly,' I whispered. 'Your gloves and apron were seized and burnt. They sprinkled you with perfume and, of course, you were generously recompensed.' Consett stared unblinkingly at me. 'I was there when it happened during the night,' I continued. 'The wooden casket and lead coffin within burst asunder, didn't they? The stench must have been hideous. You must have masked your nose and mouth with cloths soaked in spices.' I gestured at his blackjack of ale. 'Turned your stomach, didn't it? That's why you are not breaking your fast. The silver is yours. You will not be violating your oath but simply confirming what I suspect. You, my friend, can take the coins and I swear by all that is holy that you will not hear or see me ever again.'

Consett licked his lips, one hand going for the silver; I knocked it away. 'Yes or no?'

'Yes,' he breathed. 'I cannot say whether it was the jogging and shaking of the chariot or,' he glanced over his shoulder, 'the effect of some other cause. Anyway, both lead coffin and casket were ripped open, cut apart, corrupt body fat and putrefied blood seeped out on to the floor beneath. Fortunately the thick black cloths beneath the hearse soaked up this squalid mess. These were pulled away, heaped in barrows and taken out to be buried on the other side of the church. Fresh cloths soaked in all sorts of heavy perfume were brought in.'

'But the corrupt matter must have continued to trickle out?'

'A large tub, the type a washerwoman uses, was placed just beneath where the coffin was cracked. The rupture ran across the top and down one side.' He took a sip of ale. 'It was like working in a cesspit, a slimy mound of human mess. I used heavy cloths and some wood to plug the gap and repair what I could.' He waved his hands. 'Cloths, wood, sacks of sawdust and glue. Once I'd finished, others took over. The crack is now hidden by the heavy funeral drapes. They doused everything in all forms of fragrances, the fabric soaked in crushed herbs; huge pots of smoking incense were also brought in. They will hurry him to his grave now.'

'Who was in charge of this?'

'One lord looks very much like another,' he jibed, 'especially in a darkened church.'

I dug into my purse and brought out two more silver coins and placed these alongside the rest.

'Three in particular,' the fellow gabbled swiftly. 'My lords Wriothesley, Dudley and Paget. There may have been two more.' He shrugged. 'They said very little, at least in my hearing and that of the carpenters. When I had finished, Wriothesley took me up into the sanctuary, forced my hand against the Book of the Gospel and swore me to silence. I am of the old faith, master, and its ancient ways. I am learned in the horn book. Any oath taken under duress has no force either in the sight of God or man.' He moved closer, fingers not far from the pile of silver. 'There is something else,' he whispered. 'I was brought into the church during the early hours. By then, the mourners had been dismissed. They opened all the doors because of the great stink. Now the convent used to house a pack of lurchers; they still haunt their former kennels, more wild than tame. Anyway,' he picked up one of the coins, 'three of these lurchers crept into the church and managed to skulk beneath the hearse. They were lapping up the putrid mess. It took some time to drive them away.' My stomach protested at the gruesome story; no wonder Consett was not eating. I rose swiftly, trying to curb the urge to vomit. I gestured at the silver and hurried to the door leading to the privy.

When I returned, both Consett and the silver were gone.

God be my witness, I was shocked at what he had told me, as well as haunted by a sinister memory. Over a decade earlier, King Henry and his new wife Anne Boleyn had been staying at Greenwich, where the Franciscans had a house. One of these, Father Peto – now Cardinal Peto after he fled the kingdom to escape Henry's wrath – in a sermon before His Majesty compared him to Ahab the wicked king of Israel. Peto had warned Henry to his face how if he did not take greater care, he, like Ahab, would meet a macabre end and the dogs would come to lap his blood. A true prophecy? Had the King's coffin been deliberately damaged to give Peto's prediction a helping hand? Yet I'd been there in that gloomy nave when the corpse had burst asunder. Nobody had approached it. What was the true cause? Particularly if Henry's corpse had been so properly embalmed, crammed with the costliest spices by the most skilled in the kingdom?

I returned to the Bridgettine convent, seeking to speak privately to Princess Mary. We met in what used to be the prioress's cell, a cavernous, shadow-filled chamber with a writhing white Christ nailed to a cross against the wall. The princess, dressed completely in black except for frothy lace at her neck and cuffs, seemed distant. Her long, narrow face was unpainted, her red hair clasped tight to her head under a black veil; Ave beads, her mother's, curled around her fingers. She sat

on a box chair with me on a stool before her like priest
and penitent at the mercy pew. I told her what I'd seen,
heard, witnessed and felt. She dragged thin fingers down
her face and muttered in Spanish, blinking swiftly to
hide her tears.

'I remember Peto's curse,' she confessed. 'Many would
say it has come to pass. But what caused it, Will? What
did happen in my father's secret chambers?' She beat
her fists against her knees.

'They cannot have properly embalmed him,' I replied.
'Your father, according to the official record, died fifteen
days ago. Thousands of pounds were spent purchasing
a mass of spices, embalming fluids, herbs and other
materials. The most skilled practitioners worked on his
corpse. His Majesty was a man of massive proportions.
If his corpse had not been prepared properly, then it
would bloat, swell and burst, surely, the strength of the
rupture so great it would shatter both wood and lead.
And yet, as I have said, the body was supposedly
embalmed.'

'Or so we think.'

'I agree. Did they really honour his corpse, or was
your father's cadaver thrust into its lead shell and
wooden casing unprepared and swollen? Your Grace, you
did not view the corpse. I cannot discover anyone who
actually did. In short, I do not think the circumstances
of your father's death are as the official proclamation
described them.' I then confessed my doubts about
Thomas Seymour being sworn to the Council, whilst

the story about Cranmer's intervention well past the eleventh hour also seemed highly suspect.

'This present pandering,' I concluded, 'this charade is to satisfy the public whim. The churching, the prattling of requiem psalms, the masses are a liturgical sham. Where is the black marble sarcophagus your father wished to be interred in? Oh, banners fly, heralds chant, priests pray, but Your Grace, the King's death is proclaimed on a Monday, then, unseen by anyone, his corpse is coffined away by Wednesday. Now of course the Council can take its time. What the eye doesn't see, the heart can't wonder about. What happened last night must have agitated those who know the truth.'

'I agree,' Mary replied. 'Gardiner has told me how the Council have enriched themselves; my father's will virtually bribes everyone. There are gifts and grants to me and the Princess Elizabeth. Queen Katherine Parr may not be regent but she is well endowed and, if rumour be correct, already playing cat's cradle with Thomas Seymour. Oh yes,' she smiled at my surprise, 'have you noticed how the Queen both at Greenwich and on this funeral march has kept very close, deep in the shadows? That is the best way to meet her lover. There's more. According to Paget, the King promised generous grants to others on the Council, lordships of certain manors, estates, rents and revenues. Not only that, all the doctors and apothecaries, commoners like the doorkeeper Roberts, are also to be well rewarded.'

'Except me!' I declared.

'Yes, but they know that you live by the truth, whilst they are practising a great lie.'

'How are they justifying this?' I asked.

'Gardiner tells me all. Old Norfolk is not to be executed; they will leave him to the mercies of the Tower. However, to answer your question, Paget maintains that all these generous grants were recorded in a small black book which the King kept in the pocket of his gown. Of course this book can't be found, but Paget can recall every detail. Seymour is to be made Duke of Somerset, Dudley Earl of Warwick, Wriothesley Earl of Southampton. The Council was to be the protectorate, but according to Gardiner, some of them are already calling Seymour the Lord Great Master; he is set to become regent or protector. The rest of the Council and others will be bribed, more grants lavishly issued under the dry stamp.' Mary rubbed her face. 'The elder Seymour will be king in all but name. Of course that will not go unchecked. The other wolves, Wriothesley in particular, are already beginning to howl in protest.'

'Your Grace, they may have used the dry stamp without your father's knowledge, or even had a second one fashioned unbeknown to him.'

'It does not matter now, Will. Gardiner is correct. Power, money, honours, titles, Crown lands, offices and benefices pour like a waterfall over the Council.' She waved a hand. 'You are right: this farce of a funeral is very clever. The great lords hide in the background. The disgraced Gardiner leads the services, which are Catholic in both form and substance. Cranmer cannot be seen. The likes of Dorset lead the mourners. I want to know what is behind this charade. My father, his death? The dead are dead,' she added wearily. She bent closer; the redness in her cheeks had gone. I could see the dark shadows beneath her eyes; even the gorgeous hair beneath its beautiful bejewelled cap seemed to have faded. 'What they did to my father haunts my every waking moment and troubles my sleep. Did they abuse him? Yet behind that lurks another horror. If they could do that to the great Henry, what about me? Catherine of Aragon's Spanish brat, cast off by her father, once declared illegitimate? Am I to be forced into a loveless marriage to some German princeling in the frozen wastes of Prussia? Will I disappear into the Tower, suffer a fatal accident or rise from a banquet vomiting black bile?'

'Your Grace, Your Grace.' I tried to calm her, but Mary was locked into her mood of desperate imaginings.

'Do you think Dudley, Seymour or Cranmer will let me succeed? Cranmer, who dissolved my mother's marriage and pronounced me illegitimate? Dudley and Seymour, who favour the teachings of Geneva and Zurich? Edward my brother is frail; he may well die without an heir. I don't think they will turn to Catholic Spanish Mary or even my half-sister Elizabeth; Seymour would never accept her, nor she him. His sister caused the downfall of Elizabeth's mother.' Mary wrapped the Ave beads more tightly around her fingers and stroked her nose, a common mannerism whenever she becomes highly agitated. 'We have to be careful, Will, prudent. Tell no one else about what you know.' She rose to her feet. 'Let us finish this charade, this hypocrisy, and await our time.'

I took an oath that day to be careful and prudent. I will be most strict in its observance. The sham funeral with all its mock mourning continued. On Monday 15 February, the cortege left for Windsor to be greeted by a dozen white-coated knights as well as scholars from Our Lady's College at Eton. The coffin moved through the town in a sanctified atmosphere, prayers, psalms, chants, hymns and gusts of incense. In the Chapel of St George, the coffin was placed on its three-storey hearse all draped in black and gold. Masses continued to be offered in the nearby chantry chapels, culminating in a solemn requiem presided over by Bishop Gardiner. The climax of this was when the King's Serjeant of Arms, Chiddick Paul, rode in full armour, except for his helmet, into the choir and placed the King's pole-axe, point down, on the altar, where it lay on richly embroidered cloths. The mass continued. After the Gospel, Gardiner delivered a homily on the frailty of man and how the King's death was a most dolorous and heart-wounding loss. I was standing amongst the Princess Mary's ladies in the choir loft and could hardly keep a straight face at the sheer hypocrisy of being told I should thank the Almighty for having bestowed upon us 'such a Virtuous Prince'.

This Virtuous Prince, this much-trumpeted Mirror of Justice was finally laid to rest. The elaborate effigy was moved to the sacristy. Gardiner and his bishops chanted the verse 'The snares of death have surrounded me' as they left the altar. The chapel vault was opened to reveal Queen Jane Seymour's coffin. Fifteen strong Yeomen of the Guard in parties of three used coiled linen ropes to lower Henry's massive coffin down into the darkness. The bishops scattered the dust of Ash Wednesday as they loudly recited the ominous verse 'Remember man that thou art dust, and unto dust thou shalt return'. God be my witness, if there was one verse Henry didn't remember, let alone reflect on, that was it. Members of the King's privy chamber, led by Paget, then broke their white staves of office above their heads and hurled the shards into the vault. I watched Paget and Gates. Oh, they played the part, their faces heavy with sorrow, loud sighs, mumbled words of grief as the tears rolled down their cheeks. To be honest, I suspect these were more due to genuine relief than any mourning. The vault was then covered with planks. The business was finished. There would be no black marble sarcophagus, no elaborate monument or finely carved statue fashioned by the finest craftsmen out of Italy; nothing at all!

The Garter King of Arms, surrounded by all the other heralds, proclaimed the accession of Prince Edward, but already the grooms of the King's chamber were grabbing at the costly funeral cloths of precious material woven with silver and gold and studded with miniature diamonds. They would later share these out. Even as the trumpets blared gloriously for Prince Edward, Dudley was crossing the chapel to claim the great ceremonial chair draped in purple velvet and silk with its three blue cushions of precious taffeta. Others, hungry for food and drink, were bustling towards the door and the gallery leading down to the castle refectory. Here the lords of the Council gorged themselves on the finest wines and delicious food. I watched them stuff their maws, then, bellies full and warm, they collected their cloaks, went down to the bailey, swung themselves up into the saddles of the finest horses from Henry's stables and thundered swiftly back along the road to London.

Later that day, with the falling snow freezing hard and a grey dusk moving swiftly in over Windsor, I left my narrow chamber in one of the garden towers and made my way back to St George's Chapel. All was in disarray. Chairs and stools lay overturned, scraps of parchment littered the floor. The King's once magnificent effigy rested face down in the sacristy. I turned it over. This effigy was a goodly image, similar to the late king in all aspects, but now it looked battered. The black silk cap, gold crown and precious garters around throat and thigh had been torn away along with anything else of value. Someone, as a grim joke, had gouged out the eyes in the waxen mask and inserted two small roundels of charcoal, pulling down the lips on either side so it looked more like the face of a hell hound than anything else.

The candles were guttering out, though there were so many, the light was still strong. I crossed to the burial vault, moved the planks, took the workmen's ladder from the sacristy and thrust it down into that burial pit. Then I grabbed a sconce torch and carefully descended into the icy blackness. The vault is about eight feet wide and the same deep. I reached the bottom and stood holding up the torch, its glow glittering on the purple pall of the coffin. I rolled this back. Even as I did, I caught traces of that same filthy stench I had smelt at Syon. I lifted the torch. The top of the casket had been roughly and swiftly repaired. I touched the extra pieces of wood inserted in the crack and felt the bulge along the top of the coffin, proof enough that both the corpse and its lead sheath within had swollen, then erupted. I took my hand away and carefully sniffed at where the repairs had been effected. The stench was strong but so was that of the aromatics hastily packed into every crevice. I pulled back the pall, positioning it correctly, then closed my eyes and crossed myself. I had come to pay my last respects. I opened my eyes and stared at the coffin. Here lay a king, a monster I had known and served for over twenty years. All his passions, his lusts, his loves, his hates, his dreams of empire had ended here in this lonely, dark, freezing vault.

'Sic transit gloria mundi' – 'Thus passes all the glory of the world' – and 'Remember man that thou art dust, and unto dust thou shalt return'. Henry, the fearsome, ferocious, fickle lion, lies dead and buried, his plotting brought to a sudden end, his death sprung like a trap. I suppose I was obsessed with him as you would be with a half-remembered fear-drenched nightmare. He, in turn, was obsessed with himself and his kingdom to the point that Henry became England and England Henry. Now he is gone, what shall I do? Hide, probably; hide well away from the wolf pack. My days of courtly dalliance are over. Henry is gone and he will never return.

'I am sorry.' I spoke out loud. 'Your Majesty, I am so sorry that I could not make a proper farewell.' I thought of his councillors, bellies full, bodies warmed, galloping back to London to celebrate their new-found wealth, power, status and titles. 'God rest you. God bless you,' I whispered. 'God assoil you, Henry of England.' Then I crossed myself and climbed the ladder, pulling it up after me.

I returned to this chamber, warming my fingers over a chafing dish, reflecting on what had happened and wondering what the future held. Henry is dead. I promised to keep a journal. Now that he is gone, there is no need to continue, not unless I learn the truth. I shall end it here, 17 February, the Year of Our Lord 1547, at Windsor Castle.

29 September 1553

Queen Mary is crowned! England's rightful monarch is triumphant! The plotting of vipers and the cunning of other serpents has been brought to nothing. On 27 September, the day before her coronation, my beloved Queen Mary rode through the City of London to Westminster, sitting in a chariot of cloth-of-gold tissue, drawn by six horses caparisoned with the same. She was attired in a gown of purple velvet, furred with powdered ermine. On her head a caul of cloth tinsel set with pearls and stones, above this a round circlet of gold, so richly studded with precious stones that its value is inestimable. So ponderous were both caul and circlet that the Queen was obliged to bear up her head with her hand. Over the chariot was a canopy of state borne by yeomen dressed in red and gold . . .

Today, Michaelmas, the day following Queen Mary's coronation, I, Will Somers, dressed in my favourite brown and green cloak fringed with squirrel fur, my hair shorn, my face shaved and oiled, a new pair of Cordovan boots on my feet, a gift from the Queen, sauntered into the Pegasus of France, a spacious red-walled, black-tiled tavern close to the ruins of St Mary Grace's Abbey, a mere arrow shot from the harsh fastness of the Tower. Her Majesty had sent me there with all the warrants I would need to meet that shadow from her household, Master Balaam, fresh out of Flanders, Venice, Madrid, or wherever that flitting shade has travelled on Her Majesty's business. Fortune's wheel has surely turned, spinning violently to set the world upside down. The Seymours, Sir John Gates, Dudley, Denny and others are gone, as is their master, poor Edward the boy king. Bishop Hooper once remarked how the young monarch might become the terror and the wonder of the world, if he lived. He did not. Earlier this year, around midsummer, Edward, already wasting away, his ulcerated body mere skin and bone, lapsed into paralysis and unconsciousness. When he awoke, he coughed black sputum, which exuded the most offensive and putrid smell, and both his hair and nails dropped out. So desperate became the physicians that they foolishly allowed a so-called wise woman to give Edward potions, but these only made his shrunken body puff out and so choked off his vital parts. The poor young man, God rest him, died in agony on 6 July last. John Dudley, Viscount Lisle, who styled himself Earl of Warwick before elevating himself to be Duke of

Northumberland, realised that Edward's death would mean his ruin. Dudley tried to change Henry's will by publishing a so-called 'Device for the Succession', inserting that Edward's legitimate successor should be Henry's niece and Dudley's own daughter-in-law the Lady Jane Grey, and her heirs. A period of turbulence and thunder followed. Soldiers marching the roads, warships gathering off the Thames, castles fortified, the drums of war loudly beating.

In the end no one accepted either Dudley, or the Lady Jane Grey as Queen. I was with the Princess Mary when her brother died. She retreated to Framlingham in Norfolk, where she raised her standard, declaring herself to be true queen, the daughter of King Henry and, by his will and the law of Parliament, the legitimate successor to her brother's crown. The kingdom responded. Ships at Yarmouth declared for Mary. Troops raised in the shires hailed her name. The Council locked in the Tower broke out of Dudley's prison and proclaimed the same. London rose in rebellion, tearing down the usurpers' standards and great cloths of state. Dudley himself advanced to Cambridge, where he acknowledged his failure. Already his allies on the Council had deserted him, riding into Mary's camp to submit on their knees, their own daggers turned towards them. I truly enjoyed that. Paget was one of them!

Now the victorious queen had sent me secretly to this tavern where I was to await Balaam. In truth, I was highly nervous. Since the death of Henry, my beloved Jane and I had sheltered, or more correctly hidden, in the Princess Mary's household, well away from the swirling fog of London and the deadly miasma of the court, moving to Beaulieu and other lonely manors close to the Essex coast. The black water of Maldon, the stony beaches of Walton and the windswept Orwell estuary became as familiar to me as the frenetic busyness of Cheapside and Poultry. Of course we had news and heard the gossip and chatter, yet they were hard, difficult years as Princess Mary fought a lonely battle to maintain her faith, her independence and her rights. Balaam had virtually disappeared. In London he could move easily amongst a shoal of people; he could act the part and stride the boards. But in those lonely Essex manors, every going and coming was brought under the most careful scrutiny of the Council's Judas men.

Balaam, I understood from Princess Mary, became very busy in foreign parts. He played a leading role in the preparations to spirit the princess abroad after she had defied the Council on matters of religion. Dudley and the rest regarded her 'as a runnel whereby the rats of Rome could re-enter the kingdom'. They mocked the bowing and genuflecting of her priests as the gesturing of apes and ridiculed the Sacrament as 'Round Robin' or 'Jack-in-the-box', whilst her chaplains were insultingly dismissed as 'the whores of ancient Babylon'. Mary's agents, couriers and spies like Balaam fared no better, being described as 'the Misty Angels of Satan'.

Rewards were posted on their heads, especially after Corneille Scheperus and eight imperial warships hovered close off the Essex coast ready to take Mary off should she decide to flee. Instead she stood her ground, despite the bullying of the Council, who had the impudence to claim that she was subject to their will and should not attend mass. The princess roundly replied that she was subject to their will only in the matter of her marriage, and if they were right in their remembrance of her father's will as she was, they should have two masses celebrated every day for the repose of the late king's soul. Princess Mary has spent these last six years hurling stones against the wind, yet she has remained constant. Now, miraculously, in three months, her fortunes, all our fortunes have changed. I suspect the man with the far-seeing gaze has played his part in this.

I entered the red-walled garden of the tavern, a sheer square of sweet-smelling beauty. Late September is best enjoyed amongst the flowers as they come to full blossom. I love this season of the year, when you can catch the shift, the bridge between summer and the delicate onset of autumn. I certainly did in that garden, with its aromatic herb plots, brilliant flower beds and small orchard of perfumed apple trees, the fragrance of their full fruit ripening the air with its sweetness. I would have liked my beloved Jane by my side, but ever since that hideous business with Wriothesley in Newgate, the Lady Jane had begged me not to include her in what she calls my 'secret affairs'. She was now happily closeted with the mistress she adores and loves, revelling in her new-found status. The six years and more since Henry's death have been oppressive, so walking into that garden, sure and certain of the full support of the Crown, was like being liberated from a noisy, foulsome prison. I also nourished a ravenous curiosity. I suspected I was there to bring certain matters to a close, particularly the mystery surrounding Henry's death.

Balaam had not arrived, so I hired a small enclave in the garden, secret and private, a three-sided arbour, its trellis fencing covered by the most fragrant-smelling roses. A very comfortable place with stout wooden chairs, their arms, backs and seats cushioned by thick flock pushed into dark blue felt, the table heavy and well polished. Mine host the tavern master brought snow-white napery, gleaming tranchers and pewter goblets for 'the purest water' from the nearby abbey well, together with a jug of the finest Rhenish. I sat cradling my cup, lost in my own thoughts, until a shadow blocked out the sun. Balaam stood in the entrance, dressed like a fighting man in a cream-coloured shirt, a leather sleeveless jerkin and light green hose pushed into the most elegant riding boots. He unstrapped his heavy war belt with its basket-hilt sword and iron-coiled dagger, winked at me and placed these carefully on the ground. He beckoned me to stand. We embraced and exchanged the kiss of peace, then he pushed me gently away, studying me from head to toe.

'You look a little older, Will, though the years have not broken you.'

I stared back. Balaam was darker-skinned, his hair neatly cut like that of a soldier, his cunning, sallow face clean-shaven, oiled and perfumed. He still had that lazy, cynical glance, as if he knew the world for what it was and did not trust it. Oh I have glimpsed him over the years, but until that moment in the garden he was just a shadow scurrying amongst other shadows as the Princess Mary eked out her dangerous existence. But as I have written, the object of this journal is to bring matters to a close; that is why I have returned to it. The full reckoning had yet to be known about my master's death. Deep in my heart I suspected that was why we were there.

For a while Balaam and I just sat and shared the wine, reminiscing and recalling. Balaam had been every-where, even hinting that he had visited the New World. He was certainly full of stories, so extraordinary I wondered if he was telling tales like any moon man; all the time he studied me sharply, leaning over to grasp my hand or staring at me over the rim of his cup. At last he fell silent, tapping his thigh with his fingers as if listening to music I could not hear. He shifted in his seat, then turned back.

'Will, towards the end you did not trust me.' He jabbed a finger. 'You still don't.'

'For whom did you really work?'

'You will see soon enough.' The thin smile disappeared.

'First, though, I kept my promise. The dog is long dead, his soul thrust down to Hell.'

'Which dog?' I mocked.

'Wriothesley.'

'He died peacefully at his house at Ely Place, Holborn.'

'Oh yes, Baron Wriothesley, freshly created Earl of Southampton after his master's death, mad as a March hare and malicious as a demon.'

'He was disgraced,' I replied.

'True, on some trumped-up charge that could be levelled at any Lord Chancellor: misuse of the office of the Great Seal. He was placed under house arrest.' Balaam put his cup down and leaned closer. 'I visited him late one summer afternoon. I slipped like the vengeance I was into that deserted house, the scene of his former glory. The very hall where he and the other self-devouring monsters trapped and baited the hapless Surrey.' He ran a finger along the rim of his goblet. 'Wriothesley was disgraced, finished. No one truly trusted him.' He waved his hand. 'He hopped like a flea on a hot skillet, this way, that way. He was also prone to lunacy, though when clear-witted was dangerous enough. I am sure you will hear more of that soon.'

'What do you mean?'

'In a while, my friend, but back to Wriothesley. I had not forgotten how he terrified you and the Lady Jane, one of the main reasons for my visit. I pretended to be from the Council. Wriothesley, unshaven, half drunk, blubbering like a babe, welcomed me himself; his servants had long fled, taking whatever they could. Eventually he brought me into that hall; indeed I asked him to. Chattering like a friendly sparrow, I sat where Surrey had sat. I poured the wine. I toasted him to the rafters. I extolled his great work, his endless labours for the Crown. How he had not been truly appreciated, but future glory certainly beckoned. Oh, how he revelled in that! A dismal place, Will. Unpolished and ill-swept, the dust mites dancing like a host of demons in the streaks of sunlight. A summer's day, but that hall was gloomy. I wondered if the ghosts of Wriothesley's victims were beginning to gather. Of course, he just wallowed like a pig in its sty. Sottish with drink, he confessed how his sleep and waking hours were plagued by sweat-drenched nightmares. I cheered him up and told him not be frightened of shadows.'

Balaam fell silent. I closed my eyes. I recalled that long, sombre hall at Ely Place. Yes, it would be thronged by ghosts, especially Surrey's.

'Will!' I opened my eyes. 'I was there for vengeance, for you, for the Lady Jane and for Surrey, but I also came on behalf of the Princess Mary. Now that did startle him. He became sharper-witted; the old cunning returned. He challenged me about being an emissary of the Council. How could I come from both them and the Princess Mary? I told him I wanted to know the truth about the last of days. What really did happen in the old king's death chamber? He refused to reply and became very agitated. He mumbled something

313

about how dangerous it was. He turned in his chair, staring at me out of the corner of his eye. He asked if I had not heard about Sir Anthony Denny, Chief Gentleman of the Privy Chamber; you remember Denny?'

'Of course.'

'Denny was well rewarded after Henry's death, then disappeared from public office and died suddenly at his house. Anyway, Wriothesley was now suspicious. I pressed him hard about King Henry's death, what really happened? Wriothesley began to rant. He sprang to his feet, walking up and down that hall dressed in his long dirty robe. You know the way he was, fingers jabbing, chin jutting, those milky blue eyes frenetic with an unreasoned excitement. He turned on me. He called me a spy, an intruder, how he would go to the Council. I realised I would get no further sense from him so I refilled his goblet and left.'

'And?'

Balaam half smiled and leaned closer. 'You remember my days as a physician fresh out of Salamanca?' He laughed softly. 'Or wherever else it was. Well, I slipped a potion into that last goblet. A few days later Wriothesley was dead, his soul gone to God. No one will miss him.' Balaam paused. 'Wriothesley was quite frenetic. I have studied his history. This behaviour, moonstruck, lunatic, apparently began after the King's death. Oh,' he waved a hand, 'Wriothesley was always vicious, nasty as a viper, but something truly turned his wits.'

'And you killed him?'

'Executed him, Will. I executed a murderer, a torturer, an evil soul. Do you remember Anne Askew?'

I nodded.

'Beautiful woman, fair and graceful. I met her. I was much smitten with Anne. Wriothesley dispatched her to torture and condemned her to a more horrific death than his own, burnt to a blackened stump at Smithfield. If given a chance, if the opportunity ever arose, he would have done the same to you and the Lady Jane. Ah well.' Balaam turned, gazing up to catch the warmth and light of the sun. 'They have all gone into the dark, despite their bustling and busyness. Queen Katherine Parr? Henry died in January; the two turtle doves, Katherine and Thomas Seymour, were already clinging together. Henry suspected that. If he had lived any longer, Katherine would have followed her namesake to the scaffold and Seymour would have joined her. Henry was scarcely in his grave and Seymour was tripping along the midnight paths to Chelsea Place to pay court to the royal widow.'

'Mad as a pot of frogs,' I murmured.

'And just as bad,' Balaam added. 'What did one of his companions say about Seymour? "Fierce in courage, courtly in fashion, in personage stately, in arms magnificent but somehow empty in soul." He and Queen Katherine played a very dangerous game. They were meeting before Henry's death. They certainly did afterwards; betrothed by May, married in June. Then the

Lady Katherine was pregnant within a year of Henry's death. Great passion,' he breathed.

'The other councillors, Seymour's elder brother and Dudley, must have known.'

'Oh yes, they frowned on the marriage. The Council refused to hand back the jewels and property Katherine acquired as queen. The younger Seymour was like an untrained stallion; his new wife was given custody of the Princess Elizabeth but she had to send that young woman away when Seymour began to interfere with the young princess's clothing as well as appearing in her bedchamber at the most unseemly hour. Seymour secretly entertained hopes of marrying either Elizabeth or Mary.'

'I heard rumours about his plots, all brought to nothing.'

'In September five years ago, twenty months after the death of her royal husband, Katherine Parr gave birth to a baby girl and died shortly afterwards. Thomas Seymour became unhinged. Sent to fight pirates in the Bristol Channel, he entered into secret negotiations with them. He then tried to defraud the mint at Bristol and crowned all his foolishness by invading the young king's bedchamber during the dead of night and shooting one of the royal spaniels.' Balaam sipped at his goblet, 'Even his own brother could not save him from the headsman's axe. Bishop Latimer, whom Thomas Seymour asked to deliver his funeral sermon, openly declared that it was clearly evident that God had forsaken

Seymour; indeed, whether he be saved or not was a matter only God could decide. Seymour was certainly a wicked man and the kingdom was well rid of him. According to Latimer, Seymour died irksomely, dangerously and horribly.' Balaam wafted away a fly. 'As for the rest, you must have learnt what happened. The elder Seymour, who made himself Duke of Somerset and Lord Protector, failed in Scotland and stirred up rebellion in England. He was removed from power but was then executed for plotting to poison the entire Council in a banquet to be held at his London house.'

'And now Dudley has gone? What a death! He and his henchman Gates arguing in the death cart on the way to the scaffold!'

'Oh yes. When Dudley reached Cambridge and realised all was lost, Gates tried to change sides and arrest his master when he had his boots half on. In the end, both went to the axe—'

'I was there,' I interrupted. 'The Queen asked me to be her witness. Dudley was executed by a lame swordsman dressed in a white butcher's apron. He died renouncing all the reformist doctrine. He reverted to the old faith. When asked why, he replied that he'd thought best of the old religion but, seeing a new one begin, run dog, run devil, he would pursue it.' I paused. 'How fortune changes. Old Norfolk, freed from the Tower by Queen Mary, presided at Dudley's trial and execution. He enjoyed it. He wanted Dudley's beating heart plucked from his body and flung against his face.

But in the end, Balaam, why all this now? The wolf pack, that horde of mad, wild predators, turned on each other and tore themselves to pieces.'

'True, true,' Balaam soothed. 'And I ask myself would such men deliberately kill a king?' He studied my surprise. 'Oh yes, Will!' His words seemed to hang in that warm, scented air. 'That is why you and I are here. What did happen in that frost-besieged, cold, shadowy palace vibrant with all forms of devilish passions? We are queen's men, Will. We now hold the power, and God be my witness, Queen Mary wants to know the true fate of her father.'

'And how will we discover that in a rose-covered tavern arbour? Do you already know, Balaam? Did your patron on the Council tell you?'

Balaam got to his feet. 'One thing I did not learn was that, which is why we are here. We are going to the Tower, where someone will meet us.' He leaned down. 'Remember this, Will: do not act surprised if I ask you one question.'

'Which is?'

'You will tell a lie. Maintain you heard Dudley's confession after he had been shriven by the Bishop of Worcester on the scaffold. After all, you were there as a Crown witness. Yes?'

I shrugged. 'It doesn't make sense.'

'Don't worry, it shall. I cannot answer every one of your questions, but in justice, you deserve to know what I do.'

'Including Martin, the Spanish servant of the late Earl of Surrey?'

Balaam pulled a face. 'Including him. Come.'

We left that scented garden and went down an alleyway into Petty Wales, that close, narrow place around the Tower. The needle-thin alleyways were thronged with all the low life who prowl there: beggars, coney-catchers, apple squires, sewer squires, penny traders and touting tinkers, a shifting sea of red, brown, green and black. A surging shoal of common folk who pushed and shoved their way past sumpter ponies and purveyance carts, fighting their way under the shabby gable-ended houses that leaned over to black out the brilliant sun in a deep blue sky. Signs creaked danger-ously and noisily just above our heads. We breathed a heavy fog of different scents, odours and smells, which ebbed and flowed, be it the steaming, fly-infested midden heaps or the acrid smoke billowing out like the thickest mist from the many cook shops which pander to the poor, selling cat meat as venison and the offal from Newgate shambles as the sweetest stews. Mountebanks jostled with moon people in all their garish finery and cheap glittering rings and collars. An ape, trained to juggle, performed on top of a barrel, watched by no one except a tamer and his pet bear, a black, scruffy-furred animal with sad eyes and tightly tied muzzle. I also sensed the frenetic excitement, a legacy of the stir-ring times following Queen Mary's entrance into the City, the execution of her opponents and all the glory of her crowning at Westminster. A feeling of relief that the crisis had passed. People no longer felt that they had to draw their horns in. They could now give vent to their feelings, throwing their caps higher than the stars and rejoicing that the kingdom was at peace under its legitimate ruler.

I walked silently beside Balaam, feeding off the City's sights and sounds. Such a stark contrast to where I had lurked for the last five years, those lonely, gloomy manor houses of Essex. We approached the Tower. Our warrants gave us safe and smooth passage through the Lion Gate and all the other sally ports and entrances. The fortress was well garrisoned: troops from Norfolk, squadrons of Spanish musketeers and a host of royal archers. No one bothered us as we slipped along those narrow gulleys under grey, forbidding walls. The soft breeze carried a pervasive stench from the menagerie pens where the tawny-coated lions and the other great cats prowled, growled and snarled, a heart-chilling din on such a beautiful day. We reached the great water gate leading to the river, the docking place for the sealed death barges that brought the victims of Henry's rage to be imprisoned in the Tower. Few of those ever escaped, led up the great steps to where we now stood. I glanced at the narrow barred windows then down into the moat; the river was ebbing and the black, oozing mud reeked of the dead fish lying in its stinking mess.

'Surrey's prison,' I murmured. 'St Thomas's Tower.' I

pointed down at the mud. 'That's where he hoped to make his escape.'

Balaam did not reply. He had a quiet word with the guards, then led me up the steps into Surrey's chamber, a cavernous, bleak room, its plaster-white walls turning a dullish grey, the fire in the narrow hearth long extinguished and crammed with crumbling ash. Windows on either wall provided a view over the river or the Tower. A crucifix was nailed to the wall, although the figure of Christ had been ripped off. There were sticks of battered furniture: chairs, stools, tables and a narrow rope-bound cot bed. The chamber smelt musty and stale, though I noticed the gleaming flagon and goblets on the small table beneath the crucifix covered with snow-white napkins. I walked over to the retiring room which housed the garderobe, opened the creaking door and stepped inside. The room was black and shabby, the latrine primitive, a stony chute that cut down through the wall. The seat over the hole had been removed, the gap left broad enough for a man to climb in, dropping down into the muddy moat once the river had ebbed. I turned and stared back at the door to the chamber. On the night Surrey tried to escape, the guards must have returned, unlocked that door, noticed their prisoner was missing and immediately hurried across to this garderobe.

'Martin the Spaniard?' I demanded. 'That was you, Balaam?'

'Yes, I was Martin. I drifted into the Tower, posing

as one of the many Spanish mercenaries serving in London. Gates gave the impression that he didn't care one way or the other, nor did Stonor, the lieutenant. Nobody, as we know, wanted to be associated with Surrey, who had fallen never to rise again. I liked him, Will, I really did. And he favoured me. Of course he thought about escape.' Balaam pointed to the garderobe. 'That was the only way. He asked me to carry messages to his younger brother Thomas, to assemble men and supplies for him. I persuaded him not to.'

'What!'

'Think, Will. How far would Surrey have run? Who would have helped him? Oh no.' Balaam sat down on a stool. 'I had been indentured so easily into his service. I grew deeply suspicious. Gates had only acted as if he didn't care; I noticed that. When I left the Tower, I was followed. One night I hired a barge and we passed as close as we could to Traitors' Gate, as they now call it. I observed armed men in boats nearby, groups of the same on the quayside down to St Katherine's Dock. Remember, Will, Surrey was first imprisoned in Wriothesley's house in Ely Place, Holborn. Wriothesley brought him here to this prison chamber. He wanted Surrey to escape, he was hungry for it.'

'Why?'

'To draw in any other Howards, as nearly happened with young Thomas—'

'And more than that,' I interrupted, 'Henry Howard, Earl of Surrey, would have been killed trying to escape.

The mad, hot-tempered warrior nobleman. Everybody knew what he was like: his rash temper, his impetuous conduct while besieging Boulogne.'

'True. The accusations against him were feather-light.' Balaam tapped his booted foot against the ground. 'If Surrey was killed whilst escaping, there would be no need for a trial. He was intent on escape. I gave him a knife as a token of my support. However, I warned him that it was precisely what his enemies, especially Wriothesley, wanted. He would be killed, and if any of his family were implicated, they too would suffer.' He paused. 'Surrey, locked in composing his sonnets, finally agreed. He thought it would be better to establish his innocence at a trial and protect what was left of his family. He also conceded that his enemies would depict any attempt at escape as proof of his guilt. On the night in question, when in truth there was no one ready to assist him, he hid in the garderobe, the knife I had given him thrust into his belt.' Balaam spread his hands. 'He just waited until the guards returned. They found him hiding there, and that became the alleged escape – which is why so little was made of it at his trial.'

'But someone else must have informed you about what Wriothesley plotted, someone on the Council?'

Balaam held up a hand; he was staring over my shoulder.

'Of course, Will. It was me.'

I whirled around. A figure had followed us up the steps and stood in the doorway. He came into the chamber slightly lame, resting on a gold-topped cane which tapped the floor. The stranger pulled back the hood of his silver-edged deep blue cloak. I stared into the face of that arch-schemer Sir William Paget, once Chief Secretary of the Council. He had certainly aged, the silver quite plentiful in his once reddish hair, moustache and beard; his smooth pale face was creased, those clever eyes looked tired.

'Put not your trust in princes,' I whispered. 'And I said in my excess all men are liars . . .'

'We are all liars, Will. God knows we have to be.' Paget laughed abruptly. 'Those who live by the truth rarely survive long. Yet we pay the price for our lies. The years have not treated me gently.' He hobbled over, patted me on the arm, then crossed to sit on the chamber's one and only high-backed chair. I glanced accusingly at Balaam.

'Were you a Judas man?' I asked.

'Tell him!' Balaam snapped.

Paget rested both hands on his walking cane and beckoned me to a stool. I sat down.

'Will, I do not dream dreams of power like Dudley or the Seymours. I do not imagine, deep in my cups, that I might wear the Crown Imperial. No, I am the Crown's good servant.' He grimaced. 'Or at least I thought I was. You know the story of Henry's council. We turned on each other as soon as the one great fear that bound us all together disappeared for ever: King Henry of not so blessed memory. Whilst he lived, we were united not so much in purpose as in terror, like sheep who cluster together when the wolf approaches.'

'Some sheep!' I taunted. 'More wolves in sheep's clothing yourselves.'

'I agree. But we were nothing compared to Henry.' Paget pointed at me. 'I served him, Will, because I serve the Crown. Balaam is proof of that. I was determined to maintain close ties with the Princess Mary. Balaam was my man as well as hers. Mary is the Crown, the rightful heir after Edward; Romanist or not, she is our legitimate ruler. Balaam was our link. I could not tell him everything. I had to be careful. If Mary really knew all that was plotted, she might betray herself and eventually us. The likes of Wriothesley and Gates would have strangled me. Fluent in Spanish, Balaam was given false credentials. I issued him with a warrant declaring that he was a member of the Imperial ambassador's household. He could now move as he wished.'

'But you were hunting him. You said that yourself. You threatened me . . .'

'All shadow play. I had to pretend. I also had to discover where your true loyalties lay. I soon found out. Your heart was with the Princess Mary and the Lady Jane. It would have been too dangerous to draw you in. I gave you the opportunity. Thank God,' he crossed himself, 'you refused it. But,' he banged the walking cane against the paving stones, 'I also protected you when I could. Wriothesley hated you. He saw you as a grotesque gargoyle. I heard a story, whether it's true or not I don't know, that Wriothesley had a younger brother, in appearance something like yourself. Cherished and loved by his parents, he died young. They mourned him to the exclusion of their elder son. Wriothesley never forgave or forgot that memory. He wanted you dead. It was he, not me, who discovered your meeting in Whitefriars and dispatched the Council men. Wriothesley certainly proved his hatred for you at Newgate. Balaam hastened to me. I freed you. In the end neither Balaam nor I dared leave the shadows. If you had known the truth, Will, and we were unable to protect you, the likes of Wriothesley would have had you stretched out on the rack, the Scavenger's Daughter in the Tower dungeons.'

'And Surrey?'

'Surrey was his own man, brilliant but wilful. He would never accept being second, bowing to the likes of Seymour and Dudley. Civil war would have raged. Years before he died I begged, I pleaded with him to be moderate in his temper, to ally himself with Seymour and Dudley. He refused. Wriothesley was jubilant at his arrest. He believed it would be only a matter of time before . . .' Paget pointed at the garderobe. 'Surrey tried to escape. You know the rest. Balaam warned him.' He cleared his throat. 'I also did my best to save Norfolk. I argued that to end the old king's reign and mark the accession of his heir with the execution of England's premier duke would be seen as a banquet of blood.'

He rapped the cane against the floor again, peering at me quizzically. 'Ah well, now you are the master, Will. I have been summoned here to refer to you, to account for the past.'

I glanced at Balaam; he nodded imperceptibly.

'One thing only,' I retorted. 'Her Majesty demands the truth about her father's death.'

'That was proclaimed at the time.'

Balaam went over, removed the napkins and filled three goblets with white wine. He served both Paget and myself. The wine was cold and delicious. All three of us sat sipping carefully.

'We are not here to be cozened, flattered or ignored,' Balaam declared. 'Sir William, I have served you well, but there is one secret that is still owed. The Queen is prepared to return you to full office, to grant you as much power and status as you enjoyed before.'

'I submitted myself most humbly to Her Majesty.'

'After Her Majesty raised her banner to which all loyal subjects flocked,' I declared. 'You did not, Sir William. You remained in London with the other rebels. You appended your name, beside that of traitors, on a letter to the Lord Lieutenant of Essex, instructing him to move against his, and your, rightful queen. You submitted because the rebels' cause was lost.'

'I did advise you,' Balaam whispered. 'I did plead . . .'

'And I was threatened,' Paget retorted.

I stared at him. I now accepted why I had to be here. I knew the path we were about to follow.

'You will be confirmed in everything,' I persisted, 'if you tell Her Majesty the truth.'

Paget continued to tap his cane on the ground. A blast of hot air brought us the mixed odours of the Tower, the filthy ooze of the moat below us, smoke from the Tower mint and tanneries. Children laughed and shouted as they played Hob the Lost. The cries of sentries echoed above the shrill screaming from the hog pens where the pigs waited to be slaughtered. A horn brayed. Lurchers barked and horses neighed as a hunting party prepared to leave to chase the hare in Moorfields, north of the old City wall. I stared around that bleak chamber. Did Surrey's ghost walk here? Or was his troubled spirit soothed by the restoration of his family name as well as plans to move his shattered corpse from All Hallows to the Howard mausoleum in St Michael's Church, Framlingham? 'The storms are gone, those clouds dispersed': a line from one of Surrey's last poems echoed through my soul. Paget was lost in his own meditations.

'Oh, you must know,' Balaam glanced quickly at me, 'Somers also heard Dudley's last confession after he had been shriven by the Bishop Heath. Isn't that true, Will?'

Paget glanced up; he smiled crookedly at me.

'Never tell a secret,' he murmured, 'to more than one person. You, Master Balaam, must leave. My surety.' He shrugged. 'I want no other witnesses.'

'So if necessary,' I retorted, 'you can dismiss what I might say in the future as the ravings of a fool.' I drank greedily. 'I assure you, I will tell no one except Her Majesty. I also warn you, sir, I am not so fey-witted as to be unable to distinguish the nettle from the vine. Her Majesty wants the truth, otherwise,' I gestured around, 'this may become more than just your visiting chamber. Master Balaam?'

That man of subtle deceit stood chewing the corner of his lip like a merchant valuing a roll of cloth. He frowned slightly but left the chamber, closing the door quietly behind him. I rose and took my stool closer to Paget so he did not have to raise his voice.

'Let us be brief and succinct. No politicking now.'

'The King our late dead master,' Paget kept his head down, 'did not die on the twenty-eighth of January in the Year of Our Lord 1547, but four days earlier, when Sir Thomas Seymour was sworn of the Council. Now you knew, I knew, we all knew King Henry. What did he boast? There was no man he made that he could not unmake. And there was no head, however noble, he could not make fly. The King destroyed the Howards but he was preparing to clear the board. He had growing suspicions about Dudley and Seymour, their use of the dry stamp, how they were beginning to dominate the Council. He planned to destroy them and us.'

'How?'

'He kept Norfolk alive and comfortable, Gardiner under house arrest. We garnered rumours, whispers that Henry was prepared to indict Queen Katherine for her illicit liaison with Thomas Seymour; even Cranmer was suspect. On the morning of the twenty-second of January,' Paget chose his words carefully, 'you were put under arrest in your chamber. The Council met. Dudley accused Wriothesley of being part of the King's plot to move against him and Seymour.' He picked up his goblet and sipped carefully. 'Wriothesley was truly dangerous,' he gestured with his hand, 'jumping here, jumping there. We believed he was the King's key to unlock the door to a new bloody purge.'

'Of course.' I nodded. 'Wriothesley would know a great deal. He would be the Crown's witness in any treason trial.'

'Naturally Wriothesley denied all this. You see, Will, our king wasn't insane. Oh yes, I know all about Balaam's interpretation of certain paintings, but believe me, Henry had good cause to fear. Seymour and Dudley, together with other members of the Council, were ruefully reflecting on decades of bloody tyranny under Henry. They argued for a commonwealth. A kingdom ruled by a council.'

'And Henry's heirs?'

Paget gazed stonily at me. 'Think, Will. Young Edward, if he had grown to manhood, would have been as bloodthirsty and tyrannical as his father. You know there is a suspicion that Dudley poisoned him?'

I shrugged this off. 'And the two princesses?'

'Ah, that's where I and others proved obdurate. We argued that the kingdom, the people would never accept the total annihilation of Henry's heirs. Now all this is mere speculation, but I believe Wriothesley may have informed Henry.'

'That's why Surrey was removed, wasn't it?'

'Yes, the King thought he was a threat to the young prince, but Dudley and Seymour regarded him as an obstacle to their idea of a commonwealth. God forgive me, I agreed with them.' Paget rose, balancing himself on his walking cane. He stretched, then began to walk up and down. 'The Council was divided into two: those who looked forward to a new king and those who hoped for no king at all. Then there was Henry, deter- mined that no council would ever pose a threat to him and his family. The King was growing stronger. He had recovered from a fever; the burning stages had passed. He began to rant about his treasonous wife and how ill served he was. He expressed deep sorrow over Cromwell's death and regretted the execution of Anne Boleyn, who of course was removed from power because of Seymour's sister. Henry demanded that Wingfield and his Spears be always close by. What he didn't know was that we had bought Wingfield's allegiance.

'We tried to placate the King. I summoned his old comrade Francis Bryant, to no avail. Days passed. Dudley and Seymour were now deeply agitated, Wriothesley even more so. Thomas Seymour was growing increasingly fearful of the consequences of his illicit liaison with the Queen.' Paget breathed in deeply as he hobbled back to his chair. 'Abruptly Henry realised something was wrong. He demanded to see you. Dudley ordered Huicke to feed the King an opiate, the milk of poppy. Huicke had no choice but to agree, though he pointed out that such deep sleeps might invigorate His Majesty.' Paget leaned forward, both hands resting on the walking cane, eyes half closed as he went back down the gallery of the years to those warm, stuffy chambers, littered with all the plunder from Henry's victims, a constant reminder of the King's bloody outbursts.

'The Council continued divided. Dudley and Seymour were fearful that old Norfolk would be released and would be joined by Gardiner. They accused Wriothesley of being party to this. He screamed back about what he had done for both Crown and kingdom, but his savage words did not convince. The younger Seymour joined the shouting; hands fell to daggers. Wriothesley declared he would prove his loyalty and asked if there was man amongst us who would join him.' Paget shook his head. 'Wriothesley and the younger Seymour went into the King's chamber. Huicke was there; the King was fast asleep. They dragged the doctor out, slammed the door shut and locked it from inside. When they came out, Wriothesley, hands clasped together, mournfully pronounced that the King was not sleeping but had quietly slipped away.' Paget wetted his lips. 'Dudley wanted the truth of it. Wriothesley said he had now demonstrated his loyalty to the Council.'

'And the truth?' I asked.

'While Seymour guarded the door, Wriothesley seized

332

a bolster and placed it over the King's face. Henry became aroused and struggled. Seymour helped Wriothesley even as he whispered how he intended to plunder and ravish Katherine Parr's soft white body. According to Seymour, Wriothesley was giggling like some witless maid. Eventually the King lay quiet. We went into the chamber. Henry lay sprawled, head slightly to one side, eyes all glassy, mouth gaping. At the time no one even dared mention the truth about what had really happened. '

'When was this?'

'Early in the hours of the twenty-fourth of January. After the initial tumult and panic we continued the pretence. Those we could not fully trust, or did not need, remained banished from the royal chambers.'

'Like myself?'

'Like yourself. We simply continued the sham. Huicke, frightened out of his wits, rearranged the corpse as best he could. Somebody mentioned extreme unction, the need for the last rites, so Cranmer was secretly summoned. He viewed the corpse but observed nothing untoward. He performed what rite he could and left immediately. He may have suspected the truth but he could never prove it. Whether he liked it or not, he too was consenting to what had happened. And how could he object? Wriothesley hailed himself as the hero of the hour; his frenetic mood deepened. What could we do? In one way or another we were all his accomplices. To blame Wriothesley and Seymour alone would have been the greatest foolishness. I too was implicated. I urged them to be pragmatic. Henry was dead and we should all unite.'

'Murder!' I interrupted. 'Regicide! Henry the King was murdered and you were an accomplice.'

'We had no choice. Henry would have struck at us all. Think, Will. What if Henry had released Norfolk and Gardiner and made Wriothesley his creature? Wriothesley hated you and the Lady Jane. Even before the King died Wriothesley was dripping poison about you into his ears. Oh yes, Will Somers, if Henry had succeeded, I would have had a better chance at life than you and the Lady Jane.'

I could not contradict that. I closed my eyes and thought of Henry sprawled in that great bed gasping his poppy-drenched dreams. Seymour guarding the door, Wriothesley the assassin closing like a shadow, grasping the bolster and silencing that powerful king once and for all. Now I knew why Wriothesley had hauled me off to Newgate. He was terrified that I knew of his double dealing with the King and might still betray him to the rest.

'Will?'

I opened my eyes.

'I begged them all to unite and I had my way. The King's death would remain secret. Important decisions had to be made. Queen Katherine Parr would be excluded from government but allowed to keep her jewels and lands, even marry Seymour as long as they waited. But Seymour, like Wriothesley, was deeply affected by what he had done. It turned his wits. He insisted on grasping his prize immediately.'

'Did he tell his new wife what he'd done to her late royal husband?'

'I suspect he did. An act of bravado, to show how deeply he loved her. After all, they'd both desired Henry's death. He was the screech owl of their hushed conversations at Greenwich. Whether they were attempting to poison the King remains debatable; the potions and philtres Henry fed himself could have been dangerous. The King certainly misjudged Huicke; he was, first and foremost, the Queen's creature. Strange, isn't it? Huicke was with Katherine when she gave birth to Seymour's child, an act that killed her. In fact when Katherine Parr lay dying, tossing in a fever, she accused Seymour of attempting to murder her. Seymour desperately tried to quieten and soothe her. Why should Katherine think that unless she was dealing with a man, and being tended by a physician, who'd helped murder a king? So why should they baulk at killing her? Both Seymour and Wriothesley grew increasingly frenetic in their behaviour. They had to be silenced; that's why the elder Seymour signed his own brother's death warrant. Balaam took care of Wriothesley. And as for Sir Anthony Denny, Dudley catered for him lest he go to confess and be shriven by Bishop Gardiner.'

'Do you think that good bishop suspects?'

'I don't think so. Gardiner is too absorbed with his

own dreams to restore the power of Rome. Others, however, could have asked questions.'

'Hence your little black book of infamous memory.'

Paget smiled thinly. 'That was the mortar to the bricks of the house I wanted to build. Bribes, estates, titles, sinecures, benefices, gold and silver. No one was overlooked: Huicke, Wendy, Alsop, Roberts, Wingfield, Bryant and others. Once they'd taken the bribe, they were all consenting to what we had done.'

'And you truly believe the King was preparing to destroy you?'

'Us, Will, all of us! He wanted to create a realm where he was both emperor and pope. Read the classics, Will. I can point to many princes who have walked the same path, who strove for the same prize. I also understood Dudley and Seymour's plan, though I tempered it. I wanted to see England being ruled as a commonwealth where there was a king, a monarch, but subject to a council. No more would we accept that one man's will could override Parliament, statute law and even scripture itself. Wriothesley betrayed us. I have no doubt he knew about Seymour's dalliance with the Queen. We simply moved before Henry did.' He rubbed the side of his face. 'That's why Surrey also had to die. In our eyes he was just as dangerous as Henry. Surrey tolerated the King; what chance did we have with a nobleman like that? He believed that his aristocratic blood was the only licence to rule. He would have provoked the wars of a hundred years ago.'

Paget fell silent, turning his head as if half listening to the sounds of the Tower. 'Of course Henry's death did not mark a new beginning. The King was not even in his coffin and my advice was being ignored. Seymour even considered assuming the title of "The Great Lord and Master". Wriothesley, wits already unhinged, was the first to object, claiming he'd been cheated, and so the cracks widened. Young Seymour galloped off to claim his bride. Dudley and Seymour drew apart over failure in Scotland, unrest in the countryside and division over religion. And look at the future. God rest him, Will, but young Edward was a righteous prig who also saw himself as God's will incarnate.'

Paget filled his goblet and offered the jug to me. I shook my head. What these lords intended did not matter now. I was more concerned about why I had been sent here.

'And the King's corpse, Henry the once magnificent prince?'

'Not so magnificent, Will. He died on the twenty-fourth of January but the embalmers were not allowed in till the evening of the thirtieth; six days had elapsed. I visited the corpse myself. I had to go masked, my nose and mouth almost buried in a pomander. The death chamber was crammed with all forms of perfumes and fragrances. The stench was hellish, the corpse even more so; swollen like a balloon so that the belly was bloating to rupture. Corruption and rottenness were seeping from every pore and aperture, be it the eyes, mouth,

337

nose or anus. The embalmers were solemnly sworn to silence and ordered to do what they could. The King's rotting, slime-covered cadaver was washed, cleansed and waxed as swiftly and as expertly as could be done. God knows what was truly buried in that casket under the flagstones at Westminster. We thought the lead coffin and elm casket would contain all the corruption, but the long delay, the rattling of the funeral chariot . . .' Paget shrugged. 'What happened at Syon was inevitable, dismissed as an accident. I was never so grateful to see a corpse buried.'

'Did the King ask to see his family?'

'The Queen, no; the children, yes. Please tell Her Majesty so. Of course we couldn't allow that. Henry might have divulged his suspicions. Princess Mary was astute enough to act. I have no excuses now, no more than the others,' he held up a hand, 'except one. If Henry had lived, I, we and probably you, Will Somers, would have perished. And now we are back at the beginning. A new queen, intent on reversing everything Henry has done over the last twenty years. Some people will resist, some people will die, but you have what you came for. Henry died, smothered in his bed by his own ministers, who feared him more than the devil and wished him gone with that devil. They did so because they suspected Henry was plotting to do the same to them in a more heinous and barbaric way. And that is the truth of it.' Paget shrugged wearily. 'Of course, there is no proof, no witnesses. The official account is well known; it cannot be contradicted,' he smiled, 'except for a court fool and a disgraced minister.' He gestured at me. 'Remember, Will, I warned you. On the day I told you about Cranmer, I wanted to alert you to how, in the coming storm, no one would be safe. How the Princess Mary and her household were watched most closely, as well as what horrors awaited those who fell foul of the King. True,' he winked at me, 'I was being mischievous in establishing where your loyalty lay. In the end I protected you as well as I could. I never sent those council men to Whitefriars; Wriothesley did that, as he tried to break you in Newgate. I repeat, I protected you when I could. I now beg you to return the favour.' Then he was gone.

I heard his footsteps fade and followed him soon after out into the sunshine. Paget was now making his way along one of the gulleys. Balaam was close by, leaning against a wall talking to a vivacious red-haired young lady. She turned and smiled brilliantly at me. I recognised the Princess Elizabeth, garbed in a gown of blue slashed with white, head and hair hidden under a bejewelled gauze veil. She glanced flirtatiously at Balaam and stepped back with a coquettish curtsey. Balaam responded with the most lavish courtly bow. Elizabeth threw her head back, pealing with laughter, then waggled those long white fingers at him, a sign for him to withdraw to where her lady stood some distance away. She watched him go, shading her eyes, then, smiling coyly, walked slowly towards me, hips swaying as she playfully put one foot in front of the other. I know Elizabeth and I admire her, those dark eyes so bright with life and that kissable mouth slightly pouted as if she is always on the verge of bursting into laughter. A born flirt, her appearance masks a sharp, deep intellect, whilst she possesses all the charm and courtesy of a born courtier.

'Why, Master Somers.' She rounded her eyes as she stretched out a hand to be kissed. I did so, and Elizabeth gently brushed my face with her fingers.

'Your Grace?'

'Your Grace wonders why Sir William Paget should be closeted so close with my good friend Will. Why he leaves so humbly when only months ago he was one of the masters of the dance. Now he slinks from the Tower like a beaten dog. Why did he come here?' She smiled and waved her hand airily. 'To this "royal palace" as my good sister calls it, where I reside as her beloved guest.'

'Till better days come, Your Grace.'

'Oh Will, will they come, will they?' She laughed at the pun on my name, then stepped closer, the smile gone, the eyes searching. Oh Lord, save me, I recognised that look, the set of the mouth which reflected the steel in her soul. 'Paget, what did he say?' She leaned even closer. 'My father? His death?'

I glanced to where Balaam flirted with her ladies. 'Your Grace,' I bowed, 'what I know is only for the ears of the Queen.'

'Is it now, Will?' She moved from side to side in a flurry of dress and petticoats; I caught the scent of her heady perfume. 'Will, look at me.' I did so. 'For the ears of the Queen only?'

I nodded.

'So when I am Queen it will be for my ears as well?'

'Of course, Your Grace.'

Elizabeth pecked me on both cheeks. 'There, Will, that's for you and the Lady Jane.' She fluttered her fingers in goodbye, walked away, then turned. 'Oh Will?'

'Yes, Your Grace?'

'Remember . . .'

Will Somers's journal ends here.